⚜

Dear Reader:

   In HarperPaperbacks's continuing effort to publish the best romantic fiction at the best value, we have taken the unusual step of pricing nine of our summer Monogram titles at the affordable cost of $3.99. Written by some of the most popular and bestselling romance writers today, these are magical and exciting stories that we hope you will take to your hearts and treasure for a long time to come.

   Open the pages of these wonderful books and give yourself the gift of a reading experience like no other. HarperPaperbacks is delighted to present nine extraordinary novels—at a very attractive price—by favorite authors who can bring the world of love alive for you.

Sincerely,

Carolyn Marino

Carolyn Marino
Editorial Director
HarperPaperbacks

⚜

Books by Carolyn Lampman

Murphy's Rainbow
Shadows in the Wind
Willow Creek
Meadowlark
A Window in Time
Silver Springs

Published by HarperPaperbacks

Silver Springs

⚒ CAROLYN LAMPMAN ⚒

HarperPaperbacks
A Division of HarperCollinsPublishers

This is a work of fiction. The characters, incidents, and dialogues are products of the author's imagination and are not to be construed as real. Any resemblance to actual events or persons, living or dead, is entirely coincidental.

HarperPaperbacks   *A Division of* HarperCollins*Publishers*
10 East 53rd Street, New York, N.Y. 10022

Cover illustration by Aleta Jenks

First printing: August 1996

Printed in the United States of America

HarperPaperbacks, HarperMonogram, and colophon are trademarks of HarperCollins*Publishers*

❖ 10 9 8 7 6 5 4 3 2 1

To my "twins," Ann and Barbara. I am truly in awe of your talents.
And to everyone in Riverton, Wyoming, who loves Silver Springs Gulch as I do.

Silver Springs

1

Wyoming Territory 1872

"There's a gentleman wants to see you, Miss Angel." The bartender glared toward the back of the casino. "I put him in your office."

Angel was surprised. Sam rarely disapproved of anyone. "Who is it?"

"Said his name was Goff."

"Never heard of him. What does he want?"

"I don't know. Said he'd only talk to the owner of the Green Garter." Sam's eyes narrowed. "Want me to throw him out?"

Angel raised an eyebrow. "Don't you think I should find out what he wants first?"

"Maybe. I ain't so sure I'd want to know."

Angel could hardly wait to meet this Mr. Goff and see for herself who had ruffled the taciturn Sam's feathers. "Don't worry. If he needs to be bounced out of here, I'll be sure to let you know."

"Can't wait," Sam muttered.

"By the way, Sam," Angel said, as she headed toward the back, "will you tell Peg I want to see her when Mr. Goff leaves?"

"Why, she done something wrong?"

"Nothing for you to worry about. Just send her in."

Angel walked into her office without waiting to hear the protest she knew was coming. She smiled to herself as she closed the door behind her. Sam protected the women who lived and worked at the Green Garter as if they were his own daughters.

"Good afternoon, Mr. Goff," she said pleasantly to the man sitting in front of her desk. "What can I do for you?"

He jumped to his feet. "There's been some kind of mistake. I'm here on business, not pleasure. However," he said, giving her an appreciative once-over, "after I've talked to your boss, I'm sure you and I could think of some way to while away the afternoon that we'd both enjoy."

"I doubt it." Angel walked calmly around her desk and sat on the only other chair. "My bartender said you wanted to see the owner of the Green Garter, and that's who I am."

"But you're a woman!"

"How very perceptive of you to notice," Angel said. "At the risk of repeating myself, what can I do for you?"

He sat down uncertainly. "I've never done business with a woman before."

"There's a first time for everything."

"Very true." He steepled his fingers and gazed at her. "I want to buy this place."

"The Green Garter is not for sale."

Mr. Goff smiled confidently. "You haven't heard my offer yet."

"That's also true. However, I doubt it would change my mind."

"Not even for ten thousand dollars?"

Angel blinked. "I must admit that's a very attractive offer. Nevertheless—"

"Naturally, that includes all the equipment and stock," he continued, as though she hadn't spoken. "As well as the girls."

"The girls?"

"Of course. You have one of the nicest stables I've ever seen. That's one of the things that impressed me about this place."

"My *girls* are not for sale either," Angel said coldly. "In case you missed it, President Lincoln abolished slavery nine years ago."

"Oh, come now, we both know they sell themselves for a living. I suppose the next thing you'll be telling me is that you don't take a percentage of their earnings."

Angel stood up. "I'm sorry you've wasted your time, Mr. Goff. The Green Garter is not for sale."

"Don't be so hasty. You're not likely to get as good an offer from anyone else."

"It wouldn't matter if I got a *better* offer. The fact remains: This place is not for sale. Now if you'll excuse me, I have some rather pressing business to attend to."

Mr. Goff rose reluctantly. "All right, but at least give my offer some thought."

"I will," she said, walking him to the door. "But it won't make any difference."

"You might change your mind."

"If I do, you'll be the first to know."

He smiled. "Good. I'll be at the Sherlock Hotel for the next couple of days. I'm sure you'll reconsider."

"Right," she murmured as he walked away. "When hell freezes over."

"Since he's walking out of here in one piece, I guess the offer he made you wasn't what it sounded like," said a deep voice from the shadows.

Angel whirled and peered into the dark hallway outside her office. "Ox?"

"Who else?" he asked, sauntering out into the light. "How's my favorite redhead?"

"I ought to box your ears," she said. "You scared me half to death. How did you get in here anyway?"

"Sam let me in the back door so I could put your supplies in the storeroom." He grinned. "I got your new roulette wheel."

Angel's eyes lit up. "You did? Where is it?"

"It's out in the freight wagon. Found it in Omaha."

"No wonder you have the reputation for being the best freighter around. I didn't figure there was one within a thousand miles."

"At Bruford Freight Lines we do everything we can to please our customers," Ox said. "I suppose you want to see it?"

"What do you think?"

He made a sweeping motion toward the back door with his hand. "After you."

"Hold on a second." Angel ducked back inside her office and grabbed her coat. Her heart was still pounding as she walked by Ox a few moments later, but it had more to do with Ox Bruford himself than the fright he'd given her. Those gorgeous green eyes and that tall broad-shouldered body always made her feel like a giddy debutante, a silly girl in the throes of her first love. One look at that heart-stopping grin of his and she'd catch herself daydreaming about running her hands through his thick brown hair and tracing the hard line of his jaw with her fingers. Luckily, he had no idea of the effect he had on her. The last thing she needed was for him to discover her weakness. "I suppose this is going to cost me a small fortune," she grumbled, to hide the vulnerability he made her feel.

"Actually, I got it secondhand. Even with the cost to ship it to Rock Springs by rail, it was less than you budgeted for." He followed her outside. "Of course, it's going to cost you extra for bringing it up the mountain in the dead of winter like this."

Angel glanced over her shoulder at him. "Oh, Lord, I'm almost afraid to ask."

"How about an apple pie to go with supper?"

Angel stopped and put her hands on her hips. "Now where am I going to get apples in South Pass City this time of year?"

"I just happen to have a dozen right here." Ox reached under the tarpaulin that covered his load and pulled out a flour sack. "A widow down in Green River gave me some of her winter's store out of undying gratitude."

Angel cocked an eyebrow. "I don't think I want to know what you did to deserve them."

"A trifling service," Ox said, waving his hand.

"I'll bet." Angel had no doubt the widow didn't consider the matter trifling. All that masculine appeal was pretty hard to resist, especially when it came with a heart as big as Wyoming Territory. Angel found it in her to feel a little sorry for the widow. "All right, I'll bake you a pie. I take it you're planning on staying the night?"

"Of course. Since you're the only customer who gives me room and board for bringing in supplies, I have to take advantage of it when I can."

Angel gave an unladylike snort. "I figured it would be a lot cheaper than paying those exorbitant rates you charge. But the way you eat, I'm not sure I got the better end of the bargain."

Ox's eyes twinkled. "Sorry, it's too late to change now. A deal's a deal. Anyway, this should make you feel better about it." He threw back the tarp. "Madam, your new roulette wheel!"

"Oh, Ox!" she cried. "It's mahogany, how beautiful."

"Story is, it came off a riverboat, one of those floating palaces."

Angel ran her hand reverently over the polished wood, delighting in the rich red hue. "You know, I might have to bake you an extra pie to take with you for this. It's far nicer than I hoped for."

"Who's that unsavory-looking character across the street?" Ox asked suddenly. "I don't like the way he keeps staring at you."

Angel glanced up and followed his gaze across the street. "Oh, that's just Jim Dugan," she said, wrinkling her nose.

"I don't think he's one of your admirers," Ox said, spitting a stream of tobacco juice into the street. "In fact, he looks distinctly unfriendly."

"Can't say I'm surprised." Angel frowned. "He got a little too rough with one of the girls last night. I had to ask him to leave."

"He looks angrier than that."

"I suppose it could have something to do with the way I got my point across," Angel admitted. "He was as ornery as an old boar grizzly, refusing to go, making a nuisance of himself. He made the mistake of grabbing me."

"Where was Sam?"

"Downstairs at the bar where he belongs. It didn't matter. A well-placed knee took care of the problem."

Ox winced. "Ouch. That's hardly the way to endear yourself to your customers."

"I can do without customers like Jim Dugan, thank you." She pushed herself away from the wagon. "And I have better things to do than stand here chitchatting about him all day. Do you have other deliveries to make in South Pass City?"

"Nope, you're the last, and all I have left of yours is the roulette wheel. Where do you want me to put it?"

"Right where the old one was. I'll send Sam out to give you a hand."

"We'll have it set up and working by suppertime."

He rubbed his hands together. "I'm looking forward to that pie."

"You've earned it," Angel said, over her shoulder. She stopped in surprise just inside the back door. A young woman stood against the wall, looking as though she wanted to fade into the woodwork. "Good heavens, Peg. What's wrong?"

"Sam said you wanted to see me."

"I do, but I promise you it's nothing to be afraid of. My plans just changed so I don't have time to meet with you right now, though. How about dropping by my office right after closing tonight?"

"I guess so."

"Oh, for goodness' sake, Peg. Don't look like that. You have nothing to worry about, I promise. Now cheer up!"

Peg gave her a fleeting smile. "All right."

"That's much better." Angel glanced at the gold watch pinned to the bodice of her green taffeta dress. "Would you mind getting a bath ready for Ox? He always likes to take one as soon as he gets in off the trail."

"I'd be glad to, but don't you usually do that?"

"Yes. However, today I have something more pressing to attend to." She smiled and held up the sack of apples. "I have a pie to bake."

It was well after midnight when Peg nervously entered Angel's office. "M-my last customer just left," she said.

"Good. Have a seat." Angel closed the door. "Rumor has it you and young Fenwick are thinking about getting married."

Peg, who had just settled gingerly on the edge of the chair, jumped to her feet in alarm. "He pays for my time just the same as everyone else!"

"Relax, Peg. Nobody's accusing you of anything." Angel put her hand on the other woman's shoulder and gently pushed her down onto the chair again before walking around behind the desk. "Do you plan on marrying him?"

"He's asked me." Peg glanced miserably down at her hands, clasped tightly in her lap. "But we'd have to start over somewhere else, and that takes money."

"If money weren't a problem, would you marry him?"

"Quicker'n a cat could lick its ear."

"Good." Angel opened her safe and pulled out a small leather pouch. "I went to the bank this afternoon and made a withdrawal for you."

Peg gave her a blank look. "I don't have any money in the bank."

"On the contrary, you had seven hundred dollars," Angel said with a smile. "I hope you don't mind gold dust."

"Seven hundred dollars!" Peg's eyes widened in astonishment. "But where—?"

"This is my cut of your earnings; I've been keeping track since the night you started." Angel pushed the pouch across the desk. "I make my money off the casino, not what the brothel brings in. You and the others are the drawing cards here; I don't figure I have any right to the money you make. Other than a little I take out each month for food and expenses, it's all here. "

"I-I don't know what to say."

"You don't have to say anything. Just take it and start your new life as Mrs. Fenwick. I do ask that you keep this to yourself, though. Don't tell Billy until you're well away from South Pass City. Sam doesn't even know."

"But why?"

"I have a reputation as a hardheaded business-woman to protect. No one is going to believe it if they

find out I do this for my girls." Angel smiled as she rose
to her feet and walked around the desk to the door.
"Unless my eyes deceived me, your young man was
waiting for you at the bar."

"Oh, Miss Angel," Peg cried. Tears running down
her face, she hugged the other woman. "Thank you
with all my heart!"

"You're welcome," Angel said, hugging her back.
"And good luck to both of you."

Angel walked back to her desk, pulled out a small
ledger, and smiled as she wrote *Paid in full* across the
column marked *Peg*. She'd helped almost twenty
women over the years, giving them a chance at a normal life.

Six had been working at her first casino, and she
hadn't known what to do with them. If she closed
down the brothel, they'd have had no place to go, but
the thought of making money from prostitution was
repugnant. That's when she'd come up with the idea of
"freedom money." When there was enough to give
them a new start, or an opportunity like Peg's arose,
Angel presented what she'd put aside for them with no
strings attached.

"Here's today's receipts," Sam said, walking in and
slapping the papers on the desk. "I'm closing down the
casino for the night."

Angel raised an eyebrow. "From the look on your
face, I take it you're not too happy with me."

"Peg and Billy Fenwick just went upstairs to collect her things." Sam glared at Angel. "I think she
said she was leaving, but she was crying too hard to
be sure."

"We've had this conversation before, Sam. What happens between the girls and me is none of your business."

"No, but that doesn't mean I have to approve."

Angel winced as he slammed the door behind him.
She'd probably get the cold shoulder for a few days

until he calmed down. Sam's soft heart was one of the things she loved most about him.

Three quarters of an hour later, Angel put her paperwork away. She stood and stretched wearily before blowing out the lamp. Darkness greeted her as she opened her office door and stepped out into the hallway. Sam must really be angry. He always left a light burning on the bar so she could find her way upstairs.

Suddenly a hand covered her mouth while another jerked her arms behind her and dragged her into the storeroom. A rope snaked around her body and legs, completely immobilizing her.

"Watch those knees of hers," said a voice out of the darkness. "She's got a kick like a damn mule."

"Don't worry, Jim, I got her all right and tight," replied another voice.

The door slammed. "There, now, she can scream her head off and nobody will hear her. All the whores sleep on the other side of the building. Nothin' above us here but the cribs."

A match flared in the darkness, and Angel saw the man's features for the first time. Her mouth went dry: Jim Dugan!

"Nobody in the cribs this time of night," he said, touching the match to a lantern wick. "Everybody's done their screwin' and gone home." He leered at Angel. "Everybody but us, honey. Don't reckon we need one of them fancy beds, though. The floor will work just fine for the likes of you." Dugan ran a dirty finger around the neckline of her dress. "Can't hardly wait to see all that pretty white skin."

Angel gathered every drop of saliva she could and spit in his face. "Pig!"

"Why, you little—"

The hard slap snapped her head back against the wall, and a blinding pain burst in her head. There was a loud crash, and a roar echoed through the room. At first Angel thought it was from the agony in her head. Then the hands holding her jerked away, and Ox's face, contorted with rage, swam into view.

Angel slid down the wall to a heap on the floor, unable to focus on the fight that was going on. By the time her vision cleared, Dugan lay unconscious on the floor and Ox was involved in a fistfight with the other man. As she watched, Ox began to get the upper hand. With one final punch, he smashed his fist into the other man's face.

As Ox's adversary crumpled, Angel suddenly caught a movement out of the corner of her eye. "Look out, Ox!" she yelled. "Dugan's got a knife!"

Ox turned just in time to deflect the murderous lunge aimed at his back. The knife slashed upward, slicing his cheek. One blow from the big fist sent Dugan crashing to the floor, just as Sam appeared at the door with his shotgun.

"What the hell?"

"Go get the sheriff, Sam," Ox said, stumbling across the room to where Angel was trying to get up. "This scum attacked Angel."

"Oh, Ox!" she cried, as he unwound the rope from her body.

"It's all right, Angel, they can't hurt you now." Ox kicked the rope away and swept her up in his arms. She sobbed against his shoulder as he carried her across the hall to her office, where he sat down with her still cradled against him, rocking back and forth, whispering soft words of encouragement until she stopped crying.

For the first time in her life, Angel felt safe in a man's arms. Yet she knew it was an illusion. Any man, even a well-intentioned one like Ox, would try to dominate her if he had the chance. It was just the way they were.

"I'm sorry," she said, sitting up and wiping her eyes. "I've never cried like that before."

"You've never been attacked like that before, either."

"No, I—Ox, your cheek!" Angel stared in horror at the blood dripping down his face.

"It's nothing."

"Don't be ridiculous, it's a knife cut and needs to be attended to." She squirmed off his lap. "My bandages are in the kitchen. I'll doctor it there." She grabbed his hand and pulled him to his feet.

In the kitchen, she filled a bowl with water from the kettle on the back of the stove. "Here, sit down. I hope you don't need stitches. Doc Caldwell is out of town, and I'm not much of a needlewoman."

"You sure know how to make a man relax," he said sarcastically, as she sponged the blood away.

"I never professed to be a nurse." Angel bit her lip as she washed away the last of the blood. Instead of the clean slice she'd been hoping for, she saw a jagged puncture wound, the most dangerous kind of all. She had to prevent infection at all cost. "Looks like he just nicked you. What were you doing down here anyway?"

"I heard some news I thought might interest you."

"Really? Open that bottle of whiskey for me, would you?"

"Sure. Is it so bad you need a drink?"

"Don't be silly. I'm out of iodine and I need something to clean the cut. Now, what was this important news?"

"I was talking to some of the hard-rock miners. They're planning on pulling up stakes and leaving— Jesus Christ, Angel!" The air whistled in through his clenched teeth as she poured whiskey on his cheek. "That hurts worse than when he cut me! What are you trying to do?"

"You saved my life. I'm just returning the favor."

She resisted the urge to hold his hand and pillow his good cheek against her shoulder until the pain faded. "Be glad I was out of iodine."

"It's a good thing I didn't dive out in front of a runaway buggy to save you. I wouldn't have lived through your gratitude."

"What did the miners tell you that was so all-fired important?"

"The mines are shutting down."

"What? The assays say there's gold ore all over this mountain."

"Right, but it's too expensive to process. There's no profit in it."

Angel frowned. "Then South Pass City will be a ghost town before long."

"Looks that way."

"Sheriff Lucien is rounding up Dugan and his friend," Sam said, from the kitchen door. "Are you all right, Miss Angel?"

"Thanks to Ox, I am." Angel poured Ox a glass of whiskey. "Sam, first thing tomorrow I want you to go to the Sherlock Hotel and tell Mr. Goff I want to see him."

"What for?"

She put the cork back in the whiskey bottle. "Hell just froze over."

2

Angel paused in front of the Green Garter and glanced down the deserted street. Who would have believed South Pass City could die in a mere three months? With a sigh, she turned and went inside the empty casino. "How's the inventory coming along, Sam?" she asked, closing the door behind her.

"Almost done. I saved this for you." Sam frowned as he rubbed his thumb across the label on the bottle of whiskey. "This is the last of your private stock. I thought you might like to keep it for a special occasion."

Angel smiled. "Good idea. Maybe we'll use it to christen the new place when we get set up."

"I figured we'd do that with champagne."

"Why, Sam, I would never have expected such extravagance from you."

He grinned. "Nothing will be too good for the Palisade Palace. It won't be in a mining town like South Pass City, either. We'll find a place where the customers have a little class and lots of money." Sam's smile disappeared as he set the bottle on the bar and glanced around. "Aw, who am I fooling? I love this place. There will never be another Green Garter. Maybe I should have bought you out."

"Don't get maudlin on me, Sam. South Pass City is all but empty now; in six months it will be a ghost town. I was lucky to find a buyer."

"I guess so. I couldn't run it without the girls anyway. I still can't believe none of them wanted to go with us."

"Mmm, well, maybe they have something better to do," Angel said noncommittally as she picked up the bottle of whiskey. "I'll be in my office if you need me for anything."

She left her office door ajar and moved purposefully across the room. Setting the bottle on the corner of her desk, she took out her small ledger and sat down with a satisfied sigh. She flipped open the book, dipped her pen in ink, and wrote *Paid in full* across the four remaining columns with a flourish.

Then she leaned back in the chair and permitted herself a rare moment of celebration. Another victory in her secret crusade. Four more women with a new chance at life, free to start over, to find happiness. When she called them into her office this morning, they had all expected their walking papers. Instead she'd given them their freedom money and a chance to put their past behind them.

"Howdy, Sam," said a familiar voice through the half-open door. "Do you know anybody named Angelica Brady?"

Angel's head jerked up. What in God's name did Ox want with Angelica?

"Can't say I ever heard of her," Sam said, after a moment. "Why?"

"A man in Rock Springs gave me a letter to deliver. Seemed pretty sure I'd find her here."

"Some of the girls don't use their own names. Could be Miss Angel knows who she is."

"Good thought. Where is she?"

"In her office. Go on back."

Willing her heart to stop pounding, Angel stuffed the small ledger into a drawer and grabbed her pen. By the time Ox stuck his head through the door a few seconds later, she was diligently working on her business accounts.

"Hope I'm not interrupting anything," he said.

Angel looked up with a smile. "Nothing that can't wait until later."

"How's my favorite blackjack dealer?" Ox asked cheerfully, as he took off his hat and sat down across the desk from her.

"Out of business, in case you couldn't tell."

Ox grinned. "The place did look a mite empty when I came through. I thought maybe you were doing some redecorating in the three weeks since I was here last."

"Of course. Vacant casinos are all the rage now," she said sardonically. "How was your trip up the mountain?"

"About the same as usual, except I only had about half a load." Ox sighed. "This is my last run. There's not much sense in hauling freight when there's nobody left to buy it."

"You'll find another route easy enough."

"I know, but I always kind of liked it here. I suppose you'll be leaving soon too."

"As soon as I tie up all the loose ends. The girls are already gone. Sam and I should be finished up by next week. I have to admit, though, I'm real tempted to wait around until Mr. Goff arrives to take possession of his new casino. He hasn't been back since I agreed to sell to him three months ago."

"After you got done with him, he probably figured you'd try to get out of the deal." Ox grinned. "He was convinced he'd taken gross advantage of you."

"I know, and he wound up paying me twice what it was worth. Maybe it will teach him not to underestimate women."

"That reminds me. I've got a letter here for somebody named Angelica Brady. Do you know where to find her?"

"I can see she gets it."

"I thought you probably could." He pulled the letter out of his pocket and looked at it. "Funny how much Angelica sounds like Angel."

She shrugged. "Coincidences like that happen all the time."

"I guess so," he said, as he handed her the letter. "You know, it's kind of strange. I don't think I've ever heard your last name."

"Don't use one." Let him speculate all he wanted. Unless she admitted to being Angelica Brady, he'd never be positive his suspicions were correct.

"That's kind of peculiar, isn't it?"

"In my business you don't need a last name. Besides, it's no worse than being called Ox." Angel glanced at her sister's familiar handwriting on the envelope and wondered if it contained bad news. Alexis's letters had been increasingly agitated lately. She nonchalantly dropped it on her desk as though it held no interest for her. "Do you expect me to believe your mother actually named you after an overgrown steer?"

Ox chuckled. "You know what I love about you, Angel?"

Her heart lurched. Why did he have to say things like that? "I haven't got a clue."

"Nobody's ever dented that armor of yours. Nothing seems to bother you."

"Life's too short to worry about what other people think."

"That's true enough." He nodded toward the bottle on her desk. "Planning on getting drunk?"

"Hardly. It's the last bottle in the place." Angel pulled two glasses out of a drawer. "Join me in a drink?"

"That depends. Is this some of the private stock you keep under the bar or the rotgut you sell to the miners?"

"What do you think? Sam just handed it to me and suggested I save it for a special occasion."

"Ah, the good stuff. Shall I do the honors?"

"Please."

Angel watched Ox open the bottle and pour the amber liquid. Dented? Hell, he was the one man who could cut right through her armor and steal her heart.

Ox smiled his big lovable grin as he handed her a glass and raised his own in a toast. "To the best friendship I ever had. May neither of us ever forget it."

"To friendship." Friendship? Lord, how could feelings like these be so one-sided? Instead of wallowing in "if onlys" as she was tempted to do, Angel sipped her drink and studied the depression in one rugged cheek. The scar hadn't marred his face a bit. In fact it looked almost like a dimple, one that deepened beguilingly when he smiled. It was going to be tough to say good-bye.

"Why so serious?" he asked.

"Oh, I was just thinking how much I'm going to miss all this." She waved her hand to encompass the room. "The Green Garter has been good to me."

"I know. I almost feel like I'm losing my home."

"You should. You've stayed here often enough."

"Pretty hard to resist the deal you made me. A soft bed whenever I was in town and as much food as I could stuff in." He patted his stomach. "You're about the best cook in Wyoming Territory. If you ever get tired of running a casino, you can open a restaurant."

"I tried that once. It may be more respectable, but it isn't anywhere near as profitable, especially in a place like this where men would rather gamble than eat. I run an honest game and they flock to my tables. As long as there aren't many players like Swede, who wins more often than he loses, I make good money."

"I don't remember you ever telling Swede he wasn't welcome here."

"Of course not," Angel said. "He was good for business. Seeing somebody win like that all the time makes people more willing to part with their money. I haven't had near the take since he and Becky left town. I got a letter from them last week, by the way. They send you their regards."

"Things are going well for them?"

"They seem to be. Swede bought his grandfather's blacksmith shop, and Becky's expecting again."

Ox chuckled. "Somehow that doesn't surprise me. Those two will probably have a dozen babies before they're done. How's our goddaughter doing?"

"Talking a blue streak and into everything. Becky says she's a sore trial."

"And they wouldn't trade her for all the gold in South Pass City."

Angel smiled softly. "No."

"Ah, those two could almost make a man believe in marriage."

"Nothing could make me believe in marriage," Angel said decisively.

"No. It's not something I ever care to try again either."

Angel raised an eyebrow. "Again?"

A look of pain crossed his face. "It's ancient history. It only lasted long enough to convince me a wife and children weren't for me. Still, Swede and Becky do make you wonder if there isn't something to it after all," Ox added, with a touch of wistfulness.

Angel shook her head. "I think marriages like theirs are few and far between. Most husbands and wives don't even like each other. Becky and Swede were friends long before they were lovers."

"That's true enough. Maybe being friends first is the key." He gave her a crooked grin. "What do you say, Angel? Shall we get married and see if we fall in love? Just think, we could roam the world together, seeing the sights, having one adventure after another."

For a fleeting instant she was tempted to take him seriously. Then reality intruded. Even if Ox loved her as much as she loved him, she wouldn't give up her hard-won independence. No man was worth that. "Sure, why not?" she said flippantly. "We might make it clear into next week before we drove each other crazy."

"Probably, but it would sure be fun while it lasted." Ox's smile faded as he regarded his drink pensively. "Have you decided where you're going?" he asked, after a moment.

"No. Sam and I have been sorta thinking of Denver or California somewhere. What about you?"

"I don't know yet either. There are a few things I have to take care of first."

"Well, you can go just about anywhere you want. This country's wide open, and everybody's going to need supplies hauled in."

"Actually, I'm thinking of looking into a less strenuous profession. I'm getting kind of tired of the freight business. Sleeping under the stars in all kinds of weather and eating my own cooking is beginning to lose its appeal. It might even be time to settle down in one place." He downed the last of his drink and gave her a heart-stopping grin as he set the glass on the desk. "Then again, maybe not. At any rate, I'd better get moving. I have supplies for Fort Stambaugh and Miner's Delight. I'm going to have to hurry to get there before dark."

"You're not staying the night?" she asked, trying to hide her disappointment.

"Nope. I'm on a pretty tight schedule. I probably shouldn't have stayed this long."

"I'll walk you to the door." Angel picked up the letter. "I need to deliver this anyway."

There was a twinkle in Ox's eye as he rose to his feet and put on his hat. "I trust Angelica will be easy to find."

"I imagine I can track her down."

"I'm sure you can."

They walked though the casino wrapped in pleasant camaraderie, though each was aware of a deep feeling of melancholy. Angel stiffened her spine as Ox stopped to say good-bye to Sam. There was no way either of them was going to see her cry.

By the time Angel and Ox got to his wagon outside, she had herself well in hand. She was prepared for anything, or so she thought.

"Damn, I'm going to miss you!" Ox said, leaning down to give her a kiss. The feel of his lips on hers took Angel so completely by surprise she didn't stop to think, she just responded. All her feelings for him rose in a tide, surrounding them in a bright velvet haze and rocking them both clear down to their toes. Ox put his arms around her and she sagged against him in total surrender. It was all she had ever dreamed of and more.

When she finally broke away, Angel was breathless and bemused, but she came to earth with a jolt when she saw the utter astonishment in Ox's eyes. Oh, God, what had she done?

"Good Lord, Angel, that felt more like hello than good-bye," he said.

Angel forced herself to give him a blank look. "What are you talking about?"

"Didn't you feel it?"

"Feel what?"

He stared down at her for a moment, then shook his head. "My imagination must be playing tricks on me." He gave her one more bewildered glance and climbed into his wagon, picked up the reins, and took the whip out of its socket. "I guess this is good-bye, then."

"I hate good-byes." She smiled as she reached up to take his hand in a farewell clasp. "I prefer auf Wiedersehen. Until we meet again."

"Auf Wiedersehen it is." He returned the pressure of her fingers and lifted his hand to her face. *"Vaya con Dios,* Angel," he said, softly tracing the curve of her cheek with the backs of his knuckles. Then, with a flick of his whip over the leaders' heads, he was gone.

"May God go with you too," Angel whispered, watching the wagon rumble down the street.

When he finally disappeared around a bend, Angel sighed and turned her attention to the letter in her hand. It didn't take long to read. As usual, her sister's note was filled with dramatic threats of imminent disaster and very little real information. They were twins but almost complete opposites in everything but looks. Still, Angel sensed an unusual urgency in the way Alexis begged her to come to Cheyenne as fast as she could. That as much as the tearstained page convinced her.

"Sam," she said, as she walked decisively through the front door of the Green Garter, "do you think you can finish up here by yourself?"

"Sure thing, Miss Angel. Is there a problem?"

"No, I just discovered some out-of-town business I need to attend to. I'll be leaving early tomorrow morning."

Angel spent the rest of the day putting her business affairs in order so she could turn the final details over to Sam. The sun had long since set by the time she wearily climbed the stairs to her room.

The events of the day crowded in on her as she began to remove the thick layer of makeup she wore. As her flawless white skin emerged, her gray eyes seemed to take on a luminescent shine, and the years disappeared as if by magic. Angel made a face at herself in the mirror. Perhaps it was a good thing she was leaving. Usually she shed the persona of the cynical casino owner with the greasepaint she used. But lately she'd had a harder and harder time finding herself when she finished. Going to Cheyenne was probably exactly what she needed. Whatever her sister's problem, it was sure to make Angel forget her own troubles.

She glanced through her sister's letter again and tried to concentrate on the sketchy information it gave her. It was useless; a pair of green eyes kept intruding. After several minutes she dropped the note on her dressing table and stared into the mirror again.

What would Ox Bruford think if he could see her like this? Would it change his perception of her, or would he still look at her with indifference? No, not indifference, friendship. God, how she hated the word! As she picked up her hairbrush and pulled it through the fiery mass that caressed her shoulders, she thought of the kiss they'd shared. She touched her lips with two fingers. Her reaction had shocked her as much as it had him. No man had ever moved her that way before.

Surely Ox had felt the power of that kiss just as she had, though his reaction had hardly been loverlike. He couldn't have been more astonished if one of his mules had suddenly started singing opera and dancing the minuet. It was obvious he saw her more as a crony than a potential sweetheart. Not that she found that particularly surprising. No man with a respectable background like Ox would even consider falling for the madam of a whorehouse.

Angel shook her head. What difference did it make? It wasn't likely she'd ever see him again, which was just as well. The last thing she needed was a man who would take away her freedom and control her life, a man like her father. Good riddance. Her life would be much less complicated without him underfoot. Someday she'd be glad.

Her lower lip quivered slightly in the mirror. The tears that had threatened all day suddenly spilled over and ran down her cheeks. With a sob, Angel dropped her face to her folded arms and let them flow unchecked. Someday, maybe, but for right now all she could think of was how much she was going to miss him.

3

"Alexis, are you in there?" Angel pushed open the door and peered cautiously around the inside of the little cabin. The place looked as though it hadn't been disturbed for a while. For the dozenth time she wondered why her sister had insisted they meet here instead of the beautiful big home Duncan Smythe had built for his young wife. With a sigh, Angel walked inside and shut the door.

Angel had sent a message as soon as she arrived in town but, knowing Alexis, her sister probably wouldn't be out of bed yet. Then she'd need to get dressed and have Martha do her hair. It could be a very long wait. But she barely had time to remove her hat before she heard the sound of a carriage outside. Seconds later the door burst open and Alexis arrived in a swirl of taffeta and perfume.

"Oh, Angel, you came!" she cried, enveloping her sister in a lavender-scented hug.

Any irritation Angel felt disappeared as she returned

her sister's embrace wholeheartedly. Being with Alexis was like rediscovering a part of herself. "Well, of course I did, you goose. Did you think I wouldn't?"

"I was afraid you wouldn't get my letter way out there in the wilderness."

"I've gotten every letter you ever sent. Besides, South Pass City isn't exactly the wilderness," Angel said dryly. "Now that I'm here, why don't you tell me what's going on?"

"Oh, Angel, my life is over unless you help me." Alexis released her sister and gave a dramatic sigh. "I've fallen in love!"

Angel blinked. "What?"

Alexis glared at her. "Why is that so unbelievable? Just because your heart is made out of stone doesn't mean mine is."

"Oh, I believe you're in love, all right. I just don't understand why it's a difficulty. You've been a widow for months now, and Duncan was almost seventy years old. Nobody will blame you for getting married before your full year of mourning is over."

"That's not the problem."

"Oh?" Angel raised an eyebrow. "Then what is?"

"Father!"

"Ah, I might have known. He doesn't approve of your swain, does he?"

"He doesn't even know about Brandon."

"Then I don't see—"

"Father has arranged for me to marry someone else."

Angel closed her eyes. "Oh, Lord, how bad is it?"

"I'm not sure, I've never met him. All I know is that he's thirty years old and graduated from Harvard with honors."

"I'll bet he's rich, too."

"His grandfather is."

"Then he's probably insufferably arrogant and self-centered. Well, at least he isn't as old as Duncan."

"That's not the point. Duncan was very kind to me." Alexis took an agitated turn around the room. "Anyway, I don't care what James Treenery is like. I don't want to marry him!"

"Not if he's Father's choice, you don't. Still, I don't see where I come into all this."

"I want you to convince Father that this match will never do."

"You want me to what?" Angel laughed. "My dear sister, I think love has muddled your brain. In case you've forgotten, I haven't spoken to Father in almost ten years, not to mention the fact that he disowned me and pretends I never existed."

"I know. And that's precisely the reason it will work."

"What are you talking about?"

"I wasn't positive until I saw you but—oh, come here. I'll show you." Alexis took off her hat and led Angel over to the mirror on the wall. "What do you see?"

Angel peered into the dirty glass. "About four pounds of dust and the life's work of a very diligent spider."

No, not that," Alexis said in disgust, as she wiped away the worst of the grime with her lace handkerchief. "Now what do you see?"

"You mean besides the ruined handkerchief you're going to have a hard time explaining to Martha?"

Alexis's answer was a glare. Angel obediently removed the grin from her face and turned back to the looking glass. "I see two women staring at themselves in the mirror."

"Right, and we're as alike as ever," Alexis said with satisfaction.

"I think you have a tad more hair, though it's pretty hard to tell with it pulled back that way," Angel said with a grin. "And you wouldn't be caught dead wearing this particular shade of blue or such a scandalous dress."

"But besides all that, we still look exactly alike."

"We *are* identical twins, you know."

"That's right. If we dress alike no one can tell us apart."

Angel turned to look at her sister with dawning comprehension. "Oh, Lord. You want me to pretend to be you?"

"Exactly."

"Forget it. I'm not going to travel all the way to New York to see Father, not even for you."

"You don't have to. He's here in Cheyenne. They came when Duncan died and have been with me ever since."

"He's here and you didn't tell me?"

"I knew you wouldn't come."

"I suppose Vanessa is here too?"

Alexis nodded. "And the children. Father even brought a tutor along for them."

"If that isn't just like him. Not only does he come in and take over your home before your husband is cold in his grave, he expects you to feed and house his servants as well."

"Shannon and Jared took care of that for me. They convinced the tutor to leave right away." Alexis grinned. "In fact they've managed to drive off three since they've been here. Father finally said they could spend the rest of the term studying by themselves. I think he's sorry he brought them along."

"He's not one to stay calm when things don't go his way either. I'll bet he had a fit when they read Duncan's will and found out he couldn't touch a penny of your money."

A brief smile crossed Alexis's face. "I didn't know a person could turn that color of purple. He didn't realize a woman could own her own property in Wyoming Territory." Her smile faded and the earnest expression returned. "All you have to do is meet James Treenery, decide you dislike him the way you did Duncan, and refuse to marry him. I'll bet you could even convince James he doesn't want to marry *me* if you put your mind to it."

Angel rolled her eyes. "Why don't you just tell Father you're in love with someone else?"

"Father won't care. He'll force me to marry James Treenery no matter what I say."

"Come on, Alexis. Duncan left you a very rich widow. Father no longer has a hold on you."

"Maybe not, but I can't stand up to him like you can. He'll yell at me, threaten all kinds of awful things, and I'll crumble."

"I don't see why you give in to him. You don't even have an allowance he can cut off."

"Thanks to you. If you hadn't convinced Duncan I should have control of my own money, Father would have that too."

"Father isn't nearly as powerful as you think he is."

"Not to you, but Vanessa says that's because the two of you are so much alike."

Angel frowned. "There's no need to insult me."

"I wasn't. In fact, I've always envied you your strength. You won't give in no matter what pressure Father puts on you." She smiled brightly. "If you make him mad enough maybe he'll disown me too."

"That's crazy. You'd hate being cut off from the family, and it's only when he's trying to run your life that you dislike Father. Besides, we're like sugar and salt. We may look alike, but in reality we're as different as can be. I'd never be able to pull off actually *being* you."

"Yes, you can. We did it all the time when we were children."

"That was years ago, and we didn't do it for more than a few hours. We'd never fool Martha and Vanessa."

"Martha will be on our side. That's the thing about

servants that have been with the family forever. As for Vanessa, she'll never know the difference."

Privately, Angel had to agree. Their stepmother was far from perceptive. "I don't know any of the people you do. If I went out in public I'd be sure to give myself away."

"I haven't been in Cheyenne long enough to have any friends. Duncan and I spent most of our last year in Europe. About the only people I know are the wives of Duncan's business partners at the bank, and they barely speak to me. Anyway, we have two weeks for me to teach you everything you need to know."

Angel frowned. "Two weeks?"

"Father is giving a party welcoming James to Cheyenne. That's when we're supposed to meet. It shouldn't take you more than a week to convince him the match will never do, and you can work on Father at the same time."

"Forget it, Alexis. It's a crazy idea and I'm not doing it."

"Angel, you have to help me!"

"You haven't thought this through. If we got caught, you'd be worse off than you are now."

"I couldn't be," Alexis said, her lip quivering. "If you turn your back on me, it will happen exactly like it did eight years ago. I'll wind up marrying James Treenery the same way I did Duncan, and I'll never have a chance at happiness."

Guilt washed over Angel. Though her sister never mentioned it, they both knew it was Angel's fault Alexis had been forced to marry Duncan Smythe. If she lived to be a hundred, Angel would never forget her rage when she discovered her father had accepted Duncan Smythe's offer for her hand. To Richard Brady, Smythe's fortune and consequential connections were important. The fact that he was over sixty was not.

The wedding plans progressed rapidly in spite of

Angel's efforts to stop them. Finally, in desperation, she decided to run away and start another life somewhere else. Alexis insisted she take the only thing of value the twins owned, their mother's jewelry. So, with many tears and the first pangs of soul-deep loneliness, the twins had parted for the first time in their lives.

It was nearly three months before Angel was able to make contact with her sister again. In the meantime Richard Brady had offered Alexis to Duncan Smythe and he'd been just as smitten with her as he had been with Angel. Alexis had become Mrs. Duncan Smythe in less than a month. Angel had never forgiven herself, not even after she and Duncan became friends and he admitted he was far happier with Alexis.

It all played through Angel's mind now. This was Alexis, her sister, her best friend, the kindest sweetest person she'd ever known: Alexis, who had never let her down, who was everything she was not, her other half.

"Oh, Alex," Angel said, putting her arms around the other woman comfortingly, "if it means that much to you, of course I'll do it."

"You will?" Alexis cried joyfully. "I knew I could count on you. You're the best sister anybody could have."

"I hope you still feel that way when this is all over. I have a feeling we'll probably both live to regret it. Our chances for success are pretty slim, if you ask me." She released her sister and looked around the cabin distastefully. "Well, I guess if I'm going to stay here until I meet this beau of yours, we'd better get the place cleaned up. Why don't you send your driver after Martha while you and I get started?"

Alexis grinned. "Martha's waiting in the carriage."

"I should have guessed. Was she going to convince me if you failed?"

"No, she said I'd have to do that myself."

Angel raised an eyebrow. "Oh? Then she doesn't approve of this little escapade either?"

"Not entirely, but she did say she'd help us if you agreed. I don't think she believed you would."

Thank heavens for Martha, Angel thought, as Alexis hurried out to get her maid. Maybe between the two of us we can keep this from getting completely out of hand.

"I can't believe you actually agreed to this plan," Martha muttered when she walked through the door. "Always figured you for the one with sense."

Angel smiled. "Since you're here, it looks like she talked you into it too."

"Humph. I'm just a servant. I do what I'm told."

Angel and Alexis exchanged a grin and a wink behind Martha's back as she looked around the room in disgust.

"Well, what are you two waiting for?" Martha asked, draping her shawl over the back of a chair and rolling up her sleeves. "This place is a pigsty."

There was much for Angel to learn in the next week and a half, from memorizing the distinguishing features of all the people she might meet to mastering the latest gossip so she could converse knowledgeably with her stepmother. Angel completely immersed herself in her sister's life. It was more a matter of shedding her South Pass City persona than learning anything new. Alexis's mannerisms soon became her own again, and she began walking with small feminine steps instead of her usual direct stride. Angel even switched perfumes, changing from her favorite rose water to her sister's lavender.

Physically there was little to change. In spite of their dissimilar lifestyles, the twin's figures were still exactly the same. In fact about the only difference was their hair. Since Alexis's was longer, they decided to cut both to match. They left the actual haircuts until the day before the switch. That way Alexis's hairstyle would still be so new, everyone would attribute any difference they noticed to the haircut.

"What do you think?" Alexis asked, after Martha finished cutting the waist-length red hair. She turned her head this way and that, studying her image in the mirror.

Angel walked around her sister surveying it critically. "I like it. What about you, Martha?"

"I think it's about the best I can do without whacking off more hair than Alexis is willing to part with. Sit."

Angel obediently took the chair next to her sister and started to remove the pins from her coiffure.

"Uh-oh," Martha said. "It's a different color from Alexis's."

"No, it isn't." Angel closed her eyes and ran her fingers through her hair to shake it free. "It's just a tint I put on to make the color look artificial. You'll cut off most of it." When she opened her eyes, both Martha and Alexis were staring at her with identical stunned expressions.

"Why do you want people to think you dye your hair?" Alexis asked in a strangled voice.

"It's all part of the image I wanted the people of South Pass to see. I wear heavy makeup too."

"But surely they can tell it isn't real."

"Of course they can, but they assume I do it to look younger. If anyone even suspected my true age, I'd have a very difficult time running my business. Men don't have much respect for a young woman."

"Oh, my poor Angel," Alexis said, reaching out to touch her arm. "I never really thought how dangerous it is for you there." She shuddered. "I hate to think of the things you see every day."

Angel shrugged, but the disgust in her sister's voice hurt. Suddenly her life seemed shameful and depraved.

"You have no call to look down your nose at Angel," Martha said, picking up a comb and scissors. "Your sister is a successful businesswoman, plain and simple. She makes a good living and doesn't hurt a soul in the process."

Alexis was instantly remorseful. "I didn't mean it that way. I just worry that something will happen."

"I can take care of myself," Angel said with a brittle smile. "And my bartender makes a pretty good bodyguard."

"Oh, Angel, I'm sorry. I didn't mean to hurt your feelings. I could never have supported myself the way you have. It's just that I worry about you and I want you to be happy."

"I *am* happy. Besides, I sold the business."

Alexis shook her head. "Someday you'll want to get married and have children. I don't see how you're ever going to find a decent husband among all those terrible men."

"A husband is about the last thing I want. I left home to get away from one man's domination," Angel said dryly. "The last thing I'm going to do is subject myself to another's." But even as she spoke the words the image of a man who was both good and decent popped into her mind. Once again she could feel his lips whisper across hers in a kiss that rocked her soul. What would marriage to Ox be like? Angel savored the picture for a moment and then pushed it away in irritation. She needed a husband about as much as she needed a wooden leg.

4

"*Well, James, it's about time* you put in an appearance," James Oxford Bruton Treenery said with good humor. He stood behind his desk near the window, one hand grasping the lapel of his coat, every inch the influential business tycoon.

James Treenery III scowled at his grandfather, unimpressed by the older man. "I had a few things to take care of first."

"Ah, yes, that little hobby of yours. Really, James, you're wasting your time there."

"It's a business, not a hobby, and my name isn't James."

The elder Treenery's face darkened for a moment; then he shrugged. "All right, then, Jamie: I'll be damned if I'll call you by that other heathenish name."

"Suit yourself." The younger man sat down on a chair and put his feet up on the polished surface of the desk. "I'm a busy man, and I don't think you brought me here to discuss my name. Why don't you get to the point?"

Only the tightening of the muscles in his jaw gave any indication James Treenery was having trouble keeping his temper. "It's time you stopped playing at being a common man and took your place in my empire."

"If you summoned me here to sing that song, old man, you've wasted your time," Jamie said, picking his teeth just to annoy his grandfather.

"Actually, I have a proposition for you."

"I can hardly wait."

"All in good time." His grandfather visibly relaxed as the sound of footsteps came from the hallway. "Right now, I think there's someone here to see you," he said, smiling complacently.

"Jamie!"

Jamie straightened in surprise as the door burst open. "Mother?" He surged to his feet.

"Oh, Jamie, you're finally here!" The tiny woman threw herself into his arms. "When Papa Treenery said you were coming I just had to brave the trip out from Chicago."

"He talked you into coming here?" Jamie glared over her head at his grandfather.

"Of course not, dear. In fact, he tried to talk me out of it. He said Cheyenne wasn't the place for a delicately nurtured female."

"He's right. This place isn't fit for anyone but hoodlums and riffraff."

"Now, Jamie, you know that isn't true. You opened your new stage line here, after all."

"He told you I opened a new stage line?" The look Jamie gave his grandfather was positively murderous.

Sarah Beth Treenery patted her son's arm. "Don't blame Papa Treenery. He wasn't going to tell me at all until I wheedled it out of him. I had a terrible time getting him to talk."

"I'll bet," Jamie said dryly.

His grandfather shrugged. "You know how your mother is. She just wouldn't rest until I explained why you decided to give her a whole new wardrobe."

Jamie raised his eyebrows. "You hadn't planned on telling her, I'm sure. My generosity quite overwhelmed you."

"It did indeed. You're a very dutiful son." The elder Treenery reminded Jamie of a snake who knew its victim was completely helpless in its coils and was fully enjoying the death struggles.

"You really shouldn't spend your money on me that way," Sarah Beth said.

For the first time Jamie's smile was genuine as he gave his mother a tender look. "There's no one in the world I'd rather spend my money on."

"That's only because you don't have a family. When you get married again and have children to spoil, you'll feel different."

"I'd feel different, all right," Jamie said with an amused smile. "A wife and a gaggle of children would send me running for the high country. I'd build myself a cabin in the wilderness and only come out once a year for supplies."

She smiled up at him. "You just haven't met the right woman yet."

"The right woman doesn't exist."

"Nonsense." She gave him a hug. "At any rate, I think you should reconsider buying me my own house in Chicago. It was very generous of you to offer, my dear, but I'm perfectly happy at your grandfather's."

"Ah . . . well, perhaps we'd better leave the discussion of that for another time." Jamie felt his grandfather's coils tighten about him as his mother gazed up at him worshipfully.

"Oh, dear, I wasn't supposed to know yet, was I? No matter, I'll forget I ever heard anything." She gave Jamie another hug. "I'm sure you and your grandfather have a great deal of business to discuss so I'll leave you to it. Will you be joining us for dinner before the ball?"

James took Sarah Beth's arm and escorted her to the door. "Of course he'll be dining with us. And you two will have plenty of time to visit before that. I won't keep him long."

"Thank you, Papa Treenery. You're so good to me."

Jamie crossed his arms and regarded the older man sardonically as the door closed behind his mother. "You enjoyed that, didn't you?"

"It's always a delight to see a son so concerned with his mother's happiness. Oh, did I mention you've given her quite a substantial increase in her quarterly allowance too?"

"All right, you wily old bastard, what is it you want from me?"

"Why, what I've always wanted. My only grandson shoulder to shoulder with me at the head of a thriving company."

"The new stage line my mother mentioned, no doubt."

"The Flying T, to be precise. Not only do we have the government mail contract, our line is the only public transportation from the railroad here in Cheyenne north to the mines in Silver Springs Gulch and beyond. It's a guaranteed moneymaker. We've been in business less than six months, and already we've made back most of our original investment."

The elder Treenery's eyes took on a familiar gleam as he began to talk about profit. Jamie could barely contain his disgust. He'd never seen his grandfather show that much emotion for any person living or dead. "It doesn't sound like you need me."

"On the contrary, you are exactly the person I need. I can't stay here to run it; I have far too many other investments to look after. You have plenty of experience, though admittedly it is with freight rather than passengers. You know what sort of drivers to hire, the kind of stock to buy, what supplies would be needed. . . . In short, you could walk in and run the whole operation tomorrow."

"Any number of people have that same kind of experience."

"True, but we need someone with . . . special qualifications."

"We?"

"I have a partner, Richard Brady. He's a man after my own heart."

Jamie's mouth twisted. "He's crooked then?"

"In fact," his grandfather said, ignoring Jamie's remark, "he has the same problem I do. He can't devote as much time as necessary to the business either."

"And he's willing to let me handle it?"

"Not exactly, and to be honest, I wouldn't consider handing it over to his heir either."

"Then what precisely is it you want me to do?"

"It's quite simple, really. We decided if two of the younger members of our families formed a partnership, we could confidently leave the running of the stage line to both of you."

Jamie was incredulous. "You expect me to go into business with a man I've never met?"

"No, we had a somewhat different partnership in mind."

"From the tone of your voice I can tell I'm not going to like this. I suppose the son is just like the father?"

James Treenery Sr. took a cigar out of the humidor on his desk and calmly bit off the end. "Actually, it isn't his son we were proposing you go into partnership with. It's his daughter Alexis."

"His daughter—" Suddenly, Jamie understood exactly what his grandfather wanted, and white-hot anger exploded in his chest. "Marriage? Christ, I thought Deanne would have been enough to convince you I'm not husband material," he said tightly.

"Deanne died in a carriage accident," James reminded him. "There was nothing wrong with your marriage."

"You'd naturally think that, since you arranged it."

"At any rate, it's ancient history and has no bearing on this."

Jamie thought he might choke on his anger. "It does to me, old man. I'll be damned if I'll marry again just to make you happy."

"My happiness isn't involved," his grandfather said. "It's your mother I'm thinking of."

"I can take care of my mother without your help," Jamie snapped.

"Perhaps, but she'd have to give up all those luxuries she's come to expect, not to mention the house you promised to buy. It means a lot to her, you know. She hasn't had a place of her own since your father died." The elder Treenery lit his cigar. "I know how much you sold your little business for. It wouldn't even pay her allowance for a year."

"And you'd cut her off just like that."

His grandfather shrugged. "You forget, she's only my son's widow—no kin of mine. Besides, I wouldn't have to. All I'd need to do is tell her the truth, and she'd refuse to take another penny of my money. I'd do my best to convince her to stay, of course, and she'd leave thinking I was the most generous man alive." He puffed on his cigar and watched the smoke drift toward the ceiling. "Personally, I feel sorry for the poor woman. Her son has lied to her almost constantly for the last ten years."

"That's blackmail!"

"I prefer to think of it as hedging my bet."

"You can't force me to marry Brady's daughter."

"The wedding need not be right away. She's still in

mourning for her husband, though I doubt she'll be wearing black for much longer."

"A widow? Oh, Christ, this gets better and better. Is she old or just ugly?"

"Her name is Alexis Smythe." James went on as though his grandson hadn't spoken. "You'll meet her at the party her father is giving tonight in your honor."

"You're going to look pretty stupid when the guest of honor doesn't show up," Jamie snarled as he strode to the door.

"Your mother is renting a small house near the Grand Hotel," his grandfather called.

"Good, I'll stay there too," Jamie said, and slammed the door behind him. He certainly wasn't going to stay in the same hotel as his grandfather.

"Damn it to hell," Jamie muttered, stalking down the hall. His grandfather had him over a barrel, and they both knew it. A year from now he could have laughed in the old bastard's face. By then he'd have enough money in the trust he'd set up for his mother to support her in style and would be beyond his grandfather's reach.

One year, damn it, that's all he needed. Jamie didn't doubt for a moment that his grandfather would carry out his threats. The man didn't have a bit of interest in anybody or anything except money. There had to be some way to outsmart the old coot.

And then he knew. All he had to do was convince his future bride she wanted no part of him. By the time he reached the street, Jamie was grinning. His years in the freight business had given him a repertoire of obnoxious habits that were guaranteed to send any delicately nurtured female running for cover. When he was done with Alexis Brady Smythe, she'd refuse to marry him if he were the last man on earth.

* * *

"There," Martha said, patting Angel's last curl into place. "You could fool the devil himself."

"Good." Angel smiled at her in the mirror. "Because I'm having dinner with him."

"That's no way to talk about your father."

Angel chuckled. "How do you know I didn't mean James Treenery?"

"Humph. What I do know is you'd better stop this tomfoolery if you want everyone to believe you're Alexis."

"Don't worry, Martha, I'm doing things her way. If it had been left up to me, I wouldn't have worn this dress." She ran her hand over her green satin skirt. "I'd have dressed in her plainest black and gone down to supper too late for Father to do anything about it."

"Yes, and you'd have given yourself away immediately. Your sister would never openly defy—" A knock at the door stopped her in mid-sentence.

"Here we go." Angel gave Martha a conspiratorial wink before answering. "Who is it?"

"It's just me, dear." The door opened, and a tall willowy blond woman swept in. "Are you about ready?" she asked in her clipped British accent.

"Hello, Vanessa," Angel greeted her stepmother. She turned back to the mirror with a worried frown. "Do you really think it's proper for me to be wearing this? I'm not out of mourning yet."

"Please don't be difficult, Alexis. You know what your father said."

"Yes, I know he wants me to make a good impression. Oh, Vanessa, the last thing I want to do is impress James Treenery!"

"You don't even know him. He may be very nice. His mother certainly was when we met her the other day."

"But it's not Sarah Beth Treenery that Father wants me to marry."

"No, of course not. Why ever would you think that?" Vanessa looked vaguely confused.

Angel resisted the urge to roll her eyes as she rose from her seat at the dressing table and crossed the room to her stepmother. "Never mind. Unless my ears deceive me, our guests have arrived."

Vanessa listened for a moment and nodded. "That does sound like a carriage pulling up in front. We'd better go." She hesitated a moment and then touched Angel's hand. "Alexis, I know you don't want this, but you may find you like him very much."

"It won't matter if I hate him. Father wants this marriage, and nothing will change his mind."

Vanessa looked troubled. "Your father loves you. He wouldn't want you to be unhappy." Her jaw hardened, suddenly making her look almost fierce. "If you find Mr. Treenery's grandson intolerable, I promise you I will speak to your father for you."

Much good that would do, Angel thought. Still, she couldn't help but be touched; the image of her stepmother standing up to Richard Brady was laughable. Impulsively Angel put her arms around Vanessa and kissed her cheek. "Have I ever told you how glad I am you married my father?"

Vanessa blinked in surprise. "Why, thank you. I've always thought I was very lucky to have you and Angelica."

It was Angel's turn to be startled. "Both of us?"

"Well, of course. You know how I feel about Angelica. If only she and your father weren't so much alike. I swear I could just shake the two of them."

"I think you just did," Angel heard Martha mutter behind them. She smiled as she thought of the severe lecture Martha had delivered less than an hour ago on letting her unruly tongue give them away. Angel wasn't the only one who was going to have to be careful.

"I guess we'd better go. Our guests are waiting,"

Angel said. She felt a sudden surge of nervous anticipation about seeing her father again after all these years. Richard Brady was standing at the bottom of the stairs waiting for them. He was still a handsome man, though the gleaming black hair was shot with silver and he appeared to have put on a few pounds. Angel felt an unexpected wave of affection as he smiled up at them. For the first time in years she remembered how much she'd loved him when she was a child. It wasn't until she grew up and he began trying to control her adult life that she'd turned her back on him.

"I'm sorry we're late, Richard," Vanessa said, a trifle breathlessly, when they arrived at the bottom.

He kissed her forehead. "It's quite all right. You two lovely ladies were worth waiting for." His gaze swept Angel from head to foot. "I'm glad to see you decided to wear the green dress after all. You look quite stunning. I'm sure James will be impressed."

Richard Brady missed Angel's glare as he turned to a nearby servant and gave directions for dinner to be served in fifteen minutes. How dare he order Alexis's help around as though it were his house? Her earlier affection was replaced by righteous anger. Richard Brady thought of his daughters as poker chips to be used on the bargaining table, nothing more.

Unaware of Angel's displeasure, he took an arm of each woman and led them forward to meet the Treenerys, who were just entering the front door.

Angel was less than gracious but no one noticed, as James Treenery gave a rather vague excuse as to why his grandson had been delayed. Rather than being insulted, Angel was grateful. Dinner with her father was going to be difficult enough.

To her relief, Vanessa had seated her as far away from her father as possible. Instead she was surrounded by Treenerys, with Sarah Beth on her left and James on her right. She liked Alexis's prospective mother-in-law immediately. The older woman even seemed vaguely familiar, though Angel couldn't figure out why. The elder James Treenery was another matter. Though he was not unattractive and was unfailingly polite, there was something about him that made her skin crawl. He reminded her of an eel, slippery and viscous. If his grandson were like him, Angel would move heaven and earth to keep him away from her sister.

At last, the interminable meal was over and they moved back to the entrance to welcome the ball guests. Duncan Smythe had spared no expense when he built his home. Although Cheyenne was a raw frontier town, he'd insisted on a ballroom, certain there would eventually be some sort of society here. And what society there was came in droves. Angel experienced a moment of sheer panic when it became obvious they were going to have a formal reception line. As hostess, it would be her job to introduce all the guests to the Treenerys. A moment later she was relieved to discover Richard Brady intended to usurp her position once more. Without resentment, she stepped aside and let Vanessa take Alexis's rightful place.

Richard and Vanessa Brady welcomed everyone graciously, but Angel could tell James Treenery was far from impressed by the guests. She added snobbery to the long list of things she didn't like about him. His grandson was probably worse; third-generation money usually was.

The guest of honor still hadn't put in an appearance when it was time for the ball to begin, so Richard Brady did the honors with his daughter. The close proximity to her father made Angel nervous, but he didn't appear to notice anything unusual.

Angel never lacked for partners and she found herself thoroughly enjoying herself, for she had always loved to dance. As midnight approached and the younger James Treenery still hadn't appeared, she began to hope he wouldn't. Not even Richard Brady could blame her for refusing to marry a man who insulted her so. She was drinking a glass of champagne and chatting with a handsome young man when Vanessa suddenly appeared at her elbow.

"Mr. Treenery's grandson finally came. Your father's bringing him over right now," Vanessa whispered. "Oh, Mr. Treenery. We're so glad you could make it," she said, a second later, in her breathless voice.

This was it, the moment Angel had been waiting for all evening. So much depended on his first unfavorable impression of her. Angel took a deep breath and fixed a bored look on her face. With deliberate nonchalance, she turned and found herself staring right into the startled green eyes of Ox Bruford.

5

"*It's a pleasure to meet you,* Mrs. Smythe,"
Ox said, in a strangled voice. "May I have the honor of
this dance?"

He didn't wait for an answer. Before Angel even had
time to blink he pulled her into his arms and swept her
out onto the dance floor.

"Well, well, this is certainly a surprise," he said, as
the strains of a waltz surrounded them. "Are you going
to tell me what the hell is going on?"

Angel's tongue seemed frozen to the roof of her
mouth. Ox Bruford was James Oxford Bruton Treenery
III, the man her sister was to marry? A marriage
between the two of them didn't bear thinking of. Alexis
enjoyed the luxuries of her wealth as much as Ox rel-
ished his solitary, nomadic lifestyle. They'd be thoroughly miserable with each other.

Suddenly she remembered her last conversation
with Ox. Was marrying a rich widow what he'd
been talking about when he said he was thinking of

giving up the freighting business and taking up a less strenuous career? If she admitted who she was, Ox would probably insist on meeting the real Alexis and they'd all be right back where they started. In that moment, Angel decided to play it out the way she and Alexis had planned. She gave him a blank look. "Mr. Treenery?"

"Mr. Treenery?" His voice was heavy with sarcasm. "If we're about to become betrothed, don't you think you should call me Ox, at least when we're alone?"

"O-Ox?"

"It's always been good enough before. At the risk of repeating myself, what the hell is going on?"

"P-perhaps if you told me what you were referring to . . . ?" She allowed her voice to trail off with just the right amount of nervous confusion. It wasn't all faked. Ox in full formal evening attire was dazzling and completely unfamiliar. Angel felt she was treading on uncharted ground.

"What I'm referring . . . how about how you managed to make my grandfather think you're Alexis Smythe?"

"I *am* Alexis Smythe, and I only just met your grandfather last week."

Suddenly Ox's eyes narrowed. "Oh, Lord, he followed me to South Pass City. What did he hire you to do?"

Angel didn't have the slightest idea what Ox was talking about. What she did recognize was the pain in his eyes. He thought she'd betrayed him somehow. Something constricted painfully in her chest. "South Pass City? Oh, my goodness!" She gasped as though she had just put it all together. "You must know my sister, Angelica!"

"Angel's your sister?"

Angel nodded. "We're twins. Most people can't tell us apart. She lives in South Pass City."

"Actually, I know her quite well. In fact I just saw her a couple of weeks ago."

"How was she?" Angel asked eagerly.

"Well, she'd just sold out and was planning on leaving South Pass City within the week." His eyes narrowed. "I can't believe two people could look so much alike."

"We're identical, you know, like a pair of bookends." She smiled, but inside her heart was pounding so hard she wondered if he could hear it. The shock of seeing him had completely muddled her mind. She struggled to concentrate on what Alexis would have done if she were really here. "Did Angel say where she was going?"

"I don't think she'd decided yet."

Angel frowned. "You know, she's told me a lot about her friends but I don't remember her mentioning anyone named James."

"What about a bullwhacker named Ox Bruford?"

Angel looked pensive for a moment. "Well, as I remember, there was a freighter with a rather peculiar name . . . I think maybe it was Ox. Is that you?"

"It's the name I go by."

"Why?"

"It's my middle name, sort of." The corner of Ox's mouth quirked as the music stopped and he led her off the floor. "Angel never questioned it. Besides, I didn't know her real name either. In fact when I discovered it by accident she pretended it was someone else."

"How . . . odd."

Ox shrugged. "I guess it was, though I never really thought about it."

Angel cocked her head to one side. "Isn't the freighting business a rather unusual profession for a Yale graduate?"

"Harvard. I see my grandfather's been sharing all the family secrets again." He grimaced. "My college years were a lifetime ago. I've come to view the world much differently since then." He glanced around, looking for an unobtrusive place to spit. With the idea of being obnoxious in mind, he'd taken a healthy bite off a plug of tobacco before he came inside. Suddenly his original plan of spitting on the floor no longer seemed like such a good idea.

"Is anything the matter?" she asked.

"Er . . . no. Would you like something to drink?"

"Yes, please."

"Name your poison."

She gave him a bewildered look. "I beg your pardon?"

"What would you like to drink?"

"Oh. Some punch, I think."

He handed her a glass of punch from the refreshment table and led her to a pair of chairs near the wall. Angel would have known exactly what he was talking about. Still, it was hard to believe.

Angel glanced furtively toward her father and the elder James Treenery, who were both standing near the door wearing self-satisfied expressions.

"Something wrong?" Ox asked, following the direction on his gaze. His jaw hardened when he saw the two men.

"Not really." She bit her lip. "But it might be better if you don't tell my father you know Angelica."

His eyebrows rose a fraction. "Why not?"

"They . . . they had a fight years ago and she ran away. He hasn't spoken of her since."

Ox looked closely at her. When he'd first seen her the only difference he could detect was that she wore no makeup. Now that he looked, he realized they were different in other more subtle ways. Alexis's hair was a softer shade of red, her movements slightly more graceful, her voice a trifle less strident. It was hard to believe two people could look so much alike, and yet it was even more difficult to think of Angel, his closest friend, in cahoots with his grandfather.

"Are you and Angel estranged too?" he asked.

"Oh, no, in fact she moved to South Pass when my husband and I came to Cheyenne so we could be closer to each other."

"Why didn't she just come to Cheyenne?"

Angel pretended to be perplexed. "You know, I'm not sure. She said it had to do with her business, but I'm sure she could have done as well here."

"Maybe she thought there was more money to be made in South Pass City. Then again, it might have something to do with what she does for a living."

"A living?"

"Her job. You know, the work she does."

"Angel owns a business of some sort, but I don't think she actually works."

The ghost of a smile flitted across his face. "Somehow I don't think she'd appreciate hearing you say that."

"Probably not. She seems awfully sensitive about it for some reason." Angel shrugged. "Anyway, she always spends a day or two with the children and me when she can get away."

Ox raised an eyebrow. "You have children?" Funny his grandfather forgot to mention that. Probably because he knew how much Ox disliked the little beasts.

"No," she said, with a smile. "My father has three children from his second marriage. Even though they're much younger, we're all very close. They always spend the summer with me, and Angel comes to visit when she can."

"She loves children," Ox said, taking another surreptitious look around to locate a spittoon. Surely they had one someplace. This was the West, for God's sake.

Angel gave him a startled look. "What makes you think so?"

"Just the way she acts." He smiled tenderly as he

remembered the first time he saw Angel with Becky Ellinson's baby. There was an almost ethereal quality about her as she cooed to the infant in her arms. She'd fairly glowed, and Ox had felt the most peculiar tightening in his chest. "She has a goddaughter she dotes on."

"Oh, yes. Alaina, isn't? Angel has mentioned her a few times. Tell me, Mr. Treenery, how do you like children?"

"Wrapped up in twine and tied to a tree," he answered promptly. It was the sort of nonsense he and Angel shared when their conversation became too serious, but Alexis obviously had a different sense of humor.

"Excuse me?" There was no mistaking the horror in her face.

"It was just a joke," he said, feeling rather foolish. "Actually, I haven't been around many. I was an only child."

"Your grandfather seems to think you're quite anxious to have children of your own."

Ox frowned. "I see my grandfather's been even more informative than usual."

"He was a most enlightening dinner companion."

"I'm sorry I missed it," Ox said dryly. "I suppose you found him entertaining as well?"

Angel looked away. "He's . . . ah, he's rather difficult to converse with."

"Only if you want to add something to the conversation."

"I'm sure he has your best interests at heart," Angel said uncertainly.

"I think it's fairly safe to say James Treenery is his main concern."

"Your mother seems quite close to him."

"He's been very good to her since my father died." And will continue to be as long as I do what he wants,

Ox thought. He quickly surveyed the room again. If he didn't find a place to get rid of the noxious fluid in his mouth soon, he was going to be in big trouble.

Angel glanced around. "Goodness, Mr. Treenery, I've been monopolizing you. As the guest of honor you should be meeting everyone. My stepmother will probably be quite put out with me for not bringing you to her sooner." She rose.

"Then by all means let's go find her," Ox said as he got up too. He caught a glimpse of his grandfather across the room. The man was nearly glowing with self-satisfaction. With a start, Ox realized he'd spent the better part of an hour with Alexis Smythe and hadn't once been the obnoxious boor he'd intended to be. In fact he'd apologized for the one off-color thing he said and was nearly strangling to keep from embarrassing himself in front of her. This wasn't going at all as he'd planned.

He glanced down at his companion as she led him through the crowd. She just reminded him too much of Angel. When she'd first turned around and he'd seen the face of his dear friend, his immediate reaction had been one of overwhelming joy. Then when he thought his grandfather had somehow subverted her, the pain had been devastating in its intensity. Now he found he simply couldn't be rude to her twin.

"You remember my stepmother, don't you?" Alexis was saying to him.

"Certainly, Mrs. Brady," he said, smiling at the tall slender woman.

"I'm sorry I've kept Mr. Treenery from the party for so long, Vanessa. I know you've been wanting to introduce him to everyone."

"I have?" She gave her stepdaughter a blank look.

"Yes, dear. I'm sure Mrs. Coombs and her daughters are just dying to meet him."

Ox couldn't see Alexis's face, but he was certain her

expression gave Vanessa Brady a very strong message. He was hard put not to laugh. If he hadn't been convinced of her identity before, he was now. Whenever Angel tired of his company, she told him to go bother someone else for a while or informed him she had better things to do than shoot the breeze with him all day. Her sister wasn't quite so straightforward, it seemed.

Vanessa Brady blinked a couple of times. "Oh, of course, how silly of me. She was just asking when I was going to bring him around." She looked at her stepdaughter uncertainly. "Were you planning to come with us?"

"I'm afraid I have a bit of a headache. If you don't mind, I think I'll make an early night of it."

"I hope it's nothing serious," Ox said, with a touch of cynicism. "It would certainly be too bad if one party wore you out."

"I'm sure I'll be fine in the morning. It was just all the last-minute switching we had to do at dinner and the uncertainty of whether all the guests would arrive. It tends to put one out of sorts."

Ox smiled. He'd just been firmly put in his place. Maybe Alexis was more like Angel than he thought. "I'm sure the culprits have been properly chastised."

"I certainly hope so. Good night, Mr. Treenery."

"Good night, Mrs. Smythe. It's been a most entertaining evening."

"I'm glad you've enjoyed it. Oh, by the way," she said, as she started to leave, "the spittoon is over behind the door."

Ox grinned as he watched her walk away. Angel would have just let him swallow it.

Angel's thoughts were in a turmoil as she climbed the stairs to Alexis's room. Ox Bruford! Lord, as if the plan weren't difficult enough already. Without her cynical casino owner persona to protect her, how was she going to keep him at arm's length when his very nearness sent her emotions into a spin? Playing cat-and-mouse with him was not what she had bargained for either. He knew her far too well. It wouldn't take many exchanges like the last one to give her away. His remark about the twine and children had nearly been her undoing. Pretending to be aghast instead of laughing had been far from easy. Drat the man anyway.

Martha met her at the door of Alexis's bedroom. "Well, did young Treenery ever arrive?"

"Oh, yes, and we've got trouble."

Though exhaustion dogged her steps, Angel resisted the temptation of going to bed and gave Martha a quick rundown of the evening instead. While she talked, she shed her ballgown and donned Alexis's riding habit.

Martha's brow furrowed with concern as she watched Angel complete her preparations. "Are you sure you're going to be all right? This town isn't safe at night."

"Compared to South Pass City, Cheyenne is positively boring." She slid a lethal-looking knife into the sheath strapped to her calf and dropped a derringer into the pocket of her cape. "Don't worry, Martha, I know how to stay out of trouble. Besides, this is the only time Alexis and I can meet. I'll be back in an hour or so."

The trip out to the cabin took very little time, and Alexis was soon welcoming her inside.

"I see you've had a visitor," Angel said, removing her cape.

"How did you know that?"

"You don't smoke." Angel nodded toward a cigar butt, still smoldering in a dish by the fireplace. "Brandon?"

Alexis blushed and nodded. "He was in town to get supplies."

"In town? He doesn't live in Cheyenne?"

"No. He has a ranch north of here."

"A cowboy? Good Lord, how did you manage to meet him?"

Alexis's eyes flashed. "You don't have to be such a snob, Angel. So what if Brandon works for his living? So do you, and nobody thinks any less of you for it."

It never ceased to amaze Angel how little her sister understood about her life. Nobody thought less of her? Even the man she loved couldn't see through her chosen profession to the woman inside. "I'm sorry, Alexis," she said, rubbing her forehead. "I didn't mean it to sound like that. He just doesn't seem like the sort of man you'd be likely to run into. Why didn't you tell him to stay so I could meet him?"

"He had to get back," Alexis said, avoiding her eyes. Angel couldn't help wondering which one she was ashamed of, her lover or her sister.

"Maybe next time," Angel said, plopping down in a chair.

"Yes, maybe so." Alexis poured a cup of coffee and sat down in the other chair. "How did it go?" she asked, handing Angel the cup.

"You were right about his grandfather and his mother. I couldn't stand him and I loved her." She took a sip of coffee. "James Oxford Bruton Treenery the Third is going to be more of a problem than we thought."

"Is he old?"

Angel smiled. "No, in fact he's not much older than we are."

"Ugly then?"

"Hardly. He has wavy brown hair, gorgeous green eyes, and a set of shoulders that would make the girls back at school swoon."

"Then he's stuck-up?"

"Hasn't got a conceited bone in his body."

Alexis raised an eyebrow. "It sounds like you're in love with him already. Is that what you're worried about?"

"The problem is that I know him. More importantly, he knows me."

"Oh, dear. How well?"

Angel sighed. "Well enough. Do you remember me mentioning a man named Ox Bruford?"

"The muleskinner?"

"That's him. I haven't quite figured out what's going on, but he's definitely Treenery's grandson."

"But this is wonderful, Angel! We'll just tell him I don't want to marry him and that will be that."

"I don't think that's going to work."

"Why not?"

"I know Ox, and this isn't like him at all. He's in trouble somehow, maybe even being blackmailed by someone. If my suspicions are correct, there's more at stake here than our little charade, and he won't be easily dissuaded." Angel closed her eyes and pinched the bridge of her nose. "I'm afraid he's marrying you for your money."

6

"Ahhgh!" Martha screeched and jumped back as a very large, ugly bug dropped onto the dressing table in front of her.

Angel looked at it critically for a moment and then picked it up and popped it into her mouth.

Martha recoiled. "Lord have mercy, girl, what are you doing?"

"I know marzipan when I see it," she said, chewing the sugary confection with obvious enjoyment. "All right, you may as well come out. We're on to you."

The curtain next to the dressing table parted and a little girl's freckled face appeared. "Angel?"

"Of course it's Angel." A dark-haired boy crawled out from under the bed. "Alexis would still be screaming her head off."

Angel glanced up at Martha. "So much for fooling my brother and sister."

"Humph. I might have known," Martha said. "These two are both cut from the same bolt of cloth as you."

"Why, thank you, Martha."

"I didn't necessarily mean it as a compliment."

Angel just grinned as she rose from her seat and moved toward her half-siblings. "Let me look at you two. Heavens, Jared, you're nearly as tall as I am!"

He stood a little taller and puffed out his chest. "I turned twelve, you know."

"That's right. Goodness, you're growing up so fast you'll be a man before I know it. Come here and let me give you a hug."

"Aw, Angel, that's for little kids."

"And big sisters. Don't worry, Martha and Shannon won't tell." Angel gave him an enthusiastic embrace and smiled when he returned it wholeheartedly.

"I don't mind hugs." Shannon stepped out from behind the curtain and made a face at her brother. "Jared wouldn't either if it weren't for that stupid Thomas next door. He says only sissies let girls hug them."

"He's obviously misinformed," Angel said, embracing her ten-year-old sister happily. "I do believe you get prettier every time I see you, Shannon. Alexis is going to have to step aside as the family beauty, one of these days."

"I still have freckles, Angel."

"So did Alexis and I at your age. They'll be nothing but a memory in a few years." She cocked her head to one side. "Is this a new hairstyle I see?"

Shannon looked doubtful. "Mama said I should try curls instead of braids."

"I think it's very nice."

"It gets in the way," Jared said with disgust. "Yesterday, she caught it on a branch when she was climbing a tree. She screeched like a mountain lion till I got her loose."

"Did not!" Shannon was indignant.

"Maybe we can come up with something to keep it

out of your way," Angel said. "In the meantime, I don't see any reason why you can't go back to braids when you need to on occasion."

"She could stop climbing trees," Martha pointed out. "Though I don't suppose there's much hope of that."

"Well, of course not. What an idea." Angel dismissed the notion with a wave of her hand. "Life is too short to spend it earthbound."

"Does Father know you're here?" Shannon asked.

Angel avoided looking her in the eye. "Ah—well, no, not exactly."

"Don't be a dunce, Shannon," Jared said, rolling his eyes. "She's here to get rid of the bothersome beau."

Angel was startled. "The bothersome beau?"

"You know, the man Father wants Alexis to marry. She said she'd die first, and Father said she was an unnatural daughter, and—"

"I get the idea," Angel put in hastily. "But what makes you think I could get rid of him?"

"Alexis says you can do anything you set your mind to," Shannon said. "It's just a matter of getting you to set your mind to it. That's why she wanted you to meet Tree—Tree—whatever his name is instead of her. Then she can marry Brandon."

Angel's eyebrow rose another fraction of an inch. "Alexis told you all this?"

"Not exactly." Shannon and Jared exchanged a guilty glance. "We sort of overheard it."

Martha looked down her nose at them. "Overheard it, my eye. It was eavesdropping plain and simple."

"It seems the two of you have picked up some bad habits." Angel crossed her arms and tried to look severe. "I certainly hope I'm not going to have to worry about you two listening to every conversation I have."

Jared grinned. "Oh, no. We only listen to the interesting ones."

Angel laughed. "I guess that put me in my place." Then she sobered. "The truth is, eavesdropping is very rude and inconsiderate. It's also very embarrassing if you get caught."

"Besides, eavesdroppers never hear good of themselves," Martha said primly.

The two miscreants tried to look repentant, though they weren't very successful. "Does Mama know you and Alexis traded places?" Shannon asked after a moment.

"No. Only you two and Martha know. If Father finds out it will all be for nothing."

"I guess he'd be pretty mad, wouldn't he?" Jared said.

"Furious."

Shannon and Jared looked at each other. "We won't tell," they said in unison, solemnly raising their right hands and looking expectantly at Angel.

For the first time Angel felt a sting of guilt. Shannon and Jared were offering to take the Brady oath, a tradition she and Alexis had started when they were children. Though it was a child's game, she knew her brother and sister took it very seriously. They were essentially promising to keep her secret even if it meant lying to their parents. "I don't know if that's necessary—"

"Come on, Angel," Jared said.

She sighed. "Oh, all right, but it only means you don't tell. I wouldn't want you to actually lie for me." She lifted her right hand and linked her little finger with theirs.

"One for all and all for one, we Bradys stick together. Through blood and pain and tortured screams this secret is ours forever," they chanted. Then they all spit in their right palms and slapped them together high above their heads.

"That ought to do it," Martha said sarcastically.

Jared looked pensive. "We better not tell Betsy. I don't think she'd understand."

Angel shook her head. "No, I don't imagine she would. She's only four, after all. Where is she, by the way? You two aren't supposed to be watching her, are you?"

"No, she's taking a nap."

"Is Alexis going to marry Brandon?" Shannon asked suddenly.

Angel raised a brow. "She didn't say. Have you met him?"

Jared shrugged. "Once, but it was just to say hello. He promised we could come out to his ranch sometime, but she never took us."

There was a knock at the door. Then it opened and Vanessa swept into the room. "Alexis—oh, what are you two doing in here?"

"We were just chatting," Angel said. "I haven't seen them for so long."

Vanessa looked confused. "But you spent most of the day before yesterday with them."

"Yes, but that was before the party," Jared put in quickly. "She was telling us all about it."

"I liked the dancing," Shannon added. "And all the pretty dresses. I especially liked Mrs. Dayton's."

"It's too bad we didn't think of letting the two of you stay up and take a peek from the top of the stairs," Angel said dryly. She was rewarded with a unrepentant grin from her brother and sister.

As usual, Vanessa was oblivious to the interchange between the three. "I'm so glad you decided to go along with your father's wishes, Alexis. He was very pleased with the way you treated Mr. Treenery."

"My aim in life is to please my father."

"I must admit Mr. Treenery was something of a surprise," Vanessa said candidly. "He's seems quite nice, and so handsome, too."

Angel had to bite her lip to keep from grinning. Apparently Vanessa hadn't expected much of her husband's choice either. "I'm still not interested in marrying him."

"Certainly not, you only just met. I told your father he'd have to give the two of you a chance to get to know each other first."

"And I'm sure he was willing to do that."

"Well, of course. Your father isn't an ogre, you know. Oh, heavens, here I am chattering on like a magpie and he's waiting for you downstairs."

Angel frowned. "My father?"

"No, silly, Mr. Treenery. I think he's very taken with you."

Angel's heart jumped to her throat. Ox was waiting for her downstairs? Willing herself to stay calm, she walked back to the dressing table. "I'll be down in a few minutes as soon as I finish my hair."

"All right, dear, but don't keep him waiting long. You children run along now," Vanessa said, shooing her offspring toward the door. "Alexis doesn't have time to visit."

Angel glanced back over her shoulder. "They don't have to leave."

"It's all right. We have something we need to do anyway," Jared said.

Shannon looked surprised. "We do?"

"Yes." Jared gave her a little push toward the door. "And we have to get started right away."

A slight frown marred Vanessa's brow as she watched them go. "What do you suppose they're up to?"

"No good, I'll wager." Martha picked up the hairbrush and started on Angel's hair again. "If there's no trouble to get into, those two will make their own."

"I best go see."

Vanessa hurried out after them and Angel smiled. "Do you think she'll be able to thwart whatever Jared has planned?"

Martha snorted. "Not likely. In fact, if I know those two she'll probably wind up helping them without realizing she's doing it. Stop your fidgeting or I'll never get this done."

"I'm sorry." Angel forced herself to sit still. "I'm just not used to having anyone do my hair for me." In truth, it was difficult not to jump up and pace the room. How ridiculous for the mere anticipation of seeing Ox to set her heart pounding in her chest like this. It wasn't as if she was a silly schoolgirl, for heaven's sake. By the time Martha secured the last hairpin, Angel had calmed herself, at least outwardly. It was a very serene widow who entered the parlor a few minutes later and greeted Ox Bruford.

"Good afternoon, Mr. Treenery."

He flashed her his heart-stopping grin. "Please, call me Ox. I never could abide being called Mr. Treenery. It sounds too much like my grandfather."

"Very well—er, Ox." Her tone left no doubt she thought it was a peculiar name. "Won't you sit down?"

"Actually I came to ask if you'd like to go for a buggy ride."

Angel glanced toward the window. A gorgeous early spring day beckoned. This might be a good time to begin trying to find out why he needed to marry for money. Besides, a buggy ride with Ox was too tempting to resist. "I suppose I have time for a short one. Just let me get my wrap—"

"Alexis, Alexis!" The door burst open and a small whirlwind dashed into the room.

Angel bent down and scooped the little girl up in her arms. "What is it, precious?"

"I go with you?"

"Who said I was going anywhere?"

"Shannon and Jared."

Angel swallowed a smile. So that's what they were up to. They couldn't have provided her with a better chaperone. "Er . . . , Ox, this is my youngest sister, Elizabeth. Betsy, this is Mr. Treenery."

"Howdy do, Mr. Treenery." She stuck out her hand.

He cleared his throat uncomfortably, then reached out and shook her hand awkwardly. "It's a pleasure to meet you, Miss Brady."

"I go with you and Alexis?"

"Er . . . well, I guess you could," he said, with a wary smile. "If you want to."

"I do!"

A startled expression crossed Ox's face as Betsy withdrew her hand from his larger one. He glanced down at his palm, and his brows rose a fraction.

"Please, Alexis," Betsy begged, putting her hands on either side of Angel's face and looking earnestly into her sister's eyes.

Angel reached up and pulled a blond braid. "I don't know, brat, will you be a good girl?"

"I be perfect."

"You promise not to scare the horses, or jump out of the buggy, or cry when it's time to come home?" Angel asked.

"I promise," Betsy said.

Though most of her attention was on the little girl in her arms, Angel couldn't help but notice Ox watching them with rapt attention. How peculiar. He always maintained he couldn't stand children. "All right, then, let's go ask your mother," she said, setting Betsy on her feet. "We'll be back in a few minutes Mr.—I mean, Ox."

"Take your time." Ox's grin was even bigger than usual.

"Is something wrong?" Angel asked suspiciously.

"Well, I wouldn't call it wrong exactly." His eyes danced with ill-concealed humor. "But you might want to —ah, check your hair before we leave."

Mystified, Angel followed Betsy out into the hall.

She was still wondering what Ox's problem was when they reached Alexis's sitting room, where Vanessa was working on her embroidery.

Angel glanced in the mirror that hung outside the door and froze in dismay. No wonder Ox was amused; it was amazing he wasn't laughing outright. Check her hair indeed! There wasn't a thing wrong with her coiffure, but her cheeks were another matter. They were covered with two perfect handprints outlined in sticky purple jam.

7

"*Be careful, Betsy,*" *Angel* said, as her sister bounced up and down on the buggy seat. "You'll fall out if you don't sit still." Though all her attention appeared focused on the little girl, she was vitally aware of the man sitting next to her. In all the time she and Ox had been friends, they'd never done anything like this. Maybe there were some advantages to pretending to be Alexis.

"Look, Alexis, a moose!" Betsy said, leaning precariously over the side.

"No, sweetheart, that's a cow," Angel said, pulling her back.

"I ride it?"

Ox chuckled. "People don't ride cows."

"Why not?"

"I guess because people milk them instead."

"Why?"

"Well," Ox said thoughtfully, "maybe because the saddles don't fit."

"I ride it without a saddle?"

Ox shook his head. "No, that's not a good idea. Cows aren't trained like horses. Anyway, ladies never ride bareback."

"Angel does."

"She does?"

"Uh-huh. I be like Angel."

Angel rolled her eyes. "I promise you, Angel never rode a cow."

"You let me ride a cow, Mr. Treenery?"

"No." A look of consternation crossed his face as Betsy's inquisitive blue eyes filled with tears.

"Er, maybe I'll take you for a horseback ride one of these days."

The tears instantly disappeared. "Tomorrow?"

"Tomorrow? Well, I don't know. . . ."

Angel bit back a grin. If Shannon and Jared were like her, Betsy was the image of Alexis. It was all Angel could do not to laugh as she watched her baby sister skillfully wrap Ox around her little finger.

"Please?" Betsy pleaded, staring up at him earnestly.

Ox raised an eyebrow. "If Alexis comes along, I will."

Betsy switched around and gazed up at her sister beseechingly. "Please, Alexis, please. I want to go with Mr. Treenery!"

"We'll see," Angel said. "And you don't need to try those fake tears with me because they won't work."

"Well, what do you say, Alexis, shall we let this little one have her way and go for a ride tomorrow?" Ox asked.

"I think she gets her way too often as it is."

Ox grinned. "Then once more won't hurt."

"No, I suppose not."

"May I take that as a yes?"

Angel shrugged. "I guess so."

"With enthusiasm like that, I'm tempted to suggest a picnic too," Ox said, with a twinkle in his eye.

The warm smile set alarm bells ringing in Angel's head. What was she doing flirting with him when she was supposed to be convincing him he didn't want to marry Alexis? "Picnics aren't my style. I don't like eating in the dirt."

She watched his smile fade with a certain amount of satisfaction. A man who lived and worked outdoors the way Ox did was sure to be offended by such a statement. It wouldn't take long to convince him how inappropriate Alexis would be for a wife.

"Would you mind my asking you a personal question, Alexis?"

"That would depend on the question."

"I was just wondering how long you've been interested in the stage business."

"The stage? Why, never, really, though I've always thought acting might be fun if it weren't socially unacceptable."

"Acting?" It was Ox's turn to look surprised. "Oh, no, I didn't mean that kind of stage. Stagecoach."

"What on earth would make you think I was interested in stagecoaches?"

"My grandfather told me you wanted to take over your father's half of the Flying T."

"The Flying T?"

"The stage line your father and my grandfather are partners in."

Angel shook her head. "I can't imagine where your grandfather got such a notion. My father would never even discuss business with me, let alone actually let me participate."

"My grandfather said that was the reason for this proposed—er, partnership."

Angel laughed. "If your grandfather believes my father will give up one ounce of power to anybody, he's doomed to disappointment."

"Not even to his daughter?"

"Especially not to his daughter. My father controls everything and everybody around him. He'd never let me make business decisions; he wouldn't even let me choose what I wore to the party last night."

Ox raised an eyebrow. "Has he always been like this? I mean, I can't imagine anyone telling Angel what to do."

"He tried. That's why she left." She gave him a direct look. "If I know my father, this is probably a way for him to get more control of the company instead of less."

"It seems your father and my grandfather have the same flaw," Ox observed. "That might just be their downfall."

"Wouldn't I love to see that!"

"Maybe you will," Ox said pensively. "Maybe you will."

Angel was still wondering what he meant when she paid her nightly visit to Alexis shortly after dinner. Predictably, her sister was less concerned with what plan Ox might have in mind than how long it was going to take Angel to persuade him to give up his suit. She laughed aloud when Angel told her about the jam fiasco.

"We should have realized Shannon and Jared would jump into the middle of things. Who else would have thought of sending Betsy along as a chaperone?" Alexis said with a grin.

"I have to admit it was pretty clever of them." Angel took a sip of tea and relaxed in her chair. "Though I wasn't nearly as impressed with the rest of it."

Alexis giggled. "It's too bad Betsy didn't leave her jam on Mr. Treenery instead."

"A little jam won't stop Ox."

"What will?"

Angel sighed. "I'm not sure, but I think you're going to be very silly tomorrow," she said.

"Will he believe it?" Alexis asked doubtfully.

"He doesn't know you. Besides, the world expects rich widows to be brainless simpletons."

"Thank you," Alexis said. "I'm glad I won't be there to witness myself as a total idiot."

Angel grinned. "It's your own fault. You decided to let me play the part." Then she sobered. "I just wish I knew what Ox is up to."

"He's trying to convince you to marry him."

Angel shook her head. "I don't think so. There's nothing the least bit loverlike about the way he's acting."

"You probably wouldn't recognize it if there were."

"Well, of course I would," Angel said, with a touch of irritation. "I know a man with marriage on his mind when I see one."

"Sure, that's why you never realized John Stikes was trying to court you until he proposed," Alexis reminded her. "You just assumed he thought of you as a good friend."

"I was eighteen!"

"And how many men have courted you since?"

"None."

"See?" Alexis smiled triumphantly. "There were probably dozens. You just didn't know it."

"Alexis, I've spent most of that time running casinos!"

"Right, casinos frequented by men. Surely there were some who looked at you as something other than a businesswoman."

"I'm sure there were, but it wasn't marriage they were thinking of."

"You don't know that. Anyway, I don't think you can trust your instincts on this, Angel. You've got to try harder to keep Mr. Treenery at arm's length. I don't want to wind up married to him."

"If you don't like the way I'm doing things, why

don't you just end this stupid charade and do it yourself," Angel snapped. "I'll be glad to step aside."

Alexis bit her lip. "I'm sorry. I didn't mean to sound critical. I just don't want anybody to get hurt, including your friend."

"Don't worry, I know what I'm doing. I know exactly how to handle Ox Bruford."

But her sister's words kept running through Angel's mind. She'd know if Ox was seriously pursuing her . . . wouldn't she? Suddenly she wasn't so sure. Maybe it wouldn't be a bad idea to put a little more distance between them, just in case.

Ox felt the crazy urge to whistle as he rode up to Alexis Smythe's house. There was no guarantee she would agree to help him, yet he couldn't shake the positive feeling he'd had ever since the idea occurred to him. Angel would have embraced the plan wholeheartedly, for it was just the sort of challenge she thrived on. If Alexis was as much like her twin as she seemed, she'd jump at the proposition he was going to offer her.

His feet had barely touched the ground when the front door burst open and Betsy came flying down the steps.

"Mr. Treenery!" she yelled. "I ride with you?"

"Not if you scare my horse."

She came to an abrupt halt and started toward him again on tiptoe. "I be very quiet," she whispered. "Alexis said she be right out. Can I talk to the horsey?"

"If you're very careful and don't make any quick movements." Ox watched in amusement as Betsy petted the animal and whispered nonsense to it in order to make up. It was no wonder she was a trifle spoiled, she was such a cute little thing. Even the rented horse seemed to like her.

Time passed slowly as Ox waited for Alexis to appear. Betsy kept up a steady stream of chatter, though she eventually lost interest in the horse and moved on to the sticks and gravel along the side of the road. Ox's glances toward the house became more frequent as she asked him a barrage of questions about castles and dragons. He was on the verge of losing patience when the door finally opened.

Ox looked up and caught his breath in surprise. Though he had never seen Angel in a fashionable riding habit, he was struck by how much Alexis looked like her today. It would be virtually impossible to tell them apart.

The image disappeared the moment she joined him. "I'm sorry I'm so late," she said petulantly, "but my maid just couldn't get my hair right this morning."

"It looks fine."

She touched the elaborate mass of curls with one hand and made a face. "It's very nice of you to say so, but I know I look a fright. If Betsy weren't looking forward to this ride—" She broke off with a dramatic sigh.

"I wouldn't worry too much. No one's likely to see us once we leave town."

"I suppose you're right. This is the most godforsaken country."

Ox frowned. "I like to think of it as wide-open spaces."

"You sound just like my sister," she said, with a tinge of disgust. "Angel loves it here."

"Apparently you don't agree with her."

"You'll find that Angel and I frequently don't agree, Mr. Treenery."

"I thought we had progressed beyond Mr. Treenery and Mrs. Smythe yesterday."

She shrugged. "Mule is such a peculiar name. Couldn't I just call you James?"

"My grandfather's name is James. I prefer not to use

it. And my name is Ox, not Mule," he said, with a touch of irritation.

"Oh, yes, of course, how silly of me. Ah, here's my brother with the horse now." She smiled as the boy led a pretty dappled-gray mare around the corner of the house. "Thank you, Jared. Did you have any trouble getting her saddled?"

The boy looked surprised. "But you—" A look from his sister stopped him in mid-sentence. He gave Ox a guilty glance and began again. "No trouble at all, Alexis."

"Good. Mr. Treenery, I'd like you to meet my half-brother, Jared. Jared, this is Mr. Treenery."

"Ox," he corrected, reaching out to shake the young man's hand. "I'm a friend of your sister Angel's."

Jared's eyes widened. "Angel?"

"He knew her in South Pass City," Angel put in. "Are you and Shannon ready to go?"

"Mama said we couldn't. I think she would have made Betsy stay home too if the little brat hadn't thrown such a fit. Mama doesn't think you need company."

Great, Angel thought with a frown. All she needed was for Vanessa to play matchmaker. "Never mind. I'll be fine."

The boy looked worried. "You're sure?"

"Positive." She patted his shoulder and turned to Ox. "Shall we collect Betsy and be on our way, Mr. Treenery? I hope you don't mind, but she insists on riding with you."

As the morning progressed it became obvious to Ox that Alexis was avoiding him. By continually riding out ahead, she managed to stay far enough away that he couldn't talk to her. Good. It appeared Alexis didn't like being a pawn any more than he did and was trying to thwart her father's plan by repulsing her suitor.

Ox tested his theory the first chance he got.

"Alexis," he called, as she came within hailing distance, "Betsy and I need your help."

"With what?" Angel asked, as she turned and rode back to them.

Ox held up the two halves of Betsy's pinafore sash. "This . . . thing on her dress came undone."

"Oh, for goodness' sake, all you have to do is tie it."

Ox looked slightly perplexed for a moment. Then he shrugged and tied the sash in an intricate knot.

Angel had to fight the urge to laugh as she watched. The knot was one Ox used to tie down the canvas covers on his freight wagons. "What in the world is that?"

"A clove hitch. I figure if it can hold a tarp on a load it ought to keep a dress on a little girl," Ox said, looking at her over the top of Betsy's head. As their gazes met, something sweet and warm uncurled in the pit of his stomach. For a split second he saw a reflection of that warmth in her eyes before she turned her horse away with a jerk.

"I think I'll ride to the top of that hill," she said, over her shoulder. "I'll bet the view is spectacular." With that she was gone.

It was the last time she let him get close. Every time he came within speaking distance she was off again to take a closer look at this or that. Ox's amusement deepened. He was beginning to think he was going to have to put off his proposal until another day when Betsy provided him with the opportunity he'd been waiting for.

Unable to answer the call of nature by herself, Betsy summoned her sister. By the time they emerged from the bushes, Ox had dismounted and was leaning against a tree. Angel's eyes narrowed as she took in the sight of the horses grazing contentedly on the prairie behind him.

"Why did you hobble the horses?" she asked suspiciously.

"This is such a pretty place, I thought you and Betsy might want to rest awhile before we start back."

"We're just fine."

"What do you think, Betsy?" Ox said, hunkering down to the little girl's level. "Shall we head right back or do you want to play for a while?"

"Play," she answered promptly.

"That's what I figured," he said with a smile. "Why don't you go pick some of those flowers to take home while your sister and I talk?"

"All right," she said, and was off before Angel had a chance to stop her.

I don't know what we'll find to talk about," Angel said uneasily as Ox straightened and moved toward her.

"On the contrary, we have a great deal to discuss."

"I can't imagine what." She took three steps backward. "We hardly know each other."

"Perhaps not, but we have a common goal." His voice was soft and deep as he closed the distance between them. "In fact, I have a proposition I think you'll find hard to resist."

"You've obviously misunderstood me, Mr. Treenery." She kept backing up until she suddenly came up against a tree. "I have no intention of—"

"Ah, but you haven't heard my proposition," he interrupted, bracing his hand above her head on the tree and looming over her.

She closed her eyes. "N-no. You don't understand."

"I understand perfectly. That's why I need to ask you an important question," he whispered. The soft silkiness of his voice against her ear was as devastating as an intimate caress.

"I don't want —"

"Alexis," he interrupted again, his voice a soft, sexy rumble, "will you stop running away if I promise I won't ask you to marry me?"

8

"*What?*" *Angel's eyes flew* open in shock.

Ox raised his brows slightly. "That's what's going on, isn't it? You're afraid I'm going to propose so you're making darn sure I don't get the chance. I just wanted to relieve your mind so you could stop all this shilly-shallying."

As Angel looked up into his eyes and saw the familiar twinkle in the green depths, she realized he was teasing her. "Talk about shilly-shallying! Why didn't you tell me that in the first place instead of all this elaborate folderol?" She reached up to cuff his shoulder. "Now stop breathing down my neck before I box your ears."

The moment she saw the startled look on his face, Angel realized her mistake. It was the way she had always reacted to his foolishness. From his expression it was clear he was dangerously close to seeing through her little masquerade. She had no choice but to brazen it out. "What's the matter, didn't my sister ever put you in your place?"

"All the time. It's just that—my God, you sounded so much like her just now!"

Angel shrugged. "We react the same under pressure. If you ever meet Martha you'll understand why."

"Martha?"

"She was my mother's maid until Mama died, and she's been bullying my sister and me ever since. Martha is the kind that berates you for not washing behind your ears while she's helping you put your life back together."

Ox smiled. "A little on the abrasive side, is she?"

"You might say that. It's her way of showing us she loves us."

"Sounds a lot like Angel. She uses cynicism to hide her feelings."

It was Angel's turn to be startled. Ox was more perceptive than she ever imagined. More perceptive and far more dangerous. "You didn't bring me out here to talk about Angel," she said, slipping out from under his arm.

"No." He leaned against the tree and crossed his arms. "After our conversation yesterday, it occurred to me that you aren't any more anxious for this arranged marriage than I am."

"You don't want to marry a rich widow and settle down to a life of indolence?"

"Not particularly, though it has nothing to do with you." He grinned. "In fact, as rich widows go, you're a cut above the rest."

She raised an eyebrow. "You have a great deal of experience with them then?"

"Nope, you're the first. But I don't think many as young and pretty as you stay single for long."

"Thank you—I think."

"It was meant as a compliment," he assured her; then his smile faded. "I know it's forward of me to ask, but am I right in assuming you're being forced into this by your father?"

"Yes, though I never had any intention of bowing to his wishes." She cocked her head. "Your grandfather is doing the same to you?"

"He's trying to."

"How? I can't see him being very successful by threatening to cut off your allowance."

Ox's expression hardened. "Not mine, my mother's. My grandfather sets his traps well." As Ox described his grandfather's threats and his skillful manipulation of the truth, Angel's dismay grew.

"The man is diabolical!" she exclaimed.

"I can think of a few other choice descriptions." A muscle in his jaw flexed. "I've spent most of my adult life being a thorn in his side, irritating him at every opportunity, thwarting every plan he comes up with."

"That's why you call yourself Ox Bruford," Angel said, with a flash of insight.

"Exactly, it infuriates him. He calls it a bastardization of an old and noble name." Ox snorted. "It's neither old nor noble. He's the first one with it, and I intend to be the last."

"I'd say he has a rather formidable adversary in his grandson."

"Perhaps, but he is clever, I'll give him that. Until yesterday I really wasn't sure how I was going to get out of this one."

"But now you know?"

The smile Ox gave her did not bode well for his enemies. "With your help I plan to teach my grandfather and your father a lesson they'll never forget."

"I like it already, and I haven't even heard your idea. What are we going to do?"

He grinned. "Everything we possibly can to make the Flying T lose money. I can't think of anything that will get our point across better."

"Neither can I. We'll be hitting them where it hurts the most, in the bankroll. What did you have in mind?"

"I came up with a few ideas last night, but the possibilities are endless. To start with, my grandfather put me in charge of buying stock and keeping the stations in supplies. He's such a miser he'll be pleased when I buy from second-rate suppliers. Just think of all the complaints we'll get about weevily flour and tainted meat. If well-fed passengers are happy passengers, I suspect the reverse is true as well."

"Not bad," Angel said.

"As for the horses, a few showy-looking animals with no stamina scattered all along the route will cause endless problems. On top of that we can arrange all kinds of minor delays that will throw the schedule off. We could even hire people to pretend to attack the stage and scare the passengers. If the line gets a bad reputation nobody will want to ride it, even if it is the only transportation to Silver Springs Gulch."

"The only transportation to Silver Springs Gulch," she repeated thoughtfully. "You know, if we work it right we could do a lot more than make the Flying T lose money." Angel looked up at him with shining eyes. "We could put them out of business!"

"Wait until you hear my news!" Angel cried, bursting through the door of the cabin an hour later. "Alexis?"

Alexis rolled over on the bed and blinked up at her sister. "Angel, what are you doing here this time of day?"

"I didn't want to wait." Angel sat on the edge of the bed. "What's the matter, love, aren't you feeling well?"

"I'm fine. Just a little tired, that's all."

Angel frowned as she reached over and felt her sister's

forehead. "Since when do you take naps in the middle of the day?"

"Since I started staying up late every night to wait for you." She stretched and sat up. "Now, what's this news?"

"Ox and I have come up with a way to break Father's hold on you once and for all."

"I don't think anything short of murder will do that."

Angel's eyes sparkled. "By the time we get done with him, you'll be lucky if he ever speaks to you again."

"Good heavens! What are you planning now?"

"It's quite simple. You and Ox are going to start your own stage company and put the Flying T out of business."

"We're *what*?"

Angel launched into a detailed explanation of the plan, her enthusiasm obvious as she paced around the room. In her excitement, she didn't even notice Alexis's horrified expression. "And the best part of it is that you can go back to being yourself, because Ox has no intention of marrying you," she finished, with a pleased smile.

"You're crazy!"

Angel blinked in surprise. "What?"

"I can't do that."

"Why not?"

Alexis jumped to her feet. "All it would accomplish is to convince Father I can't be trusted to handle my own affairs."

"That's the beauty of it." Angel flopped down in the overstuffed chair. "Father won't even know you're involved until it's all over."

"He's not going to know I'm involved because I'm not going to do it."

"But you have to."

Alexis shook her head. "No, I don't. You said yourself

Ox doesn't want to marry me. In case you've forgotten, that's what this was all about. Not even Father can force me to marry a man who doesn't want me."

"What's going to stop him from finding you another unwanted husband?"

Alexis shrugged. "Maybe he'll give up after he realizes he's failed."

"That'll be the day," Angel said, rolling her eyes. "Even with Ox out of the picture, there will be someone else soon enough. I wouldn't put it past Father to decide you should marry Ox's grandfather!"

Alexis was aghast. "He wouldn't!"

"You want to bet? He's decided his wealthy eligible daughter is the way to get more solid control of that stage line, and it's going to take some pretty powerful convincing to change his mind."

"I don't see where my marrying the elder Mr. Treenery would gain Father anything."

"Not now it wouldn't, except that family ties are harder to sever than business connections. But you have to remember James Treenery is an old man with no heirs except a grandson who wants nothing to do with him. When Treenery dies, Father would have the whole stage line, not to mention all that lovely money. I can just see Father licking his chops over the fortune that would come to you in a few years."

"That's what he was thinking when he made me marry Duncan, but he never saw a penny of that money," Alexis pointed out.

"Don't fool yourself. Father won't be tricked the same way twice. He'd make damn sure he was the executor of Treenery's will. I wouldn't put it past him to figure out a way to get hold of Duncan's fortune, too."

Alexis gave her a bleak look. "He would, wouldn't he."

"I'd put money on it."

"I can't do what you're asking me to, Angel," Alexis said, in a defeated whisper. "I don't know the first thing about a stage line."

"Ox does. That's why his grandfather wanted to put him in charge. He knew Ox would do a good job of running it."

Alexis closed her eyes. "And he figured I'd be useless, so Ox wouldn't have any interference."

"Then he made a serious error of judgment. And that's exactly what's going to defeat both Father and him. You and Ox will bring them to their knees."

"I think you overestimate my abilities."

"And I think you grossly underestimate them. You'll never know what you're capable of if you never try." Angel stood up. "Once we go talk to Ox tomorrow you'll feel more confident."

"We're going to talk to him? Oh, Angel, what are you thinking of? He'll be so angry that we lied to him."

"Probably, but if we don't tell him he'll figure it out on his own. The only reason we've been able to fool him is because he's never met you."

"I don't know about this."

"Don't worry, Alexis. Ox is my best friend. I know you'll like him."

"Won't this take a long time?"

"We're figuring six months at the very least and probably closer to a year. That's why I think we should trade back. We never intended me to take your place for an extended period."

"And where will you be while all this is going on?"

Angel grinned. "Right here. You don't think I'd miss the chance to participate in Father's downfall, do you?"

"I hope it doesn't turn out to be ours instead," Alexis said with a frown.

"Have I ever let you down, Alex?"

"No."

"Then stop fretting. I promise everything will work out fine."

"You're really excited about this, aren't you?"

"Of course," Angel said, giving her a quick hug. "And you will be too, once you think it over. Be ready tomorrow at eight o'clock, and we'll ride out to meet Ox."

Alexis's answering embrace had a hint of desperation in it. "I love you, Angel, remember that."

"I know. And I love you too."

A strange sense of melancholy dogged Angel's steps as she prepared to trade places with her sister again. In spite of her encouraging words to Alexis, she wasn't completely sure what Ox's reaction would be when he found out she'd been lying to him. How was he going to feel about her playing him for a fool?

Worse yet was the realization that she'd have to revert to the Angel he'd known in South Pass City. It was as much an act as her portrayal of Alexis, and one she really had no desire to go back to. The Angel from South Pass had kept Ox at arm's length; she was hard-bitten and cynical. As Alexis she'd been able to relax a little. In spite of the uncertainty, the last few days had been fun. It was the first time since she'd known him she'd even come close to being herself.

Sleep eluded her until nearly dawn, when she finally fell into an exhausted slumber that was disturbed less than two hours later when Martha woke her up. Heavy-eyed and irritable, Angel was less than pleasant as she dressed and finished packing the few personal items she hadn't borrowed from her sister.

"You're going to get wet if you go out," Martha informed her dourly. "There's a storm brewing, sure as shootin'."

"Then I'll get wet. I'm not sugar and I'm not salt and I won't melt."

"Maybe not, but you'll be nursing a cold before the week's out. You'll have a devil of a time playing your sister then. Your father would know immediately. Even Vanessa could figure it out. Alexis is a decent sort even when she's sick, not like some."

"Meaning me, I suppose? Don't worry, Martha, I'm taking precautions," Angel said, throwing a heavy cloak over her arm. "Besides, Alexis and I are switching back today anyway, remember? If I get the sniffles I'll be out at the cabin with nobody to be grumpy at but myself." She kissed Martha's cheek and headed for the door. "Alexis will be back after lunch sometime."

"Humph," she heard Martha mumble. "As though I'd let her be sick out there all by herself. The very idea."

Angel had to agree with Martha's weather prediction. They were almost certain to get a good drenching if they went out as planned. Even so, Angel was determined to get Alexis to the rendezvous with Ox if she had to drag her.

But when she arrived at the cabin, it only took Angel a moment to realize Alexis had packed her things and left. There was a note on the mantel, and she read it with a sense of defeat.

Alexis had decided Angel was right about teaching their father a lesson, though she herself was not up to it. Angel was better suited to the task and would be a much more useful partner for Ox. The note went on to beg forgiveness, explaining she'd be staying with friends, and gave an address where she could be reached if Angel needed her.

Angel sighed as she refolded the note. Alexis wouldn't be there to support her when she told Ox who she really was. Suddenly it seemed an impossible task. No wonder Alexis had fled. Angel felt like running away herself.

As she stared dejectedly at the empty fireplace, she realized she really didn't have to tell him. After all, if the plan was going to work, she'd still have to maintain the deception in order to fool her father and James Treenery. It would actually be easier if she never stepped out of character, she told herself. The part of Alexis wouldn't be as difficult to play as the caustic saloon owner. Ox would think any similarities were because Alexis and Angel were twins. He'd have no reason to suspect there was only one of them.

The next few months would be difficult, of course. She and Ox would be working shoulder to shoulder, spending hours at a time in each other's company, sharing ideas and problems. It was an intoxicating picture. For the first time all morning, Angel felt like smiling.

9

"*I was beginning to think* you weren't coming," Ox said, as Angel arrived at their prearranged rendezvous near the now-flooded creek.

"Believe me, I gave it serious thought."

"So did I. Only an idiot would come out in this weather." Ox pulled the collar of his coat tighter against the pouring rain. "I guess you know what that makes us."

"Wet!"

Ox laughed. "Can't argue that."

"Come on. I know a place we can dry off and talk."

"Close, I hope." Ox put a muddy foot in the stirrup and swung up into the saddle. "Otherwise we'll need a rowboat to get there."

Though the cabin wasn't far, the roads were so bad it was almost fifteen minutes before they arrived. "Thank goodness the woodbox is full," Angel said, unbuttoning her cloak. "Why don't you start a fire to dry out our clothes and I'll get some water heating for coffee?"

"Just point me toward the kindling." Ox glanced around the interior of the cabin curiously. "Who lives here?"

"No one now, though this is where Duncan lived when he first came to Cheyenne. He was going to sell it after he built the house, but I convinced him it might be useful to have. This is where Angel always stays."

Ox looked surprised. "She doesn't stay with you?"

"No, she says she's more comfortable out here."

"Why?"

"I don't know. We have words about it every time she comes to visit." Angel was conscious of his curious gaze on her back as she busied herself at the small cookstove. "She says she likes the quiet."

"That's probably true enough. The Green—er, her place was pretty noisy most of the time. Lots of people coming and going."

"She always said business was good."

"Oh, it was. Angel went out of her way to make her customers happy. A lot of lonely miners found a home there."

Angel smiled to herself, inexplicably warmed by Ox's sugar-coated description of the Green Garter. He made it sound more like a tea parlor than a casino and brothel. "Have you known my sister long?"

"A couple of years. We're good friends."

"How good?" Angel was aware she was treading dangerous ground but couldn't seem to help herself.

"About the best I ever had. I think that's why South Pass City was my favorite stop. If I had to lay over somewhere for a couple of days, I tried to do it there. I usually made sure I had at least an overnight stay."

His words gave her an unexpected spurt of pleasure. "It sounds like you were very close."

"We weren't lovers, if that's what you mean, though I sometimes wonder. . . ." Ox's voice trailed off.

Angel knew she should drop it but couldn't resist one more question. "Why not? I mean, if you liked each other so much."

"It never occurred to me at the time. I'm not sure I'd have had the courage to try even if it had. Angel isn't exactly the type a man feels comfortable cuddling up to." He stopped talking suddenly and cleared his throat. "This place seems pretty well stocked for a guest house."

"Martha's doing," Angel said smoothly, as she turned to look at him. Alexis would certainly have had something to say about such an improper conversation, but Angel took one look at his red face and decided Ox had suffered enough. Besides, it had been her own doing. Though his words stung her feminine pride a bit, they weren't unexpected. It was the reason she'd adopted a prickly attitude in the first place. Not even Ox was brave enough to try cutting through it. "Do you want coffee or tea?"

"Coffee."

She took a tin off the shelf and poured beans into the grinder. "Did you talk to your grandfather?" Angel asked, as she ground the coffee and placed it in the pot.

"A little. I asked a few roundabout questions. If I act interested in the Flying T too soon he'll be suspicious. How about you and your father?"

"Not yet." Angel sat down and tugged off a wet boot. "I think I'll wait until he asks me. He'll probably send my stepmother to sound me out."

Ox stood up and warmed himself in front of the fire he had just built. "Do you think he'll believe you've decided to accept my suit?"

"It hasn't occurred to him yet that I might not." Angel got down on her hands and knees and looked under the bed. "I knew she'd forget them," she said with satisfaction, as she pulled out a pair of slippers and put them on. "My father has a way of ignoring anything that doesn't fit in with his plans. As far as he was concerned, my reluctance was merely a temporary inconvenience."

"Pretending we're courting may not be easy."

"Don't worry, Angel says I was born knowing how to flirt." She batted her eyes at him.

Ox grinned. "Uh-oh, does this mean my bachelorhood is in jeopardy?"

"Not hardly. I have no more desire to get married than you do. Father will insist on setting a wedding date, but we'll think of some kind of delaying tactics to put him off."

"Can we get away with saying a year from now?"

"I doubt it, but I can say I won't even think about it until my year of mourning is over. If we still need more time we can set the date then."

"Well, now, will you look at this?" he said, picking a framed miniature up off the mantel. "It's you and Angel!"

"Our father commissioned it for our eighteenth birthday. I've always liked it."

"So do I," Ox said, gazing down at the picture in his hand. "Which one are you?"

Angel smiled. "See if you can figure it out. Not many people ever have."

"Hmm." Ox studied the painting intently. "To tell you the truth, I don't know. I'm tempted to say the one on the right is Angel, because she gets that look in her eye when she's up to something. But I've seen you with the same expression."

Angel was startled, for he had identified her correctly. Only Martha and Duncan had ever been able to tell them apart in the painting. As long as Ox never met Alexis, he'd have no reason to suspect a switch had been made. But if he continued to study the picture, there was a possibility he'd figure it out. The miniature would have to disappear.

She focused on his clothing. "You'd better get out of those clothes before you catch your death."

"You're not going to tell me which one is you?" he asked in surprise.

"Nope. We never tell anybody." She took the picture out of his hand and set it back on the mantel. "Meanwhile, you're dripping all over my floor."

"I don't suppose Angel left a change of clothes behind like she did her slippers," he said.

"None that would fit you anyway. Hmm." She glanced around the cabin until her gaze lit on the bed. "Just the thing," she said, crossing the room and pulling off the quilt.

Ox turned red. "I can't wear that."

"Oh, for pity's sake, Ox. This is no time for modesty. You'll be completely covered. Now sit down so I can help you get those boots off."

"You're doing it again," he said with a chuckle.

"What?"

"Acting like Angel."

"You mean Martha," Angel said, as she pushed him down on the chair. "You're lucky she isn't here. You'd already be out of those clothes, sitting with your feet in a tub of hot water, and saying yes-ma'am no-ma'am as meek as a lamb." Angel grabbed the heel and pulled off the first boot.

"Lord, I can hardly wait to meet this dragon."

"Count your blessings." She grunted as the other boot came off. "You can change behind the screen, and I promise I won't peek."

Angel took herself severely to task as he took the quilt and disappeared behind the screen. This was never going to work if she kept slipping like that. By the time Ox emerged again, she had poured two cups of coffee and had her Alexis mask firmly in place. She kept her back turned until he settled himself on one of the chairs she'd placed by the fireplace. Only then did she join him, her gaze fixed on his face as though the sight of his clothes drying by the fire embarrassed her.

"So what's our next step?" she asked, taking a sip of her coffee.

"We need the basics of a stage line."

"You mean like horses, drivers, stations, that kind of thing?"

"Stagecoaches would be nice too," Ox said with a grin.

Angel laughed. "I suppose that *is* one of those little extras the customers appreciate."

"Right, but not just any coach will do. We need a Concord coach."

"Why?"

"There's no way we'll be able to compete with the Flying T unless what we offer is noticeably better. Concord coaches are the best coaches in the world. There are none faster or more durable, not to mention the comfort."

"Now there's a revolutionary concept, a comfortable stagecoach."

"It's all in the suspension. The body sits on two thoroughbraces made of three-inch-thick leather straps so it sways instead of jolting. It's like riding down the road in a cradle."

"I take it the Flying T doesn't use Concord coaches."

"Nope. Their coaches have steel springs. A trip in one of them is a bone-jarring ordeal you wouldn't want to repeat if you could help it."

"Well, then, we'll definitely buy Concord coaches," Angel said decisively. "How many do we need?"

Ox grimaced. "That's the problem. We may have a tough time getting even one. New coaches sell for twelve hundred dollars."

"What?"

"I think I know where we can get a couple of them

for a lot less," Ox said. "They're both over ten years old, but they're still in good shape."

"Can we run it with only two coaches?"

"We can if we start small. We can begin with a run between here and Silver Springs Gulch and branch out later, when we have more working capital. The problem is going to be coming up with enough money to get started."

Angel looked thoughtful. "I could invest a fairly large sum right now."

"There's a great deal of risk involved, but that's the way business operates. Generally, the more you risk the better the payoff. Unfortunately, the coaches are only part of what it takes to put a stage line together. We'll also need horses, drivers, stock tenders, stationmasters, freight wagons, bullwhackers, supplies, feed for the animals."

"In other words, we need money and lots of it," Angel said. Alexis could finance the venture and never even feel the pinch, but she wasn't here. If Angel invested all her money from the Green Garter and their venture failed—she pushed the thought away. They weren't going to fail. "All right, then," she said, going to the desk for paper and a pen. "Let's see what we can do. How much do you figure it will cost for the horses?"

An hour and five sheets of paper later, Angel stretched and rubbed the back of her neck. "We're cutting it awfully close, but it looks good on paper anyway." The plan they had come up with would take every penny they both had. If it was successful, they would double, maybe triple their investment. If not—

"It all depends on whether we can get those coaches or not," Ox was saying. "And we need to start thinking about a front man."

"A front man?"

"Somebody needs to appear to be running the business for us, since we have to stay hidden. It will have to be someone we can trust. Once we find him, we'll set it up. . . . "

Angel's lack of sleep was beginning to catch up with her. She found herself focusing on Ox's mouth rather than his words. He had such a nice mouth, with straight white teeth and sensuous lips. And his smile; it made her go all tingly inside. She especially loved the way his eyes crinkled at the corners when he grinned.

Her gaze lingered a moment on his lips and then drifted to his strong chin and moved down his neck to the wide shoulders she had always admired. They were just as impressive without his shirt and coat. Even through the heavy flannel of his underwear, Angel could see the outline of well-defined muscles across his broad chest. Dreamily, she imagined her fingers leisurely undoing the buttons that ran down the front of his undershirt and reaching inside to explore the warm supple skin and hard muscles that—

"Alexis? Are you there?" Ox asked.

Angel jerked her mind back from its improper wanderings. She felt her face growing warm. Lord, what was she doing? "Er, I was half asleep. I was awake most of the night."

"You had such a faraway look on your face I wondered what was going on."

"Just woolgathering." She jumped to her feet and practically ran to the fireplace. "Your clothes are probably dry." It only took her a moment to scoop up his pants, shirt, and vest and return them to him.

His eyes twinkled as he accepted them and went behind the screen to get dressed. Angel wondered if he had any idea what she'd been thinking. How embarrassing!

"We're going to need a meeting place," he said, from behind the screen. "There will be a lot of planning involved that we won't be able to pass off as flirting with each other."

"How about here?"

"If your father caught us here, he'd think I'd compromised you and make us get married right away!"

"Father doesn't even know about this place."

"He doesn't?"

"No, I kept it a secret so I'd have a place to get away when he came to visit."

Ox stepped out from behind the screen as he finished buttoning his shirt. "Your father doesn't live in Cheyenne?"

"Not usually. He has a very nice home in New York, but he sort of took up residence here when Duncan passed on. I'm hoping he'll leave once he thinks I'm going along with his plan to marry you."

"We can always hope." He sat down in the overstuffed chair and held his bare feet out to the flames.

Angel stared at them. There was something curiously intimate about a man's toes. "Your feet still cold?"

"Not really, but that fire sure feels good. I think I just came up with a name for our stage line."

"Oh?" Angel pulled her gaze away. After the embarrassing episode with his mouth she didn't dare concentrate on his feet. Who knew where her eyes would wind up? "What's that?"

"The Silver Springs Express."

"Hmm," she said consideringly. "Not bad."

"We're probably crazy even to be considering this. It's kind of like David going up against Goliath."

"True, but David won, remember?"

"And so will we." He lifted his coffee in salute. "Here's to success."

"To success."

As Angel raised her cup to her lips, she reflected on how strange life was. Here she was about to embark on the challenge of a lifetime, and all she could think about was her partner's naked feet.

10

"*Alexis, dear, are you out* here?" Vanessa called, stepping into the garden behind the house.

Angel finished patting the soil around the small shrub she had just planted. "Right here. Hand me the spade, will you, Shannon?"

"Oh, my," Vanessa said, as she caught sight of her stepdaughter kneeling in the dirt. "What are you doing?"

"Just moving a few plants that were too close together. Why?"

"It's nearly teatime."

"Heavens, already?" Angel winked at Shannon. Vanessa's tenacious refusal to give up teatime was a standing joke in the family. It was the only thing besides her accent that remained of her British roots. "Oh, well, not to worry. It will only take Shannon and me a moment to wash our hands."

Vanessa eyed the front of Angel's skirt. "You'll need to change your clothes too."

Angel glanced down in surprise. Her dress was a little mussed but not really dirty. "Why?"

"You'll want to make a good impression."

"Uh-oh. Who's coming, Vanessa?"

"Your father mentioned it to Mr. Treenery this morning. He's bringing his daughter-in-law and his grandson."

"Vanessa—"

"The elder Mr. Treenery is about to escort Mrs. Treenery to her sister's in Boston." Vanessa broke in before Angel had a chance to finish her sentence. "I knew you'd want to see her again before she left."

Angel would have been delighted to spend a little more time with Ox's mother if they could have been alone. But under the watchful eyes of her father it was sure to be an ordeal. Every time she came in contact with him she took the chance of giving herself away.

Besides, this would be the first time she and Ox were around anyone else, though they'd spent plenty of time together over the last week and a half. She wondered nervously if their "romance" would be convincing enough. "I wish you'd told me sooner. I wouldn't have spent so much time in the garden."

Vanessa looked puzzled. "Whatever possessed you to come out here and dig in the dirt anyway?"

"I don't know, but it was very relaxing. Shannon and I enjoyed ourselves immensely."

Shannon nodded eagerly. "Oh, yes, Mama. An—er, Alexis was showing me all about gardening."

"I wasn't aware she knew anything about it."

"I dabble a bit, is all. I got started when Duncan couldn't find a decent gardener in Cheyenne," Angel said, brushing off the front of her dress. "Come on, Shannon, we wouldn't want to be late for tea."

"Alexis never works in the garden," Shannon whispered, when they were out of earshot.

"Well, she's going to start. I can't abide sitting

around with idle time on my hands." Angel smiled down at her sister. "You had fun, didn't you?"

"Oh, yes. Can we do it again?"

"We'll have to make sure it doesn't interfere with teatime," Angel said with a grin. "Better scoot along now or we'll both be in trouble."

Normally it wouldn't have taken Angel long to change, but today she wanted to look her best. She and Ox would be under intense scrutiny. In the end she chose an apple-green walking dress that brought out the pink in her cheeks and the sparkle in her eyes. How ironic. A mere month ago she'd been intent on persuading everyone this betrothal was impossible. Now she was just as determined to make them think it was her heart's desire. With a last pat to her hair, she took a deep breath and went downstairs to join the others.

The Treenerys had just arrived and were still standing in the hallway when Angel reached the bottom of the stairs. "I'm so glad you could come, Mrs. Treenery, Mr. Treenery," she said, trying to ignore her irrational flare of disappointment over Ox's absence.

Sarah Beth smiled brightly. "Why, thank you. I hope you don't mind that we're a little early. Your father and my son were delayed. I didn't want to wait, so Papa Treenery was kind enough to escort me. I did so want to chat with you, Mrs. Smythe."

"Please, call me Alexis."

"And you must call me Sarah Beth. Jamie talks about you and your sister Angel so much, I feel as though I've known you both for years."

"Jamie? Oh, you mean Ox."

James Treenery stiffened, but Sarah Beth's eyes twinkled in a way that reminded Angel strongly of her son. "Of course."

"I'm glad we have a chance to visit before you leave town." So Ox talked about her to his mother? The thought gave Angel a warm feeling inside. "I think my stepmother is in the parlor waiting for us."

"You know, I've never had a real English tea before," Sarah Beth confided, as they moved toward the parlor door. "You'll probably think me silly, but I'm rather excited about it."

"I don't think it's silly at all, and it will please Vanessa no end. She feels we don't give the tradition proper respect."

"Waste of time if you ask me," James Treenery grumbled. "No place for a man."

Angel swallowed a grin as she opened the parlor door. "Vanessa, our guests are here for tea."

The children had already come downstairs and were waiting patiently for the adults. Sarah Beth was delighted, but the look on James Treenery's face was anything but. He couldn't have been more disgusted if he'd found pigs romping in the parlor.

Ox's mother was an instant success with the children. Within five minutes Betsy was sitting in her lap, Shannon was watching her with worshipful eyes, and even Jared unbent enough to tell her about the tree house he and his friends were building.

Angel thoroughly enjoyed herself as Vanessa and Sarah Beth progressed from discussing the accomplishments of the Brady brood to the finer points of child rearing. The conversation wasn't particularly entertaining, but James Treenery's reaction to it was. He became more revolted by the second. As his expression soured, Angel had a difficult time not giggling.

"Your son tells me you've recently been to New York, Sarah Beth," Vanessa said pleasantly, "and that you particularly enjoyed the opera."

Sarah Beth nodded. "I was lucky enough to hear Jessica Lanford. It was delightful."

"Really? I've never had the pleasure," Vanessa said

avidly. "They say her voice is the ninth wonder of the world. Is it true?"

"It wouldn't surprise me in the least. I could hardly believe what I was hearing. Sadly, it was her last performance before she disappeared."

Vanessa's voice took on a conspiratorial note. "Isn't that the strangest thing? She said she was going to visit her mother and vanished without a trace. No one has seen hide nor hair of her since."

"Small loss, if you ask me," James Treenery muttered. "Never heard such caterwauling in my life."

Sarah Beth smiled. "Papa Treenery isn't fond of opera."

"Mr. Treenery!" Betsy cried suddenly, squirming off Sarah Beth's lap and heading for the door. Angel turned just in time to see the little girl grab Ox around the legs and hug him for all she was worth. It was hard to say who was more surprised, Ox or Richard Brady, who looked at his youngest child as though she'd sprouted horns.

"Here now, Betsy," he said disapprovingly. "Don't bother Mr. Treenery."

"It's no bother," Ox said, patting the little girl on the head awkwardly. "Hello, Betsy."

She gazed up at him adoringly. "You hold me?"

"Er, I don't know." His uncertain expression gradually dissolved into a smile as she gazed up at him with her big blue eyes. "Let me see your hands."

She held them out, and he solemnly inspected them. "No jam, I see," he said, swinging her up in his arms. "Have you waited tea for us then?"

Betsy nodded. "Mama said we had to. Can we eat now? I hungry."

"An excellent idea," put in Vanessa.

"We'll go tell Martha," Shannon said, jumping to her feet. "Come on, Jared."

Vanessa frowned as they hurried out the door. "Now what do you suppose got into them?"

"Probably too much adult conversation," Sarah Beth said with an understanding smile. "Well, Jamie, I see you and young Betsy are already acquainted."

Ox grinned. "She has a way of making herself known."

"He let me ride his horsey."

"She shamed him into it," Angel said with a chuckle. It was only when her father gave her a sharp look that it occurred to her that Alexis was more likely to giggle than chuckle. It was something she'd have to watch in the future.

Martha chose that moment to enter, carrying the tea tray. Shannon and Jared followed closely behind, with finger sandwiches and sweet cakes.

Angel swallowed a sigh of relief as her father turned his attention to his wife, who was directing Ox and himself to chairs.

Ox obediently set Betsy down and went to sit by Angel on the settee. Since they had discussed at length how to make their betrothal convincing, Angel was fully prepared for his loving smile and the tender way he touched her hand. What she wasn't expecting was the effect it had on her.

Suddenly she found it hard to breathe, and her whole body felt as though it had been dipped in warm honey. She didn't even have to fake her reaction. The slight blush and shy smile were as real as they looked.

"Set those over here by your sister," Martha instructed her two helpers. "Don't think you can get away with taking more than your share just because you helped, either. Now sit down and behave yourselves." With a sniff she turned her attention to Angel. "Will you be needing anything else, Mrs. Smythe?" she asked, very pointedly identifying her as the mistress of the house.

"No, I'm sure this will be fine. You've done a lovely job. Thank you."

"Humph, as though it's any different today than it was yesterday," she muttered, as she went to the door.

Ox leaned closer to Angel and whispered, "And I'll bet that's Martha, right?"

Only Angel heard his question, but everyone saw the way her lips quirked when she nodded and his answering grin as they shared their private joke. The looks that Vanessa and Sarah Beth gave each other were only slightly less triumphant than the ones that passed between the elder James Treenery and Richard Brady.

Angel looked up at Ox. Could he tell how hard her heart was pounding in her chest? He glanced down and gave her a little wink. For one breathless moment she could almost believe it was all gloriously real, and then reality returned as her stepmother's voice broke through the curtain of euphoria.

"Do you take sugar in your tea, Sarah Beth?"

"Yes, please."

"I'll pass the sandwiches," Shannon said, jumping to her feet. "And Jared can hand around the tea."

Angel's eyes narrowed suspiciously. Since when did Shannon and Jared offer to help with tea? They were far more likely to find excuses to be elsewhere. What were they up to?

"Were the horses to your liking, James?"

Ox permitted himself a slight smile as he answered his grandfather's question. "As a matter of fact, they're exactly what I was looking for."

"Excellent." The old man accepted a cup of tea from Jared. "I think now is the proper time to make our announcement, James, don't you?"

"I suppose it's as good a time as any."

There was a note of disgust in Ox's voice. It was too subtle to be noticed by everyone, but it was enough that his grandfather was aware of it. His jaw tightened in irritation for a fraction of a second. "My grandson has agreed to take over my half of the Flying T."

"But only when Grandfather can't be in Cheyenne," Ox added.

"Well, congratulations, my boy." Richard Brady acted as though the idea were a completely new one to him. "We need some young blood in the company."

Sarah Beth frowned. "I thought it was Jamie's to start with."

"I'm afraid you misunderstood, Mother." Ox reached for a sandwich on the tray. "The Flying T belongs to Grandfather and Mr. Brady. They only want me to run it for them."

James Treenery waved his hand. "Nonsense, my boy. It's merely a matter of—"

"Do have a sandwich, Alexis," Shannon said quietly, so as not to interrupt James Treenery.

Something in Shannon's voice set alarm bells ringing in Angel's head, but she could see nothing wrong with her sandwich. Nor could she see anything amiss with the way her sister was serving, though she watched her intensely for several minutes. So why the smug satisfaction?

When she glanced away, she was startled to find her father's gaze locked on her face. Oh, Lord, that chuckle had given her away after all. Her father wasn't unobservant like Vanessa, nor could he be convinced as easily as Ox, who had never actually met Alexis. The only thing in her favor was the absolute idiocy of what she and Alexis had done. Richard Brady was having difficulty believing it. Maybe if she did something only Alexis would do, she could put his suspicions to rest. But what?

And then she had it. So simple really, it was amazing she hadn't thought of it before. Angel yawned. It was a very small yawn and carefully hidden behind her hand, but it did the trick. Vanessa gave her a questioning glance, which Angel returned with a slight shrug of her shoulders as if to say all the talk of business bored her to tears.

Vanessa, ever the adept hostess, took the matter in hand. "Gentlemen, your tea is getting cold." It worked perfectly. Even James Treenery stopped his rather one-sided discussion of the merits of investing in stocks.

Angel sneaked a peek at her father out of the corner of her eye. The look of pure disgust on his face was unmistakable. Good. He was forever calling Alexis a scatterbrain, and Angel had just proved it to him once again.

She fought the urge to smile as she brought her cup to her lips. But when she looked up she saw that Ox was watching her in surprise. Her sudden disinterest in business would take some explaining. He quirked an eyebrow and took a bite of his sandwich. He never dropped his gaze as he chewed.

Angel felt a wave of apprehension. Would he believe she did it to fool her father? Suddenly, without warning, his face turned an alarming shade of red.

"Ox?" Angel sat forward in consternation. "Ox, what is it?" But he only gasped as though he couldn't catch his breath. "Oh, Lord, he's choking!" Angel cried, slapping him on the back.

It didn't seem to help. Tears appeared and coursed their way down his now-purple cheeks as he reached out and grabbed his teacup. He gulped the contents like a man dying of thirst. A second later he spit it all back out, spraying tea halfway across the room.

Angel was in a panic. She continued to slap his back, not knowing what else to do, but it made no difference. All at once Jared was there with a glass of water, his face as white as a sheet.

"Here, Mr. Treenery. Drink this. It will help."

Ox grabbed it from his hand and downed it all in several big swallows.

When he put the glass down at last, he took a long shuddering breath, the first he'd had since the ordeal began. He glared down at the sandwich he held in his hand. "Jesus," he rasped out. "What's in that damn thing?" Then he went off into a fit of coughing.

Angel took the sandwich from his lax fingers. Her lips thinned as she pulled the bread apart to look inside. Then she picked up Ox's cup, dipped a finger into the tea, and stuck it cautiously in her mouth. "Yuck!"

"What is it?" Sarah Beth asked fearfully. "Will he be all right?"

"He'll be fine," Angel said, rubbing Ox's arm as he collapsed back against the settee. "He just ate something he shouldn't have."

Vanessa gave her a bewildered look. "But we all had the same sandwiches and tea."

"That's right, but somebody," she said, glowering at Shannon and Jared, "put pepper in *his* sandwich and alum in *his* tea."

11

"*We didn't mean to hurt him,* Angel, honest," Jared said earnestly.

Angel frowned at him. "Maybe you should tell Mr. Treenery that."

"We tried, but his mother said he was too sick for visitors." Shannon's eyes were wide with worry. "He *is* going to be all right, isn't he?"

"No thanks to you two, he is. There was enough pepper and alum in his food to bring a full-grown buffalo to his knees."

They both stared miserably at their feet. "We put in just a little at first," Jared mumbled, "but then I went back and put in some more."

"I did the same thing," Shannon confessed, "because I didn't know Jared had."

Angel rolled her eyes. "No wonder he nearly choked to death. Whatever possessed you to tamper with his food anyway?"

"W-we were just trying to help."

"Help what? Shorten his life? He's never done a thing to either of you."

Jared scuffed his foot on the floor. "It was because of the Brady oath."

"The Brady oath?" Angel repeated. "All you swore to was not to tell Father who I really am. It had nothing to do with Mr. Treenery."

"He wants to marry Alexis," Shannon whispered. "We were trying to change his mind."

"You said yourself you were here to get rid of the bothersome beau," Jared reminded her. "We Bradys stick together."

"Oh, dear." Angel bit her lip in consternation. With those two after him, James Oxford Bruton Treenery III didn't stand a chance. She couldn't very well tell them what she and Ox were up to, but she definitely needed to put a stop to their so-called help. "It turns out Mr. Treenery doesn't want to marry Alexis after all."

"Are you sure?"

"Yes, I'm sure. He told me so himself."

"Does he know you're really Angel?"

"No, he still thinks I'm Alexis, but it wouldn't matter. He doesn't want to marry either of us."

Jared crossed his arms and looked down his nose, a perfect copy of their father. "Then why is he spending so much time with you?"

"And why does he watch you with that funny expression on his face?" Shannon added.

"We're trying to fool everybody into thinking we're falling in love."

Shannon and Jared looked at each other. "Why?" they both asked at the same time.

"Because then they'll let us run the Flying T for them without any interference."

Jared scratched his head. "Do you want to do that?"

"Yes, we do."

"Where's Alexis?" Shannon asked suddenly. "Does she know what you and Mr. Treenery are doing?"

"Alexis is staying with friends and, yes, she knows what's going on."

"Oh, I see." Jared nodded wisely. "She got tired of Father telling her what to do and decided to let you handle it for a while."

Angel resisted the urge to sigh in relief. At last an excuse they'd believe. "I suspect that has something to do with it. She said she needed some time away."

Shannon frowned. "What if Mr. Treenery really falls in love with you? Wouldn't he be mad if he found out you'd been lying to him all this time?"

Angel laughed. "Don't worry. Ox has known me for two years and hasn't fallen in love with me. He isn't attracted to me that way. As far as he's concerned, I'm his close friend and nothing more. Besides, he isn't the type to settle down."

"Martha said you like him a lot."

"She did?" Angel was startled. "When?"

"When Jared asked why you were spending so much time with him."

"Well, for once she's right. I do like him. We're very good friends."

"Martha also says good friends make the best husbands."

"That may well be, but husbands and wives should be in love too. Since I'm not going to fall in love with him, you can stop worrying so much." Angel fixed a stern look on her face. "Now then, about my mission here. Your mother sent me to tell you you're both banished to these three rooms for the remainder of the week. She assures me you have plenty of schoolwork to catch up on since you ran your tutors off."

"But this is the nursery," Jared protested. "We're too old to stay here."

Angel shrugged. "Since there have never been any

babies but Betsy here, I don't suppose this is really a nursery. Besides, you always sleep here when you come to visit Alexis, so I fail to see what difference it makes."

"Is that our only punishment?" Shannon asked in a small voice.

"No. You'll be expected to apologize fully to Mr. Treenery for tampering with his food and to your mother for ruining her tea party. Martha also has a long list of chores for you to do."

Jared's face fell. "Knowing Martha, we'll be busy for another week at least."

"You're lucky Father didn't take time to discipline you himself." Angel crossed her arms and looked down at them. "And no more help with the bothersome beau. Promise me."

"Promise," they said together.

"Good. Now I can assure Mr. Treenery he's quite safe from the two of you. I have an appointment, so I'll leave you to your studies."

Shannon and Jared watched the door close behind her. Then they looked at each other and grinned as they brought their crossed fingers out from behind their backs.

Usually Alexis was already at the cabin by the time Ox arrived, but today he was a few minutes early and found it deserted. He looked at the mantel, hoping to find the miniature of the twins, but its place was still empty. The painting had mysteriously disappeared after his first visit. Alexis seemed to think it had been misplaced when Martha came to clean and would show up eventually. Unfortunately that hadn't happened. With a disappointed sigh, he sat down to wait.

A pair of pink slippers peeking out from under the bed caught his eye and brought a smile to his lips. They represented the enigma that was Alexis. One minute she'd been completely matter-of-fact about wearing them and getting him out of his wet clothes. The next she'd tucked her feet out of sight and been too embarrassed to even look at him.

Everything she did was like that. Sometimes she was so silly she set his teeth on edge. Just when he'd decided Angel had gotten all the brains, Alexis came up with a financial plan that still amazed him. Her business savvy was nothing short of amazing, but she'd been completely bored by yesterday's teatime discussion about stocks and bonds. He never knew if a teasing remark would be met with a sarcastic rejoinder or a blank stare. All in all, Alexis Brady Smythe was a bewildering collection of inconsistencies—one that utterly fascinated him.

As if he had conjured her up with his thoughts, the door swung open and Alexis swept in.

"Sorry I'm late. I was having a long talk with my brother and sister. I don't suppose you're quite ready to receive their apologies yet?"

"Frankly, I'd rather never see them again."

She grinned. "I can't say I blame you. However, they did promise me there'd be no more nasty surprises like the last one."

"Thank God. I'm not sure I'd live through another one."

"It wasn't personal, you know. They were just trying to help me."

Ox cocked an eyebrow. "Help you what? Do away with me?"

"More or less. They overheard Father and me arguing about the betrothal and knew I didn't want to marry you. I guess they were trying to scare you off."

"Damn, I'd hate to see what they'd do if you were really threatened."

"They're very protective of Angel and me."

That got a laugh. "Angel too? Now that's funny."

"Why?"

"Angel needs about as much protection as a grizzly bear."

"What's that supposed to mean?"

"Nobody but nobody tangles with Angel," he said, with a chuckle. "It's kind of like kicking a cougar in the backside. If you're stupid enough to do it, you'd better be prepared to run for your life."

"You make her sound like some kind of monster."

"Hey," Ox said, reaching out and touching her cheek. "Angel's my friend, remember? I'm kind of proud of the way she stands up for herself."

"But she's not the type you'd feel comfortable cuddling up to, right?"

"Well, I —"

"Never mind." She turned away, her entire body rigid with anger. "Your note said you had a surprise to show me."

"Alexis, I didn't mean—"

"Look, Treenery, this is a business relationship, right?"

"Yes, but—"

"So it really doesn't matter what you and my sister were to each other, does it?"

"No, I guess not."

"Good. Let's drop it and get on with the business at hand. I take it this surprise isn't here?"

"No, it's at a barn I'm renting outside town."

"Fine. Let's go."

Ox frowned as he followed her outside. What in the hell had gotten into her? You'd have thought he'd insulted her sister instead of bragging about the way she could take care of herself. It wasn't as if he didn't like Angel.

They rode the mile and a half in almost complete silence. By the time they finally reached their destination

Ox was convinced Alexis was right. Keeping their relationship purely business-oriented was best.

"Here we are," he said, swinging down from his horse next to the corral. It was obvious the eight horses inside the fence had been bred with strength and endurance in mind. They weren't flashy matched teams, nor would they win any beauty prizes. But what they lacked in comeliness they more than made up for with broad chests and sleek muscles. They were powerhouses. "The first of our horses," Ox said proudly. "We'll need about a dozen more like them, to start with."

Angel dismounted and walked over to the fence. "Are these the ones Father took you to see yesterday?"

Ox grinned. "Not hardly. These are for the Silver Springs Express. They're the best horses I could find."

"And the ones you and Father went to see?"

"Are exactly what I wanted for the Flying T. Showy but with very little stamina. There weren't more than half a dozen in the whole bunch that are worth a tinker's damn. Neither your father nor my grandfather knows beans about carriage horses." As Ox reached up and lifted her down from her horse, he had the irrational desire to put his arms around her. Would she fit the curve of his body as well as he thought she would? He set her away from him before he could give in to the impulse.

"And you bought the other horses for the Flying T?" she asked.

"Lock, stock, and barrel. What choice did I have? Your father thought they were just what we needed, and he *is* the owner of the Flying T, after all."

She giggled. "No wonder he looked so smug when the two of you came in. He thinks he can control you."

"Exactly. He also hinted that he'd be more than willing to lend me any amount of money to tide me over, since we're about to be related and he knows how tight my grandfather is."

"At a ridiculously high interest rate, no doubt."

"We never got around to discussing it, but I wouldn't doubt it." He smiled down at her. "Are you ready for the surprise?"

"There's more?"

"Oh, definitely." Ox walked over to the barn and threw open the big double doors. "Look at this!" he said, stepping back out of the way.

After the bright sunlight it took Angel's eyes a few minutes to adjust to the shadowy interior of the barn. Then she caught the faint gleam of polished brass. "You found a coach!" she cried, hurrying inside to examine it.

"Yup, and the other one will be delivered sometime next week. The two of them together only cost us seven hundred dollars. They belonged to an old friend of mine who used to own a stage line until Ben Holliday put him out of business back in the sixties. He was glad to sell them to me."

He opened the door and she climbed up on the step to peer inside. "Oh, Ox, it's even better than we hoped for. It will carry a dozen people."

"Only nine on the inside, but more can ride on the roof."

"Can we take it out for a ride?"

Ox rubbed his chin thoughtfully. "Is there any possibility we might meet your father?"

"He went to Denver and won't be back until the end of the week."

"Good. My grandfather left with my mother this morning. That means we're perfectly safe. It'll take me a minute to catch the horses. Normally we'll run six to a team, but we might as well give all eight a workout, since we're just going for fun."

"I'll sit here until you're ready."

Ox smiled as she climbed into the coach's roomy interior without waiting for him to help her. It was probably just as well. He was still a little unsettled from the last time he touched her.

When he came back with the horses she was ready to climb down but hadn't lost an ounce of her exuberance.

"It's wonderful inside, all nice leather and comfortable padding. You know, Ox, I was thinking: we can provide lap robes and warming bricks for the passengers' feet in the winter. I rode in a coach like that once."

It wasn't long before Ox's pleasure in her obvious delight began to fade. By the time the horses were hitched to the stage, he was ready to wring her neck. Alexis hadn't stopped chattering during the entire process and showed no signs of running down. The worst of it was, she hadn't said one consequential thing in all that time. Lord, would the woman never shut up?

"Let me help you back inside," he said. "You'll want to experience it just like a passenger would."

"No, I want to ride up on the box with you."

He shook his head. "I'm not sure that's wise. The horses don't react well to—er . . . "

"To what, magpies? Don't worry, I've quite run out of things to say."

"That'll be the day," Ox muttered under his breath. He could have sworn he caught a twinkle in her eye as she walked past him.

"Is this where we go up?" she asked, studying the rungs on the front side of the coach.

"Yes, but—"

"Good. Give me a hand, will you?"

Ox made a face behind her back but obediently went over and boosted her up to the first step. With surprising agility she clambered to the top and settled herself comfortably on the seat.

"Well, what are you waiting for?"

"Not a thing." Ox was practically glowering when he climbed up beside her and picked up the reins. As he gave the leaders the signal to go he had the distinct impression she was highly amused about something.

Out on the open road, he kept waiting for the flow of babble to begin again, but she seemed quite interested in the passing scenery. After several sidelong glances, he gradually relaxed and enjoyed the drive. When she finally did speak, it was a complete surprise.

"Amazing," she said in awe.

A glance at his companion found her staring at his hands with rapt attention. He looked down at them but could see nothing unusual. "What?"

"The way you handle all those reins at once. I've never seen anyone drive an eight-horse hitch before."

Ox shrugged. "I'm a muleskinner, remember?"

"It's not the same thing."

"No, but horses aren't all that different. I've actually driven twelve, but I don't think I'd want to do it again. I almost—uh-oh," he said, pulling back on the reins.

"What's wrong?"

"It looks like some kind of accident up ahead."

As they drew closer they could see a stagecoach overturned beside the road, the familiar bright red and gold shining in the sunlight.

"Oh, Ox, it's one of the Flying T coaches!"

"Damn. It looks like we're in business, partner."

She looked at him in surprise. "What do you mean?"

"The Silver Springs Express is about to take on its first passengers."

12

"Whoa, there." Ox brought the horses to a halt next to the overturned coach. Chaos reigned as a man who didn't look much more than eighteen tried to calm the frightened horses that were tangled in the traces.

"Grab the bridle and pull his head down!" Ox called, as one of the horses tried to rear. "It's the only way to control him. Then get those tugs unhooked from the coach if you can."

While the young man scrambled to follow Ox's instructions, the sound of sobbing suddenly rose from inside the coach. "My God, there are people in there," Angel whispered. She started to climb down.

"Wait, Alexis," Ox said urgently. "I can't leave the horses. They'll never stand with all this noise."

She didn't even pause in her descent. "And I'm completely useless up here. Can't you take the horses down the road a ways and hobble them or something?"

"I can try." He winced as she jumped the last few feet to the ground. "Careful."

Angel raised her hand in a brief acknowledgment and hurried over to the other coach, where the horses were finally starting to quiet. "How many people are inside?"

The man didn't even look her way. "Two."

"All right, I'll see what I can do to get them out."

She came to a man lying on the side of the road. His neck was twisted at an odd angle, and she knew without stopping that it was too late for him. Fighting down nausea, she stepped around the body and moved to the open door. "Hello in the coach," she called. "Can you hear me?"

"Y-yes." The female voice quavered, as though trying to control sobs. "We . . . we need help."

"Hang on." Angel bit her lip. With the coach on its side the way it was, the door was above her head. Unless the other woman was very tall, she wouldn't be able to pull herself out through the opening. First things first. "Is either of you hurt?"

"Sam is."

"How bad?"

"I . . . I don't know. He hasn't opened his eyes since we crashed."

"Is he breathing?"

"Yes, b-but his head's cut and it's all bloody."

"Do you have something you can use to stop the bleeding?"

The other woman took a deep shuddering breath, and her hiccuping sobs subsided. "You mean like my handkerchief?" she asked after a moment.

"Perfect. Hold it against the cut and press as hard as you can."

All at once Ox was beside Angel. "Thank God you're here," she murmured with heartfelt relief.

"How bad is it?"

"I don't know, but they aren't going to get out without help."

"We'll have to get the horses unhitched first."

Angel nodded. "I know. I'll stay here with her until you're ready."

"Good girl." He gave her shoulder a reassuring squeeze and was gone.

"My name is Alexis," Angel called to the woman in the stage. "What's yours?"

"Jessie."

"Well, Jessie, help is on the way. The men will be here in a few minutes. The horses have to be unhitched so they can't jerk the coach while we're getting you out."

"I understand."

"Where are you headed?" Angel asked.

"Cheyenne. Sam is taking me to a friend of his."

"Well, you haven't far to go, then. Cheyenne is less than five miles from here." Angel kept up a flow of small talk with the unseen woman, hoping to keep her distracted. She jumped when an unexpected gunshot rang out but kept right on talking. By the time Ox and the other man joined her, her throat was beginning to hurt.

"Here they are, Jessie," she said, as Ox joined her. "It will just be a few more minutes now."

Ox wasted no words as he made the introductions. "Alexis Smythe, this is Frank Thompson. He was riding shotgun." As the two murmured polite hellos, Ox looked up at the open doorway and frowned. "Damn, I wish we had a rope. I guess we'll just have to make do without."

"I think the two of us can manage," Thompson said. "I'll go up first."

"Did you find out what caused the accident?" Angel asked Ox, as Thompson began the climb.

"Whiskey."

"What?"

"The driver was drunk." Ox scowled fiercely. "It happens quite a lot, unfortunately, though most of the time they manage to keep the coach on the road. If he hadn't killed himself, I'd have fired him on the spot."

Angel glanced toward the body and shivered. "Isn't there a rule against drinking while they're on duty?"

"Not on the Flying T. My grandfather figures he can pay his drivers less if he doesn't saddle them with a lot unnecessary regulations." He sighed. "He'll probably be more concerned with the fact that we damaged a coach and lost a horse."

"Was that the shot we heard?"

"Broken leg."

"We were lucky it was only one."

"Right." Ox glanced up at the man on top of the coach. "Guess we better get this rescue operation under way. We'll bring the injured man out first."

Angel nodded. "Let's hope it's not serious."

"Here, you may need my coat to put over him." Under the cover of removing his coat and handing it to her, Ox leaned close, his lips nearly brushing her ear. "As far as Thompson is concerned my name is James Treenery, understand?"

"All right." Angel stared after him in surprise as he climbed up to where Frank Thompson was looking down through the open door. After a short discussion, they decided Ox would be the one to go inside since he was the taller of the two. A moment later he disappeared through the hole.

In a matter of minutes, the injured man was lifted out and Angel's hands flew to her mouth. "Oh, God, not *my* Sam," she said in a horrified whisper. There had been no mention of his coming to Cheyenne when they'd said good-bye at the Green Garter in South Pass City. Why was he here? Something had to be very wrong.

"Be careful," she snapped, as Thompson lowered him to the ground. "Can't you see he's badly hurt?" Angel dropped to the ground and cradled Sam's head in her lap. There was a large purple lump over one temple and a cut on the opposite cheek. Though the cut didn't look serious, it had bled profusely, covering the front of his shirt with blood. Her eyes filled with tears for her friend.

Angel paid little attention to the rescue effort that continued on without her. Still dabbing ineffectually at Sam's injury, she wasn't even aware of Jessie until the other woman knelt next to her.

"Is he any better?" she asked hopefully.

"I don't know. He seems to be breathing easier." Angel looked up and was stunned by what she saw. Even with her hair hanging down in thick mahogany tangles and tear tracks streaking through the dirt smudges on her face, Jessie was quite possibly the most beautiful woman Angel had ever seen.

"If anything happens to him I'll never forgive myself," Jessie said, picking up his hand and holding it tightly. "He wouldn't even be here if it weren't for me."

Angel couldn't help wondering why tears turned Jessie's cornflower-blue eyes into brilliant jewels instead of making them bloodshot the way they did most women's.

First Frank and then Ox jumped off the coach and hunkered down next to the unconscious man. "Sam," Ox said loudly. "Sam, can you hear me?"

"Oh," Jessie cried. "I think he's waking up!"

Angel looked down just as Sam opened his eyes and stared up at her.

"Angel?"

"Not quite, Sam," Ox said in relief. "This is her sister Alexis. Alexis, meet Angel's right-hand man, Sam Collins."

"H-how do you do?" Angel stammered. She had

momentarily forgotten the part she was playing. If Ox hadn't spoken first she'd have given herself away.

"Not Angel?" His voice was thin and confused.

"They're twins."

"Twins?"

"Don't worry, Sam," Ox said comfortingly. "It will make more sense later. How do you feel?"

"Like the devil." He closed his eyes. A moment later they popped open again. "Jessie?"

"I'm right here." She gripped his hand tighter.

He focused on her. "You're hurt."

"No, just a little shook up."

"Blood," he said, reaching out to touch the stain on her shoulder.

She shook her head. "It isn't mine."

"Angel's?"

"No, Sam, it's yours." Jessie lifted his hand to her cheek. "You're the one who's hurt."

"Damn, I ruined your dress."

"Oh, Sam, it doesn't matter in the least."

"I think we'd better get him back to town and have the doctor take a look at him," Angel said.

Ox nodded. "I'll go get the other stage. Thompson, come give me a hand with the extra horses. We'll tie them to the back of the stagecoach."

"Huh? Oh, right." Frank Thompson pulled his bemused gaze away from Jessie's face and started after Ox. He glanced over his shoulder three times before he'd gone fifteen feet.

"Hurry," Angel said anxiously.

Sam rubbed his forehead in confusion. "What happened?"

"There was an accident," Jessie said, smoothing his hair back.

"I remember. The driver was going way too fast. Man ought to be horsewhipped."

Angel made a face. "It's too late for that. He's dead."

"If Mr. Treenery and Alexis hadn't happened along when they did we'd still be trapped in the coach," Jessie added.

"Treenery." Sam looked confused. "Mind's muzzy. Could have sworn it was Ox Bruford pulled me out. Don't know why he'd be here, though."

"You've had a nasty bump on the head, Mr. Collins," Angel soothed. "Just relax."

He looked up at her with narrowed eyes. "Miss Angel's sister, huh?"

"That's right."

"Where is she?"

"Er—well, I'm not sure."

"She said she'd be in Cheyenne." Sam closed his eyes. "I need her."

"What's wrong?"

"Something only Miss Angel can help me with."

"Well, maybe if you told me—"

Sam shook his head stubbornly. "Miss Angel would have my hide if I shared her business with anyone, even her sister."

Angel bit her lip. Sam's loyalty was unshakable. If he thought Angel wanted him to keep a secret, torture wouldn't drag it out of him. She was wondering if she dared tell him the truth when Ox drove up with the other coach.

"Can you hold all eight?" Ox asked Frank Thompson.

"Yes, sir, Mr. Treenery."

"Good. This won't take long." Ox handed the reins to the younger man and descended from the driver's seat.

"All right, Sam," he said cheerfully, "let's get you on your feet. There's no way these two women and I can lift you into the stage without your cooperation. Here, I'll help you stand up. Put your arm around my shoulder."

"Ox! I knew it was you," Sam said, as the other man

hoisted him to his feet. "They told me your name was Trainery or some such thing."

"I'll explain later," Ox said in a low voice. "In the meantime just concentrate on putting one foot in front of the other. Alexis, get his other side, will you? Jessie, open the door."

"I feel weak as a kitten."

"You took a pretty good bump on the head," Angel pointed out. "Where are we taking him, O—er, James?"

"I was thinking the cabin for the time being, if that's all right with you."

"The cabin? Certainly, though I don't see—"

"I don't want to be no trouble," Sam said.

"You won't be any trouble at all," Ox said. "In fact, my friend, you are the answer to our prayers."

Angel looked at Ox in surprise. "He is?"

"He most certainly is." Ox gave her one of his beautiful smiles. "This, my dear, is our front man."

"Oh!" Of course. Sam would be absolutely perfect! Angel was amazed she hadn't thought of it herself.

"Is there something you want me to do?" Sam asked.

"I'll explain that later too," Ox said. "Basically, we want you to work for us."

"Can't do that until I talk to Miss Angel. Do you know where she is?"

"No. Do you, Alexis?"

"Well, I'm not exactly sure—"

"It's real important," Sam said pleadingly. "Please."

"If you can't tell me what's going on, can you at least tell Ox?"

He was adamant. "Nope. Only Angel."

"It has to do with me, I think," Jessie put in shyly. "It isn't that important."

"The *hell* it isn't—er, pardon me, ladies." Sam blushed but continued. "It'll be real important to Miss Angel, believe me. Besides, she's the only one who will know what to do."

Angel frowned. Sam Collins was one of the most stoic individuals she'd ever met in her life. For him to come all the way to Cheyenne in a panic was nothing short of alarming. If he thought his news would be that important to her, she had no doubt he was right. He wasn't the type to get shaken up over trifles.

It was also abundantly clear that Sam was not going to give his news to anybody but Angel. Nor would it be safe to tell him who she was. Though she knew he'd never tell Ox if she asked him not to, she was afraid he'd inadvertently give her away. There was only one solution. Angel was going to have to make an appearance.

13

The next morning, Angel was no closer to knowing what Sam's urgent business was. She'd spent half the night sorting through the possibilities, but the few that made sense didn't require secrecy. By the time Ox arrived for their morning ride, Angel had decided to make her appearance that night.

"Have you located your sister yet?" Ox asked, as she joined him at the stables.

Angel placed her foot in his cupped hands and sprang into the saddle. "No, but I did send her a message when we got home yesterday. How's Sam?"

"Other than cuts and bruises, he says he's none the worse for wear." Ox mounted his own horse and turned toward the road. "I suspect he had a pretty good headache when he woke up this morning, though."

"Did he tell you any more about why he needs to see Angel?"

"Nope, won't even talk about it."

"Neither will Jessie, though I'm not sure she really knows."

"It was nice of you to take her in."

"I have plenty of room. Besides, I don't think she'd survive very long on her own." Angel shook her head. "I can't figure out if she's stupid or has spent her life wrapped in cotton wool. I never met such a pea brain in my life."

"A woman who looks like Jessie doesn't have to have brains," Ox said.

Angel gave him a look of pure disgust. Leave it to a man. As though all a woman needed to survive was good looks. In her experience, beauty worked against a woman as often as it worked for her. "Do you think we'll be able to talk Sam into joining for us?" she asked, changing the subject.

"I have no idea." Ox sighed. "He won't even discuss it until he talks to Angel. Do you know how long it will take her to get here?"

"I'm not even sure where she is. I wouldn't look for her until the end of the week at the earliest."

"Damn—er, sorry. We could almost be ready to go if Sam was willing to take the job. If we have to find somebody else, it could be weeks. Is there any chance Angel could show up sooner?"

"Maybe, but I doubt it. Did you find a place for the depot in Silver Springs Gulch?"

"Sure did. It's just down the street from the Flying T station. Couldn't be better."

Angel frowned. "You know, Frank Thompson saw us both with that stagecoach yesterday. If my father or your grandfather should ever think of talking to their employees, they might trace the Silver Springs Express back to us."

"I already took care of it. I offered him a job as horse tender." Ox's eyes twinkled. "Unfortunately, the only opening the Flying T has is clear up north."

"He didn't mind going?"

"Nope, not after I gave him a raise."

"You are a devious one, aren't you?" Angel said admiringly. "I almost feel sorry for our adversaries."

"You're rather formidable yourself. I'd never have thought of going into competition with them and beating them at their own game."

"We *are* a good team, aren't we?"

Ox flashed her his heart-stopping grin. "That we are, partner, that we are."

As their gazes met and held, blood thrummed through her veins with an effervescent tingle that turned her skin hot and cold by turns. She found it strangely difficult to breathe, yet she'd never felt so fantastically alive. It was bewildering, frightening even, but also incredibly wonderful.

Angel had no idea how long she sat there staring at him in bemusement before she realized it had been too long. From the expression on his face, it was obvious he was beginning to wonder what was going on. "Come on!" she yelled, applying her heels to her horse's flanks. "I'll race you to the big cottonwood down by the creek."

The sun had barely set when Angel sat down at Alexis's dressing table and began the transformation back into Sam's Angel. "I'd almost forgotten what a pain this is," she grumbled, as she smeared the thick greasepaint over her face.

Martha paused in the process of picking up Angel's discarded clothes. "Humph. Waste of time, if you ask me."

"The Angel that Sam knows has to put in an appearance tonight," Angel explained, adding a little more makeup to the side of her nose. "He won't tell anyone else what's wrong. Besides, we need him if this venture is going to work."

"Why don't you just tell him the truth?"

"He might give it away to Ox."

"Wouldn't that be too bad?" Martha said sarcastically. "Then we'd have to quit all this tomfoolery."

"I can't tell Ox I've been lying to him all this time."

"Only because you don't want to," Martha said. "When you're Alexis you have the freedom you never allow yourself otherwise."

Angel stopped in the middle of dabbing powder on her nose. "What are you talking about?"

Martha's eyes met hers in the mirror. "I think you like playing Alexis because you can let yourself go, feel all there is to feel. For the first time in your life you're finding out what it is to be a woman in love."

"That's ridiculous."

"Is it?" Martha gave her a meaningful look before she turned to go. "You've been running from your emotions since the day you let your skirts down and put your hair up."

"You have a vivid imagination, Martha."

"And I say young Treenery turns you inside out," Martha said over her shoulder, as she walked out the door. "You're disgusted with your weakness, but you can't resist the temptation to be soft and natural with him. That's why you hide behind your sister's face." The door closed behind her with a definitive thump.

Angel stared after her for a moment and then sighed and finished putting on her powder. Martha was dead wrong. Being in love with Ox Bruford didn't disgust her, it scared her half to death.

The dark drive out to the cabin in Alexis's buggy only added to her grouchiness. She'd have much rather ridden Alexis's little mare, but the animal was extremely skittish in the dark. Determinedly pushing her unhappy thoughts aside, she secured the buggy behind the cabin and walked around to the front. She closed her eyes and concentrated. The woman Sam knew was almost as different from her true self as Alexis was.

After a moment she squared her shoulders and knocked on the door. "Open up, Sam," she called. "I haven't got all night!"

A heartbeat later, the door swung open and Sam was peering out into the darkness. "Angel, what are you doing here?"

"What do you *think* I'm doing here?" she said, sweeping past him into the cabin. "I got a message from my sister saying she had a contrary bartender on her doorstep demanding my presence."

Sam grinned. "Contrary?"

"I'm sure she was referring to that stubborn streak of yours."

"Which I learned from my boss."

"Flatterer." She raised a skillfully darkened eyebrow. "Is there some reason we're having this conversation in all this fresh air?"

Sam's grin broadened. "How did you get here so fast?"

"I was in Denver visiting friends, so I wasn't that far away. Now, what's this all about?"

His expression sobered. "Did you meet Jessie?"

"No, I didn't have the pleasure, but Alexis told me about her. She's as beautiful as they come but not overly bright."

"You don't have to be so critical, Angel. Jessie can't help what she is. She's been sheltered most of her life."

"My, my, aren't we sensitive? Did she get under that thick skin of yours?"

Sam ignored her sarcasm as he ran his fingers through his hair. "She's Molly's daughter, Angel."

"Oh, Lord." Angel sat down in the nearest chair with a thump. Sweet, uncomplicated Molly, whose mother sold her into prostitution at the age of thirteen, had succumbed to influenza a year ago, just a few weeks short of her thirty-fourth birthday. She was the only one of Angel's "girls" who hadn't immediately taken her freedom money when it was offered to her. "She never told me she had a daughter."

"I doubt if she told anybody. Jessie's spent most of her life in boarding schools back east."

"Where did you find her?"

"Molly wrote that she would come for Jessie sometime this year. When she didn't show up, Jessie came to South Pass City lookin' for her. Molly told her she worked as a cook at a place called the Green Garden. People figured she meant the Green Garter and sent her there."

"Molly's opium habit," Angel said suddenly. "It wasn't real."

"What opium habit?"

"She told me all her money went for opium, but it wasn't true. She was using it to support Jessie." And that must have been why she'd asked Angel to keep the freedom money for her "until the habit was broken." It was like putting the money in the bank until she was ready for it. She had been planning on starting a new life with Jessie when her daughter finished school. "Oh, poor Molly," Angel murmured, fighting the lump that suddenly clogged her throat. "Her dream came so close to happening."

"Jessie didn't have any idea her mother had died," Sam said quietly. "She took it pretty hard. I didn't tell her the truth about what Molly did for a living."

"I'm glad." Angel reached over and gripped his hand. "Thank God you were there, Sam. Think what would have happened if you hadn't been."

"I know. She's not exactly prepared for the real world."

"That's the understatement of the century."

Sam gave her an odd look. "I thought you hadn't met her."

"Well, no, but Alexis filled me in," Angel said. "The question is, what do we do with her now?"

"That's why I brought her to you."

"What exactly did you think I could do?"

"Find her a job."

Angel just stared at him. "Find her a job," she repeated incredulously.

"Why not? You're always taking in strays."

"First of all, in case you forgot, I no longer have the Green Garter. Second of all, even if I did, I wouldn't give Jessie a job. Molly would never forgive me for turning her daughter into a soiled dove after she worked so hard to keep her clear of it. Anyway, I don't believe in corrupting innocents."

"I didn't mean a job like that," Sam said, his face darkening in embarrassment.

"Well, what kind of job did you mean?"

"I don't know. Something like you gave Becky Ellinson, I guess."

"Becky Ellinson spent three hours a day mending! How much mending do you think I have, now that the Green Garter's closed? Besides," she said, jumping to her feet and pacing the floor, "Becky didn't live there. Every night she went home to her husband."

"I'm sorry, Angel," he mumbled. "I didn't know what else to do."

She stopped pacing and looked at him. "No, Sam," she said, after a moment, "I'm the one who's sorry. You did exactly the right thing. It just kind of threw me for a minute, is all. I'll think of something. I feel responsible for her." In fact, by rights she was more than responsible, as she owed Jessie a rather large sum of money. Unfortunately, Angel had invested it in the Silver Springs Express along with everything else she had. She wouldn't be able to pay her debt to Jessie for several months at least.

"How about your sister?" Sam asked abruptly.

"You mean Alexis?"

"She must know people in Cheyenne. Surely she could find someplace Jessie could work."

"I guess it's worth try—"

A knock at the door interrupted her. She and Sam exchanged a startled glance. "Were you expecting someone?" she asked.

Sam shook his head and shrugged as he stepped over to open the door.

"Good evening, Sam," said a familiar voice. "Thought you might be bored so I brought some cards and a little something to warm your innards." Ox Bruford strolled in and set a bottle of whiskey on the table. "Nothing like a game of poker to—Angel!" The look of astonishment on his face was almost comical when he caught sight of her near the fireplace.

"Hello, Ox," she said. Ox Bruford was about the last person she wanted to see right now. The whole purpose of the nighttime visit was to avoid him.

"Well, I'll be damned," he said, with real pleasure. "Alexis didn't expect you for a week or so."

"She didn't realize I was so close by."

"How have you been?"

"Good. How about yourself?"

"Never better." Ox grinned. "Did Alexis tell you what we're up to?"

"If you mean the havoc you plan to inflict on my poor unsuspecting father, that's all she could talk about."

Ox chuckled. "Alexis said you'd be pleased. Would you like to join us?"

"I wish I could. His downfall is something I'd love to participate in." She sighed. "Unfortunately, I'm rather involved in a business venture of my own right now."

Sam raised his brows. "You are?" From the hurt tone of his voice, it was obvious he thought she was deserting him.

"Yes, and when I get it all put together I fully intend for you to help me run it."

Ox hung his hat by the door. "Have you two solved the dilemma that brought Sam to Cheyenne?"

"Actually, I think we'll leave it up to Alexis," Angel said. "It appears she's in a better position to help than I am. In the meantime, she says the two of you have urgent need of Sam's talents."

"Truer words were never spoken." He pulled out a chair and sat down. "What do you say, Sam, are you ready to talk business?"

Sam looked at Angel and shrugged. "I guess so. What exactly did you have in mind?"

Angel let Ox do all the talking, since Angel wasn't supposed to know any details of his plan.

"So," Sam said, when Ox finally finished, "the whole idea is to take as much business away from the Flying T as possible and make it look like the Silver Springs Express is somehow behind it?"

"Exactly." Ox grinned. "That's where you come in. If anybody asks, and they will, you're just another paid employee. You're rather curious about who the owner really is and will speculate quite freely, I imagine."

"Dropping clues that point to either Treenery or Brady," Sam said, "depending on whose man I'm talking to at the time?"

"Of course."

Sam rubbed his upper lip. "Could work."

"Are you with us then?" Ox asked.

"I don't know." He looked at Angel. "Am I?"

"If you're referring to the matter we discussed earlier, you've done your part. I'll take care of it from here. As for the rest of it, the choice is yours, but I'd feel a whole lot better if I knew you were involved. There seems to be a lot riding on the success of this."

His gaze held hers for a long moment; then he looked down at the hem of her skirt. She had the oddest feeling that what he saw there decided him.

"All right. When do we start?"

"As soon as possible. I'll bring Alexis out in the morning and we'll make plans." Ox turned to Angel.

"Are you sure I can't change your mind somehow? We really need you."

The simple statement sent flashes of heat through her whole body. He needed her? Oh, Lord, if only it were true! "Don't see what I could do that Alexis can't. Besides, I can't spare the time right now."

"You're sure?"

"Positive." Angel could have sworn his voice had a note of longing in it but knew it must be wishful thinking on her part. She felt a sudden overwhelming need to get away from him. "Well, gentlemen," she said, standing up, "it's been a little piece of heaven, but it's time I left you to your cards and your whiskey."

Ox pushed back his chair and stretched. "Actually, I'd just as soon leave it for another night. What do you say, Sam?"

"Suits me fine. I'm for bed."

Angel gave Sam a quick hug. "Take care, old friend. I'll be in touch. Alexis will see to that other matter for us."

"All right." He smiled. "And thanks, Angel. Didn't know what else to do."

"You did exactly right." Angel hoped to slip away while the men were saying good night, but she had barely cleared the door before Ox was right behind her.

"Angel, wait. What's your hurry?"

"I wanted to talk to Alexis before she goes to bed."

"Ah, yes, Sam's mysterious errand." He picked up her hand and pulled it through the crook of his arm. "At least let me walk you to your horse."

"I brought a buggy."

"A buggy? Well, now, that *is* a surprise." She could hear the amusement in his voice. "From what Betsy said I thought you'd probably ridden bareback on the wildest horse you could find."

"Betsy? Where did you see her?"

"At Alexis's house, usually within the first few minutes

after I walk in the door. In fact, she and I have become very good friends."

"I thought you didn't like children."

"Your baby sister is pretty hard to ignore. She has a way of getting pretty much whatever she wants."

Angel smiled in the darkness. "I see you know her well. Have you met Jared and Shannon yet?"

"Mmm. You could say that. They made quite an impression on me."

"They have a way of doing that. Well, here's my buggy. I'm glad I got to see you. I wasn't expecting to." She tried to pull her hand loose but he wouldn't let go.

"Do you need a place to stay tonight?"

"Wh-what?"

"I know you always stay at the cabin, but you can't this time because Sam is here. Since your father and his wife are at Alexis's that's out too, but you're welcome to stay with me if you want."

"Stay with you?" She stared up at him in disbelief.

"Sure, why not?" he said matter-of-factly, as he studied her face in the moonlight. "Lord knows I've stayed with you often enough."

Angel's heart froze in her chest. He was hardly the first man to make her an indecent proposal, but coming from him it hurt to the point of agony. She couldn't even bring forth a scathing refusal or a flip answer the way she usually did. Her voice had mysteriously deserted her.

Ox seemed completely unaware of the devastation his words had caused her as he reached up and traced the curve of her face with his hand. "I've missed you, Angel." His voice was a soft husky rumble that went through her like a knife. "I haven't been able to get you or your good-bye out of my mind."

The last was whispered against her lips. His kiss was gentle and incredibly sweet, like the first rain of spring or the delicate inner petals of a rose. A warmth unlike any she had ever known uncurled in the pit of Angel's stomach and started to spread through the rest of her body.

As her lips parted beneath his, Angel knew if she didn't stop him now she never would. With the thought came the knowledge that she didn't want him to stop. The truth was she wanted him to make love to her more than she'd ever wanted anything in her life.

Desire rose within Angel like a tide of molten rock. With her body yearning for his, and the passion beginning to consume her, Angel did the only thing possible. She pulled back her arm and slapped him as hard as she could.

14

"*We should have done this* months ago." The surprising thought flickered through Ox's mind as Angel's lips parted beneath his in delicious acquiescence. Her mouth was warm and inviting, her body softly yielding in his arms, the essence of a dream he didn't even realize he'd had. A magical haze of longing surrounded them as she shifted in his embrace, and he tightened his arms around her.

He had no inkling of danger, no warning. One moment Angel was melting in his arms, the next a hard stinging slap snapped his head back.

"What the hell was that for?" he asked, rubbing his cheek in bewilderment.

"What do you think it was for, Ox Bruford? I don't appreciate being mauled!"

Ox's heart lurched when he saw the expression on Angel's face. Behind the mask of naked fury was a deep anguish that he was somehow responsible for.

"How dare you assume I'd sleep with you?" she cried, shoving against the solid wall of his chest.

"I didn't—"

"'You can stay with me,'" she mimicked. "Damn it, Ox, just because I used to run a whorehouse doesn't mean I fall into bed with any man who has the urge."

"Angel—"

"Don't Angel me, you Judas. I thought we were friends."

"We *are* friends."

"That's not how I treat *my* friends," she said, climbing into the buggy. "In the future, I'll thank you kindly to keep your hands and your lips to yourself!"

Ox could have sworn he saw a sheen of tears in her eyes as she untied the reins and pulled the whip out of the socket. "For God's sake, Angel!" He started to reach up and stop her, but a glare from her smoldering gray eyes halted his hand.

"Don't touch me," she said tightly, and flicked the whip over the horse's rump.

"Damn it, Angel, wait!" He reached out beseechingly, but he might as well have been invisible. She drove out of the yard without a backward glance.

"Hell and damnation!" His cheek was on fire as he stalked around to the front of the cabin where he'd tied his horse. What in tarnation ailed the woman anyway? All he did was offer her the use of his mother's empty room for the night and she acted like—He came to a sudden stop as an appalling thought occurred to him. What a fool he was. Angel had misunderstood his invitation completely because she had no way of knowing he had an extra room when his mother left for Chicago. No wonder she'd reacted that way.

Ox felt a slash of guilt as he untied his horse and swung up into the saddle. She thought he associated her with her former profession. The truth was, he hadn't ever thought of her in that light. There wasn't a man in South Pass City who didn't know Angel was off limits; even newcomers figured it out right away. Though she ran a brothel, she was definitely not part of the merchandise.

Ox hadn't planned that kiss; it had been an irresistible impulse brought on by moonlight and enchantment. The kiss and the invitation to spend the night weren't related at all. He'd been almost as surprised as Angel—but there was about as much chance of her believing that as there was of Sam taking up knitting.

Ox turned his horse toward the open prairie. As a rule a long ride on a good horse helped him get his life back in focus. Tonight it had little effect. Somehow working off anger at his grandfather was a much simpler task than dealing with the confusing emotions Angel inspired. He'd kissed his share of women over the years, but none had ever affected him this way. Until they'd said good-bye in South Pass City, he'd always thought of her as a good friend, and the thought of kissing her had never crossed his mind. Now he could think of little else.

It was long after midnight when he finally returned home, but he was no closer to understanding than he was before. Too bad he'd left the whiskey with Sam; getting rip-roaring drunk might have put things in perspective. Then again, maybe it was just as well, he thought with a wry smile. Facing a still-angry Angel with a hangover might prove to be lethal, especially with Alexis on her side, as she was sure to be.

It suddenly occurred to him the twins would be together tomorrow. Ox felt a flash of anticipation. Would the differences he thought he'd detected between Angel and Alexis stand up in the light of day? If they dressed alike and fixed their hair the same, would he be able to tell them apart even side by side? To tell the truth, he wasn't sure.

Ox grinned to himself. He might not distinguish

between them physically but he sure could if he spent any time in their company. Alexis was bound to say something silly eventually, and Angel could keep her cynicism to herself only so long.

As he undressed and crawled into bed, Ox found his mood had lightened considerably. He was really looking forward to seeing the twins together. . . .

The dream started shortly before dawn. Angel was in his arms, her kisses wildly passionate, her body molding to his in matchless symmetry. There was no slap this time, only her hands touching him, giving pleasure instead of pain. Her fingers traced the side of his face in a loving caress and then dropped to the row of buttons that ran down his chest. With slow deliberation she undid them one by one, the ordinary task becoming erotic torture in her capable hands.

Suddenly the woman in his embrace changed. Her hair softened from an elaborate coiffure piled high on her head into a respectable chignon that tumbled down around her as he pulled the pins out one by one: Alexis.

Burying his hands in the fiery waves cascading down her back, he feathered light kisses across her cheek, then explored the delicate shell of her ear with his tongue.

With a soft moan of pleasure, Alexis laid her palms flat against his naked chest and started the sensual journey up to his shoulders. Kissing the hollow of his throat, she eased the fabric of his shirt across their broad expanse and sighed as it slid down his arms.

Ox shed the unwanted garment quickly, but it was Angel who came back into his embrace. Her lips found his, and she pulled his head down in a drugging kiss. Her caresses inflamed him as he removed her clothing piece by piece.

Sometimes it was Angel and sometimes Alexis. Even in his dream state, he knew it should bother him that they kept changing, but Ox didn't care. He gave himself over to pure erotic sensation. Before long they were switching back and forth so rapidly he couldn't keep track. Suddenly, Angel and Alexis were both before him, their bodies glowing with a strange golden light. As he watched in wonder, the two fused into a single beautiful woman, who gazed at him with a soft smile on her lips. She moved forward into his arms, and he was lost in the warm sensuality of her kiss.

Ox awoke breathing as hard as if he'd run a race, with his heart pounding in his chest. His arousal was heavy and uncomfortable, but it didn't matter. Still locked in a confusing cloud somewhere between sleep and consciousness, he was filled with glorious shining joy.

It was only as reality slowly returned that his happiness faded into dismay. He rose from his bed and walked to the window. He'd once heard dreams were messages from a secret part of the mind. The meaning of this one was certainly clear. It was odd he hadn't realized the truth before. Ox leaned against the cool glass and closed his eyes. Angel and Alexis . . . Alexis and Angel. Lord, what a tangle! He was in love with them both.

"Morning, Mrs. Smythe." Sam looked over Angel's shoulder. "Where's Ox?"

"I have no idea. My sister said I was to meet both of you here."

"That's strange. I thought . . . well, I reckon Ox will be here soon enough."

"I assume so. May I come in?"

"Don't know why not."

Angel sailed in the room. "According to Angel, we need to find Jessie some sort of a job." She frowned down at the seat of the chair and dusted it off with her hand before sitting down. "Any ideas?" she asked, pulling off her gloves.

"I don't know what goes on in Cheyenne."

"There aren't very many respectable jobs for women, if that's what you mean. Her youth isn't in her favor either. You must have had something in mind."

"At first I kinda thought she could be a teacher, since she spent so much time in school."

"But?"

He rubbed the back of his neck. "She ain't exactly the teacher type. Besides, it sounds like there wasn't much learning in that school of hers that was very useful."

"It was most likely a finishing school." Angel sighed. "She can probably serve tea and make a nice sampler."

"I reckon there's something she could do. She's such a sweet little thing."

"Unfortunately, sweet isn't very useful." Angel pursed her lips. "Unless, of course, to find her a husband."

"No!"

Angel raised her brows in surprise. "No?"

"Well, I mean there must be another solution."

"Maybe, but marriage is an option all the same."

"Since when are you so all-fired set on marriage?" Sam asked with a frown. "Seems to me you're the one who's always goin' on and on about women havin' other choices now."

"I'm afraid you're confusing me with my sister, Mr. Collins," Angel said, flicking an imaginary speck off her sleeve. "I happen to think most women were meant to be wives. There *are* a few, like Angel, who think otherwise, but they are the exception rather than the rule."

Sam made a rude noise. "Your *sister*, is it? Look, Angel. Whatever your game is, you can trust me to keep your secret, but I'll be damned if I'll sacrifice Jessie's happiness for it."

"You're wrong—"

"The hell I am. There may be an Alexis Smythe somewhere, but you ain't her."

Angel stared at the determined set of his jaw for a moment and then sighed in defeat. "How did you know?"

"I suspected right from the start. When I came to after the stage accident you had tears in your eyes. Pretty hard to believe a stranger would do that."

Angel smiled. "You don't know Alexis. Oh, yes," she said when she saw his skeptical look, "I do have a twin, and we look so much alike I've managed to fool almost everybody."

"Almost?"

"My younger brother and sister knew right away. I didn't react to their shenanigans the way Alexis would. What convinced you it was me?"

"Your feet."

"My feet!" As Angel glanced down, she remembered Sam's interest in them the night before. "What about them?"

"You wore the same shoes," he said. "Kind of odd, considering how different everything else was."

Angel laughed. "I never even thought about my shoes. Do you think Ox suspects?"

"Nope. He was plumb excited when he saw you last night. Pretty obvious he thought it was the first time since you left South Pass City."

"But *you* figured it out."

"Could be I know you better. You ain't afraid of me gettin' too close." Sam crossed his beefy arms. "You gonna tell me what's going on?"

She sighed. "It's a long story."

"I ain't going anywhere."

"No, I suppose not." It was surprisingly difficult to tell Sam the rest. First she had to explain her life as Angelica Brady and how she'd wound up leaving it all behind. He said nothing, just nodded occasionally and looked thoughtful.

"Always knew you weren't what you pretended to be," he said when she finished. "You sure you made the right choice, stayin' here riskin' everything for your sister and Ox?"

"I'm not doing it just for Ox and Alexis. I'm doing it for me, too. Don't you see, I'll be free of my father's control once and for all."

"Seems to me like you've been out of his control for a long time. The only way he's going to get any of that back is if you lose your money. Isn't your freedom a lot to risk for revenge?"

Angel stared at him in dismay. Had she gambled everything she had for revenge? She was still pondering the extraordinary idea when the sound of Ox's arrival came in through the open window. Unconsciously bracing herself, she looked toward the door.

"Morning," Sam said pleasantly.

"Good morning." Ox took off his hat and hung it on the peg. "I thought I was going to pick you up at home, Alexis."

"Angel just said I was supposed to meet you both here."

He glanced around the room. "Where is she?"

"She left early this morning."

"Did she say anything?" he asked, with a touch of wistfulness.

"Just good-bye." Angel narrowed her eyes. "What happened between you two last night? She said you insulted her."

Ox shifted uncomfortably. "It was a misunderstanding."

"A misunderstanding?" Angel's voice rose. "She came home madder than a wet hornet."

"I tried to explain, but she wouldn't listen."

"You must have done something—"

"If Miss Angel left in a snit, don't reckon the two of

you can do much to change that now," Sam said with amusement. "We might as well get down to business."

Ox sighed. "I'm just disappointed, that's all. I was looking forward to seeing Angel and Alexis together."

Sam grinned. "I reckon it would be a sight to behold, at that."

"Maybe next time," Angel murmured.

"Sam's right," Ox said, pulling a chair up to the table. "We need to get started. Let's see how soon we can get the Silver Springs Express on the road."

As the three of them worked out the details together, Angel slowly began to realize it wasn't revenge that prompted her to risk everything she had. It was the challenge of putting a business together, figuring out the pitfalls and making it all work. There was nothing more invigorating.

After nearly an hour she glanced up and found Ox's gaze on her. There was speculation there and something else, something that made her feel warm and feminine and oddly shy. It was fully as exhilarating as the problem they were working on, and it scared her to death.

15

"*How was your first day* of work, Jessie?" Angel asked, as Jessie joined them for tea.

"Fine. Mrs. Warren is very nice." Her brow wrinkled slightly. "Though I'm not always sure exactly sure what she wants me to do."

Vanessa nodded. "It's that accent. I have trouble understanding it myself. She's from some heathenish place down south, you know."

"Texas is probably more civilized than Wyoming," Angel reminded her with amusement.

"Well, that doesn't say much," Vanessa observed. "It would be nearly impossible to find a less civilized place than this!"

"Do you think you're going to like making dresses, Jessie?" Jared asked doubtfully.

"Of course she will," Shannon said, flopping down on the overstuffed chair next to Jessie. "Just think how much fun it would be to design a dress."

"I don't do any of the designing," Jessie told her.

"I'm just a seamstress. Mrs. Warren tells me what to sew. I think I'll like it once I understand it better."

Angel frowned. What was there to understand? All she had to do was sew the seams straight. Mrs. Warren did all the fancy work herself. "I'm sure you'll feel more confident soon."

"Oh, yes, I'm sure I shall." Jessie smiled warmly. "I don't know how to thank you, Mrs. Smythe. You've been more than kind."

"Nonsense," Angel said briskly. "Anyone would have done as much." She felt a sting of guilt as she said the words. Kind? With Molly's freedom money Jessie shouldn't have had to work at all, at least not for a while. For at least the dozenth time, Angel reminded herself that the money wouldn't last forever and Jessie would eventually need a trade of some sort to survive. By the time Angel was able to pay her off, Jessie would have an occupation.

Vanessa gestured toward the tea tray. "Jessie, dear, would you mind pouring?"

Angel smiled to herself. Vanessa had finally found someone who gave teatime the proper respect. As she watched her protégée, Angel couldn't help thinking how well the finishing school had done its job. Jessie was the epitome of what every elegant lady should be: graceful, polite, beautiful, an exquisite ornament for any man's parlor. Angel felt a flicker of irritation. What had Molly been thinking of? Jessie was far more likely to wind up as some man's mistress than his wife.

"Good afternoon, ladies. We're just in time for tea, I see."

Angel winced as her father and Ox entered the room. Richard Brady was the last person she wanted to see today.

"Well, Alexis," he said jovially, "you certainly pulled the wool over our eyes."

"I—I did?" Angel's stomach twisted in a knot as

her father stood there, smiling benevolently. Surely he wouldn't be so smug if he knew who she was, would he?

"Your father was surprised by our news," Ox said, crossing the room to drop a kiss on her cheek. "Follow my lead," he whispered in her ear.

"What news is that?" Vanessa asked with avid curiosity.

Angel searched Ox's face looking for a clue. What was he up to?

Ox smiled as he took her hand and pulled her up to stand beside him. "What do you say, Alexis, shall we make our announcement here and now?" He squeezed her hand.

"We may as well," Angel said uncertainly. "Why don't you do the honors?"

"My pleasure." He lifted their clasped hands and kissed her fingers before he spoke. "Alexis has done me the great honor of agreeing to become my wife."

Vanessa clapped her hands together in delight. "Oh, Alexis, how wonderful! Why didn't you tell me? Gracious me, there's so much to do. I hardly know where to begin. Good heavens, what am I thinking of? I don't even know when you're going to have the wedding."

"Er—well, we really haven't talked about it yet." Angel glanced up at Ox. "Have we, dear?"

"Only that we're going to wait until your year of mourning is over."

Richard waved his hand. "No need for that. Duncan's been dead more than six months."

"He deserves the full year," Angel said, "and I intend to give it to him."

Richard's face darkened. "Alexis—" he began.

"I agree with her," Ox put in. "Alexis and I have a lifetime together. There's no sense in causing gossip by getting married too soon."

After a tense moment, Richard's glower relaxed to an indulgent smile. "You may change your mind before everything is said and done."

"Congratulations," Jessie said in her melodious voice. "I hope you'll both be very happy."

"Thank you, Jessie." For a moment as Angel stood next to Ox, her fingers entwined with his, it all seemed gloriously real. And suddenly she wanted it to be. To share everything with the man she loved, have his children, build a future with him—surely life could be no sweeter.

She glanced up at Ox and reality returned. He was playing a part just as she was. They were friends, certainly, and last week's fiasco proved she inspired lust in him, but that was all. Ox didn't love her. A hard knot formed in her throat as he looked down at her and smiled.

Angel swallowed against the lump as they sat down together. What in the world was the matter with her? She'd spent her entire adult life fighting male domination. The last thing she needed was a husband, even one with beautiful green eyes and a smile that made her feel soft and womanly. The whole idea was ridiculous. And dangerous, she reminded herself. Far too much was at stake to let silly female yearnings get in the way.

Another hand squeeze from Ox pulled Angel away from her internal musings.

"Tell me more about this new stage line that's opening between here and Silver Springs Gulch, Richard," he said. "Are they going to give us any competition?"

Richard shook his head. "I doubt it. From what I understand, they only have two coaches and a handful of horses."

"How do you know that?"

"I dropped by the station here in town." Richard accepted a cup of tea from Jessie with a smile. "The stationmaster was glad to talk to me, though he didn't know much. Apparently the operation's headquarters are in Silver Springs Gulch."

"That's odd. Why would they run the operation from there when Cheyenne is on the railroad? It seems kind of backwards to me." Ox reached for a tea cake. He glanced at Shannon and Jared sitting side by side with identical expressions of innocence and dropped his hand. "Maybe someone should make a trip north."

"Good idea." Sipping his tea, Richard eyed Ox and Angel over the rim of his cup. "You and Alexis can leave on the morning stage."

Angel sat up in astonishment. "What?"

"I thought as owner you'd like to check into it yourself, Richard," Ox said.

"No one will suspect the two of you. Alexis will be a perfect cover. What man bent on spying would be stupid enough to take a woman along?"

Angel gritted her teeth. One of these days she was going to shove those superior male remarks right back down his throat.

Vanessa frowned. "Richard, you can't have thought this through. Won't they have to spend the night in Silver Springs Gulch?"

"Probably, why?"

"What will people say?"

"Nobody's going to know. Besides," he said, with a sly glance at Ox and Angel, "they're officially betrothed. We can trust James to take good care of our little girl."

Compromise her, you mean, Angel thought angrily. It didn't take a genius to follow her father's thinking. He figured she and Ox would wind up in bed together if they hadn't already. If an unplanned pregnancy didn't force them to move the wedding date up, he probably figured pure lust would. Even when he thought he'd won, Richard Brady wanted to make sure he had total control. Angel had to bite her tongue to keep from voicing her irritation.

By eight o'clock the next morning, Angel had decided not to waste any more time being angry at her father and just enjoy the opportunity to be with Ox.

Shannon and Jared had been strangely silent. In fact, they'd been uncommonly well behaved since the great pepper incident. It made Angel distinctly nervous. She even went so far as to peer under the seat when she entered the stagecoach.

Ox watched her with amusement. "What are you doing?"

"Making sure there aren't any surprises down the road."

He chuckled. "Somehow I never pictured you as the type to look for monsters under the bed."

"Monsters, no." She settled herself on the seat. "Jared and Shannon are another matter entirely."

"I see your point. You think they might try something?"

"Who knows? They've been awfully quiet lately."

"Count your blessings," Ox said, with feeling. "It's hard enough to second-guess your father without having to deal with those two as well."

"Ah, yes, my father. You've just seen first hand why Angel left home. She couldn't tolerate the way he tries to run everyone's lives. I'm still angry about this trip."

"It doesn't make much sense, does it? Pretty obvious he doesn't see the Silver Springs Express as much of a threat. I can't imagine what he hoped to gain by sending us on this wild goose chase."

"An early wedding."

He gave her an odd look, but the opportunity to talk was lost as the coach began to fill with other passengers.

A young couple with a fussy baby sat in the opposite seat, next to a man with an impressive set of whiskers who smelled strongly of garlic. A rather large woman squeezed in to the left of Angel, shoving her tightly up against Ox.

"Too bad we didn't take the Silver Springs Express," Angel muttered to Ox. "At least we'd have room to breathe."

"Wait until we start moving," he said in her ear. "You'll really wish we'd gone on the Express."

A few minutes later they started with a jerk, and Angel soon discovered Ox had underestimated the discomfort. It was like riding over a washboard in a sardine can. Not that the ride was without its compensations. With every jolt of the carriage she was forced that much tighter against Ox, until she was practically sitting in his lap.

When Ox put his arm across the back of the seat to give them more room, Angel tried to stay upright so she wouldn't crowd him, but it was impossible. In a very short time she gave up and relaxed into the curve of his body. Though the summer day was far from chilly, Angel found it a challenge not to snuggle closer into his warmth. Far from an ordeal, bouncing from rut to rut became an enjoyable experience.

Angel was disappointed when Ox decided to ride up top with the driver and the guard after the first stop. The extra room was nice, but he could have returned when the fat lady got off at the next stop. He didn't, just helped change horses and then climbed up top again with little more than a smile and a wave to Angel.

At the little town of Rawhide they lost the young couple and "Mr. Garlic." Angel's sigh of relief at being alone in the coach had barely cleared her lips when a cowboy climbed in and took the opposite seat. If his dust-covered clothes and surly expression were any indication, he'd had a rough time on the trail.

One glance from the glacial blue eyes ended any thought Angel had of striking up a conversation. Though he was fairly young and not unattractive, he was not the type one spoke to unnecessarily. An air of danger hung about him like a smoke cloud. Even after he settled back into the corner and tipped his hat down over his eyes to sleep, there was something sinister about him.

Angel looked out the window, but there was little in the rolling landscape to claim her attention. Not that it would have mattered if there were. All she could think of was a pair of green eyes and the night to come. Ox wasn't likely to proposition Alexis as he had Angel, but she couldn't help wondering what would happen if he did.

Lost in a pleasant daydream, Angel didn't realize the man opposite her had stirred until he spoke.

"I've heard city ladies ain't real brave," he said conversationally.

"What?" Angel turned away from the window and gasped in shock. He still leaned negligently against the side of the coach, but now his pistol was lined up with her chest.

"I hope you're not a screamer," he continued, rubbing the pistol hammer with his thumb. "Never could abide a woman who screams. Makes me crazy. I'd surely hate to shoot such a pretty lady," he said with an evil smile. "Lots of things I can think of I'd rather do with you."

16

"What do you want?" Angel asked, eyeing the gun.

"Didn't expect to find a pretty little thing like you. It's hard to say what all I'll be wantin' before this is over." He reached out and traced the side of her face with his hand. The hot look he gave her left no doubt what he had in mind. "For the present, I want your promise you'll just sit there nice and quiet when my friends arrive."

Angel tightened her grip on her reticule. A robbery. She had to think of a way to warn Ox. "Why should I?"

"Because you want to live to tell your grandchildren about the day you got held up on the stage. Be a real pity if you was to die before any of them was born, now, wouldn't it? Turn around so I can tie your hands."

"P-please," Angel said in her best Alexis quaver. "D-don't hurt me."

"I ain't plannin' to. I just need to tie your hands so I

don't have to worry about you sneakin' around behind my back. Won't hurt you a bit."

"If the coach should turn over—" She shuddered convincingly.

He stared at her for a moment and then shrugged. "All right, I'll tie them in front, then."

Angel bit her lips and allowed a few tears to trickle down her cheeks as he tied her hands.

The sound of distant gunfire came in through the window just as he finished, and his smile widened. "Here comes my gang now."

"Oh!" she cried and dropped her head forward as though ducking shells.

Her companion gave a disgusted snort and slid away from her on the opposite seat. Angel turned her head slightly and opened one eye. He was taking off his boots! What in the world?

Then she understood. He was planning to climb out the window and up over the top of the stage. If he was successful, Ox and the driver would never know he was there until too late. Angel watched until his whole attention was focused on the gun battle outside. Then she struggled to lift her skirt and pull her knife from the sheath strapped to her calf.

It wasn't easy to move the knife into position with her hands bound the way they were, but she finally managed to turn it toward her and rest the cutting edge on the ropes between her wrists. As she moved the haft with the tips of her finger, the sharp blade made quick work of the rope. She retrieved the derringer from her reticule and removed her shoes and long cotton stockings. Intent on what was happening outside, the outlaw had obviously forgotten all about her.

His startled exclamation when the cold metal barrel of the derringer pressed into his temple was almost comical. "I hope you aren't a screamer," she purred. "Never could stand a man's screams. I think you'd better drop that hogleg of yours out the window. Big guns make me so nervous."

"The hell I will."

Angel's gun made a distinctive click as she pulled back the hammer. "Have it your way, then. It won't bother me at all to blow your brains out. To be honest, I can't think of a better solution of what to do with you."

"You ain't got the guts to pull that trigger."

"You think not?" she said pleasantly. She lifted the knife with her other hand and let him feel it against his neck. "Hmmm, it would be rather messy, wouldn't it? Maybe I'll slit your throat instead. That way I could push you out the door and let you bleed to death on the road. Much tidier."

He swallowed hard and dropped his pistol out the window.

"Careful," she cautioned, as a tiny spot of blood appeared where his Adam's apple brushed the blade. "You wouldn't want to cut yourself. Now, why don't you just put your hands behind your back and lie face down on the seat?"

"You're crazy!"

"That's right!" Angel said, her voice filled with pleased surprise. "I didn't think anybody had heard of me in Wyoming."

"Heard of you?"

She nodded eagerly. "Crazy Alice."

He lay down on the seat without another word.

One stocking went around his hands, the other around his ankles. Then she used his rope to tie the two together behind his back. She eyed her handiwork with satisfaction. "There, trussed up like a Christmas goose. Not a bad job, if I do say so myself."

"I didn't treat you like this," he protested, looking back over his shoulder accusingly as she leaned down to put her shoes back on.

"No, but then I'm not as trusting as you are," she said, pulling a handkerchief out of her reticule. "Besides, you had other plans for me. I, on the other hand, have no further use for you, so I'm not inclined to be nice."

"My gang will let me loose when they get here."

"I know. That's why I have to make sure they don't know you're in here. Don't worry, my handkerchief is clean"—she wadded it up and stuck it in his mouth—"I think."

Angel checked her knots carefully before leaving her prisoner to go look out the window. Though she could no longer hear gunfire, she could think of no reason the outlaws wouldn't still be chasing the stage. Praying they wouldn't start shooting again, Angel leaned as far out the window as she dared and craned her neck upward.

Of the driver there was no sign. Angel barely noticed, for Ox was locked in a life-and-death struggle with the guard who rode shotgun. Suddenly there was a gunshot and the two men froze. For a moment nothing happened, and then Ox began to slip sideways. The guard gave him a vicious shove, and he toppled from the stage.

"No!" Angel screamed as he landed with a sickening thud on the ground and lay there unmoving. Her one thought was to get to him. She was already reaching for the door handle when she realized how foolhardy that was. At the speed they were traveling, there was little chance she could escape injury if she jumped. She couldn't help him if she got hurt too.

Frantically she looked back, willing him to move, praying it wasn't as bad as it looked. She watched until the stage rounded a corner and Ox was gone from sight. He never even wiggled, just lay there in a crumpled heap like a bag of old clothes. It wasn't until she slumped back against the seat that she realized she was crying.

A first she was tempted to allow her grief full rein, to throw herself down on the seat and sob hysterically. She'd have given in to the misery but for two things that occurred to her at the same time. Crying wouldn't do a thing to help Ox, and her prisoner was watching her with avid curiosity.

She stiffened her spine and dried her tears. Getting back to Ox was the most important thing right now; all her energy had to focus on that. The outlaws appeared to have the upper hand. Angel's derringer and knife were meant for self-defense and woefully inadequate for the present situation. She'd obviously been a bit hasty in making her captive throw his gun out the window. All she had in her favor was a hostage who thought she was crazy. It wasn't much of a defense, but if she was clever it might be enough.

Calling up every ounce of acting ability she had, Angel picked up her knife and casually began to clean her nails with the point. "So, tell me, have you been holding up stagecoaches long?" She glanced up questioningly and found his gaze riveted on the evil-looking stiletto in her hand. "Well?"

He shook his head.

"No, I didn't think you had. An experienced thief knows better than to let lust distract him. If you'd been paying attention like you should have I'd never have gotten the upper hand." She sighed as she held her hand out to admire her nails. "I don't suppose you learned anything from this, though. Men usually need something to remind them."

She eyed him consideringly.

"It's too bad I tied you up that way," she said, running her fingers up and down the center of the knife. "If you were on your back I'd know exactly what to do. A nick here, a cut there, and you'd have a set of scars that would remind you every time you visited the privy. Hmm, I wonder, if I turn you on your side—"

The way his eyes widened in horror made it obvious he understood her meaning perfectly.

"Oh, dear," she said, as the stage began to slow and they could hear shouts outside. "It looks like this will all have to wait. We seem to have company."

He closed his eyes in heartfelt relief. If Angel hadn't been so worried about Ox, she might have permitted herself a small smile before turning her attention to the outlaws outside. This was going to take very careful handling.

"Where's Jake?" Someone yelled.

"I don't know," came the answer. "He got on at the last stop, but I ain't seen hide nor hair of him since. Probably diddlin' that pretty little red-haired passenger. You know how he is."

"Damn it," the first voice said angrily. "If I've told him once I've told him a dozen times to keep his pants buttoned when there's work to do."

"Sounds like you make a habit of bothering poor defenseless women," Angel said with a frown.

Jake shook his head vigorously.

"I was going to use you to get a horse, but now I'm not so sure. Maybe I should just take care of you here and now." Angel tapped the point of the knife against her thumbnail. "Guess I'll wait and see how bad they want you back." She raised her voice. "If you're looking for Jake, he's in here."

"Jake, what the hell are you doing? This is supposed to be a robbery, not a roll in the hay."

"Actually, he's my prisoner," Angel said pleasantly. "I'll trade him straight across for a horse."

There was a moment of stunned silence and then a roar of laughter from outside. "Ain't no way we're gonna trade a perfectly good horse for Jake, little lady.

In case you ain't figured it out yet, we've taken over the stage. We don't have to give you nothin'."

Angel shrugged. "Suit yourself. I was kind of looking forward to teaching him a lesson anyway." Leaning toward the other seat, she reached between his trussed-up arms and legs to slip the knife blade under the waistband of his pants. With a sharp upward slash, she cut the seam and proceeded to do the same with his shirt and vest before pulling the gag out of his mouth.

"For God's sake, Dick, get me out of here!" he yelled, with more than a touch of hysteria. "She's gonna kill me!"

Angel looked hurt. "Why, Jake, I wouldn't kill you." With the tip of the knife she gently traced intricate patterns on the bare flesh she'd exposed. "I just want to give you a little something to remember me by."

"Dick! Jesus, give her my horse, give her my cut of the money—hell, give her everything I own—just get me away from her! She's got a knife, and she's crazy!"

There was a low-voiced conversation outside that Angel ignored as she took Jake's hat off. "I don't think they're going to listen, Jake. This looks like a good place to start. You have very interesting ears," she said, tracing one with her finger. "I love ears."

With a quick flick of her wrist, Angel cut the lock of hair directly over his ear and Jake let out a bloodcurdling scream of pure terror. It was obvious that for an instant he thought she'd cut off part of his ear.

"What's it going to be?" Angel called out, praying the leader wasn't sadistic enough to let her carve up his friend. "Are you going to give me the horse and safe passage or do I keep cutting?"

"You can have the horse," Dick said quickly. "And we'll let you go your own way."

"Good." She put her derringer to her prisoner's

head and cut his feet loose. "Come on, Jake. You're my shield. Sit up nice and slow."

Figuring he'd try to get away when they left the stage, she gave him a little jab with her knife as he stepped down—not much, just enough to remind him it was there and that she meant business. Jake started to babble incoherently about Crazy Alice and knives and swearing off women forever.

"Be quiet, Jake," she said, with another poke. "You'll make your friends nervous."

He obediently shut his mouth. The other four men stared at his white face and tattered clothing in undisguised horror.

"Drop your guns," she ordered.

No one moved. Angel put the knife to Jake's throat.

"Drop your damn guns!" he said frantically. "She's not fooling!"

The big burly man in the middle nodded and the other three threw their guns down.

She focused on the obvious leader. "Pick them up, Dick. Then I want you to give one to me and toss the rest into the coach."

He stared at her for a moment, then did as she asked, slamming the door and stalking back to his men when he was done.

"Very good," she said approvingly. "Now, all of you take off your pants."

They looked at each other uneasily.

"Looks like your friends need a little prodding, Jake." She fired one shot into the air, then cocked the hammer and put the weapon against Jake's temple. "The next one goes through his head."

"*Please!*" Jake begged. Angel wondered if he was about to burst into tears.

"Damn it, Jake. I ain't real comfortable takin' my pants off in front of a woman," one of them complained.

"Oh, for pity's sake," Angel said. "You haven't got

anything I haven't seen before. If it bothers you so much, turn around so I can't see."

"Just do it!" Jake cried.

Dick was the first one to finally turn his back and start unbuttoning his pants. The others soon followed his lead.

Not even Jake noticed when Angel slipped her knife back into its sheath and headed for the horses. One minute she was standing right behind him; the next she was mounted and moving down the road.

Angel had no intention of staying around to find out if they kept their end of the bargain by not chasing her. In the time it would have taken them to pull up their pants and retrieve their guns, the stage was out of sight behind her.

A few minutes later she came to a spot she remembered seeing from the window of the stage and sighed with relief. The huge limestone outcropping was plenty big enough to hide her from Dick's gang if they decided to follow her. She dismounted and tied the horse on the other side. It wasn't difficult to find a place to hide and watch the road; there were dozens in the castlelike formation.

After fifteen minutes, Angel was satisfied that they had decided to leave well enough alone and it was safe to go to Ox. She refused to even consider the possibility that she was too late.

Suddenly, without warning, rough hands grabbed her from behind and a bearded face loomed over her. "Well, well, what have we here? If it isn't the little lady that set Dick's gang on their ear."

"So what if I am?" Angel tried unsuccessfully to jerk her arm away.

Her captor was a big bear of a man and seemed to find her struggles amusing. "You're a feisty one, ain't ya?"

"You don't want to know how feisty I am," she said.

"Right now Dick and his friends are very sorry they tangled with Crazy Alice."

"Never had much use for Dangerous Dick's opinion." He rubbed his chin consideringly. "I think I'd best take you to Mother Featherlegs."

"I have no intention of going anywhere with you."

"Don't matter much what you want. Mother Featherlegs will be real interested in you." With that, he picked her up and slung her over his shoulder like a sack of flour.

Angel pounded on his back with her fists, kicked any part of him she could reach with her feet, and yelled at the top of her lungs. She might as well have been an annoying mosquito, for all the attention he paid her. Whether she liked it or not, Angel was going to meet Mother Featherlegs.

17

"Put me down, you overgrown chunk of bear bait!" Angel yelled, pounding on the broad back under her fists. None of her insults or physical abuse seemed to have any effect on this man. He just kept on walking. Hanging upside down over his shoulder, Angel had no idea where they were going or even how far they'd come. All she knew was that her ears were beginning to buzz from all the blood flowing to her head.

"You'd best shut up," he said suddenly, as he heaved her off his shoulder and thrust her through a dark doorway. "You don't want none of the others to hear you and come to investigate."

"What others?" Angel asked, as he shut the door in her face. She could hear him turning the wooden block that was nailed to the outside doorjamb. He was locking her in! "You can't leave me here!"

"I'm going to get Mother Featherlegs," he said. "Won't take but a minute, and you'll be fine here in the meantime."

"The hell I will!" she yelled at the top of her lungs, as she pounded on the door. "This is a privy, you idiot!" She continued in the same vein for a few moments until it became obvious he was gone. Damn! There was nothing she could do but wait until he returned with Mother Featherlegs, whoever that was.

Lord, what a mess! Ox was hurt, maybe dying, and here she was locked up in an outhouse. Trying to ignore the stench, Angel reached out in the darkness to see just how big her prison was. One step to the left and she touched a wall. Two to the right and she hit the other. There wasn't even enough room to pace back and forth. Whoever had built it certainly hadn't worried much about comfort.

"What the hell were you thinking of, George?" a strident female voice demanded outside. "That's kidnapping, for God's sake!"

"Nah, I just figured someone would give us a reward for givin' her back."

"It's called collecting a ransom, and the marshal tends to take a dim view of it. The last thing we want is the law nosing around here."

Angel heard the block on the door move and stiffened her back, uncertain what to expect. It might yet be possible to talk her way out of this. If not, she still had her knife strapped to her leg.

The door swung. Angel winced as the bright sunlight flooded in.

There was moment of stunned silence. "Angel?"

As Angel's eyes adjusted, the familiar face came into focus. "Didi?"

"In the flesh. What are you doing here? Last I heard you were in South Pass City."

Angel nearly sagged with relief as she stepped out into the sunlight. "It's a long story. To put it in a nutshell, an injured man is lying on the road about five miles back." She glared at George accusingly. "I was headed back to help him when your buddy grabbed me and brought me here."

"How was I supposed to know you was a friend of Mother Featherlegs?" he asked plaintively.

Didi sighed. "I'm afraid a simple apology won't do this time, George. Take Clyde and find this injured man for Angel."

"I'd like to go along," Angel said quickly. "He's hurt pretty bad."

"Nonsense, George can be a gentle as a mama bear when he wants to be. You and I have some catching up to do."

Angel scowled. "We can do that later. Right now I think I ought to go with George. He may need help."

"Going with George won't do anything but make him nervous." Didi cocked her head to one side. "It's not like you to get so shook up over a man. He must be something special."

"He's my betrothed."

"Well, well, well, the unconquerable Angel finally got bit, did she? Come on, you can tell me all about it while I fix you a bite to eat. George and Clyde will be back before you know it."

Resigning herself to the inevitable, Angel followed Didi down the trail to a simple dugout built into the side of a hill. A brightly colored banner waved cheerfully from the roof, and a scarlet blanket covered the doorway. "Where did you get the name Mother Featherlegs?" she asked, as they entered the cool interior.

Didi grinned and hiked up her skirt to reveal a pair of bright red lace pantalets. "You oughta see these flutter in the wind when I ride a horse. Folks say they look just like the leg feathers on a chicken." She dropped her skirt. "Best advertisement I ever thought of."

"Then you're back in the profession?"

Didi nodded and made a sweeping motion with her

hand. "Welcome to Mother Featherlegs's dugout of ill repute, the only pleasure palace of its kind between Cheyenne and Silver Springs Gulch."

"What happened to Thomas? I thought you were on your way to happily-ever-after together."

Didi smiled fondly. "Ah, yes, Thomas. We lived the good life, him and me. Wore only the finest clothes, drank the best wines, ate the most expensive foods, stayed in the fanciest hotels. Best six months of my life." She sighed. "But the money ran out and so did Thomas. Last I heard he was working the riverboats, gambling his way from one end of the Mississippi to the other." There was no bitterness in her smile as she turned to the stone fireplace, only regret for a part of her life that was over.

Angel frowned in disappointment. Didi was one of her first successes, or so she'd thought. The older woman had come from Louisiana, where her two sons had been lynched for a variety of crimes. Few women over the years had been more grateful for the freedom money. Angel wondered how many more of the women she thought she'd saved had returned to a life of prostitution.

"So you had a run-in with Dangerous Dick Davis and his gang," Didi said, dishing up a bowl of stew from the pot on the fire.

"I guess so. They never actually got around to introducing themselves."

"Oh, that's who it was, all right. George said you had Jake the Snake so shook up he damn near wet his pants." Didi chortled as she set the bowl on the table in front of Angel and poured two cups of coffee. "I want to hear all about it."

"Poor Jake." Angel smiled. "I don't think he'll forget Crazy Alice for a while." As she regaled Didi with her afternoon's adventures, she surreptitiously surveyed her surroundings. The interior of the dugout contained an odd assortment of items, ranging from expensive trinkets of various kinds to kegs of nails and cases of whiskey. It appeared Mother Featherlegs dealt in more than pleasures of the flesh.

"Damn, I wish I could have seen it," Didi said with a chuckle. "Those boys needed to be taken down a peg or two."

"You know them well?"

Didi shrugged. "I've had business dealings with them now and then. Actually, I try to avoid contact with Dangerous Dick. Can't trust the man." She turned toward the doorway and listened intently for a few seconds. "Sounds like George is back."

Angel was outside in a blink of an eye. She arrived just in time to see George pull Ox off the back of his horse. "Oh, God," she whispered.

"Uh-oh," Mother Featherlegs said, coming up behind Angel. "You were too late?"

"Nope." George transferred the limp body to his shoulder and headed toward the dugout. "Leastways he was alive when we picked him up. Where do you want him?"

"I'll put out the extra pallet," Mother Featherlegs said, and hurried back inside.

"Be careful," Angel said apprehensively, following closely behind George. She could see a lump the size of a goose egg on the back of Ox's head from several feet away. Even more alarming was the red stain on his shirt. *Please don't let him be dead*!

Ox groaned as George unceremoniously dumped him on the pallet.

"He's alive!" Angel cried, dropping to her knees beside him.

"Sounds like it," Didi observed, looking over Angel's shoulder.

"Let's hope we can keep him that way," Angel said, easing Ox's shirt open to examine the bullet hole in his arm. "Oh, my God!" she whispered. His whole shoulder and upper chest were so covered with blood it took a moment to locate the wound in the fleshy part of his shoulder. "He's lost so much blood!"

"Looks like the bleeding's stopped, though," Didi observed. "Could be it ain't as bad as it looks. I'll get you some hot water and clean rags."

Angel bit her lip to stop it from quivering as she gazed down at Ox in the dim light. He was so pale. He was alive, but for how long? Tears spilled from her eyes and rolled unheeded down her cheeks.

"Ohhhhh," Ox groaned, and opened his eyes.

"Don't try to move," Angel said hastily, swallowing against the knot in her throat. "You're hurt."

"What happened?" he asked, staring up at her in confusion. "I feel like I got caught in a buffalo stampede."

Angel brushed the hair back from his brow with trembling fingers. "There was a stage holdup. As far as I could tell, the man riding shotgun was in with the gang, and you tried to stop him."

"I vaguely remember that. We fought for his gun." Ox frowned. "I lost?"

"You lost."

"My head feels like hell."

"I think you landed on it when you fell off the stage."

"Did they hurt you too?"

"No, I'm fine," she assured him. "I was able to convince them to let me go. I think they were more interested in the strongbox than anything else."

He brushed her cheek with his right hand. "Then why are you crying?"

"I can't help it." She captured his hand and entwined her fingers with his. "I was worried about you."

"Don't be. It'll take more than a bump on the head

and a hot poker in my shoulder to do me in." His eyes started to drift shut. "I'm just glad Angel isn't here to fix me up. I'm not sure I'd survive her tender mercies right now. She poured straight whiskey on my last wound."

"I'll be as gentle as I can," she said softly, as he closed his eyes.

"Is he awake?" Mother Featherlegs asked, returning with a steaming bowl of water and a pile of clean rags.

"He was, but I think he drifted off again."

Mother Featherlegs nodded philosophically. "Probably better off that way. Finding out if the bullet's still in there won't be too pleasant."

"For any of us," Angel said with a grimace. "Just pray we don't kill him."

By the time the two women had Ox's wound cleaned and bandaged, Angel was feeling much more positive. The bullet had passed clear through the fleshy part of his arm. She prayed that it wouldn't start bleeding again or become infected.

When and how they could go back to Cheyenne caused her far more concern. Even if he could travel they had no transportation, and Mother Featherlegs changed the subject every time Angel mentioned leaving. It appeared they were staying there for the night at least.

Dusk fell, and Angel helped Mother Featherlegs put up a curtain to separate the pallet from the rest of the room. After another meal of stew, Angel settled down next to Ox. The pallet was narrow and Ox's broad shoulders filled much of the available space, but Angel didn't mind. His breath on her cheek and the slow steady beat of his heart against her body assured her he was still alive. Only his wound kept her from putting her arms around him to hold him safe.

She slept fitfully, often awakening to voices on the other side of the curtain. More than once she heard the unmistakable sounds of Mother Featherlegs servicing her customers and wished she had a pillow to cover her head. Shortly after midnight a loud argument disturbed her sleep again.

"Damn it, Mother Featherlegs, it's solid gold!"

"That may very well be, but I can't give you more than two dollars for it."

"Why the hell not?"

"Too hard to get rid of. Here, look at this set of initials. . . ."

Suddenly Angel understood. That was why George had brought her here. He expected to be paid! Mother Featherlegs had a business relationship with all of them: Dangerous Dick, Jake the Snake, even George. She was a fence, the one who paid them for their ill-gotten gains. This was a hotbed of thievery, and Angel and Ox were smack dab in the middle of it!

18

"*Damn!*" *Ox muttered*, as he shifted uncomfortably on the pallet.

Angel jerked awake. "What's the matter?"

"You mean other than there isn't a spot on me that doesn't hurt?"

She propped herself up on one elbow and looked down at him. "Not only did you fall off a stage that was going full speed down the road, you have a bullet hole the size of Colorado through your arm. You're lucky to be alive."

"How bad is it?"

"If that bullet had been a little more to the right we wouldn't be having this conversation. As it is, I imagine you'll be back on your feet harassing your grandfather in no time." She put her hand on his forehead, checking for fever. "I wish I could do something to make you feel better in the meantime."

He reached up and touched her cheek. "Just having you here makes me feel better." The husky tone of Ox's voice was devastating, as his fingers moved from the side of her face to the back of her neck and gently pulled her head down. Angel didn't even think of stopping him. She'd come too close to losing him today. Her lips parted unconsciously as his breath whispered across them in a feather-light caress.

It was like satin on silk, soft and lush, as Angel's lips echoed the sensuous caress. Passion swirled between them like a spring zephyr, wildly exhilarating and completely wonderful. Their bodies shifted together, the kiss deepening and their pleasure mounting rapidly, until Ox inadvertently moved his wounded shoulder.

"Damn!" he said, sucking air in through clenched teeth.

"Are you all right?" Angel asked.

"I've been better." He winced as he eased his shoulder back down onto the pallet. "You weren't joking about that bullet wound, were you?"

"No. I had a hard time getting it bandaged."

"Was that before or after you had your way with me?"

Angel raised an eyebrow. "I beg your pardon?"

He grinned and rubbed his good hand across his bare chest. "It seemed a logical conclusion when I woke up half naked and in bed with you."

"Wishful thinking on your part." Angel tossed her head. "I never take advantage of sleeping men."

"Oh, and why is that?"

"There's no challenge in it," she said, tapping the end of his nose with her finger. "As for your shirt and coat, they were in worse shape than you were, so I got rid of them."

"Where are we, anyway?" he said, sniffing experimentally. "I could swear I smell freshly plowed ground."

"We're in Mother Featherlegs's dugout."

"Mother Featherlegs! What kind of a name is that?"

"She seems to be a friend of Angel's."

"Uh-oh," he said. "You didn't tell me we were in dubious company."

"Just because she's a friend of Angel's doesn't mean anything," Angel said, stung by his words. "Not all of Angel's friends are disreputable, I'm sure. Look at you."

"My point exactly. The Ox Bruford she knows is as disreputable as they come." He raised an eyebrow. "Are you telling me this Mother Featherlegs is an upstanding citizen?"

"Well, not exactly. She . . . ah . . . seems to do an awful lot of entertaining."

Ox grinned. "And most of her visitors are men?"

"So far all of them." She gave him a troubled look. Ox needed to know the situation. It might well take both of them to get out of this predicament. "There's more to it than that, Ox. I think she's buying and selling stolen goods."

"A fence, huh?" Ox yawned. "Sounds like this Mother Featherlegs is exactly what we need. Too bad Angel isn't here to take advantage of the situation. I doubt I'll be able to cut as good a deal."

Angel glared at him. "The things you say about my sister never cease to amaze me. Honestly, you make her sound like some kind of immoral opportunist."

"An opportunist she is, but in her case that's no insult. Angel has an uncanny knack of turning every situation into an opportunity. As often as not, both sides benefit."

"A mercenary, then."

Ox shook his head. "No, a friend. Every one of those less-than-sterling acquaintances of hers will sing her praises to the sky." He smiled softly. "Including me."

"You don't say much nice about her when I'm around," Angel said, only slightly mollified.

"Only a damn fool would compliment one woman

when he's with another." His eyes drifted closed. "I didn't say much about you when I saw her either. Of course, I don't think she'd take offense at anything I said about you."

A moment later he was asleep again, and Angel stared down at him in consternation. It sounded almost as if Ox liked Alexis better than Angel. She had an uneasy suspicion that the emotion twisting her stomach into knots was jealousy. But how could she be jealous of herself, for heaven's sake?

Angel lay back down and stared at the ceiling. What had Ox meant about Mother Featherlegs being exactly what they needed, and what kind of a deal was he talking about? Angel had the oddest feeling it might also be the way out for them. Ox certainly hadn't been unduly worried about the shaky circumstances they were in. But then she was beginning to think he had more faith in her abilities than she did.

Angel was on the edge of sleep before she figured it out. Of course! She should have thought of it herself. Ox was dead right; Mother Featherlegs *was* exactly what they needed. With her help, the downfall of the Flying T could happen twice as fast. What a perfect opportunity!

She listened to the sounds on the other side of the barrier carefully. When the last customer left, Angel rose from the pallet and peeked around the curtain. Didi was alone at the table, drinking coffee.

"Want some company?" Angel asked.

Didi smiled and nodded toward the other chair. "Grab some coffee and set a spell."

"Busy night?" Angel poured herself a cup of coffee and returned to the table.

"About usual. Thought I heard you talking a while ago. Your man wake up?"

"For a few minutes. He was in some pain, but he

seems to be sleeping now, rather than unconscious like he was before."

"He should be fit as a fiddle before long, then." Didi glanced toward the curtain. "I can see why you picked him. Even with all them bruises, he's mighty easy on the eye."

"He's a good man too." Angel took a sip of coffee. "Can I trust you, Didi?"

She was surprised by the question. "You know you can. Why?"

"Ever heard of the Silver Springs Express?"

Didi gave her a wary look. "Think so, though I ain't real sure."

"Ox and I own it."

"You do?"

"Lock, stock, and stagecoach." Angel set her cup down carefully. "We started it for one reason and one reason only. We plan to put the Flying T out of business and make its owners squirm in the process."

Didi raised an eyebrow. "Since when are you into revenge?"

"Since Richard Brady and James Treenery decided to stick their nose into my business."

Didi listened with great interest as Angel told a creative version of the circumstances surrounding the beginning of the Silver Springs Express. "Well," she said, when the story was finished, "if ever two men deserved what they get, it's those two. Just wish there was some way I could help you do them in."

Angel gave her a conspiratorial smile. "As a matter of fact, there is."

Fifteen minutes later the two women grinned at each other across the table, both extremely pleased with the deal they'd struck.

"I have the feeling this is going to be a long and profitable relationship for us all, Mother Featherlegs," Angel said, sitting back in her chair.

Didi raised her coffee cup. "To profit."

Angel raised her own cup. "And friendship."

"Can I ask you a personal question?" Didi asked, after they'd drunk their toast.

"Sure." Angel grinned. "Of course, I may not answer it."

"Does your man know about your past?"

"Not exactly."

"What do you mean not exactly? Either he knows or he doesn't."

"He thinks I'm someone else. Alexis Smythe, to be precise."

"Sounds like a schoolmarm."

"A rich widow, actually."

Didi nodded. "Good choice. Best way I know of to explain away the extra mileage."

Angel frowned down at her coffee. "You know, there is something that worries me a little."

"What's that?"

"We were due in Silver Springs Gulch this afternoon. They're bound to come looking for us soon."

"Who is?"

"Hard to say. I wouldn't put it past Richard Brady to send out the sheriff."

Mother Featherlegs blanched. "The sheriff's going to know Dangerous Dick and his gang robbed that stage. He just might decide this is where they hang out, especially when he finds the stage passengers here."

"We could tell him George rescued us."

"George ain't known for his charity."

"What if the sheriff were to find us somewhere else? He wouldn't have any reason to come here."

"True," Mother Featherlegs said, "but we can't very well dump you both on the road in the middle of the night. That man of yours ain't exactly the picture of health."

"We can't stay here either."

"What about the stage?" Mother Featherlegs asked

suddenly. "Isn't it still on the road where Dangerous Dick left it?"

"Won't do us any good without horses and a driver," Angel pointed out.

Mother Featherlegs smiled. "George could find some horses and drive the stage."

Angel raised an eyebrow. "What if he's seen?"

"Nobody pays much attention to a stage driver. Don't reckon the sheriff will even notice him." Mother Featherlegs walked purposefully to the door and pulled back the blanket. "Go get the stagecoach, George. You're going to take these two to Silver Springs Gulch.

"That's taken care of. Now all you need to do is dress your man." Mother Featherlegs crossed the room to a dilapidated old dresser. She rummaged around for a few moments and then handed Angel a worn cotton shirt. "It ain't much but it will do."

"Thanks." Angel smiled gratefully as she accepted the shirt. "I'll have him dressed and ready to go right away."

It turned out to be more difficult than she anticipated. She had to shake his good shoulder three times before he blinked groggily up at her. "Decide to have your way with me after all?" he asked sleepily.

"You have a one-track mind, Bruford."

Ox smiled. "You haven't called me Bruford in a long time, Angel."

She was dismayed for several seconds before she realized he was only half awake. "The name's Alexis," she said briskly.

"Kisses just like Angel," he murmured. "Good thing she doesn't slug the same."

"Can you sit up if I help you?"

"Think so. Why?"

"We have to get you dressed," she said, pushing his arm through the shirtsleeve. "We're leaving."

"Ouch! You don't have to be so rough."

"And you could be more cooperative."

By the time George finally returned with the stage-coach, Ox was fully dressed, had eaten a bowl of stew, and was no longer confused. He was even able to walk out to the stagecoach by himself, though George had to help him climb in.

"Sorry things happened the way they did," Mother Featherlegs said, giving Angel a hug. "But I'm glad you wound up here. I'm looking forward to doing business with you."

"Me too." Angel climbed into the stage, leaned out the window, and waved as they pulled away.

"What did she mean she was looking forward to doing business with you?" Ox asked, when Angel had pulled her head in and settled back in the seat.

Angel shrugged. "I had that discussion you suggested with her, is all. She loved the idea and accepted my terms without question."

"Oh? And what exactly were your terms?"

"We let them know which stages to hit for ten percent of the take. All deals are off if there's any killing."

"Only ten percent? No wonder she was pleased with the terms. Do you think we can trust her?"

"Of course not, but I do know she'll keep up appearances. I got what we really wanted. The Flying T will get the harassment and they'll leave the Silver Springs Express alone."

19

"*Damn it, Treenery, this* is the third time this month you've sent me one of these!" Richard Brady slammed the telegram down on the desk.

Ox laid his pen down and sat back in his chair. "I thought you wanted me to keep you informed of what was going on."

"Informed, not forced to traipse out to Wyoming every other week to take care of things. The stage line is *your* job. Should be simple enough."

Ox's face darkened. "So hire someone else. I never wanted this job in the first place."

"That's not the point."

"Then what is?"

"I want to know what the hell is going on."

"I'd have thought that was fairly obvious," Ox said, gesturing toward the telegram. "A gang of outlaws is working the road between here and Silver Springs Gulch. They seem particularly fond of stagecoaches and supply wagons."

"Especially those belonging to the Flying T!" Richard snapped. "What are you doing about it?"

"Not a whole lot I *can* do, except put on extra guards and keep our shipment schedule secret."

"It doesn't seem to be doing much good, does it?"

"I'm open to suggestions."

Richard glared at him for a minute as he considered the possibilities. "How about outriders?" he said finally.

"I'll hire some if you authorize it. My grandfather wouldn't even consider it."

"Why not?"

"Too expensive. We'd have to hire at least five men to cover all our stages, and that's if we only put one on each run. We really ought to have two for it to be effective. My grandfather thought it would cut into profits too much."

"How about alternative routes?"

Ox looked thoughtful. "That's a possibility, especially with the supply wagons. We'd still have to hit all our stops with the stage on schedule to pick up passengers, but if we took different roads whenever possible we wouldn't be as open to ambush."

"Are you ready to go, Ox?" Angel said, breezing through the door in a swirl of perfume. Her eyes widened in surprise when she saw her father. "Good heavens, Father, when did you get back to town? Vanessa didn't say a word about expecting you."

"She didn't know I was coming. This was an unplanned trip."

"Your father was concerned about a problem we're having with the Flying T," Ox said, rising from his chair and coming around the desk. He took her hands and smiled lovingly down at her before dropping a kiss on her forehead.

"Oh, pooh," Angel said petulantly, as she stripped off her gloves. "All you ever talk about is that stupid stage line."

"That's what your father and my grandfather hired me to do."

"I know, but it takes up so much of your time. Last week all I heard was how wonderful Concord coaches are."

Richard gave her a sharp look. "Concord coaches?"

"That's what the Silver Springs Express runs," Angel explained. "Ox says they're the best coach money can buy."

"Is that right? You seem to know a lot about our competition, Treenery."

"It's always wise to know the competition," Ox replied.

"How have they been fairing with the outlaws?"

"I have no idea. They don't exactly confide in me."

Angel looked confused. "I thought you said they hadn't been hit."

"That's just what I heard. I don't know if it's true or not."

Brady frowned. "Don't you think it might be worth checking out?"

"I can if you think it's necessary," Ox said, "but I really don't see what difference it would make."

Richard Brady looked disgusted. "Never mind. Have you heard anything from your grandfather?"

"No, but that isn't unusual."

"His grandfather is on his way to California and won't be back for a couple of weeks. How much longer are you going to be, Ox?" Angel asked. "You promised to take me shopping."

"I don't know, sweetheart. Your father came a long way to discuss business with me."

"Oh, darling, you promised," Angel said, with her best Alexis pout.

"I'm sorry—"

"Go ahead and take her," Richard said in disgust. "I'm leaving anyway."

"But you just got here," Ox protested.

"I found out what I needed to know."

"Will we see you at tea?" Angel asked her father.

"Tea . . . I'm not sure. There's something I need to do this afternoon. I'll be leaving in the morning, Treenery, and I want to take a look at the books before I go."

"You can look at them now if you want."

"You don't have time now," Angel said, tugging on Ox's arm. "We need to get going. There was the cutest little hat downtown. I want to get there before someone else does."

Richard gave his daughter a withering look. "I'll look at those books first thing in the morning, Treenery. Have an enjoyable afternoon," he said sarcastically, as he walked out the door.

Angel went over to the window and peeked out. She watched her father ride away and turned back to Ox with a wicked grin. "You owe me six bits, *sweetheart,*" she said, batting her eyes. "I told you my father would respond faster than your grandfather."

"Sorry to disappoint you, *darling.*" He pulled a telegram out of his desk drawer and pushed it across the polished surface toward her. "I received this less than an hour after I sent mine to him."

Angel picked up the paper and scanned it. "My, my, he sounds most upset. Hiring a Pinkerton detective, no less."

"I suspect that's an exaggeration, but I have no doubt some sort of detective will be here before the week's out."

"From the look on Father's face, I'd say he'll have one nosing around before too long as well."

"Especially after you got done with him." He grinned. "It's strange I don't remember promising to go shopping with you."

"Don't you? Hmm, it must have been the same time

we discussed your grandfather's trip to California and Concord coaches. Now then, about that hat—"

"Sorry, I have pressing business I can't put off."

"It figures." Angel sighed dramatically. "You men have no understanding of the truly important things in life."

Ox chuckled. "Ah, yes, the frivolous widow, guaranteed to drive her father crazy. So much safer than the shrewd businesswoman he's never allowed to see. I can't help but wonder which one of you is the real Alexis."

Angel closed her eyes as if in great pain. "Choosing a hat is *not* frivolous. Though you obviously don't realize it, selecting and buying a proper hat takes as much shrewd business sense as anything else I do."

"Sure it does."

"Come with me and see," Angel challenged, tossing her head.

"Alas, duty calls," Ox said regretfully. "I really do need to ride over to Silver Springs Gulch and warn Sam. Want to come along?"

"No, thanks. That little excursion last month was plenty for me. In fact it was one trip too many, as far as I'm concerned."

Ox flexed his fingers and rotated his shoulder. "Didn't enjoy it much myself. I have to admit, though, our plan is moving along twice as fast since you found Mother Featherlegs."

"True. It made the trip worthwhile . . . almost. Well, I'd best be on my way."

"Give Jessie my regards."

Angel's smile faltered for an instant and then came back as brightly as before. "I'll do that, and you tell Sam hello for me," she said, pulling her gloves back on.

Ox walked her outside and helped her into the buggy. "Good luck with the great bonnet hunt."

Angel gave him a pained look. "Hat, my love, hat. There's a great deal of difference, you know."

"And too difficult for a mere man to comprehend, no doubt," he said with a grin, as she picked up the reins.

"I wouldn't be surprised. Have a good trip," she said, blowing him a kiss. "I'll see you when you get back."

"Right. Good-bye." Ox leaned on the hitching rack and watched her drive down the street with a soft smile on his face. There was no doubt she'd be sporting an extremely frivolous hat the next time he saw her. Sometimes her streak of silliness set his teeth on edge, but the way she handled her father was nothing short of masterful.

It was times like this when she reminded him strongly of Angel. And, he admitted to himself as he straightened and went back into the office, it was times like this when he loved her the most.

Angel drove the short distance to the millinery shop with a frown on her face. How she wished she were going there on the trifling errand Ox thought she was. Miss Jones's terse note this morning requesting an interview filled her with foreboding. She had a feeling she was going to have to find Jessie another job.

This one had seemed so promising. All Jessie had to do was keep the workroom straightened and bring the customers refreshments. There was very little thought involved. At least she hadn't come home in tears as she had from the dressmaker's, when she'd ruined an expensive dress and been fired on the spot. She'd tearfully explained that no one had ever taught her how to sew.

Looking for a place to tie her horse, Angel glanced up and down the street in surprise. Every available space was taken. How odd. Usually only saloons and brothels drew such crowds. There was nothing here but a few quiet businesses.

With a shrug, she dismissed the strange occurrence and turned her mind to the meeting ahead, tying the reins to the brake lever and climbing down from the carriage. She had the distinct feeling this was going to be anything but pleasant. Mentally preparing herself for a confrontation, Angel stepped through the door and stopped in amazement.

The store was filled to overflowing with men of every size and description. Jessie moved among them, pouring tea and offering cakes. "Miss Jones will be glad you're finally here," she said with a smile, when she noticed Angel. "We expected you much sooner."

"I had to stop and see Ox for a minute. Do you know what Miss Jones wanted to talk to me about?"

Jessie gave her a troubled look. "I'm not sure, but she said to send you to the back room when you arrived."

"All right." Angel had difficulty squeezing through the crowd, but she managed to reach Etta Jones's sanctuary.

Etta breathed a sigh of relief as Angel pulled aside the curtain. "Oh, Mrs. Smythe. Thank goodness you're here!"

"What's going on?" Angel asked, letting the curtain fall behind her.

"You can ask that after walking through my shop?"

"It does seem a little crowded," Angel said. "Surely that's not a problem."

"It wouldn't be if they were women, or even if they were here to buy, but they're not. All they do is drink my tea and take up room. No self-respecting woman will step foot in the place, and I can't say I blame them. With all those men out there, this place is beginning to feel more like a saloon than a hat shop."

Angel winced. "Is it because of Jessie?"

"Well, I don't think it's my hats that are attracting them. It started yesterday after Horace Fredrickson came in with his sister. He must have spread the word, because there's been a steady stream of men of all ages ever since." Miss Jones sighed. "Jessie is a good worker and a delightful young woman, but I'm afraid I'm not going to be able to keep her. I'm very sorry, Mrs. Smythe, but quite frankly she's ruining my trade."

"I understand." Angel bit her lip. "But if I take her home right now it could cause a terrible ruckus. There must be some way. . . ." Suddenly her face split into a smile. "Miss Jones, prepare yourself. You're about to do a booming business."

With a wink at the other woman, Angel stepped around the curtain. "I need a hat for my stepmother," she said, over her shoulder. "Perhaps your assistant could help me select one."

"I'd be delighted to," Jessie said, setting the tea tray down. "What did you have in mind?"

"I'm not sure exactly. Let's see what you have."

Jessie picked up a delightful confection of feathers and lace. "How about this one?"

"Hmm. I'm not sure. Maybe if I could see what it looks like on. Would you mind trying it on for me?"

The hat looked lovely on Jessie, but Angel shook her head. "No, I don't think so. It's too . . . feathery."

"Oh." Jessie's face fell. "I thought it was rather pretty myself." Regretfully, she took the hat off and looked at it sadly.

"I'll buy it." A cowboy stepped forward from the crowd. "Fer my mother," he added self-consciously.

His face was bright red and his Adam's apple bobbed nervously, but Jessie didn't seem to notice as she bestowed a brilliant smile on him. "Oh, how sweet. I'm sure she'll be very pleased." She handed him the hat. "Your mother is very lucky to have such a thoughtful son."

Angel wondered if he was even aware of digging the money out and handing it to Miss Jones. He was still smiling foolishly as he left the shop with his purchase.

And so it went. Jessie tried on hat after hat, only to have Angel find some imaginary fault with it. Each rejection brought a frown of disappointment to Jessie's face and another man to her side. They bought hats for sisters, mothers, sweethearts, even wives.

By the time the last of them left, Miss Jones was nearly delirious with joy. "That was absolutely incredible, Mrs. Smythe. I've never sold so many hats all at once in my life."

Angel smiled. "Think of all the women who are going to be surprised when they receive one as a gift today. I fully intended to buy a hat myself. Unfortunately you don't have many left."

"I do have one," Miss Jones said doubtfully, "but I don't know. . . . Here, let me get it for you." She hurried into the back room and returned with the hat. "The governor's wife designed it, but she decided it was too ostentatious."

Ostentatious! It was horrible. A monstrous mix of organdy and lace, bedecked with ribbons, bows, and flowers, it was the sort of creation Angel wouldn't buy on a bet. She was trying to think of a way to decline gracefully when her conversation with Ox suddenly popped into her mind. She could just imagine what he would think of this hat. "On the contrary," she said. "It's perfect!"

20

"*Hurry up, Shannon,*" *Jared* said, "or we'll be stuck here until after tea."

"Don't worry," Shannon replied, as she finished braiding her hair. "Mama and Martha are busy. Father sent Mama a telegram saying he'll be here tonight. They weren't expecting him because he was just here two weeks ago." Shannon tied a ribbon around the end of her braid. "There, I'm ready."

"Finally! Come on. Let's go before they decide you need a lesson in pouring tea or something. We better use the secret escape route so no one sees us."

"Right."

The two crept down the hall to Alexis's dressing room. Jared pushed open the servants' door and cautiously peeked in. He scanned the empty room and then gave Shannon the all-clear sign. They quietly closed the door behind them and headed for the window.

"What are you two up to now?"

The unexpected voice brought Jared to such a sudden halt that Shannon crashed into him from behind. "Blast it, Angel, you scared us half to death!" He glared at his older sister, who stood with her arms crossed, leaning against the door into Alexis's bedroom.

"Oh, dear, I *am* sorry," she said.

"What are you doing here anyway?"

"Funny, I was just going to ask you the same thing. I suppose if I hadn't been here I'd have found a frog in my bed or something."

"We weren't going to do anything to your bed," Shannon said. "Why did you think that?"

"I don't know, maybe because I can't imagine any other mischief you could be up to in here."

"We were just on our way through," Jared explained.

"Of course, how silly of me not to realize it." Angel glanced around the small room pensively. "Odd, the only other door seems to be the one you came in through. Now where could you two be headed, I wonder?"

The two children exchanged a glance. "What do you think, Shannon?" asked Jared.

"Well, it *is* Angel. We can trust her."

Jared's eyes narrowed, and he stared at Angel for a moment before giving a decisive nod. "All right, but you'll have to take the Brady oath."

Angel was surprised. "Good heavens, why?"

"Because if the adults know about it they'll make us stop."

"You're doing something you're not supposed to?" she asked.

"Nobody ever told us we couldn't," Shannon assured her.

"It's dangerous, then?"

Both children shook their heads. "It's the sort of thing you used to do when you were our age."

"All right," Angel said at last. "I'll take the oath not to tell, but I reserve the right to make you stop if I think it's necessary."

Shannon's answer was to hold up her little finger. Jared and Angel followed suit, and the three of them recited the solemn oath.

"All right," Angel said, after they'd slapped hands. "Now what's this all about?"

"Just our secret escape route," Jared said, walking over to the window.

"We use it when we want to get out of the house without anybody seeing us," Shannon put in. "It's perfectly safe."

Angel frowned and looked out the window again. There was little to see; the view was nearly blocked by a large cottonwood tree. "I don't know—oh, for goodness' sake! You're going down the tree, aren't you?"

Her siblings nodded and Angel studied the tree critically. The thick branches seemed strong enough, and the trunk forked about five and a half feet off the ground. "I guess it's all right. But the minute I find you sneaking out when you shouldn't be or taking Betsy down that way, it's over. Understand?"

"We would never do that." Jared sounded offended that she would even mention such a possibility.

"No, of course not," Angel said, ruffling his hair. "Now get out of here before I change my mind."

They shinnied down the tree with the ease of long practice and waved when they reached the bottom. Angel smiled and waved back as they sprinted off across the yard and around the far corner of the house. Suddenly, the carefree days of her own youth seemed eons ago. With a sigh, she went to change for her ride with Ox.

"You're going to wear that hat again today?" Ox asked an hour later, as he watched her in amusement.

Angel stood in front of the hall mirror and adjusted

the monstrosity she'd bought two weeks earlier. "Of course. Why wouldn't I?"

"Aren't you afraid it will scare the horses?"

She threw him a look of disdain. "There's nothing wrong with this hat, as you well know. If you had come with me to buy it you'd know it was the nicest one in the shop."

"I'll bet."

For about the dozenth time, he glanced around the hallway. Waiting for a glimpse of the beautiful Jessie, no doubt, Angel thought with a pang. No man could resist her. "Did you lose something?" she asked irritably.

"No, why?"

"Then what are you looking for?"

"I—er, I thought maybe Betsy would like to go along."

"Betsy!" Angel couldn't have been more surprised if he'd said he was waiting for George Washington. "I thought you hated children."

"Hate is a bit strong. I'm just not real comfortable around them. But Betsy has a way of growing on you."

"So does mold," Angel said, turning back to the mirror. "I'm sure Betsy would love to go. Unfortunately, she and Martha are having words in the nursery."

"Uh-oh, I suppose someone told her to take a nap."

"Nothing so mundane, I'm afraid. She drew some very interesting pictures on the wall, and Martha said she had to scrub them off. Betsy had other ideas."

Ox laughed. "Who do you suppose will win that argument?"

"Who do you think? Not even Betsy is a match for Martha." Angel tilted her hat to the side. "It's going to be a battle, though. I was really glad to get your message. This house is not going to be a very pleasant place for the next hour or so. Shannon and Jared already made their escape."

"Ah, domestic tranquillity," Ox said, with a grin.

"Why, Mr. Treenery, you're just in time for tea," Vanessa said, coming down the stairs.

"Thank you, Mrs. Brady, but I'm afraid I'll have to decline. I came to take Alexis for a ride."

"Oh. Well, maybe next time."

"Perhaps."

"Enjoy your ride then." Vanessa smiled at them.

"We will, and thank you."

Angel glanced at him in the mirror as the parlor door closed behind her stepmother. "You know, Angel would hardly recognize you," she said, driving the last hatpin into place.

"Oh? How do you figure that?"

"Those lovely manners of yours." She placed her hand on his arm and allowed him to escort her to the door. "Every day I see less and less of the crude mule-skinner and more of the polished gentleman."

Ox grimaced. "All those years at Harvard coming out, I'm afraid. Guess I'll have to practice swearing and spitting before I lose the art." He glanced at her head. "I could make rude remarks about your hat if you like."

"I thought you already had."

Ox chuckled. "Only very gentlemanly ones, I assure you. I could compare it to the back end of a bear, or a very large wet buffalo chip. To tell you the truth, I've had mules that were prettier than that hat."

"I'll thank you to keep your observations to yourself, Mr. Treenery," Angel said haughtily. "It just so happens this hat was designed by the governor's wife herself."

"Good thing she married a man with money," Ox observed, as he gave Angel a hand up onto her horse. "She'd never be able support herself as a milliner. Which reminds me, have you found Jessie another job yet?"

"Yes, and I think this one will be more successful. She's serving food at Clancy's restaurant. Mrs. Clancy isn't likely to be disturbed if Jessie draws a crowd."

"No, I don't suppose she will. Might have to hire another cook to keep up, though," Ox said with a chuckle. "Helen of Troy may have had a face that launched a thousand ships, but I doubt she had anything on Jessie."

Angel squelched her annoyance. Why couldn't anyone see past Jessie's beauty? "I take it you have something important to tell me in private," she said abruptly.

"Maybe I just wanted to go for a ride with you."

"Could be, but I don't think so. You're restless as a spider in a frying pan."

Ox grinned. "That must be one of Martha's expressions. But you're right, I do have news."

"Good, I hope."

"The best. My grandfather paid me a visit today with the results of his investigation."

"And?"

"It seems the owner of the Silver Springs Express has gone to great lengths to hide his identity."

"Is that a fact? Now why would anyone want to do that?"

"My grandfather thinks it's because the Silver Springs Express is a front for someone who plans to put the Flying T out of business."

"No!" Angel said in a shocked tone. "Who would do such a thing?"

"Richard Brady, of course."

"What a surprise. You agreed with him, I suppose?"

Ox looked offended. "Of course not. I told him the truth."

"And that is?"

"That someone is only making it look like Brady to cause discord between them." Ox chuckled. "As usual, he didn't believe me and is now thoroughly convinced your father is behind the whole thing."

"Just as you expected," Angel said admiringly. "I think I'm glad you're on my side, partner."

"We make a good team. Any progress with your father yet?"

"I'm not sure. He sent Vanessa a telegram saying he had business in Cheyenne and to expect him this evening. I suspect he'll be meeting his investigator sometime today."

"Probably. According to Sam there were two of them nosing around Silver Springs Gulch last week. Is there any way for you to find out what the investigator tells him?"

"Who knows? I'll keep my eyes and ears open. Do you want me to send you a message as soon as I know something?"

Ox shook his head. "Too risky. Can you get away after dinner?"

"I don't see why not."

"Good. Meet me at the cabin tonight and we'll— what the hell?"

Angel followed the direction of his gaze. "It's Jared and Shannon. What in the world are they doing with that calf?"

"Beats me. Do you think we should investigate?"

"Definitely."

As they drew closer it became obvious the calf was not about to cooperate with whatever Shannon and Jared had in mind. It bucked and fought them at every turn.

"They've hitched it to that little cart," Angel said suddenly. "Oh, Lord, if one of them gets in—"

"Oh, hell! Betsy's with them," Ox said, spurring his horse forward. "She must have snuck out."

The two older children looked up as the adults came galloping down the road toward them. Betsy took advantage of their inattention to get close to the cart and peek in.

"Betsy, *no!*"

Angel's cry came just as Betsy leaned forward and

toppled head first into the cart. Terrified by the loud thump, the calf snorted and took off as fast as it could, straight across the road toward a steep gully on the other side.

Betsy's screams froze the blood in Ox's veins and sent his heart thudding. Please, God, let me get to her in time, he thought. The cart careened along at an alarming speed, but the calf was no match for his long-legged gelding. He caught up in a matter of minutes.

Praying his cinch was tight enough to keep the saddle from slipping, he grabbed the horn with his right hand. Slowly, so he wouldn't throw his horse off balance, he leaned his entire body off the left side and snaked his arm around Betsy, but the moment he plucked her from the moving cart he knew they were in trouble. In the heat of the moment, he'd forgotten all about his recent injury and the weakness that still plagued him. With Betsy's added weight on his arm, he couldn't straighten up.

Just as he began to wonder how long he could hold on, his horse miraculously slowed and came to a stop. Within seconds Alexis was there, lifting Betsy from his arms and pushing him back up into the saddle.

As she collapsed on the ground with her little sister clutched tightly in her arms, Ox realized Alexis had ridden alongside, grabbed the bridle, and stopped his horse. No small feat in the best of circumstances, from a sidesaddle it must have been incredibly difficult. Apparently Angel wasn't the only horsewoman in the family.

By the time he dismounted, Shannon and Jared had arrived, white-faced and frightened. "Is she all right?"

"No thanks to you two. What in the world were you thinking of? Of all the harebrained, idiotic stunts!"

Ox hunkered down next to Alexis as she lectured her shamefaced siblings. He couldn't resist touching Betsy's hair, just to reassure himself she was all right.

Without warning, the little girl reached up to Ox's neck and hugged him. "You catched me, Mr. Treenery."

"Yes," he said, folding her in his arms and hugging her back, "and I'm glad I did."

"I do it again?"

He looked down at her in astonishment. "What?"

"I ride again? It was fun!"

For the first time Ox realized the screams that had frightened him so badly were cries of excitement, not fear. He glanced at the pony cart and the terrified calf that Jared and Shannon each had a firm hold on. Suddenly, their crime didn't seem so large. In fact, their ingenuity was rather impressive. "You know, Alexis, the pony cart isn't such a bad idea."

"Are you insane? They could have been killed. If you think—"

He held up a hand. "I just meant if they had a proper pony and were taught how to drive, it might give them something to do with their time here."

"You mean keep them out of mischief?"

"It's a possibility."

"You'd reward them for this fiasco?"

"If we hadn't come along when we did, they might have pulled it off. I'm sure they'd have never put Betsy in it alone. Besides, it wasn't a complete disaster. They did me a big favor."

"What are you talking about?"

With a grin Ox nodded toward the road. "They accomplished something I've been wanting to do for the last two weeks."

Angel followed the direction of his gaze and gasped as she reached up to her bare head. Damaged beyond repair, her hat lay in the middle of the road like a squashed bug.

21

"Alexis, do stop your pacing," Vanessa said, looking up from her embroidery. "You've been nervous as a cat ever since dinner."

"I'm sorry." Angel sat down with a deep sigh and tapped her fingers on the arm of the divan.

Jessie watched her sympathetically for a moment. "Is there something wrong?"

"Not really. I'm just restless this evening. I think it must be the weather." She glanced toward the window, where the wind howled just beyond the leaded panes. "We're in for a thunderstorm, unless I miss my guess."

"Your father was jumpy this evening too." Vanessa bit off her thread and chose another color from the bright array on the table next to her. "I wonder if it has anything to do with his mysterious visitor."

Angel swallowed a smile. If his visitor was the detective he'd hired, Richard Brady would soon be in a tearing temper. In the meantime she needed to figure out what was going on and how to sneak out to meet Ox without anyone seeing her.

"This may not be the best time to bring it up," Vanessa said, rethreading her needle, "but I think I'll go back to New York with your father."

Angel's fingers stilled. "Oh?"

"I haven't been home in a long time, and I miss my friends."

"Are you taking the children?"

"Not unless you want me to." Vanessa smiled slightly. "I'd have a battle on my hands if I tried, especially now they're going to get a pony. They really love it here."

"The country air is good for them. Anyway, I enjoy having them around."

"I know you do." Vanessa studied the pattern on her embroidery closely. "Although the summer is half over, with your father and me out of the way, Angelica can come for her usual visit."

Angel froze. How did Vanessa know she spent a few days every summer with Alexis and the children? Had Alexis told her or was she guessing? It was impossible to know, and a wrong response could give the whole game away.

"You don't have to look like that," Vanessa said after a moment, as she calmly took a stitch. "I've known about it almost since the beginning."

"You have?" Angel asked faintly.

"Duncan told me. He knew how distressed I was about the disagreement between Angelica and your father." Vanessa sighed wistfully. "Anyway, I'm glad it hasn't kept her from you and the children. You will give her my love, won't you?"

Angel had difficulty finding her voice. "I . . . of course I will. She . . . she cares about you too."

Vanessa smiled affectionately. "I know."

Martha brought the surprising conversation to an

end as she opened the door and pinned Angel with a fierce scowl. "His royal highness wants to see you in *your* study. I told him you'd be along when you were finished here."

Vanessa bit her lip. "Oh, Martha, you didn't argue with him, did you?"

"Humph, I'm just a servant. It's not my place to argue with anyone. I'll leave that pleasure to his daughter." With that Martha shut the door with a resounding thud.

"You know you really should do something about her."

"What do you suggest?"

"Well, I don't know. Couldn't you speak to her or something?"

"Come on, Vanessa. You know as well as I do that I could talk to her until my face turned blue and it wouldn't make the slightest difference."

"Surely she'd listen to her employer," Jessie protested.

"She might if she considered me her employer," Angel said with a grin. "Unfortunately, she sees me as an overgrown child still in need of guidance."

"How very odd," Jessie murmured.

"Not really. She and my mother grew up together and were very close. When Mother got married, Martha came along as her personal maid. Just before she died, my mother begged Martha to take care of her babies. Martha has been diligently carrying out that promise ever since."

"But you're all grown up now."

"My sister and I realized a long time ago that Martha won't feel she's completely lost my mother as long as we still need her." Angel smiled again, a little sadly. "And I guess we've always felt that way too."

"Maybe that explains why your father never fired her," Vanessa said pensively. "I've always wondered."

"It wouldn't have done him any good if he had; Martha's one person he can't intimidate. She won't leave us until she's good and ready. Anyway," she said, rising to her feet with a determined air, "I'd better go see what he wants before he has an apoplexy."

"It's probably some small household matter he wants to discuss," Vanessa said calmly. "You'll be back before you know it."

"I'm sure you're right," Angel said, though she knew different. Richard Brady was probably ready to chew nails by now. She wasn't sure if the butterflies in her stomach were from anticipation or dread as she walked the short distance down the hall to the study.

"Martha said you sent for me?" she said, shutting the door behind her.

"Took you long enough to get here," Richard said with a growl.

Angel resisted the urge to make a sarcastic remark about having better things to do with her time. "I'm sorry," she said, trying to act meek the way Alexis would. "What was it you wanted to see me about?"

"Treenery."

Angel's eyes widened in surprise. "Mr. Treenery? The last I heard he was in California."

"Not him," Richard said in irritation, "his grandson."

"Ox? Oh, no! What's happened to him?" Angel's hand went to her throat. "He's not . . . dead, is he?"

"For God's sake, Alexis, don't be such a pea brain. I didn't say anything was wrong with him."

"Thank goodness!" Angel closed her eyes in relief and sank gracefully into an armchair. "You scared me half to death."

"I swear, you get sillier every day," Richard said in disgust.

Angel wondered if she'd overdone it as he rose to his feet and walked over to the window.

"How often does he go to Silver Springs Gulch?" he asked finally.

"Once every couple of weeks or so."

He frowned. "You're sure?"

"Positive. He always stays the night when he goes. The men he needs to talk to usually come to Cheyenne to see him, so he doesn't have to make the trip."

"Oh?" Richard frowned. "What men?"

"I don't know any of them by name, and I never paid much attention to what their business with Ox was."

"Then how did you know they came from Silver Springs Gulch?"

"They usually mention Sam."

"Sam? Who the hell is that?"

Angel looked confused. "Isn't he the stationmaster at Silver Springs Gulch?"

"No."

"I could have sworn Ox said . . . oh, well, I must have misunderstood."

Richard gave her a thoughtful look. "How much time do you spend with Treenery?"

"Time? I don't know. A couple of hours a day, I suppose."

"That's not enough. I want you to spend every possible minute you can with him."

"Why? You've already accomplished what you were after. The marriage will take place as you wanted. Even if we spent every second together, we wouldn't move up the date."

"This doesn't have anything to do with your wedding date."

"No?"

Richard shook his head impatiently. "This is far more important than any silly love affair. I have to know his schedule, where he goes and whom he meets."

"Why don't you just ask him?"

Richard rolled his eyes. "Because I don't want him to know I'm on to him, obviously. He apparently doesn't see you as any kind of threat, so he won't try to hide anything."

"You want me to spy on him?" Angel was aghast.

"Let's just say I have a vested interest in his comings and goings."

"What for? I thought you trusted him. He works for you, for heaven's sake."

"A man in my position can't afford to trust anybody, especially where a lot of money is concerned."

"You think Ox is stealing from you?"

"In a manner of speaking. I think he and his grandfather are behind all the problems the Flying T has been having."

Angel sat up straight. "That's ridiculous. You have nothing to base it on."

"Oh, no?" Richard crossed to his desk and picked up a sheaf of papers. "This says differently."

"What is it?"

"I've had a man investigating your fiancé and the way he runs the stage line. This is the report. It makes very interesting reading."

"Why, what did he find out?"

"Just what I suspected. The Flying T has more than its share of trouble with outlaws. In fact, nine out of ten attacks are against our stages or supply wagons, and the Silver Springs Express is never touched. Putting on extra guards and changing schedules only made things worse. The outlaw gang seems to know our every move."

He slammed the report down on the desk and went to the sideboard to pour himself a drink.

"Then there are all the unexpected misfortunes that seem to beset us. We run into rock slides where there have never been any before. Mail and luggage disappear, only to show up where the trip began. Wheels fall off coaches. Horses go lame for no apparent reason."

"What does all that have to do with Ox?" Angel asked indignantly.

"My investigator reached the obvious conclusion that the Flying T is being deliberately sabotaged from the inside."

"And you suspect Ox?"

"I don't just suspect him. I know damn well he's behind it, he and that grandfather of his."

"That makes no sense. Ox and his grandfather have as much invested in the Flying T as you do. Why would they steal from themselves?"

"How did I wind up with such a simpleton for a daughter?" he muttered in exasperation. "If the Flying T loses money, it also loses value. Treenery could eventually buy me out for very little and have the entire business for himself. I'll be damned if I'll step out of the way and give him full ownership of the Flying T. There's too much money to be made."

"Ox would never be party to such a thing!" Angel cried. "He's a fine, decent man."

"A few kisses and a handsome face have blinded you to his true character," Richard snapped. "He's as money hungry as that grandfather of his. Why do you think he wants to marry you so badly?"

Angel jumped to her feet. "That's not true. It's you who's blinded by greed. Ox loves me, not Duncan's fortune."

"Is that right? Shall I tell him the conditions of Duncan's will? How long do you think he'll stick around once he knows he'll never touch a penny of your money?"

"It won't make the slightest difference to him!" she cried.

"Are you certain of that?" Richard swirled the brandy in the bottom of his glass. "Have you ever discussed it with him?"

"N-no."

"Well, I have, many times. He's has big dreams for a man with no expectations. Would you like to know the plans he has for your money?"

"P-plans?"

"He's going to build a very expensive house in Chicago, for one thing. I'll wager he never mentioned it."

"You're lying!"

"Am I? What about the sizable increase he gave his mother on her quarterly allowance and the expensive new wardrobe he just bought her?" He took a swallow of his drink. "At least he said it was for his mother. I don't know of any other women in his life. Do you?"

"I . . . I'm sure there's a good explanation." Angel covered her face with her hands. "He loves me. I know he does."

"Frankly, I don't know why you're so upset," Richard said. "Not only are you marrying the man you say you love, you have enough money to keep him under control."

Stunned by the cruelty of his words, Angel nearly gave herself away with a scream of rage. She managed to keep her temper, but just barely. Realizing she risked everything if she stayed in the same room with her father, she did the only thing she could think of. She ran out of the room.

It wasn't until she slammed the door of Alexis's bedroom behind her that she realized that's exactly what her sister would have done. It was one of the biggest differences between them. Alexis ran away from their father in tears, and Angel stayed to fight.

Angel was still standing with her back against the door, fuming, when she heard a noise. She held her breath for a moment to hear better and then headed for the bed at a run. Her father was coming up the stairs.

She was lying on the bed sobbing noisily into her pillow when he spoke to her through the door. "I'm sorry,

Alexis," he said heavily. "But you needed to know the truth."

"Go away!"

"I will. When you get over being hurt you'll realize this is for the best and we can get on with what needs to be done. I hate to do this, but it's for your own good. I can't have you running off to your lover before you have time to think it through."

My lover, Angel thought wistfully. How I wish he were. The unmistakable sound of a key grating in the lock brought her out of her reverie and up off the bed in a heartbeat. "Don't you dare!"

She ran to the door, but an experimental twist of the knob was useless.

"Let me out of here!" she screamed, pounding on the door with both fists. "Martha! . . . Shannon! . . . Jared! . . . Anybody!" Angel listened intently. Nothing. Her father obviously wasn't coming back and everyone was downstairs, too far away to hear her.

Angel glanced around in frustration. There had to be some way to escape her prison. Ox was waiting for her. Her gaze lit on the window in her dressing room, and she began to smile. Jared and Shannon's escape route. Of course!

Within a few minutes she had changed into a simple dark skirt and jacket and stood at the window staring out at the huge cottonwood tree. Now, with the wind whipping the branches about, her idea wasn't nearly as inviting. Her days of shinnying up and down trees were long behind her. Angel hoped it was the sort of thing one never forgot.

The window opened so smoothly, Angel suspected her siblings had oiled the hinges. She stuffed her stockings firmly into her shoes, wrapped them in her cloak, and dropped the whole bundle out the window. Nervously, she sat on the sill and swung her legs over the edge. The ground seemed a long way down, and the wind tugged at her relentlessly. Still, the heavy bark was reassuringly rough against her hand as she reached out to grab a limb.

Taking a deep breath, she put both arms around the tree and swung out of the window. For a moment she clung to the limb for dear life; then she sighed in relief. In spite of her fears to the contrary, the tree was stout enough to support her. Though the wind was making it sway rather alarmingly, she felt secure in her perch. Her descent was unremarkable and it wasn't long before she stood on the ground, slightly shaken but safe.

Avoiding the rectangle of light coming through the window of the library, she skirted the house and made her way to the barn. In a short time she had the buggy hitched up and was headed down the road to her rendezvous with Ox.

22

The rain started when she was about halfway to the cabin. Angel pulled her cloak tighter around her, but the wind seemed to drive the cold and wet right through. It was not a night to be out and about. She sighed in relief when she saw the light in the window. At least Ox hadn't given up waiting and gone home. He opened the door, spilling golden light out in warm welcome as she drove up.

"I was beginning to think you weren't coming," he said, leaning against the doorframe.

"I wasn't so sure myself for a while. My father locked me in my room."

"Good Lord. How did you manage to make him that mad?"

She grinned as she threw a protective blanket over the horse. "He was trying to keep me from running straight to you with his suspicions. Apparently, he thought an evening of seclusion would change my mind."

"But Martha let you out, right?"

"Nope. I'd still be there if I hadn't used Shannon and Jared's secret escape route."

"Now there's a scary thought." He moved out of the way to let her pass. "Dark tunnels and cobwebs, I suppose."

"Nothing so dramatic. There's a very large tree outside my window. It was a simple matter of descending it."

"You never cease to amaze me," Ox said with a chuckle, as he shut the door. "First outwitting outlaws on the road, then performing daring rescues on horseback, and now climbing down trees in the middle of the night."

"Coming down was easy. The problem will be when I have to go back up. I'm hoping Martha will have figured out where I am and leave the back door unlocked." Angel stripped off her gloves. "That fire sure looks inviting."

"I figured you'd be chilly after coming through that storm, so I lit a fire."

"It doesn't exactly feel like the middle of July right now, does it?" She flopped down on the settee and glanced toward the table. "What are my goblets doing out?"

"They were in the cupboard, so I commandeered them to go with the cognac."

"Cognac! Where in the world did that come from?"

Ox grinned. "Compliments of my grandfather's private supply, of course. It's the best to be had this side of the Mississippi."

Angel laughed. "And he donated it to help celebrate our triumph, no doubt."

"That's right." Ox brought his hand out from behind his back. "And this, my lovely partner, is for you," he said, handing her a single red rose with a flourish.

"Oh, Ox, I love roses!" Angel held the blossom to her nose. "How did you know?"

"It was a guess. Angel once told me it's her favorite flower. I thought you might share her taste." He gave her a soft smile. "Anyway, it reminded me of us. James Treenery and Richard Brady are only beginning to feel our thorns."

"Beware the danger beneath our innocent cover," Angel murmured, as she watched Ox open the bottle of cognac.

"They won't realize where the danger is coming from until it's too late," Ox agreed, pouring the deep-amber liquid into the glasses. "What did the investigator tell your father?"

"It appears someone is systematically destroying the Flying T from the inside."

Ox handed her a glass as he sat down. "Imagine that."

"Here's to sabotage." She raised her glass in a toast.

Ox grinned and clinked his glass against hers. "To trickery and subversion."

The potent liquor slid over Angel's tongue and down her throat, leaving a trail of warmth behind. "Whew!" she said, as the glow spread from her stomach outward. "It's got quite a kick to it."

"That's true enough, but it should warm your insides."

"It does that, all right." She took another sip. "I can see how a person might acquire a taste for cognac, especially on a chilly night like this."

"My grandfather would be pleased you approve. He's very proud of his wine cellar." Ox settled himself more comfortably. "I assume your father called off our betrothal during his tirade?"

Angel shook her head. "Just the opposite. I'm supposed to spend every possible minute with you so I can report your movements to him."

Ox looked surprised. "And he thought you'd do it without question?"

"My father may not have a very high opinion of my intelligence, but he's not that stupid. He used his persuasive powers to make me see you in a bad light. You're marrying me for my money and supporting a mistress in style on the prospects."

"Good Lord! How's that supposed to make you want to be with me? Seems to me you'd want to kill me."

"At the very least, but my father thinks only in terms of power. He figures I should be happy that I now have a way to control you."

"I don't get it."

"It all has to do with my late husband's will. He left his entire fortune completely under my control. I can't pass that control on to anyone else even if I wanted to. My father fully expected to get hold of the money when Duncan died, and he's still furious about it. I think the only satisfaction he gets from the situation is that if I remarry, my husband can't touch it either. In my father's mind, if I control the purse strings I also control the man."

"Do I detect Angel's hand in your husband's will?" Ox asked pensively.

Angel was startled. "How did you know?"

"It sounds like something Angel would suggest. It's a rather radical idea, not one a man the age of your late husband would be likely to come up with."

"It *was* Angel's idea, but Duncan rather liked it. He had Father's measure by then and knew he had to protect me somehow. Anyway, I'm pretty sure we've convinced Father ours is a love match."

"What makes you think that?"

"Because he tried to blackmail me tonight. There wouldn't be any sense to it if he thought I was still against marrying you."

"Blackmail! About what?"

"He said if I didn't cooperate with him, he was

going to tell you about the will. When I ran to my room, he locked the door to give me time to think it over."

Ox got to his feet and walked to the window. "Christ, I hate manipulators who bully other people."

"So do I, but I think in this case it will work to our advantage. I'll be properly chastised by morning and will do as he asks."

Ox frowned. "Will he trust you?"

"No, of course not. I'd venture to guess someone will be sent to spy on me as well. We'll need to proceed as if we're being watched every minute."

"Good point. By the way, how would you feel about another partner?"

"That would depend on who it was."

"Sam asked if he could buy into the business today. He doesn't have a fortune to invest, but he sees the possibilities in what we're doing."

Angel nodded. "Angel has said she'd trust him with her life. That's good enough for me. Besides, he's almost acting as a partner anyway."

"That's what I thought too, and to be honest we could use the money. I'll tell him next time I see him."

"Good," Angel said, running her finger around the rim of her glass. "In the meantime, what's our next step?"

"I think, it's time we became more than an irritant."

"I agree. What did you have in mind?"

"That's an excellent question; I wish I had the answer. It has to be something pretty dramatic that will hit the Flying T at the heart of its moneymaking power."

Angel gazed into her glass pensively. "If only there were some way to get the mail contract away from them. It's their one steady source of income. Without it, they'd have to depend entirely on passengers."

Ox stared at her. "You know, you may have something there." He took a quick turn around the room as he considered the possibility. "We'd have to extend the route north of Silver Springs Gulch. Then it would be a simple matter to drop a few hints in the right ears and maybe grease a few palms here and there. By God, I think we could do it!"

Ox pulled her up off the settee and whirled her around the room. "You're a genius, Alexis!"

"Ox, my drink," she protested laughingly. "If you keep this up you'll be wearing it."

He took the glass from her hand and set it on the table. "That's easily taken care of. What do you think? Can we manage to put an extra stage on yet?"

Angel did some quick figuring. It would mean putting off paying Jessie her money several more months. She squelched her feelings of guilt with the rationalization that Jessie wasn't ready to be on her own yet and seemed perfectly happy where she was. "If we keep putting everything we have back into the business and add Sam's money, I think we can."

"It might mean losing everything we've invested so far," Ox warned.

"I'm willing to take that chance if you are. You can't win the game if you never take risks."

"Damned if you aren't the best partner a man could have!" he said, and gave her an exuberant kiss.

The current that sizzled between them took them both by surprise. Arms tightened and lips parted without conscious thought as the innocent kiss deepened into something more. A delicious warmth spread through them both, a molten desire that they were powerless to stop.

When it finally ended, they stared at each other in wonder. "Oh, my God," Angel whispered, reaching up to caress the scar that dimpled his cheek.

Ox caught her hand and kissed the palm before returning to her mouth. Her lips parted in response to the gentle urging of his. Desire, hot and insistent, flowed through Angel, melting her resolve and dissolving her better sense. All the reasons for not sleeping with Ox disappeared in a flood of intense longing as he swept her up in his arms and carried her the short distance to the bed.

Angel put her arms around him and pulled him close as he lay down next to her and sought the intoxicating sweetness of her kiss. As her tongue danced with his, she was rewarded with a moan of pure pleasure. The sound sent ripples of unrestrained excitement thundering through her, intensifying her passion to fever pitch. The taut muscles of his back felt warm and supple under her fingers as she followed the strong line of his spine down to the waistband of his trousers and back up again.

The tiny buttons on Angel's clothing barely slowed him down. In a matter of minutes his lips were tracing patterns down the column of her throat and the soft sensitive skin below. He nuzzled the tip of one breast with his lips, sending shock waves of sensation to the pit of her belly.

It soon grew too intense. Angel pushed Ox over on his back and rolled on top of him. "Now it's my turn," she said in a husky whisper, as she unbuttoned his shirt and pushed the material aside. She kissed the hollow of his throat and began her own sensuous journey of exploration. His entire body was superbly muscled. Angel delighted in discovery after delightful discovery as she worshiped it with hands and lips. Never had she imagined the mere touch of her hand on another person's body could produce such a fever in her own.

Unable to lie still, Ox slipped his hands inside her blouse and traced the curve of her back, his breathing ragged as she pushed him to his limits. With one fluid movement he rolled her beneath him and became the aggressor once more. Ox dispatched her clothing with little trouble, tossing each garment aside as he removed it. When she was naked at last, he rose to his feet, shed his pants in record time, and rejoined her on the bed.

Lost in a whirlpool of passion, Ox felt all his dreams had come to life as she shifted and moved beneath him in glorious abandon. At last he could stand no more and put his knee between hers. "Open for me, sweetheart," he whispered. "I'll take us both to heaven." His mouth found hers again, his tongue delving eagerly into its silken warmth. She wrapped her arms even more tightly around him as her legs parted.

Ox had the vague impression that she was bracing herself, but it had no meaning for him as he entered her body with a single smooth thrust. A second later he pushed through a thin barrier that had no business being there.

"What the hell?" He pulled his mouth away and stared down at her in undisguised horror.

"It's nothing for you to worry about."

"Nothing for me to worry about! Are you crazy?"

"I want you to make love to me." Angel wiggled her hips erotically. "Are you going to make me do it all?"

Ox gritted his teeth against the nearly overwhelming pleasure her movements caused.

"Please, Ox," she whispered. "Someone will do it eventually. I want it to be you."

"Oh, Lord. . . ." The rest was lost as she moved insistently against him, destroying any thought of restraint. After that he couldn't have stopped if he wanted to, and stopping was the last thing on his mind.

It was like nothing he had ever experienced before, wildly passionate but deeply fulfilling as well. As their bodies shifted and moved together in the ancient rhythms of love, it was as though she reached out and touched his very soul. Her release rocked him to the very depth of his being and pushed him over the edge into his own. As he shattered into a million fragments of blind ecstasy, he cried out her name.

Alexis! The name slashed through Angel like a sword. "Oh, Lord, what have I done?" she cried, scrambling from the bed.

"What's the matter?" Ox tried to gather his wits as she hurriedly pulled on her skirt and blouse.

"How could I have been such a fool?" she cried, grabbing her cloak.

"Alexis, wait!" He rose from the bed and grabbed her arms. "Don't be embarrassed. I'm sure it had nothing to do with you. Duncan certainly wasn't the first old man who couldn't perform his marital duties."

Her beautiful gray eyes swam with tears as she stared up at him. "Oh, Ox, I'm so sorry!" She reached up and touched his scarred cheek. "Forgive me." With a sob she turned and ran.

Two strides took Ox to the door, but it was too late. She sprang into the buggy and headed down the road toward town.

"Alexis!" he called desperately, but she didn't even pause. As she disappeared from sight, the wind-driven rain hit his naked chest like small icy blades. He slammed the door, stalked across the room and pulled on his pants. What the hell was that all about? he wondered, flopping down on the settee. First she begged him to make love to her, then she ran away like a scared rabbit when he did. Damn it all anyway. The woman was making him crazy.

As Ox stared broodingly into the fire, he gradually became aware of something poking the bottom of his right thigh. He glanced down and then grimaced as he moved his leg to pick up the rose he'd given her. It lay in his hand like a mangled corpse, the petals as bruised and broken as his heart.

23

"*He's downstairs asking for* you again," Martha said, carefully arranging roses in a vase by the window. "This time he brought you a present to go with the flowers."

Angel glanced up from her book with feigned nonchalance. "Who's that, Martha?"

Martha snorted. "Same one who's been here twice a day for the last week. Who do you think?"

"It's only been three days." She went back to her book. "Tell him I'm still sick."

"He'll know I'm lying just like he has from the beginning. I don't know what happened between the two of you, but you can't run away forever. You're going to have to face him sometime." Martha watched her for a moment as she pretended to read the page in front of her. "It's because he's falling in love with you, isn't it?"

"He isn't falling in love with me."

"Oh, no? Then why do I have him underfoot every

morning and every night, asking about you, bringing you flowers and presents, acting like a lovesick pup?"

Angel stared unseeingly at the wall for a long moment. "It's not me he's falling in love with," she said quietly. "It's Alexis."

"Balderdash! He's never even met Alexis."

"No, but he hasn't seen the real me either."

"He sees you every day," Martha said in disgust. "You may be pretending to be Alexis, but there's far more of you than your sister in this disguise."

"It's fooled my father."

"Only because you never relax your guard around him. Besides, he's so blamed arrogant he can't see beyond the end of his nose. The children figured you out right off the bat," Martha reminded her. "I think even Vanessa knows."

Angel gave Martha a startled look. "She does?"

"You forget, Vanessa and Alexis have spent a good many hours together over the years. They share the same interests, which don't include gardening or gallivanting all over the countryside on a half-broke horse. Even Vanessa is bound to notice something so obvious." Martha gave her a shrewd look. "Which is all entirely beside the point. We were discussing your being in love with young Treenery."

"We were discussing him being in love with Alexis," Angel said, slamming her book closed.

"You mean the woman he *thinks* is Alexis. This charade wouldn't last two minutes if you and Alexis were to trade back right now. He'd know immediately, because it's you he's in love with, not the part you play."

"Wishful thinking, Martha." Angel stood up and walked to the window.

"Is it? He told me Angel was the best friend he ever had."

"That's exactly right. Friend."

"But—"

"Martha, just go tell him I'm not up to seeing him today," Angel said stonily. "It will all be over soon anyway. I've written to Alexis. When she gets back from visiting her friends, we'll switch back."

"She's taking her own sweet time," Martha observed. "What if she doesn't come?"

"She will."

"And you're going to leave her to face Ox by herself?"

"Why not? If she'd done that in the first place we wouldn't be in this mess now."

"Fine. I just hope you don't live to regret it," Martha grumbled.

When the door slammed behind her, Angel's shoulders slumped in defeat. "Too late," she whispered, reaching out to touch Ox's roses. "I already regret it more than you can possibly know."

Listlessly she opened the box Martha had brought with the flowers. Nestled inside was a delightful hat of organdy and lace. "He bought me a new one." Angel gasped with genuine pleasure as she lifted it out. It was exactly the sort of hat she would have chosen for herself. She smiled into the mirror as she put it on and tied the ribbons beneath her chin. A small tasteful spray of flowers provided just the right touch. If Ox had picked this out all by himself, he had incredible taste.

Angel's smile faded with the thought. Sadly, she removed the hat and carefully placed it back in the box. After this last fiasco, it was obvious she couldn't trust herself around him. Not that she'd ever have to worry about it again. He'd be so angry when he found out about the deception they'd played on him, he'd never speak to her. She just wanted it over with. This waiting was driving her insane. What in blue blazes was keeping Alexis anyway?

* * *

Ox stared out the window as he waited for Martha to return. He was still in love with both Angel and Alexis. Time and distance hadn't brought the intelligent council he hoped for. It had brought disaster instead.

When Alexis left the cabin three nights ago, he'd been angry and hurt. But as the disappointment and confusion began to fade, he'd found himself in a horrible quandary. Though she was a widow, the fact remained he'd stolen her innocence. To a lady like Alexis Brady Smythe that meant one thing: marriage. Could he marry Alexis, knowing Angel was bound to be a close part of their lives? How incredibly awkward he would feel, becoming Angel's brother-in-law.

"She sends her regrets, but she's still not up to seeing you," Martha said from the doorway.

Ox frowned. "Did you give her my message?"

"Yes, and your gifts."

"Did you try to convince her?"

"It's not my place to convince her of anything," Martha said primly. "I'm just—"

"A servant. I know," Ox broke in impatiently. "But she listens to you, Martha."

"In a pig's eye! That girl is her father all over again. I swear I don't know how my sweet Julia produced such a stubborn daughter."

"Seems to me she produced two of them," Ox said, grinning in spite of himself. "If anything, Angel is even worse."

"That's a fact," Martha agreed handing him his hat. "At any rate, she refused to see you."

Ox gave a deep sigh. "Tell her I'll be back tomorrow."

"I don't know what good that will do, but I'll tell her."

"Thanks and keep working on her. I have faith in

your abilities." He ignored her snort as he put on his hat and walked to the door. "See you tomorrow, Martha."

Ox strode down the path to the barn to get his horse. Damned if Alexis hadn't done it again! He'd lost count of the times she'd refused to see him in the last few days. Today he thought he'd finally made some progress when Martha headed up the stairs with a militant look in her eye. Irritation was fast replacing his guilt. One short burst of lust that they had both enjoyed wasn't worth all this.

"Mr. Treenery!" Betsy came running from the barn, a small whirlwind of braids and petticoats.

Ox stooped down to catch her before she crashed into his legs. "Here, now," he said, lifting her in his arms. "What's the rush?"

"I comed to say hello." She put her arms around his neck and gave him a noisy kiss on the cheek.

Ox smiled. Obviously not all the Brady women were afraid of him. "Hello to you too. What are you doing down here this time of day, escaping a nap?"

"Uh-uh. I help Jared and Shannon. We got a pony."

"I see."

"You help too?"

"Well, I—"

"Mr. Treenery, just the person we need." Jared was all smiles as he emerged from the barn with Shannon at his heels. "Do you have time to help us with the pony cart?"

Ox eyed them apprehensively. "What sort of help?"

"Father got us a brand-new harness," Shannon explained. "Only we can't figure out how to put it on."

"We don't exactly know how to drive, either," Jared admitted. "Alexis told Father she'd teach us but she says she's sick."

"And you don't believe her?"

They exchanged a look. "Well, she *has* been real grumpy," Jared said.

Shannon nodded. "And she seems awfully sad."

"I saw her cry," Betsy added solemnly.

"I see." Surrounded by the three children, it suddenly occurred to Ox that he'd stumbled onto a veritable treasure trove of information. They probably knew things about Alexis and Angel the twins weren't aware of themselves. "You know, I really don't have to be at the stage office for another hour yet. Why don't we take a look at this pony cart of yours?"

Alexis had arrived at last. Her note had been delivered to the houses a short time ago. A sense of overwhelming relief warred with a deep feeling of sadness as she rode to the cabin. The thought of giving up the closeness with Ox, of not sharing the planning and worry of the Silver Springs Express with him, was almost more than she could stand. On the other hand, she could hardly wait to get out from under the strain of carrying on the masquerade.

As always, the anticipation of being with her sister again overshadowed all other considerations. Everything else was forgotten as she stepped through the door and into Alexis's welcoming hug.

"You sure took your time getting here," Angel said, hugging her back.

"I just got your message yesterday. People don't pass that way every day."

Angel frowned. "Your friend Mandy lives right on the road to Denver."

"Er—well, I was only there for a few days."

"Oh? Where have you been the rest of the time?"

Alexis blushed. "I went to stay with another friend. But that isn't important. What's happened? Your message said it was urgent. Has your plan failed?"

"No. In fact, it's moving along even better than we'd

hoped. Our accomplices are wreaking havoc with the Flying T, and Ox thinks he can get the mail contract. Even now, James Treenery and Father are trying to figure out how to ruin each other and get full possession of the line."

"Then what's the problem?"

Angel took an agitated turn around the room. "We have to switch back, Alexis."

"Switch back? Why?"

"I can't do it anymore."

"You've been doing it for four months. You must be about perfect by now. I'd be willing to bet money Martha would have trouble telling us apart."

"Then you'd lose. Martha says even Vanessa suspects I'm not you. It's only a matter of time until Father figures it out. He came close a couple of months ago."

"But you didn't panic then." Alexis watched her sister closely. "I wonder why you are now."

"I'm not panicking!"

"Oh, no? Then why are you pacing? You only do that when you're extremely upset."

Angel stopped immediately. "I'm just not getting enough exercise. I'm used to a lot more activity than I get here."

"Angel, this is me you're talking to," Alexis said softly. "You don't have to make excuses, just tell me what's going on."

Angel rubbed her forehead. "I want out, Alexis. I can't go on like this."

"Like what? You still haven't told me what's wrong." She looked thoughtful. "Does it have anything to do with the rumpled bed and the half-empty bottle of cognac I found when I got here?"

Angel stared at her sister for a moment. Then she sank down onto the settee. "Neither of us planned it," she said, with a small catch in her voice. "It just happened."

"Good!"

Angel looked up in surprise. "Good? Are you crazy? Don't you realize what this means?"

"Yes, as a matter of fact I do." Alexis smiled as she sat down next to her. "It means, my dear sister, you've finally let some man get under your skin. I couldn't be more pleased. I hope he did a thorough job of it."

"Of what?"

"Making love to you."

Angel blushed. "Thorough enough. I'm no longer a virgin."

"And it's about time too," Alexis said, giving Angel another hug. "Are you in love with him?"

"I—yes," Angel whispered.

"Then I don't see the problem."

"Don't you? Ox isn't in love with me."

"Are you sure?" Alexis glanced around the room. "It looks like a pretty elaborate seduction to me."

"It wasn't a seduction," Angel said irritably. "We were celebrating our success. He gave me a friendly little kiss and it kind of exploded."

"That's even better. It means he finds you irresistible." Alexis smiled brightly. "I think he *is* in love with you."

"No," Angel whispered. "He's in love with you."

There was a moment of stunned silence before Alexis burst into laughter. "You goose. He doesn't even know me."

"He knows Alexis is a respectable widow of gentle breeding and high moral standards. The Angel he knows is the madam of a notorious brothel."

"That shouldn't make any difference."

"Oh, no?" Angel gave her a bleak look. "Ox and I have been friends for two years. During that time he never once made any kind of romantic move."

"Maybe he never had the opportunity."

"He stayed at my place at least twice a month. We

ate together, drank together, talked for hours; we even share a godchild. He's told me time and again he considers me a good friend."

"Well, if he'd never kissed you before, he might not have realized how much deeper his feelings for you were. He was probably just as carried away as you."

"But he had, twice. He kissed me good-bye when we left South Pass City and again when I had to appear here as myself."

"And?"

"The first time he was appalled. The second time he made an indecent proposal. It wasn't until he thought I was you that he was stirred by passion."

"Isn't it a moot point now anyway?" Alexis asked. "He must have figured out our little ruse as soon as he discovered your virginity."

"No. He thought Duncan couldn't . . . "

"He isn't all that far from the truth, either," Alexis admitted with a sigh. "But if Ox believed you, I don't see what the problem is."

"I don't want to be you anymore."

"Angel, you have to stop running away from every man who shows an interest."

"I'm not."

"Oh, yes, you are. Every time a man starts to get close, you take off like a scared rabbit." Alexis put her hand on Angel's arm. "They aren't all like Father, you know."

"All the men I've ever met are. They all think women are brainless chattel who have to be taken care of."

Alexis raised her brows in surprise. "Is that how Ox treats you?"

"No, but—damn it, Alexis, we have to trade back. This just hurts too much."

"Oh, dear." Alexis bit her lip and looked down at her hands. "That may be a bit difficult."

"I know you'd rather not, but I can't continue this way. I've accomplished your original goal. You won't be forced into marriage, and by the time this is all finished you'll be completely out from under Father's control."

"I can't, Angel."

"What do you mean, you can't? All you have to do is go home."

"It's a little more complicated than that." Alexis lifted her gaze to her sister's. "Angel, I'm pregnant."

24

"You're what?"

Alexis winced. "You heard me. I'm going to have a baby."

"A baby! What in God's name were you thinking of?"

Alexis flushed. "I didn't do it on purpose, Angel, but I'm not going to apologize for it either."

"Who's the father, Brandon?"

"Well, of course it's Brandon. Who else would it be?"

Angel started pacing again. "How would I know? I suppose that's where you've been these last months."

"Yes, and I'm not going to apologize for that, either."

"You knew this back when you asked for my help, didn't you?" Angel said suspiciously.

"No. I suspected before I left, but I wasn't sure." Alexis sighed. "Please don't be angry, Angel. I want this baby more than I've ever wanted anything in my life. Be happy for me."

"Is Brandon going to marry you?"

"I . . . I don't know."

"What do you mean, you don't know? Surely you've discussed it with him?"

"N-no, I haven't. I was waiting for the right time."

"The right time? Good Lord, Alexis. If you don't hurry up, he'll be able to tell by looking at you. How do you think he'll feel then?"

"Hurt, I suppose." Alexis bit her lip. "I guess you're hurt I didn't tell you either."

"Hurt? That doesn't even begin to describe it. I'm your sister. Why didn't you say something?"

"Probably because she wanted to avoid a tantrum like the one I just witnessed," said a new voice from the doorway.

Angel turned in surprise to confront a stranger. The man was tall and lean, and his blue eyes snapped as he advanced on her.

"Alexis always said you had a nasty temper, but I found it hard to believe. Now I see she was dead right. It's obvious you're identical in looks only. Otherwise you'd have a little compassion for your sister. She certainly would for you. "

Alexis gasped. "Brandon!"

Brandon? Angel could hardly believe her eyes. This was Alexis's mysterious lover? When they were younger, her sister usually chose handsome ne'er-do-wells. This man was an entirely different breed. Though he was not unattractive, the weathered skin of his face and his calloused hands marked him as a man who was more than passingly familiar with hard work. Angel was impressed in spite of herself.

"Brandon, what are you doing here?" Alexis asked, in a guilty little voice.

"We'll get to that in a minute. Right now, I'm waiting for your sister to apologize to you."

"That's not necess—"

"I think it is."

"But—"

Angel put up her hand. "No, Alexis, he's right. I had no business taking my frustrations out on you, and I'm sorry. Can you forgive me?"

"You don't even have to ask. I'm sorry I didn't tell you."

"I'm sure you had your reasons, and you certainly don't owe me an explanation."

"But you do owe me one," Brandon said severely. "Several, in fact, starting with why you left this morning without telling me."

"I couldn't find you. Besides I was perfectly capable of coming by myself."

"You shouldn't have come alone. One of the men should have come with you. I'd never forgive myself if anything happened to you."

"Don't be silly. What could happen?"

"He's right," Angel said, thinking of her own narrow escape from Dangerous Dick's gang. "The roads aren't safe these days."

"Will you promise to tell me where you're going from now on?" Brandon asked earnestly.

"Of course I will. If I'd known how you felt, I'd have told you this morning. How did you know I was here?"

"I came to town on some unexpected business and thought I saw you. Figured you had come to see your sister and I'd escort you home when you were finished. By the time I arrived, Angel was already here."

Alexis bit her lip. "H-how long were you outside?"

"Long enough."

"I was afraid of that."

"I suppose I should have made myself known earlier, but the conversation seemed rather . . . personal. I didn't want to embarrass anyone," he said ignoring

Angel's blush. "I wound up discovering I'm going to be a father. It was something of a shock."

"I'm sorry," Alexis whispered. "I was afraid."

"Of what? Damn it, Alexis, you know I love you. I've been asking you to marry me for the last five months, for God's sake."

"You don't know my father."

"Only because you refuse to introduce me to him. I'm beginning to wonder if your real reason has more to do with being ashamed of me than fear of your father."

"Oh, Brandon, how could you think such a thing?" Alexis cried, jumping to her feet.

"What am I supposed to think? Angel is the only adult member of your family I've met, and that was by accident."

"Maybe it's her family she's ashamed of," Angel said, with a wry twist of her mouth. "After meeting the Bradys, any sane man would turn tail and head for the tall timber. Though if you've met the children and still want to marry her—"

Alexis stomped her foot. "Stop it, both of you! I'm not ashamed of anybody. Neither of you takes Father seriously like I do. He decided he wants me to marry James Treenery, and once he makes up his mind to something it's impossible to change it."

Angel raised her eyebrows. "The news that you're having another man's baby will surely give him a moment's pause."

"I doubt it. Knowing Father, he'd come up with some way around it. That's why I never wanted him to know about you, Brandon. I'm afraid of what he'd do if he found out."

"Your father doesn't frighten me. He's nothing more than a petty dictator."

"But you don't understand," she said tearfully. "He could easily destroy you."

Brandon scowled. "He might try. Damn it, Alexis, how many times do I have to tell you I can handle your father? It's high time you learned to trust me on this."

"You don't realize the power he wields in the business world."

"I'm not without influential friends myself. If it comes to a fight, he might find he's bitten off more than he can chew."

"Oh, Brandon, you'd be risking everything you've worked so hard for. What if you wound up having to choose between your ranch and me?"

"Then I guess I wouldn't have a ranch anymore."

"You'd sacrifice it for me?" Alexis asked in astonishment.

"Without a backward glance. I love you."

"My sister often has difficulty believing the obvious," Angel said. "You may have to convince her."

Brandon glanced at her and then crossed the room in three long strides.

Angel watched approvingly as he pulled Alexis into his arms and kissed her passionately. The more she saw of this man and the way he handled her sister, the better she liked him.

"*Nothing* is more important to me than you, Alexis," he said in a gruff voice, when he finally came up for air. "I love you, and I want you with me always. The last four months have been the best of my life."

"Mine too," she whispered, reaching up to stroke the side of his face.

"Then marry me—now, today!"

"Oh, Brandon, I can't."

He stiffened. "Won't, you mean. What about our child? Will it be born out of wedlock because you're afraid of your father?"

"Try to understand—"

"No, Alexis. I've *been* understanding, and it's gotten

me nowhere. Either you marry me now, or I'm leaving without you."

"L-leaving?"

"That's why I'm in town. I just got word that my mother is very sick, may even be dying. I'm going to Ohio tomorrow. I want you to go with me and meet my family. I love you, Alexis; I want you to be my wife, not my mistress. I'm tired of fighting this ridiculous fear of Richard Brady. He couldn't possibly be as powerful as you seem to think he is."

Alexis turned to her sister. "Tell him, Angel."

"Sorry," Angel said, "I'm afraid I agree with Brandon. You should have told Father to mind his own business years ago."

"That's easy for you to say. He doesn't intimidate you like he does me."

Angel grabbed Alexis's arm. "Will you excuse us for a minute, Brandon?"

"Well, I—"

"It will only take a moment." Angel smiled at him as she propelled her sister toward the door. "We'll be right back."

"Alexis," Angel said, as soon as they were outside, "forget about Father for a minute. If you could do exactly what you wanted, would you marry Brandon?"

"In a heartbeat."

"Then don't be such an idiot. I don't think he's bluffing. If you let him walk out that door you'll lose him."

Alexis looked stricken. "Oh, God, Angel, I couldn't bear it."

"Then what are you waiting for? Get back in there and tell him."

Alexis stared uncertainly at her sister for a moment and then broke into a huge smile. "You're right, as usual," she said, giving Angel a big hug. "I'll follow my heart and the devil with the consequences."

"That's the spirit!"

Angel waited outside while Alexis made her peace with Brandon. She had a good feeling about this marriage. It was obvious they loved each other, and Brandon wasn't the type to be bullied by his father-in-law. At least there wouldn't be a confrontation until Alexis and Brandon returned from Ohio. By then the marriage would be an established fact and Alexis's pregnancy well advanced. In the face of those odds even Richard Brady would have little choice but to capitulate.

The rest of the day passed in a whirlwind of activity that left Angel breathless and Brandon and Alexis glowing with happiness. They had little difficulty finding a justice of the peace willing to perform a wedding on short notice, but the rest was far more complicated.

The first step was to sneak home and enlist Martha's aid. Neither twin would ever consider getting married without her, but both were surprised at how pleased she was by the turn of events. She solved their biggest problem right off the bat by producing their mother's wedding dress from an old trunk in the attic. Until that moment they hadn't even known it existed. Her explanation that she'd been waiting for one of them to fall in love both astonished and delighted them.

In spite of Brandon's admonishments to keep it simple, Angel and Alexis were determined to do it right. He complained good-naturedly about the way they laughed at all his suggestions and ignored his advice. Since his advice ranged from ridiculous to absurd, Angel and Alexis just rolled their eyes and accepted the reproach in the same teasing manner it was given. Brandon earned Martha's full approval when he confided he rather enjoyed watching the twins together. He was seeing a delightful side of his lady love he never knew existed.

Flowers from the garden Angel had judiciously tended all summer were easily obtained and fashioned into a bouquet suitable for the occasion. There was no time for nerves as the foursome crossed town to the justice of the peace. As she stood next to the couple during the ceremony and listened to Martha's maternal sniffles, Angel thought she had never seen her sister look so beautiful.

It wasn't until she and Martha were standing side by side, waving good-bye, that Angel realized her own problem was fully as complicated as before. To keep Alexis's secret until the proper moment, she was going to have to maintain the masquerade.

"Well, that takes care of her," Martha said, wiping her eyes one last time. "Now, what about you?"

"What about me?"

"Doesn't look like Alexis is going to be much help with young Treenery. What are you going to do now?"

"I'll think of something. I've kept him at arm's length before."

"Maybe so. Trouble is, now you don't want to."

"I most certainly do!"

Martha gave her a knowing look. "You can story to me all you want, but you can't fool yourself. Can't help thinking about him, can you?"

Martha was right. The feel of the strong warm back beneath her fingers and his lips as they traced erotic patterns on her body were memories that haunted Angel day and night, memories she couldn't have banished even if she wanted to. The mere thought of that night made her pulses pound.

"I can handle James Oxford Bruton Treenery the Third. It's a simple matter of keeping my distance, that's all."

"What if he has other ideas?"

"Ox is a gentleman. He'll follow my lead." And that, Angel admitted to herself, was what worried her.

25

"*I hope Angel talks to him* today," Jared said, watching Ox walk up the path toward the house. "I can't figure out why she keeps telling him she's sick."

"That's because you're a boy," Shannon said scornfully. "If you weren't so stupid you'd know she's in love with him."

Jared blinked in surprise. "She told you that?"

"Don't be stupid. I'm just her little sister." Shannon gave him a superior look. "I watched her yesterday after she got back from wherever she went."

"So did I, and I didn't see anything unusual. In fact, when we told her Ox had been teaching us to drive, she said not to pester him and changed the subject."

"But did you notice how may times she looked at her roses? At least a hundred."

"Big deal."

"Angel thought they were. I even saw her touch them. She had tears in her eyes."

Jared looked confused. "If she's in love with him, why won't she talk to him?"

"Maybe they had a fight, and that's why he sent her all those flowers. Father always gives Mama presents when she's mad at him."

"Does that mean Ox loves Angel too?"

"Sure. Why do you think he asked us all those questions?"

Jared frowned. "You mean that's why he's been spending so much time with us?"

"Why else? It certainly wasn't to enjoy our company."

"I never saw anything as brave as he was when he saved Betsy." Jared sighed. "If we hadn't been so rotten to him he might have wanted to be our brother-in-law."

"He'd be a lot more fun than Duncan."

Jared nodded wistfully. "I bet Ox would even teach me how to drive the stage someday. Do you think Angel will marry him anyway?"

"They probably don't even know they're in love." Shannon scuffed her shoe in the dirt gloomily. "Too bad we can't do something."

Jared looked up in surprise. Their gazes locked for a long moment; then they began to grin.

"If we get caught, it'll mean another prison term in the nursery," Shannon warned.

Jared's eyes sparkled with excitement. "But if we're careful they'll never know."

They both turned to gaze at the house where their unsuspecting prey had disappeared.

Once again, Ox stood in front of the fireplace waiting for Martha to come back with Alexis's refusal to see him. He wondered why he even bothered. The routine was becoming too frustrating.

"Thank you for the flowers and the hat," said a familiar voice behind him.

Ox spun around. "Alexis!"

"Martha says you've been here every day."

"I was worried about you."

Angel smiled as she sat down and gestured for him to follow suit. "I appreciate your concern, but as you can see I'm now healthy as a horse. Would you care for some refreshments?"

"You can stop the lady of the manor act," Ox said sardonically, remaining where he was.

"I beg your pardon?"

"We both know your refusal to see me had nothing to do with any illness. I hope your *recovery* means you're ready to discuss our . . . unfinished business."

"There's nothing unfinished about it."

"The hell there isn't! I had no idea you were a virgin."

"I'm not anymore."

That's beside the point."

"No, it isn't. Being a virgin at my age is more of an embarrassment than anything else, especially after being married as long as I was."

"It doesn't matter how old you are, damn it. I took your innocence!"

"I'd rather not talk about it," Angel said. "I think the whole thing is best put behind us."

"Is that right? I don't happen to agree. It seems to me that a marriage proposal is in order."

"That's not necessary," she said softly. "I . . . I haven't been completely honest with you," she said, avoiding his eyes.

"No?"

She bit her lip. "Oh, dear, I don't know quite how to say this."

"How about just coming out with it?"

"You're right, of course." She began nervously pleating

the skirt of her dress. "What happened that night in the cabin was a mistake."

"I don't know as I'd call it a mistake, exactly. Neither of us expected anything like that to occur, but—"

"No, Ox, you don't understand. There's someone else."

She knows how I feel about Angel, he thought in panic. A moment later he realized it had been a statement of fact, not a question. "What do you mean, someone else?"

"I have a fiancé."

"A fiancé?" Ox stared at her in stunned disbelief. "You mean like a man you're going to marry?"

The shadow of a smile crossed her face. "Is there another kind?"

"I don't know, you tell me. It all seems kind of sudden."

"Only because I didn't tell you about it. Brandon and I have been seeing each other since shortly after my husband died. Since I never thought of us as anything but business partners, it never occurred to me to tell you about him."

"Do you love him?"

"That's a pretty strange question."

"Is it? I find it hard to believe you'd react to me the way you did the other night if you were in love with someone else."

Angel blushed. "I don't handle strong spirits well."

"Christ! That's the lamest damn excuse I ever heard. You expect me to believe a pilfered bottle of cognac was responsible for your behavior?" Ox crossed his arms and leaned against the fireplace. "Sorry, Alexis, I don't buy it. Why did you beg me to make love to you if you're in love with someone else?"

"Haven't you ever done something that made perfect

sense when you were intoxicated but seemed silly in the light of day?"

"I've never been so drunk I forgot I had a fiancée."

"I don't deny I feel a certain . . . attraction to you," Angel continued, "but our relationship is based on business, not love."

"Business! You think what happened between us that night was part of our business relationship?"

"More or less." Angel looked down at her hands. "We were caught up in a mood of celebration."

"There's a hell of a lot more to it than that," Ox insisted. "We made love to each other, for God's sake!"

"We had sex together," Angel corrected. "There is a vast difference."

"And you don't think love is possible between us?" He knew it was a stupid question, since Alexis obviously wanted no part of him, but he couldn't resist asking anyway. Ox didn't for a minute believe she had a fiancé, but he really couldn't blame her for inventing one. She belonged to the society he'd given up along with the Treenery empire. To marry him she'd have to take a large step down the social ladder. Putting it bluntly, he wasn't good enough for her.

"Did you ever stop to wonder why I was so adamantly against our betrothal before we even met?" Angel asked.

"You can't stand to be manipulated by your father."

"That's part of it, but I hate conflict even more. My father is a master at causing conflict if things don't go his way. Only desperation could force me to go against him the way I did when I first met you." Angel sighed. "I was in love with Brandon before I ever set eyes on you."

"I've never found you to be particularly chicken-hearted," Ox said. "You're more likely to spit in your father's eye than back down to him."

"You're confusing me with Angel, I think."

Angel. The mention of her name gave Ox a curious twist in his middle and brought his conversation with Alexis into sharp focus. At least it put an end to his indecision. He no longer had to worry about choosing between them. Of course, Angel had made it clear she didn't want him either.

"Can't we just put this behind us and forget it ever happened?"

He crooked one finger under her chin and lifted it so he could look down into her eyes. "Is that really what you want?"

"I . . . yes, it is. Please try to understand."

"Unfortunately, I do. I don't like it particularly, but I do understand." He sighed deeply. "So where do we go from here?"

"Business as usual?" she asked hopefully.

"Business as usual?" He shook his head in disbelief. "All right, then. We're all set to open another line north of Silver Springs Gulch."

"You found another stagecoach?"

"Four of them, in fact."

"Four! At the price we could afford, I don't suppose they're Concord coaches."

"One. The other three are Troys."

"What's a Troy?" Angel asked. "I hope not a large wooden horse of some sort."

Ox smiled. "Hardly. It's another brand of coaches that are built along the same principles as a Concord. These are older than our other coaches and aren't in as good shape, but I got them for two hundred fifty dollars apiece. With a few repairs and a coat of paint, they'll suit our purpose admirably."

"It is still better than anything the Flying T has?"

"They're not even in the same class."

"Good. Our plan depends on passengers preferring us to them." Angel studied his profile. "There's something more you aren't telling me, isn't there?"

"Nothing for you to worry about."

Angel bristled. "Look, Bruford, I'm a full partner in this venture. Everything about it is my business, and I resent your keeping anything from me."

To her surprise Ox grinned. "You know, you sound just like Angel. She calls me Bruford in exactly that tone when she's irritated with me."

"Don't try to change the subject, Treenery."

He laughed outright at that. "I wasn't. Actually, I *am* a little concerned, but it really is nothing for you to worry about unduly. Your fortune is safe."

"Meaning?"

"The thousand dollars I paid for the coaches cut way into our reserves. If things don't go exactly as planned, you might find yourself short of cash until the next quarter begins, but that's all." He grimaced. "I, on the other hand, sank every penny I had into this venture. I could lose everything."

"Then we had better not fail," Angel said matter-of-factly. Though Ox didn't realize it, she had far more to lose than he did. If the venture failed she would be destitute. A woman's employment opportunities were limited anyway. Without money they were downright grim. In spite of her experience, without investment capital Angel would never be able to start another business and support herself. She shivered as the image of Mother Featherlegs popped into her head.

26

"You've got company," Martha stated flatly. "I told him you were busy, but he insisted on coming in anyway."

Angel looked up from the ledger she was working on. Something in Martha's expression prompted her to close the book and push it under a stack of papers. A moment later the elder James Treenery stormed into the study.

"Good afternoon, Mr. Treenery," she said calmly. "What a nice surprise."

"Where's my grandson? His landlady said he headed over here an hour ago."

"I haven't seen him."

"Could be he's with the children," Martha said from the doorway. "He's been teaching them to drive that infernal pony cart all week."

Angel rose. "Ah, that's probably where he is, then."

"I suppose you'll want me to send someone to the

stable and fetch him," Martha said, with an indignant sniff.

"If you wouldn't mind."

"Wouldn't matter much if I did," Martha mumbled, turning away from the door. "You'd think I didn't have anything better to do. Probably want refreshments for the old scoundrel next."

"As a matter of fact, refreshments would be very nice," Angel said. "We'll have them in the parlor, I think. Thank you for suggesting it."

Treenery stiffened. "Did you hear what she called me?"

"Called you?" Mentally cursing Martha's unruly tongue, Angel gave him a bewildered look. "I only heard her ask if we wanted refreshments. Shall we go to the parlor?" She began to walk past him toward the door. "We'll be more comfortable there."

James Treenery had little choice but to follow her out the door and away from the incriminating ledger. Not that it mattered anyway. He had so little regard for her intelligence that he probably wouldn't have believed what he was seeing even if he *had* caught her working on the books for the Silver Springs Express. Nevertheless, she was thankful for Martha's timely warning.

"I trust you had a good trip," she said over her shoulder, as he followed her down the hall. "We haven't seen you for a while."

"I've had other business to attend to. What do you hear from your father?"

"He and Vanessa were still in New York, last I heard. I don't know what Father's plans are, but Vanessa will be staying at least until the end of next month. She says it will take her that long just to get back into civilization." Angel opened the doors into the parlor. "Please, come in and sit down."

Angel had a difficult time keeping a straight face as

James Treenery chose the chair her father habitually sat on. He'd been there often enough that she was sure it was intentional.

"Have you and my grandson set a wedding date?" he asked.

"My year of mourning isn't over."

"It will be soon, won't it?"

"Yes, but we haven't gotten around to discussing the wedding yet."

"Probably never will, either," he muttered.

Angel was startled. "I beg your pardon?"

"If you're waiting for James to make the first move, you may wait a long time. He isn't the marrying kind."

Angel frowned. What was the old conniver up to now? "You seem to forget he proposed to me."

"Yes, and he made his mother very happy when he did it."

"Are you saying he asked me to marry him just to please his mother?"

"James is a very dutiful son."

"I don't know Mrs. Treenery all that well, of course, but she didn't seem the type who would want her son to marry a woman he didn't love."

"Ah, yes, love. That's what it all boils down to, isn't it?" James Treenery sighed. "Sarah Beth was ecstatic when he proposed to you. She figured you could thaw his heart if anyone could." He shrugged. "But it's beginning to look like the scars go even deeper than we thought."

"What scars?"

"Didn't he ever tell you about his first marriage?"

"Only that his wife was dead." Angel knew she should change the subject, but she was intrigued in spite of herself. "How did she die?"

"In a carriage accident." He suddenly looked years older, as though the tragedy was still fresh in his mind. "Little Jonathan died with her."

"Little Jonathan?"

"Their son."

"Son?" Angel was shocked. "I never knew Ox had a child."

"Jonathan was the spitting image of his father. James doted on him. As far as I know he's never even thought of marrying again."

"He must have loved her very much."

"Deanne was the sort everyone loved. James—"

"Digging in the dirt again, old man?" Ox said sarcastically from the door. "What do you expect to accomplish by raking up old memories that are better left dead and buried?"

"Alexis has a right to know," Treenery said defensively.

"She has no interest in ancient history, do you, my dear?"

"N-no," Angel stammered, taken back by the stark anger in his eyes. "But your grandfather was only—"

"I know what he was doing," Ox said. "The question is why?"

Treenery shrugged. "Alexis and I were discussing your wedding date, that's all."

"And you wanted to make sure she knew what she was getting into, I suppose."

"I suspect she already knows that. You're giving her quite a taste of your bad manners right now."

"My manners, or lack of them, have nothing to do with Alexis and she knows it." He crossed the room and dropped a kiss of greeting on her forehead. "We understand each other very well, don't we, my love?"

"Perfectly." She covered the hand on her shoulder with her own and gave it a reassuring squeeze.

He squeezed her shoulder back. The simple exchange sent a surprising ripple through her.

"I'm sure you had some purpose besides muckraking when you came here," Ox said to his grandfather.

"I do." Treenery glanced at Angel. "But it's business and best discussed in private."

"Alexis and I have no secrets from each other."

"That's all right, darling," Angel said, standing up. "I have some work I need to do anyway."

She reached out and took his hand. Unexpectedly, Ox leaned down and gave her a hard fast kiss. Angel felt branded by the heat, but she didn't fool herself. The show was entirely for his grandfather's benefit.

She gazed up into Ox's glittering green eyes. Oh how she wished she could replace the cold anger she saw with his usual warm twinkle. "I'll see you later," she said, giving his hand another squeeze.

"Don't worry, my grandfather won't be staying long."

"I'm glad we got this chance to visit, Mrs. Smythe," Treenery said smoothly. "Perhaps we can finish our conversation some other time."

Angel glanced at Ox's unyielding profile. It might have been carved from granite. "I think we've already completed it. I'll leave you two gentleman to your business."

Though Angel was curious about what James Treenery wanted to discuss with Ox, she found herself wondering about Deanne Treenery instead. Ox must have loved her very much if the mere mention of her name still affected him so strongly.

Angel was halfway down the hall when the front door opened behind her. She looked over her shoulder and saw her siblings. "Well, well, what do we have here?"

"Oh, hello, Angel," Jared said, with feigned nonchalance. "How are you feeling today?"

Angel raised her brows. "Just fine, why?"

"You—er, you look a little pale." Shannon squinted at her sister in the dim light. "Are you sure you don't need to go outside for some air?"

Angel crossed her arms. "All right, you two. What's going on?"

"Going on?" They glanced at each other and then looked at Angel with identical expressions of innocence. "We just figured it was time for tea."

"Is that right? Why today, when you haven't been in for tea once since your mother left?"

"We're hungry," Shannon said.

"Hungry, huh?"

Jared nodded eagerly. "That's right. Practically starved."

"Nice try," Angel said. "Now, are you going to show me what you have hidden behind your back, Shannon, or am I going to have to come see for myself?"

They exchanged another look; then Jared gave a deep sigh. "It's supposed to be a surprise. We were going to sneak in and put it on your pillow."

"On my pillow? Oh, Lord, what is it, a frog?"

"No!" Shannon brought her hand out and showed Angel a single perfect rose.

Angel was astonished. "You brought me a rose?"

"Not exactly." Jared squirmed a little. "We promised to do it for—a friend. You weren't supposed to know where it came from. Could you pretend you never saw us?"

Ox. Angel smiled to herself. What a sweetheart he was. "I suppose so, but you can tell your 'friend' it won't make any difference."

"Difference with what?"

"Never mind. Run along now. If you're still starving, Martha is putting some refreshments together in the kitchen. She might find some extra for you if you ask nicely."

"You won't tell anyone you know where the rose came from, will you?" Shannon asked anxiously.

"I won't mention it to a soul."

Angel watched them run up the stairs two at a time

and then continued down the hall to the study. A warm glow settled in her middle and stayed there even when she got to the end of her bookkeeping chores and confirmed what she suspected all along: The Silver Springs Express was just barely solvent. As long as nothing unusual happened they'd be all right, but the slightest difficulty could prove disastrous.

She had just finished making her last notation when Ox walked in and sat down.

"We may have a problem," he said.

"Your grandfather?"

"No, your father."

Angel raised an eyebrow. "Don't tell me they got together and compared notes."

"Not as far as I know." Ox frowned. "Your father is sending a team of horses to the Silver Springs Express."

"He's what?"

"It doesn't make any sense, does it? One of my grandfather's men was following your father when he bought the horses. It was a simple matter to find out their final destination. My grandfather considers this to be irrefutable proof that your father owns the Silver Springs Express. What *I* can't figure out is why your father would send horses to the competition."

"There must be something wrong with them."

"I know, but I don't have any idea what. I guess we'll just have to keep them separated from the others until we find out."

"It will be hard to quarantine them. Our stables aren't that big."

"No, but the Flying T's stables are. That way if there's a problem it will affect them, not us."

Angel chuckled. "Once again I'm glad we're on the same side. You make a formidable enemy."

"You aren't so bad yourself." Ox's smile faded, and his expression became troubled. "I suppose you want to know about Deanne."

"Not if it's painful for you."

"It's painful, all right, but not the way you think. Her death marked the beginning of my war with my grandfather."

"You must have loved her very much," Angel said softly.

"I thought I did, but I've often wondered since then if it wasn't more of an infatuation. She was very beautiful, you see." He gave a deep sigh. "I suppose you've already guessed it was an arranged marriage?"

Angel nodded. "Your grandfather, no doubt?"

"Right, and I'll never forgive him for it. I don't know why he didn't marry her himself. It would have been a far better solution for everyone."

Angel blinked in surprise. "Surely he was too old for her."

"They were closer in age than you and Duncan."

"And Duncan was far too old for me."

A sad little smile flitted across his face. "I'll bet you led him a pretty dance too. Anyway, it was right after my father died and my grandfather was worried about an heir for his empire. I was only twenty but I'd joined the Union Army when the war between the states war started. He was afraid I'd die without a son." Ox shrugged. "I never questioned the match, even though Deanne was several years older than I and far more experienced."

"Was she happy with the marriage?"

"I think grateful is a better word. She was pregnant, you see. I didn't know it when we got married, of course, but I figured it out when the baby arrived several months early."

"Oh, Ox."

He shook his head. "I believed her story about Confederate soldiers raping her and even thought I understood why she didn't tell me about it. Actually, I was pretty happy. I had a beautiful wife who seemed devoted to me and a son I thought the world of. Jonathan looked enough like me that no one questioned his parentage."

"Your grandfather said he was the spitting image of you."

"He was, right down to the green eyes. I've often wondered if I would have figured it out eventually anyway." Silence fell as Ox gazed out the window broodingly.

"Figured out what?" Angel asked softly.

"Who Jonathan's father was." He sighed. "There was a thunderstorm one day while Deanne and the baby were out for a drive, and the carriage overturned. I found them shortly after the wreck but there was nothing I could do. Deanne didn't realize Jonathan was already dead and was frantic to tell me the truth about him before she died. If I were to have a son of my own, Jonathan would no longer be my heir. She wanted to make damn sure her son got his fair share of my grandfather's fortune."

"His fair share?" Angel frowned in confusion. "But he wasn't even related to your grandfather."

"That's what she was afraid I'd think if I didn't know the truth." A muscle jumped in his jaw as he stared out the window. "Actually, Jonathan had as much right to the Treenery fortune as I do. My grandfather was so desperate to make sure he had a legitimate heir from his own bloodline that he had married me to my father's pregnant mistress."

27

Ox's revelation put many things into perspective for Angel. His hatred for his grandfather, his aversion to marriage, even his dislike of children suddenly made sense. The agony she suffered for his pain made her realize how very much she loved him. Defeating the elder James Treenery became fully as important as getting the best of Richard Brady. When Ox sent a note three days later, she dropped what she was doing and hurried downtown.

"I got your message, Ox," Angel said, hurrying through the door of the Flying T's office. "Sam!" She came to a halt and stared at her friend. "What are you doing here?"

"We have a big problem," he told her gravely. "I didn't know what else to do."

"Uh-oh, what's wrong?"

"Some of our horses have the epizootic."

"Epi what?"

Ox looked grim. "Epizootic. It's some kind of sickness

that's been sweeping through the eastern United States
and Canada, killing horses right and left."

"Good lord!"

"It's so bad in New York and Toronto they're using
men and boys to pull the wagons and trolleys."

"New York!" Angel paled. "The horses my father
sent!"

"Exactly my thought too."

Angel frowned. "But we stopped them before they
mixed with ours."

"The horses we intercepted day before yesterday
weren't the only ones. Another five arrived last week."

"The message said they came from Ox," Sam said,
"so I didn't give it a second thought. I just turned them
in with the others."

Ox ran his fingers through his hair in agitation.
"When they started dying, Sam decided he'd better
come see me. We spent the morning sending telegrams
back east until we got some answers. We didn't much
care for the ones we got."

Angel bit her lip. "Will all our horses get sick?"

"I don't know how the disease spreads exactly, but it
goes from horse to horse."

"What can we do?"

"That's a damn good question. I wish I had an
answer."

"Ox, everything we have is tied up in the Silver
Springs Express." Angel couldn't keep the worry out of
her voice. "If we lose it —"

"We aren't going to lose it!" he said emphatically.
He walked to the window and glared through the dusty
panes as though he might find the answer to their
dilemma on the street outside.

"I've already separated the new horses from the rest
of the stock," Sam said. "I don't know what else we can
do."

Angel looked thoughtful. "We need to move cautiously. Whoever my father has watching us is going to be suspicious if we start shifting horses around."

Sam nodded. "Specially if they aren't sick yet. The last thing we want is for him to realize Ox's grandfather isn't the one behind the Silver Springs Express."

"If this sickness moves through the horses the way it did back east, our horses won't be the only sick ones for long. That brings up the problem of replacements." Angel rubbed her forehead tiredly. "Even if we had the money to buy them, where would they come from?"

"I don't know," Sam said. "It may not spread as fast out here. There's a lot more distance between towns. It could be that we can wait the epizootic out and then go north to find replacement stock once the sickness has run its course."

"That makes sense," Angel agreed. "But it still doesn't solve the problem of what to do in the meantime to keep the Silver Springs Express running. We can't very well use human power the way they are back east."

"It doesn't help the problem of how to pay for them either. Maybe—"

"What the hell?" Ox said suddenly. "Isn't that Jessie?"

Sam broke off in mid-sentence to stare at him. "Did you say Jessie?"

"Yes. She's running down the street as if she has a pack of dogs on her heels."

Angel and Sam joined him at the window and followed the line of his gaze. "Oh, dear," Angel murmured. "Everything was going so well too."

"Obviously not as well as you thought," Sam said, striding to the door.

Ox and Angel were right behind him as he crossed the street on a course that would intercept Jessie's headlong flight.

"Jessie!"

Her head jerked up at the sound of his voice. "Sam?

Oh, Sam!" With a sob she ran straight into his arms and buried her face against his shoulder.

Sam closed his arms around her in a paternal embrace. "It's all right, little one. Sam's here to protect you."

"And nobody in their right mind would challenge him," Ox murmured.

Angel glanced around. "Let's go back to the station. This is a little too public for my tastes." She glowered at a matronly woman who was whispering behind her hand to her companion as they walked past. "I've never understood what people find so interesting about the lives of strangers." Under Angel's intense scrutiny, the woman flushed and looked away.

"That one will think twice before she sticks her nose where it doesn't belong," Ox said with a grin, as they walked toward the station.

"I certainly hope so."

"What do you suppose made Jessie so upset?" Ox asked in a low voice.

"I don't know, but I'll bet it means I'm going to have to find her another job. I don't think there's any kind of respectable work in this town that we haven't tried."

Ox smiled sympathetically. "Maybe if we put our heads together, we can come up with something."

"I hate to admit it, but I'm not sure Jessie was cut out to be an independent woman." Angel sighed. "I don't know if I really want to find out what happened at Clancy's."

"Could be it was just an irritated customer," Ox said. "She seems very sensitive."

"She's that, all right, but I have a feeling it's more serious."

"Sounds like it," Ox said, as they entered the Flying T office to the sound of Jessie's disjointed explanation.

". . . followed me into the storeroom. He tried to k-kiss me, and . . . he put his hands all over me."

A muscle in Sam's jaw jumped. "Who did?"

"Mr. Cl-Clancy."

"I'll kill the bastard." Sam's voice was a menacing growl but Jessie hardly seemed to notice, as she clutched his coat lapels and sobbed against his solid shoulder.

Angel touched her elbow gently. "Did he hurt you, Jessie?"

"N-no, because Mrs. Clancy c-came in and said . . . and said . . . Oh, God!"

"It's all right, sweetheart," Sam soothed. "You don't have to tell us if you don't want to."

Jessie shook her head. "I . . . I want you to understand why I can't go back."

"All right," Angel said sympathetically, "but give yourself a minute to calm down first."

Sam hugged Jessie tighter. "She's right, little one. There's no hurry. We have all day."

Whether it was his words or his calm strength, Jessie began to quiet almost immediately. After only a few minutes she gave one last hiccuping sob and reached up to dry her eyes. "Mrs. Clancy said it was my fault, that I caused it by flirting with him," she began quietly. "Only I didn't. I went back to the storeroom to get some more potatoes. He followed me and trapped me next to the shelves. I-I couldn't get away. I was glad when Mrs. Clancy came, even though she said all those mean things to me."

"Sounds to me like they both need a lesson," Sam said. "Maybe I'll go knock his teeth down his throat for him."

Jessie gave him a stricken look. "Oh, no, please, Sam. Mrs. Clancy has always been nice to me before today. I . . . I just want to go home." She gave a pathetic little sniff.

"It's all right, little one," Sam said, handing her his handkerchief. "I'll take you right now." He glanced at Angel and Ox.

"Do you want me to come along?" Angel asked.

Jessie gave her a weak smile. "That isn't necessary. Martha will be there."

"True, and she's better at handling situations like this than I am." Angel waved her hand. "Take my buggy. Ox and I will stay here and see what we can come up with for the Silver Springs Express."

Angel gave a deep sigh as she watched Sam lift Jessie into the buggy. "So much for my ability to judge people. I thought Virginia Clancy was a good choice."

"Idiot woman," Ox muttered. "Any fool could see it was her husband that was at fault here, not Jessie."

Angel shook her head. "I'll bet she does know it. In fact that's probably why she went back to the storeroom in the first place. Chances are she had a good idea of what her husband was up to. Most men think any unattached woman is fair game, especially one as beautiful as Jessie."

"*Most* men?" Ox frowned. "I think you exaggerate."

"Only because you're not a woman. I guess I'd better teach Jessie the power of a well-placed knee."

Ox raised his eyebrows in surprise. "What would you know about such things?"

She hesitated. Alexis wouldn't know, of course. "Angel taught me. She said even a lady had to know how to defend herself. I shudder to think of the circumstances that taught her that lesson."

Ox chuckled. "A knee is the least of Angel's arsenal. Anybody fool enough to tangle with her is more likely to find a knife at his throat or a gun to his head. Your sister is not a woman to take lightly."

"Did you?" Angel couldn't help asking.

"Take her lightly?" Ox feigned shock at such a suggestion. "Not on your life! I have far too much respect for my person to do that."

"Something tells me she'd box your ears for that one if she were here."

"Or have a snappy reply. Angel sometimes draws blood faster with her words than her knife."

Angel frowned. "I thought you considered her a friend."

"I do. I've seen her reduce more than one overconfident man to a pile of ashes with a few well-chosen words."

"It almost sounds like you admire her ability."

"No almost about it," Ox said with a grin. "Angel is never at a loss. I wish I had her sarcastic wit."

Angel felt an absurd little flash of pleasure at his words. At least something about her impressed Ox, even though it wasn't one of her best qualities. "Then you must be crazy about Martha."

Ox chuckled. "Being the quiet unassuming fellow that I am, I seldom draw Angel's fire. Martha is another matter entirely. Frankly, I'm scared to death of her."

"Sure you are," Angel said with a wry smile.

"You doubt me?"

"I don't think you're afraid of much of anything, except maybe Betsy when she's in a wheedling mood."

"That would make the bravest man flinch," he agreed.

As they grinned at each other, an unexpected current passed between them, one that had nothing to do with Betsy or humor. Petals of heated pleasure unfurled in Angel's stomach and flowed outward toward her heart. It was the same feeling she got every night when she found the single rose on her pillow. Lord, how she loved him!

The thought brought her up short. That was exactly the sort of nonsense she needed to stay away from. "Well, enough of this. We'd better set our mind to finding a way to save the Silver Springs Express."

"Any suggestions?"

"Not a one. How about you?"

" 'Fraid not."

Angel sat down at the desk and pulled out a piece of paper. "Maybe we should make a list of details that are going to need our attention."

"We have to keep a close eye on the horses so we know immediately if any of them get sick."

"Right," Angel said, scribbling furiously, "and we'd better find a place to keep them well away from the others. The biggest problem is going to be replacing them. Even if we could afford to buy more, there might not be any to buy. Where are we going to find replacements?"

"That's a good question. I wish I had the answer." Ox stared out the window pensively. His eyes narrowed suddenly as if an idea had just occurred to him. "You know," he said slowly, "maybe we're looking at this all wrong. What if we don't use horses?"

Angel gave him a puzzled look. "If we don't use horses we're going to have a tough time getting the stage from one place to another. The way I see it, that's the whole problem. What exactly did you have in mind?"

"Mules!" His face lit up with a huge grin. "According to what we found out this morning, the epizootic doesn't affect burros or mules. We couldn't keep to our schedule because they're so much slower, but if it shouldn't matter too much if we post a new schedule."

"You know, you just might have something there," Angel said, catching his excitement. "We'd only use them as a last resort, if there weren't enough horses left to go around. And if that actually happens, we'll be about the only public transportation moving."

"I know where we can get some, too. The man who bought out my freight line has several hundred. He'd be happy to sell some back to me."

Angel's face fell. "That brings us back to the original problem. What are we going to use for money?"

"I'll get a job with the army as a bullwhacker for a while. They always need experienced freighters. They pay over six dollars per hundred pounds for the run into Fort Laramie."

"Why so much?"

Ox shrugged. "The Indians tend to get a little excited on occasion."

"Then it's dangerous."

"No worse than the stage run between here and Silver Springs Gulch."

"Well, that's comforting," she said sarcastically. "It seems to me you were nearly killed along that route not so long ago."

"But not by Indians. Anyway, I don't see that we have much choice. It's our only chance to save the Silver Springs Express."

"Who's going to run the Flying T and the Silver Springs Express while you're away?"

"You and Sam could handle it for a while, couldn't you?"

Angel looked skeptical. "I'm not so sure about that."

"I have total confidence in your ability. Between you and Sam, you know every aspect of the business."

"Maybe so, but how are Sam and I going to communicate without my father's and your grandfather's spies getting wise to us?"

"That does present a problem, doesn't it? We need a reason for him to visit you."

"About the only innocent reason for a man to visit a woman is courtship. That might look a little odd, considering our betrothal."

"True." Ox gazed out the window thoughtfully. Suddenly he began to grin. "By damn, it might just work!"

"What?"

"Jessie! Sam is going to fall madly in love with her and be the most diligent suitor you ever saw."

"Won't that make everybody suspicious?"

Ox chuckled. "Yup. And it's going to make you hopping mad as well. In fact, you're never going to let them be alone together. You'll probably even threaten to throw her out of your house if she continues to see him. That will give them an excuse to sneak around behind your back. No one will suspect she's your line of communication to him."

"Leaving me free to run the Flying T." Angel nodded. "It makes sense. Still, I don't know if I can handle it by myself. I'd be doing your job and mine too."

"We'll just call in reinforcements. All we need is someone we can trust who has a head for business."

"Right. And who might that be?"

He beamed at her. "I think it's time we sent for Angel!"

28

"Sorry, Mr. Weston, the best I can offer you is thirteen cents a mile," Angel said firmly. Ox smiled to himself as the familiar voice came through the open door of the stage office. Alexis had obviously taken his advice a month ago and sent for her sister. The whole time he'd been hauling freight for the army he'd been thinking about Angel, anticipating this meeting. He'd even imagined the smell of her perfume at odd moments. The scent of roses had come to him frequently as he drove along the dusty road.

"Thirteen cents a mile! That's highway robbery!" An angry male voice answered her. "You don't get that much for passengers."

"As a matter of fact, we charge fifteen cents a mile for passengers. I'm actually losing money by using available space for freight instead."

"Freight and passengers don't take up the same space."

"Of course they do. We've carried as many as six

people on the roof. Think of all the money we lose if we haul your freight instead. I don't know why you're quibbling, Mr. Weston. If you want fast delivery, you have no choice."

"Your competition down the street might sing a different tune."

Angel scoffed. "The Silver Springs Express is a one-horse outfit. Their prices are twice as high as ours."

"I find that damn hard to believe."

"Then go talk to them yourself. You'll be back."

"Don't count on it," the man said angrily. He glared at Ox as he stalked out the door. "Damnedest bunch of thieves I ever ran across."

Ox grinned to himself as he sauntered into the office and tossed his hat on the desk. "Driving our customers right into the arms of the competition, I see."

"Ox!" Angel smiled with real pleasure as she came out from behind the desk to greet him. "When did you get back?"

"Just now. Danged if you aren't a sight for sore eyes!"

He leaned forward to give her a friendly peck on the cheek just as Angel turned her head slightly to say something. His lips accidentally brushed the corner of her mouth in a tingling caress. Ox barely noticed her startled intake of breath as the unexpected contact set blood singing through his veins. He didn't stop to consider the consequences, he just followed his instincts and rained soft kisses against her lips until she yielded their sweetness to him. The kiss was a heady combination of raw power and soft sensuality.

Angel sagged against him, her breath escaping as she put her arms around him in a welcoming embrace. A sudden rush of emotion nearly overwhelmed him with its intensity. He felt at home for the first time in years, safe in the arms of the woman he loved.

Angel shifted slightly and Ox tensed for a slap that

never came. In that moment an inescapable truth burst upon his consciousness. She smelled of lavender, not roses. He lifted his head and stared down at her uncertainly. "Alexis?"

The look of bemused confusion on her face convinced him. Angel would have made some kind of biting response to such an obvious question.

"Alexis," Jessie said, bursting through the door excitedly. "I found a sign painter for you and—oh, pardon me." Her eyes widened in consternation when she saw them together. "I—I didn't realize . . . I'll come back later."

Ox dropped his arms and tried to step away casually. "There's no need for you to leave, Jessie." He cast a sideways glance at Alexis. She looked as bewildered as he felt. At least she'd known who *he* was.

"Heavens, no. We were just . . . uh." Angel cleared her throat. "Who did you say you found to do the sign?"

"Mr. Carter over at the general store. He said he'd paint it for four dollars."

Angel raised an eyebrow. "And they accuse me of highway robbery. Well, I suppose it will have to do."

"Why do we need a new sign?" Ox asked. "The old one looks just fine to me."

"Our prices have changed."

Ox grinned. "Come to think of it, thirteen cents a mile for freight and fifteen for passengers is a bit steep."

"We have no choice," Angel said with a shrug. "We've lost so many horses I had to cut our runs in half. That money has to be made up somehow."

"What do you mean, you cut them in half?"

"The stage leaves Cheyenne every Monday, Wednesday, and Friday. The same stage comes back from Silver Springs Gulch on Tuesday, Thursday, and Saturday. We rest the horses on Sunday. We're running the same schedule north and west of Silver Springs Gulch."

"What about the mail?" Ox asked. "The contract says it has to run every day."

"I can't help it. With the epizootic running rampant through the stock, every other day is the best we can do." She picked a paper up from the desk. "Would you mind running this down to Mr. Carter for me, Jessie? The sooner he gets started on that sign, the sooner we'll be able to hang it."

"I'll be glad to. Is there anything else you want me to do before I come back?"

Angel looked at Ox questioningly. "Shall I have her tell Martha to plan on an extra for dinner?"

"Is that an invitation?"

"Yes, it is." She paused. "The children have missed you."

"Only the children?"

Angel gave him an impish look. "Of course not. Martha too."

"I'll bet," Ox said dryly.

"And Jessie. Isn't that right, Jessie?" Angel said.

Jessie gave Ox a blinding smile. "Oh, yes. Mr. Bruford has always been so kind to me."

"There, you see?"

"I guess I'd better take you up on your invitation then," Ox said sardonically. "I'd hate to disappoint so many people."

"Good. Give Martha the message then, Jessie." Angel glanced down the watch pinned to the bodice of her gown. "Don't worry about coming back down. It's almost time to go home anyway."

"Are you sure?"

"Positive. I'll finish up here for the day."

Jessie glanced doubtfully back and forth between Ox and Angel. "All right, then," she said at last. "It's good to have you home, Mr. Bruford. I look forward to seeing you at dinner."

"Me too," Ox murmured, watching her walk out

the door and down the street. "I take it you put her to work," he said, looking over his shoulder at Angel.

"I needed the help."

"What about your sister?"

"I couldn't find her."

Ox glanced back outside. "How has Jessie worked out?"

"Surprisingly well, once I taught her some simple arithmetic." Angel sighed. "I honestly don't know what she learned at that school she went to, but it certainly wasn't anything useful."

"Maybe she just doesn't learn well."

Angel shook her head. "I don't think that's the case. I'll admit, at first I thought she was as dumb as dirt, but I've changed my mind. She just never had the chance to learn anything."

Ox smiled as Jessie hurried around the corner. The moment she disappeared, half a dozen men who had been standing stock-still watching her finally went on about their business. "At least she won't have any trouble finding a husband when she decides she wants one," he said. "Men will pick beauty over brains every time."

"So," Angel said sharply. "Was your trip as successful as you'd hoped?"

Ox bit back a smile. If he didn't know better, he'd think Mrs. Smythe felt a touch of jealousy for the beautiful Jessie. "I made enough money to buy some mules, if that's what you mean. They're in a pen outside of town. All we have to do now is deliver them to Sam without raising suspicions."

"That's why I invited you to dinner," Angel admitted. "Sam is going to drop by this evening. I thought you'd probably want to talk to him."

"How did you know I was coming in today?"

"I didn't. Sam's been coming over a couple of times

a week. It's a good thing you got here with those mules. The Silver Springs Express is in dire straits. We're about to the end of our horses."

"Did you cut the teams back to four each like I told you?"

Angel nodded. "Last week. But losing even one more horse will jeopardize the whole operation."

"I take it the Flying T has suffered heavier losses than the Silver Springs Express?"

Angel grinned. "Not really. The management of the Silver Springs Express is just handling the crisis a little differently. The Flying T cut back, trying to preserve the strength of the teams they've got left. The Silver Springs Express is pushing the stock to the limit, hoping for reinforcements."

"Which arrived just in time," Ox said, with an answering grin. "Now all we have to do is get them to Silver Springs Gulch and worked into the operation."

"Any ideas how to keep our spies from figuring out what we're up to?"

"I'm leaving tomorrow to find more horses to replenish the Flying T herd."

Angel raised a brow. "That will throw them off track, all right, but won't that defeat our purpose? The last thing we want is fresh horses for the Flying T."

"It might if I had any luck, but I won't. The few horses I'll be able to find won't be any threat to the Silver Springs Express. What they probably will be is expensive."

"And the Flying T is already low on cash," Angel said with satisfaction.

"Low enough to write to your father and my grandfather asking for more money?"

"I think so."

Ox gave a low whistle. "I can hardly believe we're there already. Luckily they're both so mad neither will send us a penny."

"And when they refuse to send us any we'll start selling off Flying T assets, just as we planned."

"The question is, will we be able to buy them?"

"Not all of them," Angel admitted. "Our plan is progressing twice as fast as we anticipated."

"I know. Thanks to your father and his sick horses, we're months ahead of schedule. I expected to be fully solvent by the time the Flying T had to start selling off equipment. Buying everything they're forced to sell would be sweet revenge."

"Oh, well," Angel said. "Maybe it's better to pick and choose. We really don't want any of the Flying T coaches. The Silver Springs Express has a reputation to uphold."

"I guess as long as we accomplish our final goal it doesn't matter how much we irritate them in the process," Ox said philosophically.

"I know, but I would have loved to rub their noses in it."

Ox chuckled. "If you don't sound just like your sister."

"Angel and I agree on many things," she said, with a toss of her head.

"And you're far more alike than I think you realize. The conversation I overheard when I first arrived sounded so much like her that's who I thought was in here giving Weston a piece of her mind."

"You thought I was Angel? When did you . . . ?" Her voice trailed off, an odd combination of hope and despair.

"When did I realize you were you?" Her mood was so uncertain, Ox didn't know quite how to answer. He wasn't even sure if she wanted him to apologize for the impromptu kiss or not. He certainly couldn't tell her she kissed exactly like her sister. Obviously a noncommittal answer was his best bet. "I knew as soon as I smelled your lavender perfume. Angel always wears rose water." He gave her a jaunty grin and picked his hat up off the corner of the desk. "Guess I'd better get moving if I'm going to get cleaned up before dinner. I'd rather face wild Indians than have to explain to Martha why I'm late."

"Coward," Angel said with a chuckle.

"I've always valued my skin far more than my pride."

"With Martha, it's a matter of survival." Angel chuckled again as she sat down at the desk and pulled the ledger toward her. "You'd better hurry if you're going to get a bath."

"Am I being dismissed?"

"No. It's a gentle hint."

"Are you saying I look like something the cat dragged in?"

"Certainly not. I would never say anything so unlady-like. I was merely suggesting that you might want to—ah, freshen up before dinner."

Ox laughed. "Freshen up, eh?" He slapped his hat against his thigh and sent a cloud of dust billowing into the air. "Well, I reckon I could do with some tidyin' up at that. Don't you fret none, Miz Smythe. I'll do you proud."

"See that you do," she said, with mock ferocity. "Now get out of here. I have work to do."

Ox was still grinning as he eased himself down into a steaming hot tub at the bathhouse. Their scheme to undermine the patriarchs of their respective families was bringing out the best in Alexis. The irritatingly silly socialite he had first met when he came to Cheyenne had nearly disappeared. In her place was a self-assured woman of keen intelligence and astonishing business savvy.

With a sigh, he leaned his head back against the edge of the tub, closed his eyes, and relaxed. He found himself looking forward to their dinner. It was sure to be entertaining. Instead of the inane conversations they'd had at the beginning of their relationship, they might discuss anything from finance to politics. As often as not they'd wind up trading flirtatious banter back and forth. He looked forward to it with great anticipation as the steam curled up around his face.

29

"Whoa there, Sabin." The horse pranced nervously, taking exception to the bright red pony cart careening down the road toward them. Ox had his hands full, trying to keep the spirited animal from bolting.

"Mr. Treenery, you're back!" Shannon pratically tumbled out of the cart as she leaned forward to wave.

Jared brought the cart to a stop in front of the barn, his grin nearly splitting his face. "Goes pretty darn fast for a pony, huh?"

"Sabin thinks so, anyway," Ox said dryly, as the horse rolled his eyes in terror. "Unless you want to see him blow sky-high, I suggest you lower your voices and drive yourself very calmly around the corner so I can put him in the barn."

"Sure thing, Mr. Treenery." Jared's smile was unrepentant as he snapped the reins against the pony's back. "Giddyap, Lightning."

In spite of Sabin's displeasure, the children's delight in the fat little pony brought a grin to Ox's face. He was still smiling when Jared and Shannon joined him in the barn a few minutes later. "I see you've mastered the fine art of driving, Mr. Brady."

"Yup, and Lightning's almost as fast as a real horse."

"Lightning? I thought you were going to call him Butterball."

Shannon made a face. "That was your idea."

"Alexis liked it."

"She's a grown-up," Jared said with disgust. "Besides, she'd like anything you made up."

"I'm flattered you think so," Ox said, pulling the saddle off Sabin's back and turning him into an empty stall.

"We decided to give him a regular horse name," Shannon went on. "So he'd think he was a real horse instead of just a pony."

Jared nodded eagerly. "It worked, too. He goes twice as fast as any other pony."

"All because of his name?"

"Yup. Angel believes it too. In fact, she said you should think about renaming your mules."

Ox stopped in the middle of shutting the gate. "Angel? When did you see her?"

"Actually, we didn't see her at all," Shannon explained hurriedly. "It was Alexis. I was thinking Angel because of the mules."

Ox laughed as he finished latching the gate. "Now why would mules make you think of Angel?"

"Angel likes mules," Shannon said promptly. "In fact, last summer I heard her tell Alexis that the best-looking male animal she knew was a skinny mule named Ox." She looked confused. "Do you have a mule named after you?"

Ox nearly choked on his surprise. "Er—no, but I did have one named Angel."

"'Cause it was stubborn?"

"Stubbornest, most contrary critter I ever tried to drive," he admitted with a grin. And he'd named it Angel because it was the same beautiful smoky gray as her eyes.

Shannon eyed a bouquet of flowers he'd set down on a nearby barrel. "Are you going to give those to Alexis?"

"I suppose I'd better. You and Betsy are too young for them, and Martha would probably throw them in my face."

"Alexis likes roses better."

"Maybe so, but I couldn't find enough for a bouquet. Somebody in town has stripped every bush." He picked up the flowers and gave the two children a questioning look. "Hadn't you better put Lightning away and get cleaned up for dinner?"

The two exchanged a guilty glance and then turned identical pleading looks on him. "Will you distract Martha for us?" Jared asked earnestly. "She said if we were late again she'd tan our hides."

Ox chuckled. "I suppose I can try to distract her, but you'd better hurry or it won't do you a lick of good."

He watched them scurry around the side of the barn and then walked toward the house, whistling. So Angel was attracted to a muleskinner named Ox, was she? The thought filled him with a warm glow of satisfaction.

He knocked on the door and mentally braced himself for thirty pounds of hurtling four-year-old. But when Martha answered the door, Betsy was no where to be seen.

"Heard you were back," Martha said gruffly.

"I guess that proves the old saying, Good news travels fast."

"Some might think so, anyway. Better come in so I can close the door," she said, stepping aside.

"How thoughtless of me to stay out here on the doorstep," Ox said sardonically. "The last thing you want is a house full of flies." He thought he saw the hint of a grin as he walked across the threshold, but he couldn't be sure.

Martha glanced at the bouquet in his hand. "I suppose you'll want me to put those in water."

"If you don't mind."

"The place is beginning to look like a blooming garden party," she muttered, taking the flowers from him. "You may as well go in. They're in the parlor waiting for you."

"Thanks, Martha," Ox said as she turned away.

"I live to please."

Ox smiled. It was one of Angel's favorite sarcastic remarks. "I know you do, Martha. That's what I love most about you."

"Flattery like that might turn Angel's head, but it won't turn mine."

"You really think it would work?" His eyes twinkled as he grinned down at her. "I'll have to try it, next time I see her."

"You do that," she said, turning on her heel and stalking off toward the kitchen.

Ox grinned and crossed the hall to the parlor. Again he braced himself for Betsy as he opened the door, but Alexis and Jessie were the only occupants of the room.

"Ox!"

Alexis's welcoming smile wiped out all thought of anything else, including Betsy. He was still basking in its warmth when he saw the flowers. Every one of Cheyenne's missing roses appeared to be sitting in a huge vase near the window. "That's quite a flower arrangement," he said, hoping they were Jessie's.

If anything, the welcoming smile grew brighter. "It is rather wonderful, isn't it? Someone has been sending me roses for the last three weeks," Alexis said, gazing at the flowers fondly. "Whoever he is, I hope he knows how much I've enjoyed them."

"You don't know who it is?"

"No." The smile on her face softened to one of pure adoration. "But I have a pretty good idea."

Sudden jealousy knifed through him like a sword. For the first time, Ox began to wonder if Alexis really did have a fiancé.

"Supper will be on the table in half an hour," Martha announced, showing Sam into the room. "Everybody's here but the two scalawags upstairs, who are scrubbing the dirt off."

"It's my fault they're late," Ox said, suddenly remembering his promise to cover for them. "I asked them to show me their driving skills."

"Uh-huh, and I'm the pope's mother. I know darn good and well they got here just after you did. I saw them out the window."

"Oh," Ox said sheepishly.

"I never thought I'd see you getting pulled into their shenanigans, Ox." Angel chuckled. "But better you than me."

"Humph, you're more likely to be the leader. Here are some more flowers for you, from Mr. Treenery," Martha said, setting a vase on the mantel. "Good thing nobody around here has hay fever."

"Better add mine to the rest," Sam said gruffly. He held out a small bouquet of wildflowers. "Figured if I was s'posed to be courtin' Jessie I oughta bring flowers."

"They're beautiful, Sam," Jessie said, taking them from him and holding them to her nose. "Thank you."

He blushed. "They ain't much."

"I love flowers."

Sam smiled. "So did your mama."

"You knew Jessie's mother?" Ox asked in surprise.

Jessie nodded as she tucked the flowers into her coiled hair. The effect was predictably stunning. "My mother was a good friend of Alexis's sister. That's how Sam met her."

"A friend of Angel's?" Ox glanced at Sam's mortified countenance. "I see."

"No, you don't see," Angel said. "You don't see at all."

Ox was startled by the unwarranted attack. "I didn't mean—"

"Mr. Treenery!" The door burst open as the small cyclone Ox had been expecting ran in and headed straight toward him. Steeling himself for the inevitable collision, Ox blinked in amazement when Betsy screeched to a halt two feet from him and performed a little curtsy. "I'm so pleased you could . . . could . . ." She looked at her older sister for guidance.

"Join us," Angel prompted in a whisper.

". . . could join us for dinner." She gave him a cherubic smile. "I practiced."

"Why, thank you, Betsy," Ox said formally. "That was nicely said. You're a very polite young lady."

She stared up at him expectantly for several moments and gave a deep sigh. "I don't think I like being polite. When I was a rascal, I getted hugs."

Ox laughed and scooped her up in his arms. "Who said you were a rascal?"

"Alexis."

"Is that so?" Ox glanced at Alexis and was rewarded with a smile that warmed his blood and set his heart pounding in his chest. His interaction with the youngest Brady obviously pleased her.

"That's an understatement," Martha said severely. "Now stop bedeviling Mr. Treenery and run see what's keeping your brother and sister."

"All right." She gave Ox a noisy kiss on the cheek and squirmed to get down. The minute her feet hit the floor, she was running for the door.

"You've made a conquest there," Angel said with a smile.

Sam chuckled. "Either that or Betsy has. Best look

after your betrothed, Alexis, or your sister will be stealing him right out from under your nose."

"If you ask me, her *sister* already has; she just won't admit it," Martha said.

"Very funny," Angel said, glaring at the two of them. "It seems to me we have some rather important business to discuss and we'd better get to it. Don't let us keep you, Martha. I know you have a great deal to do in the kitchen."

Martha's lips twisted into a knowing smirk. "Truth hurts," she said over her shoulder, as she left the room.

"I hope you're here to tell us you got the mules," Sam said hopefully.

"Yes," Ox said, "and they're safe in a pen just outside of town."

"Good. I don't think we could have lasted more than another few days the way we are. How soon can we get them to Silver Springs Gulch?"

"That's a good question. We need to figure out some way to make the transfer without getting anyone's suspicions aroused. If I deliver them straight to you or if you take them directly from my pen, the connection will be obvious."

"So we somehow have to make my father think you bought them for the Silver Springs Express and make your grandfather think my father did it."

Sam shook his head. "Sounds impossible to me, especially since we don't know who the spies are."

"Maybe we only have to muddy the waters a bit, so that no one can be exactly sure what's going on," Ox said. "The question is, how do we do that?"

"Why don't you just have the outlaws steal the mules?" Jessie asked, from her place by the window.

The other three turned to stare at her in astonishment. They had almost forgotten she was there.

Jessie continued embroidering as she went on. "That way when they show up on the Silver Springs Express no one will know if Ox provided them or if Sam bought them from the outlaws." She made a knot and bit off her thread before looking up expectantly.

"You know," Ox said, "it just might work."

"Of course it will work!" Angel said enthusiastically. "All we have to do is get word to Mother Featherlegs, and it's as good as accomplished. I'll send the message tomorrow morning and—" She broke off as the door opened.

"Alexis, Martha needs to see you for a minute," Shannon said, as she and Jared came into the room. "She says it's urgent."

Angel frowned. "That's odd. Martha isn't one to get excited over burnt sauce. I'd better go see what she wants."

Ox stared at the vase of roses for a long moment after she left. "Has either of you ever met Brandon?" he asked the children.

"You mean Alexis's friend?" Shannon asked.

Ox's heart sank. So much for the theory that Alexis had made him up. "Right."

"We only met him once when we were with Alexis and ran into him downtown," Shannon confided.

"What do you know about him?"

"Only that he owns a big ranch," Jared said. "He told us we could come out sometime."

"And he doesn't get to town much," Shannon added.

"Often enough to send more flowers than a woman could possibly make use of," Ox muttered darkly, as he glared at the roses. "The man obviously has more money than sense."

Shannon and Jared grinned and winked at each other behind his back.

"Sam, you've got to get out of here," Angel said, hurrying into the room.

"What's wrong?" Sam asked, jumping up.

"Disaster!" Angel grabbed his arm and dragged him toward the French doors that led to the garden. "You can go out this way and nobody will see you."

"For God's sake, Alexis, what's the matter?" Ox asked.

"The worst!" Angel made a face. "My father just arrived for a surprise visit."

30

"His royal highness hasn't finished breakfast yet, but better safe than sorry, I always say." Suiting her actions to her words, Martha looked down the hall and then carefully closed the door to Angel's office behind her. "Clyde's gone."

"Are you sure? He's supposed to stay in Cheyenne in case I need to get a message to Mother Featherlegs," Angel demanded. "He's always either at Rosie's saloon or Finnigan's."

"I didn't say I couldn't find him," Martha replied. "I said he was gone."

Angel sighed. "All right, let's start over. Where is Clyde?"

"At the undertaker's."

"What?"

"From what I gather, somebody took exception to the way he played cards last night and shot him."

"Damn!"

"You don't need to swear," Martha said disapprovingly. "I wasn't aware you even knew the man."

"I didn't, really, but he was our only link to Mother Featherlegs and her gang. We've got to get a message to them today if they're going to steal the mules."

"Can't you send somebody else?"

"I could if we knew whom to trust. Unfortunately, I have no idea who James Treenery and my father may have hired to watch our movements. One word whispered in the wrong ear would mean disaster."

"What about Ox?"

Angel shook her head. "He was supposed to leave early this morning on a horse-buying trip. He's probably already gone. Besides, my father is suspicious enough of him."

"Guess you'll have to think of someone else, then."

"I already have." Angel sat down at her desk with a determined look on her face. "The Flying T stage leaves in a little less than an hour. I'm going to be on it."

"Why?"

"The gang plans to attack it just this side of Silver Springs Gulch. I can get word to Mother Featherlegs through them."

Martha was aghast. "You can't honestly be planning to meet with them on purpose! They're nothing more than a group of thieves and cutthroats."

"That's true; however, they do know which side their bread is buttered on. If anything happens to me they'll lose the most lucrative business venture they've ever had. They aren't likely to jeopardize it."

"Are you sure?"

"Of course," Angel said, with more certainty than she felt. "Would you mind throwing a few things in a bag for me? It doesn't have to be much. I should be back on tomorrow's stage."

"Or joining Clyde at the undertaker's."

"You always think the worst, Martha."

"Maybe so, but that doesn't mean I'm wrong!"

Angel reached up and gave her hand a squeeze. "Don't worry, I'll be careful." She pulled a piece of paper across the polished surface of her desk. "In the meantime I need to write a note to Father. All I have to do is come up with a good reason why I won't be here until tomorrow evening sometime."

"How about momentary insanity?"

"Very funny. Why don't you concentrate on helping me succeed?"

"Maybe because I hate hopeless causes." With that she stalked out and slammed the door behind her.

Angel glared at the door. "Thank you for your vote of confidence," she muttered. How she wished Ox were here to help her solve all these little problems! Unbidden, memories of his kisses popped into her head. She pushed them away in irritation. The last thing she needed was to be distracted by the thought of what Ox did to her. With a resigned sigh, she dipped her pen in the ink and began to write. . . .

In spite of Martha's disapproval, Angel boarded the Flying T forty-five minutes later. As she tried to settle herself on the hard seat, she couldn't help comparing the Spartan accommodations to the luxury of the Silver Springs coaches. No wonder the Flying T was losing business. She was enjoying a feeling of smug satisfaction when the other passengers began to enter the coach.

A pretty blond woman was the first. Her eyes widened when she saw Angel sitting on the far seat. "Oh." She glanced back over her shoulder and gave Angel an apprehensive look. "H-hello."

"Good morning." Angel couldn't imagine why the other woman was so nervous. "Lovely day to travel, isn't it?"

"I . . . I guess so."

A moment later a distinguished gentleman with

graying hair climbed in. The blonde touched his arm. "You remember Mrs. Smythe, don't you?"

He cleared his throat. "Yes, of course. How nice to see you again."

They knew Alexis! Angel forced herself not to panic. They were obviously uncomfortable for some reason. Maybe she could brazen it out. "It's been quite a while," she murmured.

"Er . . . yes. Your husband's funeral, I believe."

Angel nearly sagged with relief. The two evidently knew Alexis casually. Thank heaven for that. Now, if she could just figure out why they felt so threatened by her. . . .

A second later that faded to insignificance as a fourth passenger climbed into the coach.

"Father!" she exclaimed in alarm. "What are you doing here?"

"Good morning, Alexis," he said, sitting down next to her. "I decided to go to Silver Springs Gulch with you."

"Why?"

"I'm sure carrying on the business while young Treenery is gallivanting around the country is very difficult for you, my dear."

"Thank you for your concern, Father, but I really don't need any help. It's just a routine delivery of papers."

"Nonsense. This is a man's job. Besides, I haven't been to visit our station there in a long time." He smiled at the couple on the far seat. "I see we won't be traveling alone."

For a terrified instant, Angel thought she was going to have to introduce them to her father. She was frantically searching for a way out when the other man reached across the coach and shook hands with him.

"Good to see you again, Brady."

"Pickens," Richard said, returning the greeting.

"What brings you out of the bank during the week like this?"

Angel was astonished to see the other man darken. If she didn't know better, she'd think he was blushing.

"I'm escorting Mrs. Hanford to Silver Springs Gulch to . . . ah—"

"I'm going to visit my brother," the blonde put in quickly. "Mr. Pickens has kindly offered to accompany me there, since he has business in town."

"How fortunate for you," Richard Brady said politely. "Have you met my daughter Alexis?"

Mrs. Hanford nodded. "Yes, of course. Her late husband—"

"Ah, yes, the bank. I had forgotten." Richard Brady settled back against the back of the seat. "This should be a pleasant trip, since we all know each other so well. I find myself looking forward to it."

Angel had a hard time keeping a straight face. So this was Sandra Hanford, Alexis's arch rival. Though Angel had never met her or Thomas Pickens, she knew who they were, and it wasn't hard to figure why they were so uncomfortable.

Thomas Pickens, Oscar Hanford, and Duncan Smythe were cofounders of the prestigious Smythe, Hanford & Pickens banking firm. Considerably younger than either of his business partners, Thomas Pickens had quite a reputation as a ladies' man. Rumor had it that his latest amour was the beautiful young wife of the aging Oscar Hanford.

It was small wonder Sandra was so dismayed to find Alexis traveling with them. The two women had disliked each other for as long as they'd been acquainted. No one would willingly choose to take an enemy along on a romantic tryst.

Angel stole a sideward glance at her father. From the smirk on his face it was obvious he was enjoying the tense situation. He was apparently still angry over

Hanford and Pickens's refusal to let him take over his son-in-law's place in the bank. Too bad Alexis wasn't here, she thought. Her sister would have enjoyed making Sandra squirm a bit for all the spiteful things the blonde had said over the years.

Frankly, Angel wished all three of them were anywhere else but on the stage with her. Making contact with Mother Featherlegs was going to be difficult enough without an audience that expected her to act like Alexis.

Conversation was desultory and that suited Angel just fine, as she tried to think of a scheme to pull the wool over everyone's eyes. She was still trying to come up with a plan when the first shots sounded outside, several miles short of Rawhide.

Thomas Pickens leaned forward to look out the window. "What the hell?"

"Probably outlaws," Richard Brady said tightly. "We've had a lot of trouble with them through here."

"Outlaws!" Sandra let out an ear-piercing scream and threw herself into her lover's arms. "Oh, Thomas, save me!"

"Don't worry, Snookums, I'll protect you." He wrapped his arms protectively around her and ducked down so there was no chance of their being hit by a stray bullet.

Angel glanced at them in disgust. Honestly, how some people could be so cowardly was beyond her. Sandra was even worse than Alexis. With the thought came the sudden realization that she needed to show a bit of hysteria herself. Alexis was not the type to sit calmly waiting for outlaws to overtake the stage.

"Oh, Lord," she moaned, rocking back and forth in the seat. "I'm too young to die."

Richard Brady gave her a revolted look. "For Christ's sake, Alexis, pull yourself together. They'll be much more interested in the strongbox than in you."

"Are you certain of that?"

"No self-respecting bandit is going to bother with a hysterical female when there's money to be had." He reached into his coat and pulled out a six-gun. "Now if this character will just get close enough so I can shoot him." Richard's voice was nearly a growl as one of the outlaws rode up beside the coach.

Angel caught just a glimpse of the man but it was enough. Only George was that big. If her father succeeded in shooting him, she wouldn't be able to contact Mother Featherlegs. "Father, be careful!" she cried, throwing herself against him as though for protection.

The force of her body jarred his grip loose, and the pistol fell out the window. "Alexis, what the hell are you trying to do?"

"He could have shot you!"

"Or I could have shot him. Damn it, Alexis, I swear you haven't got the sense God gave a piece of hard tack."

"I'm sorry," she mumbled, staring down at her hands.

"It completely baffles me how I ever wound up with such a dunderhead for a daughter. Even your mother had more sense than you do."

Angel curled her fingers in her lap. How did Alexis put up with this kind of abuse? She'd been with her father less than three hours and already she was strongly tempted to strangle him.

Right now she needed to concentrate on passing on her message without giving everything away to her father. Still staring down at her lap, she opened her eyes as wide as she could. The dry dusty air coming in through the window soon did the trick, and her eyes filled with moisture. By the time the stage came to a halt, the tears were starting to trickle down her cheeks.

Angel knew the teariness wouldn't last any longer than the irritation that caused it, but it would be enough for effect. "I'm frightened," she whimpered. "What's going to happen to us?" The plaintive question ended on a scream as the door next to her crashed open.

Her startled shriek was completely convincing because it was real. Like the rest of the passengers, Angel had expected the attack to come from the side where the riders appeared. Fear skittered down her spine as the sun glinted off the barrel of a Colt .44 pointed straight at her.

"All right, everybody out!"

Swallowing nervously, Angel lifted her gaze to a pair of glacial blue eyes. Even with the lower half of his face obscured by a bandanna, she recognized him with a shiver of apprehension. Jake the Snake in the flesh.

An instant later his eyes widened in recognition. "Crazy Alice," he whispered in a horrified voice.

Angel could have sworn he paled as he backed away. Hoping Sandra's noisy sobs were distracting the men enough to cover Jake's peculiar reaction, Angel climbed out of the stage and cowered against the side. "Please don't hurt us," she whimpered loudly enough for her father to hear.

"We have nothing of any value," Richard Brady, said following her out of the stage. "I'm afraid you've wasted your time."

Jake paid no attention as he continued to stare at Angel in wide-eyed horror. "I didn't know," he mumbled, backing away even farther. "Honest."

Angel pretended to shrink away in fright as she searched frantically for George or even Dangerous Dick. If one of them didn't put in an appearance pretty quick, Jake would be begging *her* not to hurt *him*.

"What's the problem, Jake?" a gruff voice asked from overhead. "Get their valuables and stop playin' around."

Jake looked up and Richard Brady took advantage of his inattention by diving at him. The two of them hit the ground and the fight was on.

Sandra's screams brought George around the side of the stage in a hurry. He watched the men rolling around on the ground for a moment before giving the passengers a cursory glance. A second later his gaze swung back to Angel in startled recognition.

From the corner of her eye Angel could see that Sandra and Thomas were both watching the fight on the ground. Unobtrusively, she opened her hand so George could see the note hidden in the palm.

George gave her a nearly imperceptible nod as Jake finally got the best of Richard Brady and pulled him to his feet.

"Look out below," said the gruff voice from above, and the strongbox came tumbling down from the top of the stage. Another man Angel had never seen before jumped down right behind it. "I think we struck pay dirt. It's heavy as hell!"

"You're wasting your time," Richard Brady said, between his gasps for air. "The payroll isn't in there. You attacked the wrong stage."

"Then how come you were so protective of it?" Jake asked suspiciously, as he shoved Richard Brady back against the side of the coach.

"I was protecting my daughter, not the strongbox."

"Daughter?"

Richard nodded toward Angel as he wiped a hand across the bloodied corner of his mouth. "You can see what a courageous soul she is," he said sarcastically

As George inched closer and closer, Angel frantically searched for a way to pass him the note. With her father standing at her elbow, a simple transfer would be impossible.

The third outlaw nudged the strongbox with his toe. "Pretty heavy to have nothing in it."

"It's filled with rocks," Richard Brady admitted. "I thought we might run into trouble and I figured the thieves would just take the strongbox with them and not try to open it."

"So how come you're being so helpful now?" Jake was still suspicious. "Doesn't look to me like you want us to open it."

"I don't, not here anyway." Richard shifted uncomfortably. "There are three sticks of dynamite right next to the lock. If they get jarred, we'll all blow sky high. I don't know how they survived the fall from the top of the stage."

"You set a trap?" George asked in surprise.

Richard shrugged. "You've been hitting us pretty hard."

"And I say it's a bluff." Jake pulled his pistol and fired at the lock three times in rapid succession.

Sandra screamed and Angel fainted—right into George's arms. "Get this note to Mother Featherlegs as quick as you can," she whispered in his ear.

"Stop that!" Richard Brady said, clearly worried.

George lowered Angel to the ground. "I didn't do nothin' to her," he protested, as she slipped the note into his vest pocket. "She fainted."

"I was talking to your idiot henchman," Brady said angrily. "I'm not ready to die."

Jake twirled the pistol around his finger and stuck it back in his holster. "Figured he was lying about the dynamite."

"Damned show-off. Any fool knows you can't shoot the lock off a metal box," George muttered, as he lumbered to his feet. "All right, grab the strongbox and let's go."

"What for?" The third outlaw looked at him in confusion. "It's full of rocks."

George rolled his eyes. "If you believe that you're dumber than Jake, though I'm not sure that's possible.

Now pick up that strongbox and let's get the hell out of here. Could be the sheriff's right behind 'em."

Less than five minutes later, the stage passengers were watching the three disappear down the road in a cloud of dust.

"Damn it to hell!" Richard cursed, kicking the wheel of the coach. "There goes a small fortune."

"But there wasn't any money inside," Angel said in surprise.

"Shut up and get in the stage."

"I heard you tell Ox last night the strongbox would be empty."

"That's what I wanted him to believe. I figured it would be safe to transport the payroll if Treenery thought it was empty."

"You purposely misled him?" Angel's expression was properly bewildered, though deep inside she was delighted. Ox had predicted her father would try something of the sort and hadn't bothered to cancel the planned attack. The loss of a full payroll would be devastating to the Flying T.

"Everything would have been fine if you hadn't fouled it all up with your caterwauling," Richard grumbled. "This is all your fault."

Angel fought down a surge of anger. Sandra had made twice as much fuss as she had. How Alexis had put up with their father all these years was a minor miracle. Angel could hardly wait to see his face when Alexis and Brandon showed up. It would be almost as satisfying as shutting down the Flying T. Revenge was going to be sweet for both twins.

31

"*They got away with the* payroll *and the* mules?" James Treenery shouted, pacing back and forth in the tiny office of the Flying T.

"We don't know it was the same gang."

Treenery stopped pacing a moment to glare at his grandson. "What difference does that make? All that matters is Brady won this round."

"I'm still not convinced he's behind it."

"Oh, he's behind it, all right. Who else would have cause?"

Ox shrugged. "Any thief looking for a quick dollar. With the epizootic running rampant, those mules probably brought in as much cash as the payroll."

"So how did they wind up pulling the Silver Springs Express if Brady had nothing to do with it?"

"The Express probably offered the most money. When the sheriff investigated, they produced a legitimate bill of sale."

"Forged, no doubt."

"Most likely, but it was good enough for the sheriff." Ox shook his head. "I couldn't even prove they were the mules I got from the army."

"Brady probably has the sheriff in his pocket too. He'd have to in order to protect that bunch of cutthroats he's got working for him."

"I still think someone else is masterminding all this. Look at all the trouble he took to keep the outlaws from taking the payroll. Why would he do that if he wanted them to steal it?"

"To fool us into thinking he had nothing to do with it!" James said in exasperation.

"You're too suspicious."

"And you're too trusting. I think that bit of fluff you're playing with when your fiancée isn't looking has softened your brain." Treenery shook his head. "I'm surprised Alexis hasn't put a stop to it."

Ox frowned. "If you mean Jessie, there's nothing to put a stop to and Alexis knows it."

"So you say."

"Look, old man, if you came here to abuse me, you're wasting your time. We have more important matters to discuss, like money to run this business."

"No."

"Does that mean you won't discuss it or that you're not putting any more into the line?"

"I'm not putting another penny in until Brady makes his move."

Ox raised an eyebrow. "What move is that?"

"Either he'll figure out another way to attack the Flying T or he'll try to buy me out."

"I still don't see what letting the stage line go bust will accomplish for either one of you."

"Don't fool yourself," Treenery said crossing to the window. "Brady has no intention of destroying the Flying T. He's just lowering his offering price." He glanced at his grandson. "I see you still don't believe me."

"It does sound a little farfetched."

"Then why don't you ask him for money?"

"I already have." Ox sighed. "He refused even faster than you did."

"There, you see?"

"What I see is that this stage line is going to go broke unless someone is willing to put a little money back into it," Ox said in exasperation. "The replacement horses I bought just about cleaned us out. There isn't enough left to make up the payroll we lost. If neither of you will fund it, I'll be forced to start selling off assets."

"Then so be it," Treenery said with a shrug. "Just be sure you tell Brady that's what you intend to do. When he comes through with his half of the money, I'll kick in mine."

"And if he doesn't?"

"Then we'll be that much closer to buying *him* out."

Ox glowered at his grandfather. "I have a better idea. Why don't I just resign and let you two fight it out between you?"

"Go right ahead. I'm sure your mother won't mind the inconvenience of moving to Cheyenne, though you'd better do it soon. You wouldn't want to endanger her health with winter coming on."

"You'd use my mother as a pawn in your little game with Brady?"

James Treenery made a helpless gesture with his hands. "You leave me no choice. The only chance I have of beating Brady is with you here to watch out for my interests." He consulted his pocket watch. "My train leaves in ten minutes. I'd best be off."

"What if Brady doesn't come around to your way of thinking?"

"Don't worry, he will. I'll be back in a couple of weeks. In the meantime keep me informed."

With an expression of intense loathing, Ox watched

his grandfather stroll down the street. "You can come out now, Alexis. He's gone."

"He sounded just like my father did two weeks ago," Angel said, coming out of the back room. "After the holdup, all he could talk about was how he wasn't going to let those damn Treeneries get the best of him."

"Good. As long as they concentrate on each other, we'll beat them."

Angel frowned. "Do you think he'd really throw your mother out if you refused to do what he wanted you to?"

"I wouldn't put anything past the old devil."

"Then what's he going to do when he finds out you've been behind all this?"

"I don't know. Once he figures out I'm beyond his control I'm very much afraid he'll take it out on her. Originally I figured the Silver Springs Express would be lucrative enough that I could take care of her when the end came. I didn't anticipate the downfall of the Flying T happening quite so fast."

"Who would have thought they'd go after each other this way? I swear they're doing more damage than we are." Angel crossed her arms and leaned against the wall. "I guess we'll just have to figure out a way to keep your mother out of his reach when the time comes."

"Right. If worse comes to worst, she can go stay with my great-aunt. Even my grandfather won't tangle with Aunt Thelma." Ox smiled. "At least we won't have to pretend to be betrothed much longer."

"No." The thought caused a surprising wrench. When had she begun to relish the part she played?

"I'm sure Brandon will be glad to see the end of it."

A slight smile flitted across her face. "I think it's safe to say Brandon is looking forward to the end of the deception almost as much as I am."

Ox sat back in his chair and gazed at her speculatively for a long moment. "Have you thought about what we're going to do after you're married?"

"Do?"

"Well, I assume you'll be living out at his ranch."

"I suppose so," she said cautiously. "Why?"

"I doubt that Brandon will want you to continue helping run the Silver Springs Express."

"No, I don't guess he would at that."

"Good. I want to buy you out."

Angel blinked in surprise. "What?"

"I want to buy your half of the Silver Springs Express. I won't be able to do it all at once, of course, but if profits continue to grow the way they are I should be able to swing it by the end of next year."

Angel's heart plummeted. The loss of the business was almost as devastating to contemplate as the thought of how Ox was going to react when he discovered she'd been lying to him. She'd probably never see him again. "Wh-when do you want to dissolve our partnership?"

"After the final confrontation with my grandfather and your father. At top market value, I expect you'll increase your original investment substantially."

"I hadn't even thought about it."

"With your business sense I find that hard to believe." Ox smiled. "It's no wonder your husband didn't appoint anyone to look after your fortune for you. He knew you could take care of it on your own."

"Actually, Duncan figured on Angel helping me."

"Frankly, I think you're fully as capable in the business world as your sister is."

A ghost of a smile crossed her face. "I'm sure my sister would be amazed to hear that."

"How is Angel, anyway?"

"Fine, as far as I know. The last I heard she was too

busy to get away even for a few days." Angel thought she detected a flash of regret in Ox's eyes, but it was gone in an instant. "What makes you ask?"

"A conversation I had with the children the other day got me to thinking about her is all. I just wondered."

"Ox," Jessie cried, bursting through the front door. "You have a telegram from Sam!"

"A telegram!" Angel said in astonishment, as Ox took the message from Jessie's hand. "What on earth could be so important he'd risk sending it so publicly?"

"Well, I'll be damned," Ox said. "This is great news!"

Angel peered down at the note in Ox's hands: OXEN HEAR. UNCLE'S LETTERS COME BY EXPRESS. She looked up at him in confusion. "That makes no sense at all."

He grinned. "It's a code Sam and I worked out. Notice this was sent to Jessie, not me."

"But Oxen hear means to tell Ox," Jessie said eagerly.

"That makes sense, I guess," Angel agreed, "but what's all this about your uncle's letters?"

"That, my dear, refers to Uncle Sam. It seems he's decided to send his letters on the Silver Springs Express rather than the Flying T."

Angel's eyes widened in disbelief. "We got the government mail contract?"

"It appears that way."

"Oh, Ox!" Jessie cried, throwing her arms around him. "The Silver Springs Express is going to make it!"

He chuckled at her exuberance. "At least now we have a fighting chance."

"I never realized our ultimate success was so important to you, Jessie." Angel had to fight the insane urge to jerk the other woman out of Ox's embrace and rip the hair from her head.

"It means so much to all of you," Jessie said, with a

shy smile. As if suddenly realizing where she was, she blushed and stepped back. "I'm sorry I got so carried away."

"My pleasure," he said with a grin. "This calls for a celebration."

"I suppose you keep champagne handy for just such an occasion."

Angel's biting sarcasm brought a smile to Ox's lips as he pulled a bottle out of his desk. "Close enough." He popped the cork and filled three glasses. "I use this particular bottle of cognac only for celebrations." His gaze met Angel's as he handed her a glass. "It has special significance for me."

The air fairly sizzled with memories and unspoken emotion as Angel raised her glass in a toast.

"Here's to success."

"And to happily ever after," Ox said softly, as he lifted the glass to his lips.

Once again, the cognac burned its way down Angel's throat, but this time she didn't respond to its mellow soothing. Her dreams had been destroyed with a few innocuous words from the man she loved. She really couldn't blame Ox for being so ready to end their association. The Alexis he knew had gone out of her way to make him feel that way. As painful as it was for her, it had been necessary. At least now when the real Alexis returned as a married woman, he wouldn't discover he'd fallen in love with a myth. Of course, there was no getting around how angry and betrayed he was going to feel when he found out about the masquerade.

Even so, some resilient little part of her kept insisting Ox had a very real interest in Angel. Maybe she'd misinterpreted the negative things he'd said about her over the months. All the other possibilities kept swimming around in her head until she felt she'd go mad.

For the first time she dreaded the day she would give Alexis her life back. It wasn't too difficult to figure out why. Angel's world was about to fall apart, and there wasn't a thing she could do about it.

32

"Look, Jared," Shannon said, as she negotiated a difficult turn on the driving course Ox had helped them build. "Angel's here."

"Hello," he said, waving wildly, as Shannon brought the pony cart up to Angel at a smart trot. "Did you come down to watch us?"

Angel glanced around at the deserted homestead. It was half a mile from anything. "Of course not. Martha sent me to the store for some molasses. If I go home too soon she'll find something else for me to do. Your little course was on my way and seemed like a good place to hide from her. Why else would I be here on such a cold day? We might even get snow before evening."

He grinned at her. "To make us happy."

"What an idea," she said, seating herself on a stump. "As though I cared whether you two were happy or not. Now, which of you is going to demonstrate your driving skills first?"

For the next fifteen minutes Angel was an appreciative audience, calling encouragement and applauding at the appropriate moments. When Jared and Shannon joined her at last they were both glowing.

"You two are incredible!" she told them truthfully.

"Ox taught us all the difficult tricks," Jared admitted.

"Maybe so, but you must have been practicing every free minute to become so accomplished."

Shannon nodded. "We come here every day."

"We started doing that when Ox was teaching us, but we've kept it up even when he stopped coming."

"He doesn't come anymore?" Angel asked.

"Sometimes, but not as much as when we first built it. He used to come to watch and talk just like you did today."

"What did you talk about?" she asked casually.

Shannon and Jared exchanged a meaningful glance, as Angel pretended to study the deserted barn that stood nearby. "Horses, mostly, though he used to ask lots of questions about you and Alexis."

"Oh? What kind of questions?"

Jared shrugged. "Mostly boring grown-up questions like what you do for fun, what you do when you come to visit, and things like that."

"But sometimes he told us stuff too." Shannon sat down next to Angel on the stump. "Did you know he had a mule named Angel?"

Angel raised an eyebrow in surprise. "He did?"

"Yup." Jared nodded in agreement. "Because she was the stubbornest, most contrary critter he ever tried to drive."

Shannon glared at her brother. "But he never said that's why he named her Angel."

"Did so. He would never even have told us if you hadn't said she liked mules."

Angel blinked. "Whatever made you think I like mules?"

"I heard you tell Alexis so last summer."

"You did?"

Shannon nodded emphatically. "I remember cause I thought it was real strange. You said you liked a skinny mule named Ox."

Angel groaned. "Oh, Lord. Please tell me you didn't give Ox that little piece of information."

"Why not? He thought it was funny."

"Oh, yes, I'm sure he—" Angel broke off suddenly and listened intently. Someone seemed to be singing scales in the abandoned barn. "Who on earth is that?"

"Oh, that's just Jessie. She comes here every day to exercise her voice."

Angel stared at them in astonishment. "To what?"

"Come on," Shannon said, jumping to her feet. "We'll show you."

"You have to be real quiet, though," Jared cautioned, "'cause she needs to concentrate."

The lovely contralto voice surrounded them as they entered the barn. Jessie stood near the center of the building, trilling her way through the scales, completely oblivious of her audience. Angel was incredulous. Jessie made simple scales as delightful to listen to as any song.

As the last note echoed off the rafters, something in a conversation between Sarah Beth and Vanessa niggled at Angel's mind, but she couldn't quite remember what it was. Then Jessie launched into a song, and Angel ceased to think at all.

The music flowed around her, sweet and intense, more beautiful than Angel had ever thought possible. She didn't understand one word of the song, but it gave her gooseflesh and brought tears to her eyes. When it was over at last, she just stood there, scarcely able to breathe around the knot of emotion in her throat.

They say her voice is the ninth wonder of the world.

All at once Sarah Beth and Vanessa's conversation came back with sudden clarity. *She said she was going to visit her mother and vanished without a trace. No one has seen hide nor hair of her since.*

Angel felt weak in the knees. No wonder Jessie had never learned anything useful in school; she was too busy training that incredible voice. To the rest of the world, Molly's poor orphaned little daughter was the incomparable Jessica Lanford.

"Is that another one of those foreign areas?" Jared asked, as the last note died away.

Jessie smiled at him. "If you mean an aria, yes, it is: an Italian one."

"I think I liked the one you did yesterday better," Shannon admitted.

"That's because it's—oh!" Jessie stopped in midsentence when she turned and saw Angel standing by the door.

The two women stared at each other for a long moment before Angel spoke. "Shannon, Jared, why don't you two run along so Jessie and I can have a chat?"

"Aw, come on," Jared said. "We won't be in the way."

Shannon took his arm and pulled him toward the door. "Come on, Jared, they don't want us to hear what they have to say."

"I'd better not catch you eavesdropping outside the door either," Angel called after them. "You shouldn't leave Lightning standing too long anyway."

"We always miss the good stuff," Jared grumbled, following his sister outside.

Angel waited until they were out of earshot before she spoke. "You're Jessica Lanford, aren't you?" she asked softly.

"I—" Jessie hesitated, then slowly nodded. "Yes."

"Oh, Jessie, why didn't you tell me?"

Jessie blushed and looked down at her hands.

"I wanted to be just plain Jessie for a while. If you had known, everything would have been different."

"I wouldn't have done a thing differently if I'd known the truth."

"Oh, no?" Jessie lifted her eyes. "Do you really think you'd have treated me the same?"

"Well, of course I—" but as she said the words, a dozen images flooded Angel's mind and she realized Jessie was right. "No, I guess I wouldn't have. Lord, I feel such a fool."

Jessie smiled. "Why? You've never been anything but kind to me. Besides, I was curious to see if I could make a living without my voice. You gave me the opportunity to find out."

"I think you could do anything you wanted to if you had the training for it," Angel said. "A little experience in the world is all you need."

"I certainly found skills I didn't know I possessed. In fact, my only regret is that I've never gotten to meet Angel," Jessie said wistfully. "Do you think there's any chance that I can? More than anything I want to tell her how much her friendship meant to my mother."

Angel felt a stab of remorse for Jessie's obvious disappointment. Suddenly, the urge to confess was more than she could stand. "Your mother's friendship meant a lot to me too," she said quietly. "I was with her when she died."

Jessie's eyes widened in astonishment. "Angel?"

"In the flesh."

"*That's* why Sam kept telling me that knowing Alexis was as good as knowing Angel! I wonder why he just didn't tell me the truth."

"Sam's as protective as a mother wolf."

"I know," Jessie said. "I think he brought me here because he was afraid someone would take advantage of my inexperience and I'd wind up following in my mother's footsteps."

"You know—?"

Jessie smiled. "That she was a lady of the evening? Of course. I lived with her until I was ten. We spent most of that time at a place called Delilah's. It wasn't much as whorehouses go, but Delilah didn't mind having me there as long as I stayed out of the way."

"I didn't realize—"

"I know you didn't, and neither did Sam. Mama said I should always tell people she worked as a cook, so Sam thought I didn't know. He so wanted to protect me from the truth that I didn't have the heart to tell him I'd grown up in a brothel. I even started doing a few jobs for Delilah when I got older, like emptying chamber pots and running errands."

"And one day Delilah noticed how pretty you were," Angel murmured.

Jessie nodded. "Mama refused to let her take me on as one of her girls, and they had a terrible fight. The next thing I knew I was in boarding school. I have no idea how she managed to come up with the money for my voice training, but she did."

"She never said a word to me."

"No, but she told me all about you. Mama saw right through that cynical shell you wore. She said it was a disguise you hid behind so people wouldn't get too close and see the heart of gold underneath."

"I never realized what a vivid imagination your mother had," Angel said.

"Did she imagine the freedom money too?" Jessie smiled at Angel's shocked expression. "Mama tried to give it to me as soon as you told her about it. I refused to have any part of it unless she came to live with me. She finally agreed to come."

"But she never did."

Jessie shook her head sadly. "She didn't write much,

so I didn't think too much about it when I didn't get any letters. Then she didn't show up when she'd promised, and I figured she was going to need convincing. So I decided to take some time off and come get her. I never even considered the possibility that she wouldn't be alive when I arrived."

"I wish I had been there."

"Sam took me under his wing." Jessie smiled. "Besides, you had enough on your mind without me."

"I suppose you're wondering why I'm pretending to be Alexis."

"It has crossed my mind."

Angel sighed. "It started out simple enough, but somewhere along the way it got complicated." As she poured her story into Jessie's sympathetic ears, Angel began to relax for the first time in weeks. It felt so good to share it with someone.

"I think my mother was exactly right about you," Jessie said, when she was finished. "You began this against your better judgment to help your sister and wound up turning it into an opportunity."

Angel made a face. "I turned it into a disaster, you mean."

"Sam says the Silver Springs Express will provide a good living for all three of you. I wouldn't call that a disaster."

"It will if we don't go under first."

"I'm not very smart about numbers or business ventures, but from what little I've seen working down at the office, I don't think that's likely. You and Ox are incredible together."

Jessie's words brought images of togetherness that had nothing to do with business. Angel tried to ignore the warmth that flowed through her. "I'm glad you feel that way, because the money I owed your mother is invested in the company. You stand to lose a rather substantial sum if we fail."

"I hope this means I'm considered an investor," Jessie said enthusiastically. "I'd like that."

Angel was surprised. "Do you dislike being an opera singer?"

"No, but I was glad to see another kind of life."

"I hope you aren't going to try and convince me you prefer those other jobs."

"No, but some of it was rather fun." Jessie grinned. "The day we sold all Miss Jones's hats, for instance."

"I had a terrible time keeping a straight face," Angel admitted.

Jessie giggled. "So did I, especially when you showed Ox the hat you wound up with. He was appalled."

Angel chuckled. "If you think that was funny, you should have seen the look on his face when it was destroyed. I've never seen a man more pleased about anything. He gloated for the better part of a week and then bought me a new hat without a clue that I'd been teasing him all along."

"He's such a sweet man."

"I've called Ox Bruford many things over the years, but I don't think sweet was ever one of them," Angel said, a trifle tartly.

Jessie smiled. "But then the two of you are such very good friends."

"What's that supposed to mean?"

"Only that friends tend to take each other for granted."

"You think I take Ox for granted?"

"You take each other for granted," Jessie said. "I don't think either of you has taken a good hard look at your feelings for each other in a long time."

"And what do you suppose we'd find if we did?"

Jessie smiled. "I don't know. Why don't you try it and see?"

Angel shrugged. "Maybe I will someday when I'm bored." She glanced down at the watch pinned to her bodice. "Uh oh, I had no idea it was so late. I'm supposed to pick up some molasses for Martha. I'll be in big trouble if don't get moving."

"Good-bye, then. I'll see you at supper."

"Right. And maybe afterward we can have a long talk about Molly."

With a wave, Angel left the barn. Jessie was dead wrong. Angel knew exactly how she felt about Ox, and it wasn't anything as tepid as friendship. Unfortunately, she also knew how he felt about her. He couldn't wait to dissolve their partnership and get on with his life.

33

"About time you got here." Martha met Angel at the door with a predictably sour expression.

"I'm sorry," Angel said, handing Martha the bottle of molasses. "I went to watch Jared and Shannon for a while. I thought you said it wasn't urgent."

"I'm not talking about the molasses. You've got company."

"Who?"

"See for yourself."

"Honestly, Martha. Sometimes I think you're the most exasperating person on the face of the planet."

"Takes one to know one," Martha said over her shoulder, as she walked down the hall.

Angel straightened her dress. Heaven only knew what awaited her in the parlor. A knock on the front door stopped her in mid-step. "Martha?" But the housekeeper was long gone. With an annoyed sigh, Angel went to answer it.

"Well, this is a surprise," Ox said, when she opened the door. "To what do I owe this honor?"

"Who knows? Martha's in a snit about something." Angel frowned. "What are you doing here anyway? I thought you had a poker game tonight."

"I got a message saying I was needed here urgently. You didn't send it?"

"I just got home. Martha said I had company in the parlor." Angel paled. "Oh, Lord, you don't suppose it's my father and your grandfather?"

"If it is, their timing couldn't be worse. I got a telegram from Sam this afternoon. He just tracked down the last of the original suppliers for the Flying T. There is still a fairly substantial debt."

"Will they sell?"

"Without a qualm. I don't think my grandfather made a very positive impression on them when he contracted with them for supplies."

"At last we have them right where we want them."

Ox smiled. "We do indeed. The Flying T owes more than it's worth. I plan on sending out one more plea for money to cover what we owe. When they both refuse, we can start calling in our debts. Have you heard any shouting through the door?"

Angel shook her head. "No, but then I don't know how long they've been in there. If it is them, they might have gotten around to identifying the real culprits by now."

"They might suspect, but they can't have any real proof. We'll just have to brazen it out." Ox reached down and squeezed her hand. "Don't worry. We're an unbeatable team, remember?"

She gave him a brave smile and squeezed back. "Here's to teamwork."

Angel and Ox walked through the doorway together and stopped on the other side in astonishment. Nothing had prepared them for the sight of Sarah Beth

Treenery, Jared, Shannon, and Betsy, all focused on a gray-haired man who appeared to be folding a piece of paper into a small boat.

"Mother?"

"Oh, Jamie, you're here at last," Sarah Beth cried, jumping to her feet. She flew into his arms and hugged him. "I'm sorry to surprise you like this, sweetheart. I hope you'll forgive me."

"I'd forgive you anything," he said, hugging her back. "But a surprise visit hardly warrants an apology."

"That wasn't what I was talking about."

"Uh-oh," he said, with an indulgent grin. "That sounds ominous. What did you do, sell the family silver?"

"As though that would bother you." She grabbed his hand and led him over to the man getting up from the sofa. "Do you remember Theodore Collicott?"

"Of course I do," Ox said, shaking hands with the man. "You used to live close to Aunt Thelma."

"Still do, as a matter of fact. Flattered you remember. Only met you that one time when you were about the age of our friend here." He nodded toward Jared.

Ox grinned. "How could I forget? Alexis, I want you to meet Captain Collicott, formerly of the U.S. Navy. We spent three glorious days building and sailing the best little wooden ships you ever saw. Captain Collicott, my betrothed, Alexis Smythe."

"Charmed," he said, bowing over her hand.

She smiled. "Welcome to Cheyenne, Captain."

"And thank you for escorting my mother all the way out here," Ox added.

Collicott turned red and cast a helpless look at Sarah Beth. "Didn't exactly escort her. That is to say, I did, but not for the reason you think."

Sarah Beth smiled and took his hand. "What Teddy is trying to say is that we came together." She gazed up at the captain adoringly. "We wanted to tell you in person."

Ox looked from one to the other in confusion. "Tell me what?"

"Your mother has done me the very great honor of becoming my wife," Captain Collicott said. "Hope you don't mind."

Ox's mouth dropped open. "You're married? My God, why didn't you tell me?"

"There wasn't time," Sarah Beth admitted. "Teddy quite swept me off my feet."

"Popped the question, she said yes. Went to the justice of the peace the same day, then headed out here to tell you."

"Good heavens!" Angel exclaimed. "You haven't even had time to celebrate."

"When you get to be our age you don't worry about little details like big weddings," Sarah Beth said. "You live every minute to its fullest." Her gaze never left her son, who was still staring at them in astonishment. His expression was unreadable as he flexed his hands unconsciously. "Jamie?"

"Have you told my grandfather yet?"

"Er—no. We wanted you to be the first to know." Sarah Beth bit her lip. "Jamie, please don't be angry."

"Angry? Don't be ridiculous." His face broke into a huge grin as he picked his mother up and spun her around. "You got married! I never even thought of that." He laughed as he set her back on her feet and hugged her again. "Damn, but I'd love to be there when you tell my grandfather!"

"Then you don't mind?" Captain Collicott asked cautiously.

"Mind?" Ox pumped his stepfather's hand enthusiastically. "Lord, I couldn't be happier. Did you hear that, Alexis? My mother is married!"

"Yes, of course I—oh!" Suddenly the reason for his overreaction became clear. Sarah Beth had just removed James Treenery's one and only hold on his grandson. "Oh, Ox, this is wonderful!" she cried. "Do you realize what this means?"

"It means Captain Collicott will be sort of like my grandpa when you and Ox get married," Jared said excitedly.

"It also means we can finally get rid of this bottle of champagne that's been cluttering up my kitchen for these past two years," Martha said, coming into the room. She set a tray of glasses on the table and handed the bottle to Ox. "You better do the honors."

"You're a fraud, Martha," Angel said softly, as Ox made a ceremony out of popping the cork and pouring the champagne. "That bottle was what you were looking for when I came home, wasn't it?"

"Humph, you can believe what you like. I have work to do." With that she turned on her heel and stalked out.

A mood of celebration permeated the gathering from then on. Jessie was drawn into the festivities when she returned home. Even Martha relaxed enough to join the group in an after-dinner toast to the bride and groom.

When the meal was over, they returned to the parlor, where Captain Collicott was soon entertaining Angel, Jessica, and the older children with stories of his adventures at sea. After a quick hug and a kiss, Betsy squirmed off Ox's lap and ran across the room to join the others. For the first time all evening mother and son had a chance to talk.

"I don't know about this new husband of yours," Ox joked. "He seems to have stolen my best girl."

Sarah Beth glanced at her son in surprise. "You really like her, don't you?"

"Betsy?" Ox chuckled. "Kind of hard not to."

"I'm so glad. After little Jonathan I was afraid you'd never enjoy being with children again."

"Neither did I, but Betsy wore down my defenses in short order."

Sarah Beth smiled. "From the way Jared and Shannon sang your praises, I gather you've spent quite some time with them too."

"They have a way to getting you to do things for them." He crossed his arms and studied the group across the room. "Not unlike their older sisters. I can't see a nickel's worth of difference in the four of them."

"Are Alexis and Angel a great deal alike, then?"

"So alike I sometimes find it difficult to tell them apart." Ox's face took on a faraway look. "Did you ever wish for the impossible, Mother, even though you know it could never happen?"

"Everyone does occasionally. Why?"

"I guess I just needed to know I'm not the only fool in the world."

"Unattainable dreams have been known to come true upon occasion," she said, with a fond smile. "Maybe yours isn't as impossible as you think."

"It would take a miracle to make mine happen," Ox said. Then he smiled down at his mother. "Enough about me. What about you and your Prince Charming over there? Isn't this all kind of sudden?"

"Not really. We've known each other for years. In fact, I almost married him before I met your father." She sighed. "In those days there was no room in Theodore's life for anything but the sea. I didn't think he'd ever come back to me. I guess mine was one of those dreams we were just talking about."

"Are you truly happy then?" he asked gently.

"Oh, yes. I know this isn't easy for you, Jamie, but I do love him so."

Ox tucked her arm through his. "On the contrary, I find the thought of my mother as a blushing bride highly pleasing." He glanced at the Captain across the room, where the Bradys were hanging on his every word. "I just wished you'd married him sooner."

"Thank you, sweetheart. Have you and Alexis set a date yet?"

"No." He felt a pang as he looked down at her. She wanted so badly for him to be happy. "I'm not sure there's ever going to be a wedding," he admitted.

"Maybe that's just as well."

"I thought you liked her," he said in surprise.

"Oh I do, and I'd love to have her for a daughter-in-law."

"But?"

"But I think you're in love with Angel."

"You've never even met Angel!"

"No, but I've heard about her in almost every letter I've gotten from you in the last two years. Personally, I think you'd be well advised to look that way for a wife."

"I don't think she'd have me."

"Have you asked her?"

"No, but—"

Sarah Beth put her fingers against his mouth to stop his protest. "You'll never know for sure unless you try. She'd have to be crazy or stupid to turn you down."

"You just think that because you're my mother," Ox said with a smile, as he gently pushed her hand away.

"That doesn't necessarily mean I'm wrong, though, does it?"

"No, I guess it doesn't."

"Give it some thought." She glanced across the room. "I think it's time I pulled my husband away from his audience. He'll go on all night if I let him."

Ox remained there after his mother left him. She'd given him much to ponder. Angel had been constantly on his mind for months. What was the worst that could happen if he asked her to marry him, another rejection? Surely it was worth the risk. He was still considering his mother's words when Jessie sat down beside him.

"Ox, could I have a few minutes of your time?"

"Sure. What's on your mind?"

"I need your help."

"Oh?"

As Ox and Jessie talked, Jared and Shannon watched them from across the room.

"Uh-oh," Jared said in a low voice. "This looks serious. What do you suppose Jessie's telling him?"

Shannon bit her lip. "I don't know, but I don't like her talking to him all alone like that."

"Jessie's awful pretty. What if Ox falls in love with her?"

"What do you think?" Shannon said in disgust. "Ox'll marry her instead of Angel, and we'll never have him for a brother-in-law or Captain Collicott as a pretend grandpa."

"We better do something."

"Right, but what?"

Jared pursed his lips. "The flowers on her pillow and the perfume-soaked rags under the seat of his wagon and in his desk are working pretty good. They give each other goofy looks when the other one doesn't see."

"But it's taking so long!" Shannon said.

"Maybe if they got stuck alone together somewhere—"

"That's it!" Jared cried, then blushed as several pairs of adult eyes turned his way questioningly. "I'll tell you later," he whispered to Shannon. "If this works, they'll be married before the week's out!"

34

"Hello?" Ox looked around curiously as he entered the deserted barn. "Is anybody here?"

"Who's there?" A muffled voice came from the back of the barn.

"It's Ox, Jared," he called, peering into the darkness. "Where are you?"

The sound of scuffling drew him farther inside. "Jared?" Ox walked all the way to the back of the barn but found no trace of the boy. Even when his eyes grew accustomed to the darkness, he could see very little in the dim interior.

Ox could hear someone calling outside. "Is that you, Alexis?" he yelled.

"Ox?"

"I'm in here," he said, walking to the front of the barn. "I got a note from Jared saying he needed my help down here immediately. I figured it had something to do with the pony cart."

"That's odd. I got one from Shannon saying that

Jessica needed me. What do you suppose . . . *ooof!*"
Without warning, Angel fell forward into Ox's arms.

"Alexis!" he cried in alarm. "What—?"

"Somebody pushed me!" she said indignantly, as she struggled to get back on her feet. "Wait until I get my hands on—"

Just then the barn door slammed shut and total darkness surrounded them. "What the hell?" Three strides took Ox to the door, but no amount of shaking could budge it.

"Open this door!" he yelled but there was no response from outside. "I'll kill them," he said as he rattled the door.

"Oh, no, you won't."

"Look, Alexis, I know they're your brother and sister, but this time they've gone too far. They don't deserve your protection."

"Protection, hell. By the time I get done with them, there won't be enough left for you to do anything with! I suppose the windows are locked too," Angel said, moving toward the nearest one. She'd only gone a few feet when she tripped over something in her path. "What's this?" As she reached down, her hand connected with the smooth metal of a lantern. "Ox, I found a light."

"Small comfort," he said. "I didn't think to bring any matches or kerosene with me. Did you?"

"No. . . . Well, I'll be darned. Here's a packet of matches and a tinderbox." A moment later a match flared, piercing the darkness, as Angel fumbled with the lantern cover. A second match ignited the lantern wick, and a mellow light spilled out into the darkness of the barn.

Ox raised a brow. "Full of kerosene, too. How convenient."

"It is, isn't it. What do you suppose those two are up to?"

"God only knows. They obviously want us out of the way for some reason."

"Makes your blood run cold thinking of all the possibilities, doesn't it?"

"That it does. We'd better find a way out and soon."

Angel rattled the shutters on one of the windows. "Locked from the outside. I suppose they all are."

"Probably." Ox glanced around. "You know there's usually an old tool or two in a place like this. I'll bet they never thought of that."

"Good point. You take a look while I check all the doors and windows. They might have missed one." Angel rattled every window and both doors with little effect. "They did a good job of locking us in," she said finally.

"But they were careless," Ox said with satisfaction. "Look what I found."

Angel eyed the dusty wooden wheel blankly. "What are you going to do with a wagon wheel, roll it through the door?"

"Alexis, Alexis, use your imagination," he admonished with a grin.

"It seems to be temporarily paralyzed. Why don't you enlighten me?"

He swung his leg over a barrel and sat down with the wheel between his knees. "It may take me a while to tear it apart, but one of these spokes should make a pretty decent lever."

"Oh, you mean to pry open the door with."

"Actually, I was thinking more of a window." He jiggled one of the spokes with his hand. "Unfortunately, this wheel seems to be in pretty good shape. Those spokes are really tight. I wish I had something to stick in there and wiggle it loose."

Angel watched him struggle for a few moments and then sighed and hiked her skirt up to her knee. "Here, use this," she said, removing her stiletto from its sheath and handing it to him.

Ox stared at it for a moment in astonishment. "You carry a knife?"

Angel shrugged. "This country may look tame but there are all kinds of predators out there, especially the two-legged kind. I started wearing a knife after Angel was attacked one night in her own place."

"I remember that night well," he said. "A couple of drunk miners waylaid her in the hallway outside her office. If they'd been sober she and I would have both been in big trouble."

"I know," she said softly, as she reached up to touch the scar dimpling his cheek. "Angel told me all about it. She's never forgotten what you did for her that night." She dropped her hand. "And neither have I. That's why I carry the knife."

Ox stared at her. "How did you know about my cheek?"

"You don't think Angel would leave out her part in it, did you?" she asked, with a twinkle in her eye. "According to the story I heard, she was a regular Clara Barton. Without her nursing skill, you'd have died of blood poisoning at the very least."

Ox inserted the point of the stiletto into the hole at the top of the wheel. "Maybe so, but her rapport with her patients leaves something to be desired."

Angel's lips twitched. "I wonder what else is in this place," she said, wandering back into the shadows.

"Hard to say. It looks like it's been empty for a long time. You might want to watch out for rats."

"Let the rats watch out for themselves."

"I almost feel sorry for them," he said with a chuckle.

"With friends like you . . ." Her voice trailed off as she opened the lid of a feed box. "What in the world? Oh, for heaven's sake!"

Ox glanced over his shoulder. "What did you find, a giant rat's nest?"

"Not even close." She leaned over and pulled out a

large basket. "It's full of food. At least Jared and Shannon don't want us to starve."

Ox grunted as he jerked on the loosened spoke. "They must plan on keeping us here a long time," he said, as it popped out of the rim.

"I don't think so. They know Jessie comes here every day." Angel dug down into the basket. "Besides this looks like a picnic. Look, here's a blanket to sit on and a bottle of wine."

"A picnic! In a deserted barn?"

"Who knows what they were thinking? Might as well take advantage of their generosity." She spread the blanket. "By the time you break us out of here we're going to miss supper."

"True, and I have a feeling Martha won't save us anything." Ox stood up and leaned the spoke against the side of the barrel. "Although come to think of it, she just might send out the militia if we don't show up on time."

"Knowing that brother and sister of mine, she probably thinks we decided to go to Clancy's for dinner. Oh, look, Ox, your favorite: fried chicken."

Ox peered down into the basket with interest. "Is it too much to hope that there are some of Martha's biscuits in there?"

"Right here," Angel said, peeking into a tidy bundle done up in a napkin. "And there's a dish of her chokecherry jelly to go with them."

"Looks like suppertime to me." He settled himself on the blanket and picked up the bottle of wine. "You want me to open this?"

"Be my guest. I'll set out the food."

"Where are the glasses?" Ox asked, popping the cork out of the bottle.

"You aren't going to believe this," she said pulling two long-stemmed crystal glasses out of the basket. "Look what they sent."

"Good Lord. This is beginning to look more like a seduction than a kidnapping."

"Jared and Shannon wouldn't think of something like that!"

"I'm not sure I'd put anything past those two," he said, handing her a glass.

Angel's lips quirked. "Who's supposed to be seduced here, you or me?"

"I see what you mean," he said after a moment. "I guess they wouldn't think that way, would they?"

"Not yet anyway." She raised her glass. "Here's to the rats. May they suffer a thousand agonies."

"Two-legged or four?"

"I feel the same about both kinds right now."

Ox chuckled as they clinked glasses. "I'm glad I'm not in Jared and Shannon's shoes."

"They're going to regret this night's work," she muttered darkly. "Here, have a piece of chicken."

"I was coming to see you this evening anyway," he said, selecting a drumstick. "I have news."

"Oh?"

"Both your father and my grandfather refused to send me the money to pull the Flying T out of danger. It's time for the owners of the Silver Springs Express to call in all the debts."

"Good. We can set up a meeting later this week to deliver our ultimatum," Angel said with satisfaction. "Did Sam agree to go as our representative?"

"Sure did. After all, he has his life savings invested in this venture too. He also suggested we send Joe Simkins along to make it look more official."

"Joe Simkins? Who's that?"

Ox paused with the drumstick halfway to his mouth. "He's a lawyer Sam knew in South Pass City. Simkins was pretty inexperienced back then, but Sam assures me he's improved a lot in the last year. Sam thought it would make a bigger impact if he had a lawyer along with an impressive vocabulary."

"It couldn't hurt, anyway. I just wish I could be there to see your grandfather and my father's faces when they realize they haven't been fighting each other all this time."

"Me too." Ox's smiled faded as he watched Alexis in the soft glow of the lantern. It was peculiar how the subtle light played tricks with his mind. He could almost swear he was with Angel. After all this time he should be able to tell them apart, damn it.

Her fiery hair shone in the glow of the lantern. Though the style belonged to Alexis, the halo of highlights reminded him of Angel's gloriously unrestrained curls. Ox longed to reach out and touch their silken richness. Instead, he searched her face for some sign of Alexis and found an image that filled him with frustrated longing. Here was an exquisite blending of the two women he loved; Alexis without the frivolous nonsense that set his teeth on edge and Angel without the hard-bitten cynicism and wariness she wrapped herself in.

Angel glanced up and caught his gaze upon her. "What's the matter?" she asked suspiciously. "Do I have jelly on my nose?"

"No, I was just thinking how much I'm going to miss all this."

"Picnicking with the rats?"

Ox chuckled. "That too. Jared says the three of them will be leaving before long to go back to school. Didn't think I'd miss your brother and sisters, but I will." His smile faded. "I suppose you'll be getting married soon."

"In the very near future," Angel said. There was no use denying it. Alexis and Brandon would be home any day now, and the whole charade would be over.

"You don't seem very happy about it."

"You're not the only one who's going to miss this. We've had quite an adventure, but I guess all good things have to come to an end sometime."

"Do they?" he asked softly.

Angel stared at him in breathless wonder. "I . . . I don't know."

"I hate to let you go." His voice was a husky caress that sent warmth flooding through her entire body. "You're the best partner I ever had."

Their gazes met and held. For a moment they seemed suspended in time.

"Maybe"—she swallowed—"maybe Angel would buy me out. She's been looking for a business to invest in."

Ox blinked, almost as though he'd forgotten where he was. "I can't see Angel buying into something so tame as a stage line," he said with a forced laugh. "It's not exactly her style."

"You might be surprised."

"I might at that." He drained the last of his wine and got to his feet with a mighty stretch. "Well, guess I'd better see what I can do about breaking us out of here."

"Don't you want a piece of pie?" She looked up at him hopefully. "It's apple."

"I'll admit it's tempting, but I've had about all the good food I can handle for a while." With one last smile at her, he picked up the wagon spoke and walked to one of the windows.

As she packed away the remains of their picnic, the sound of splintering wood filled the barn. Angel wondered if it was the window shutters breaking or her heart.

35

"*Did you hear something,* Jared?" Shannon asked, wrinkling her brow in concern.

He looked up from the game they were playing, listened intently for a few seconds, and shook his head. "Not a sound. Hurry up, it's your turn."

Shannon turned her attention back to the cards and tried to concentrate. "There it is again," she said after a moment. "It sounded like someone coming up the back stairs."

"Oh, come on, Shannon. You're letting your imagination get the best of you. Just play."

"I heard something," she insisted.

"So what? It's probably just Martha. There's no way they could—"

"Could what?" said a menacing voice as the door swung open.

Shannon screamed and Jared's face lost all its color as Angel stomped into the room with Ox right behind her. "I want an explanation and I want it now!"

"An . . . an explanation about what?" Jared quavered, trying to look innocent.

"We'll start with why you locked us in the barn out by the track," Angel said.

Shannon's eyes widened. "Someone locked you in the empty barn?"

Angel folded her arms and glared at her sister. "As if you didn't know!"

"We were here all evening, weren't we, Jared?"

He nodded emphatically. "Ever since before supper. You can ask Martha."

"They obviously crept out the back way when Martha wasn't looking," Angel said to Ox, "pulled off their little stunt, and sneaked back in."

"We know it was you two, so you might just as well admit it and tell us what you're up to." Ox pinned them with a stern look. "What I'm most curious about is why you thought it was necessary to take our horses."

"You can't leave horses standing all night," Jared protested. "It isn't good for them."

"So much for pretending it was someone else," Angel murmured. "I guess we'd better get tough, Ox."

He sighed as he shut and locked the door. "I was really hoping we could avoid this, but I guess you're right. They leave us no choice."

Jared swallowed nervously. "What are you going to do?"

Ox shrugged. "Whatever it takes to find out what's going on. I assume we've got all night before anyone comes looking for us. That gives us plenty of time to get the truth, one way or another."

Shannon and Jared exchanged an uneasy glance. "We were going to let you out in the morning," Shannon blurted out.

"What were the two of you doing that you wanted us out of the way?" Angel asked.

"Nothing," Jared said. "I swear. We came home, ate dinner, and came straight upstairs to play cards."

"Then why did you lock us in?"

Shannon hung her head. "We didn't know how else to get you to spend the night together."

"*What?*" Ox asked.

Angel just stared at the two of them in mute amazement. Jared and Shannon scooted closer together.

"We knew you'd never do it on your own," Jared said defensively.

"Why did you want us to spend the night in the barn?" Ox asked. "Is there a ghost haunting it?"

"A ghost?" Shannon said in astonishment. "Whatever gave you a crazy idea like that?"

"If it was a ghost, they'd have stayed there themselves," Angel said sardonically. "Were you punishing us for some reason?"

"No!" The suggestion obviously appalled both Shannon and Jared. "We just wanted you to spend time together."

Angel gave Ox a bewildered look. "Does any of this make sense to you?"

"Not a bit."

"John Madison and Sharon Thomas spent the night together in a cabin last year," Jared explained. "They said they got trapped by a flood."

Shannon nodded. "Her father said they had to get married. Mama said it was scandalous."

Angel raised an eyebrow. "So—?"

"So we thought if you spent the night together in the barn, Martha would make you get married too."

"Jesus Christ!"

Ox's horrified whisper sent an arrow straight to Angel's heart. Clearly marriage to her would be a fate worse than death for him. "John and Sharon were still living with their parents," she said. "It's different with people like Ox and me because we've both been married before."

"Why?"

"I don't know; it just is. Nothing can force us to get married if we don't want to. It's unfair of you to try."

"Why?" Shannon asked bluntly. "Didn't you say marriage should be based on love? Isn't that what your big fight with Father was all about?"

"Yes but I don't see—"

"Don't you? Even Jared and I can tell you love each other."

Color flooded Angel's face. Lord, were her feelings so obvious?

"It may seem like it," Ox was saying, "but it's all a game we've played to fool my grandfather."

"I don't believe you," Shannon said stubbornly. "The flowers and the perfume were working too well."

Angel's face went from red to purple. "The flowers?" she said in a strangled voice. "It was you two?" Her hands formed into fists. "I'll—I'll—"

Ox watched her with growing alarm. She almost looked as if she were choking. "Alexis," he said, slapping her on the back. "Are you all right?"

"They—they—ohhh, I'll kill them!"

"What's she so mad about?" Ox asked the children. "What else did you do?"

Jared had the grace to look embarrassed. "It was Shannon's idea."

"But you came up with the perfume," she retorted.

"Will one of you please explain what the hell you're talking about?"

"We—ah, we put a rose on her pillow every night," Shannon confessed miserably.

"And we sort of let her believe you'd paid us to do it," Jared added.

"All those roses," Ox murmured. "And the perfume?"

"We soaked rags with her perfume and hid them under your wagon seat and behind the drawer in your desk at the station so you'd smell it and think of her all the time."

Ox frowned. "That's why I kept thinking I smelled perfume."

"Look, neither Ox nor I want your help," Angel said angrily. "We're plenty old enough to make up our own minds about who to marry. We hardly need advice from a couple of children."

"But you love him," Shannon protested. "I know you do."

"You don't know a thing about it," Angel snapped. "I don't understand why my sisters are both so sure they know my heart better than I do."

"Sisters?" Shannon said in confusion. Then her expression cleared. "Oh, you mean—"

"Shannon, if you plan on living until tomorrow you'd better close your mouth right now and keep it that way," Angel said. She glared at Jared. "That goes for you too."

"But we want Ox for a brother-in-law," Jared said.

"You'll just have to be satisfied with Brandon! I think I'll go to bed," she said, stalking to the door. "I'm too mad to figure out what to do with you two now. We'll discuss it at breakfast. Good night!"

"Whew," Jared said as she slammed the door behind her. "She was really mad. I thought she'd find it kind of funny."

"I think we embarrassed her," Shannon said. "Didn't you see how red her face got?"

"So she thought all those roses in the parlor were from me," Ox said pensively. "No wonder she thanked me for the flowers."

"She kept them in her office so she could see them all the time. Then there got to be too many, so she moved them to the parlor."

Ox rubbed his forehead. "Alexis says she's going to marry Brandon."

Shannon nodded. "I know, but—"

"Shannon!" Jared grabbed her arm. "We took the Brady oath, remember?"

Ox looked from one expectant face to the other in frustration. "What is it she doesn't want me to know?"

Jared gave a disappointed sigh. "Sorry, Ox, that's all we can tell you. We took an oath."

They all jumped as the door opened and Martha came in. "It's time you two were in bed." Her eyes widened as she saw Ox. "What in the world are you doing here?"

"Alexis and I were having a chat."

"Pretty peculiar time for a visit, if you ask me." She fixed Shannon and Jared with a fierce stare. "What have you two been up to now?"

"Alexis will probably tell you all about it in the morning," Ox said, taking pity on the two miscreants.

"Does this have anything to do with her snapping my head off not five minutes ago for no reason?"

"Probably." Ox glanced at his pocket watch. "Looks like I'm too late for my appointment tonight. If I leave a note for Alexis, could you see that she gets it in the morning?"

"Sure, why not. I just love tangling with her first thing in the morning," Martha said sarcastically. "It gets my day off to a good start."

Ox grinned as he scribbled out a note on a piece of paper from the children's desk. It was fitting that she be the one to set up the meeting for the final confrontation with Brady and his grandfather anyway. The only thing that could make the victory more complete for her would be to share it with Angel. Both twins should be here for the final confrontation.

"This note should make Alexis happy. It's what we've been working for. I thought I'd be able to do this myself, but something has come up that I need to take care of." He folded the note and handed it to Martha. "Where did you say Angel's putting up in Denver?"

"I didn't." Martha regarded him suspiciously. "What do you want to know for?"

"It occurred to me she might like to be in on the kill."

"Alexis can send her a telegram."

Ox smiled disarmingly. "I know, but I want to be the one to give her the good news."

"I don't suppose it will do any harm," she said finally. "She's staying at the Carriage House. Her friend Sally owns it."

"Thanks, Martha, you're a peach," he said, bending down to give her a swift kiss on the cheek.

Martha glared at him. "How many times do I have to tell you to save your shenanigans for Angel? You don't impress me in the least."

Ox chuckled as he put his hat on and turned to go. "I know it. That's why you're so irresistible." He blew her a kiss and shut the door behind him.

Resisting the urge to whistle, Ox walked down the hall to the stairs. Just when life seemed the blackest, the sun broke through the clouds. Right in the middle of his most frustrating moment, it had suddenly occurred to him there was one more person who knew Alexis's secret.

Angel woke with a splitting headache and a grouchy outlook. She hadn't slept worth spit anyway, and disturbing dreams had riddled what little sleep she did get. She was sitting at her dressing table staring gloomily into the mirror when Martha came in with her coffee.

"My, don't we look pleasant this morning."

Angel glanced at her in the mirror. "If you're trying to make me feel better, forget it. I'm not in the mood."

"I wouldn't waste my time," Martha said, setting the coffee on the dressing table. "If you're so dead set on making yourself miserable, who am I to spoil your fun?"

"I think maybe I'm getting sick. I don't feel very well."

"All that ails you is a bad case of stubbornness. Why don't you just tell him who you are and be done with it?"

"He's going to find out soon enough anyway. Alexis and Brandon will be here next week." Angel stared bleakly into the mirror. "He'll never speak to me again."

"Either that or he'll ask you to marry him."

Angel gave a bitter laugh. "Oh, Martha, you're such an optimist."

"And you are the most pigheaded stubborn woman I ever saw in my life. It's no wonder you butt heads with your father. You're just like him."

"I love you too."

Martha rolled her eyes. "I think I'll go do something pleasant like empty the chamber pots. Here's a couple of notes for you."

Oh?" Angel looked at them curiously. "Who from?"

"Jessie and Ox. I suppose next you'll be wanting me to read them for you."

"I'll manage." Angel opened the first note and raised her brows in surprise. "Did Ox say what came up that he had to leave?"

Martha looked thoughtful. "Just that he missed an appointment last night."

"That's odd. He never said a word." Angel shrugged. "Oh, well, I can certainly send the telegrams to my father and his grandfather." She smiled with smug satisfaction. "In fact, I'll relish it."

"That's what he figured. Well, this has been a little piece of heaven, but I have work to do, so if you'll excuse me?"

Angel hardly noticed the other woman's departure as she read her second note. Jessica, it seemed, was so desperate she'd finally decided to take things into her own hands. The note went on for several more lines in the same dramatic vein without imparting any real information. Apparently expressing herself in writing was another skill Jessica had never mastered. Though Angel couldn't quite decipher the reason, one thing was clear. Just when everything they'd all worked so hard for was coming together, Jessica and Ox were both gone.

36

"*Treenery!*" *Richard Brady's* angry voice filled the small office of the Flying T. "Damn it, Treenery, where are you?"

"I'm right here, Brady."

"Well, well, well," Richard said, as James Treenery stomped in. "I might have known you'd be here."

Treenery glared at his former partner. "I was under the impression that was what you wanted."

"I assumed your double-dealing grandson would handle this, just like he has everything else."

"Don't waste your time trying to insult me, Brady." James Treenery tossed his hat on the desk. "Let's just get down to business, shall we?"

"Fine by me. You may as well know I have no intention of selling out to you."

Treenery gave a humorless laugh. "What a surprise. Is this when you offer to buy my share of this worthless business?"

"That's almost funny, coming from you," Brady said.

"All right, Treenery, enough of this nonsense. Your telegram said we were here to discuss terms. Let's just get to it."

"I didn't send you a telegram." Treenery frowned. "In fact, I headed out here when I got *your* message."

"What message?"

"The one that said the Flying T was going on the auction block to pay off its creditors," Treenery said. "Was there another?"

"I didn't send that, you did."

"Nice try, Brady. We both know otherwise, don't we?"

"Hell, no!" Richard Brady said. "You—"

"Good morning, gentlemen," interrupted a third voice as Joe Simkins and Sam walked in together. "We weren't expecting you to arrive so early." Simkins set a small satchel on the desk.

"Who the hell are you?" Treenery asked, glowering at the newcomers.

"The big one is the front man for the Silver Springs Express," said Richard Brady. "As if you didn't know."

"How the devil should I know who he is?" Treenery demanded. "He obviously works for you."

"Of all the unmitigated—"

Simkins held up his hand. "Gentlemen, gentlemen, there's no need to argue. We don't work for either of you; we represent the owners of the Silver Springs Express. My name is Joe Simkins and this is Sam Collins. Please, have a seat and we'll get down to business."

Brady and Treenery looked at each other.

"You don't own the Silver Springs Express?" James Treenery asked Brady suspiciously.

"Hell, no! I thought you and that grandson of yours did." Brady frowned at Sam. "Is it yours then?"

Sam allowed himself a brief smile as he sat down. "Only a small part of it."

"Then who owns the rest?" Treenery demanded.

"All in good time, gentlemen, all in good time." Simkins opened the satchel and took out a sheaf of papers. "This shouldn't take long."

With another bewildered glance at each other, Treenery and Brady sat down.

"As you are aware, the Flying T is in desperate financial difficulty," Simkins said, handing them each a sheet of paper. "This is a list of outstanding debts which both of you have repeatedly refused to pay."

Richard Brady scanned the sheet and focused on the figure at the bottom of the page. "Jesus Christ, that's more than the business is worth!"

James Treenery leaned back in his chair and studied Simkins intently. "It's not uncommon for a business like this to operate in the red for short periods of time. This doesn't necessarily mean the end of the Flying T. Besides, I fail to see what it has to do with the Silver Springs Express. At the risk of being rude, none of this is any of your damn business."

"It wouldn't be except for one small detail." Sam couldn't quite keep the smug look off his face. "The Silver Springs Express Company paid all your bills. That means you owe every penny to them."

"What!" James Treenery looked like a giant trout as his mouth opened and closed in astonishment.

"So the owners of the Silver Springs Express essentially have control of the Flying T?" Richard Brady asked angrily.

"That's correct," Simkins said, "and that's the whole reason for this meeting. The owners of the Silver Springs Express are calling in your debt."

Treenery suddenly found his voice. "What if we refuse to pay it?"

"Then the Flying T goes on the auction block and the two of you will be personally responsible for any debts that aren't covered by the sale."

"What?" Brady slammed his fist on the desk. "You can't do that."

"We can and will unless you accept our deal."

Brady frowned. "Deal? What deal?"

"Sign everything over to the Silver Springs Express, and all debts will be forgiven."

Treenery jumped up from his chair. "The hell I will. You can't force us to sign away our company."

"That's true," Simkins said, gathering up his papers. "Selling out would be far more beneficial to my clients anyway. As you pointed out, you owe more than the company's worth. If it goes on the auction block and you have to pay the remainder, they stand to make a sizable profit."

"You expect us to believe you don't want the assets of the Flying T?" Treenery snapped. "Acquiring them would give you three times the coaches and horses."

Sam shook his head. "They're all useless to us. That's how the Silver Springs Express managed to put you out of business in the first place. We have better horses, better coaches, and better prices."

"You will, of course, want to consult your own people to make certain our figures are correct," Simkins said, picking up his satchel. "We will expect your decision by tomorrow afternoon. My clients wish to sign the final papers on Friday."

"That's only three days away!" Treenery exclaimed.

"Nevertheless, the final papers will be signed on Friday."

"I won't sign anything until I meet these clients of yours face to face," Richard Brady growled.

"My clients are anxious to meet with you as well. They fully intend to be here at the appointed time. Good day, gentlemen."

"Don't worry," Sam said with a grin, "they wouldn't miss it for the world."

*   *   *

"For pity's sake, will you sit down?" Martha said, looking up from her dusting in exasperation. "Duncan paid a lot of money for that rug you're wearing out with your pacing."

"I can't help it," Angel said. "This waiting is driving me crazy."

"Don't worry, Sam will let you know what happened at the meeting. You've done everything you could. The rest is up to your father and James Treenery."

Angel walked over to the window and pulled the curtain aside to look out. "That's what worries me. What if they come up with some way around us?"

"Then you and young Treenery will come up with something else the way you always do," Martha said. "I think there's more than that on your mind."

"I'm worried about Jessie. She's been gone the better part of a week with no word."

"She can take care of herself."

Angel stopped pacing to stare at Martha. "You can't be serious!"

"Jessie came all the way from New York to South Pass City alone," Martha pointed out.

"I hadn't thought of that."

"I'm not surprised. Your mind has been on other things." Martha gave Angel a shrewd look. "So what are you going to do about him when he gets back?"

"Who?"

Martha rolled her eyes. "General Lee. Who do you think?"

"There's no need to be sarcastic, Martha. It was a simple question."

"Right, as though you hadn't spent every free minute the last four days thinking about the same man. You know exactly who I mean."

Angel sighed. "If you're referring to Ox, I don't need

to do anything about him. We're friends and business partners, and that's all."

Martha snorted. "If you say that often enough, maybe you'll convince yourself and then you can feel safe again."

"That's ridiculous. I'm not threatened by Ox."

"No? Then why haven't you told him who you are? I know what the real problem is here even if you don't."

"And that is?"

"Your fear of men."

Angel was astonished. "My what?"

"More precisely, your fear of falling in love with a man. Ever since you were old enough to realize that boys were different, you've done everything in your power to keep them all at arm's length. You even took up a profession guaranteed to remind you of every male weakness there is so you wouldn't be tempted."

Angel crossed her arms and leaned back against the window frame. "This theory of yours is fascinating," she said. "Tell me, why have I developed this hatred of men?"

"I didn't say you hated them. You'd like to, I think, but you don't."

"That doesn't answer my question."

"It's simple enough. You're terrified of winding up with someone like your father who will dominate you and take away all your freedom."

"You mean like he did to my mother?" Angel asked bitterly.

"It may surprise you to know your mother enjoyed being married to your father."

"She did?"

"As far as Julia was concerned, her husband was the most important thing in the world, next to her home and her babies." Martha smiled a little sadly. "She really wasn't comfortable making difficult decisions and was quite happy to let her beloved Richard do it for her. Freedom would have been frightening for her."

"She sounds just like Vanessa," Angel said in surprise.

"She was. I've often thought that's what attracted your father to Vanessa. Anyway, your mother married Richard for precisely the same reasons you would reject a man like him."

"Your point being?"

"Young Treenery isn't like your father."

"No fooling."

"He likes you in spite of all the barricades you've built against him." Martha smiled knowingly. "The problem is, you like him too, and it scares you to death. That's why you pretend to be your sister and why you keep running away from him when he gets too close."

"I don't run away!"

"Oh, no? How about the night you went to see Sam as yourself?"

"Ox made me an indecent proposal."

"Good for him." Martha smiled. "You wanted to take him up on it too, I'll bet."

"Martha!"

"Then there was the night you came tearing home like the hounds of hell were on your heels and immediately sent for Alexis. He almost succeeded that night, didn't he? That's why you've used Brandon as an excuse ever since."

Angel flushed. "You have a good imagination."

"Do I? Then tell him who you are and see what happens."

"I know what will happen," she said gloomily. "Precisely nothing. I'm a great friend, nothing more. He even named a mule Angel because it was contrary and stubborn."

"You ought to be flattered. The man was a mule-skinner. He was probably very fond of his mules."

"Nice try, Martha. If he cares at all, he'll feel

betrayed when he finds out how I've lied to him. He'll hate me."

"He won't hate you. If ever I saw a man crazy in love, it's young Treenery."

Martha paused and listened carefully. The sound of someone knocking on the front door came through clearly this time. "I wonder who that could be."

"I hope it's Sam with good news. Are you done lecturing me, or should I go answer the door for you?"

"Humph, I might as well be talking to myself anyway. You won't listen; you never do. I just hope you don't wind up a lonely old woman."

"I'm more concerned about winding up a destitute young woman. For God's sake, Martha, go see who's at the door!"

Alexis's expensive Turkish rug took another beating from Angel's pacing as Martha went to answer the door. Maybe the older woman had a point. Alexis had said almost exactly the same thing before she left with Brandon. When Angel looked back over her relationship with Ox, the ridiculous notion became a serious possibility. They'd had a comfortable friendship in South Pass City, but it wasn't until she became Alexis that she actually showed him her true self. Had she deliberately misled him simply because she was afraid of having a serious relationship? Would Ox turn away, when he found out who she really was, or sweep her into his arms as Martha seemed to think? Maybe the time had come to find out.

"Jessica's back," Martha said from the open door.

Angel looked up in surprise. "We've been worried about you. Is everything all right?"

"It's better than all right." Jessica gave her a beautiful, glowing smile. "Oh, Angel, I'm married!"

37

"*You're married!*" *Angel* said in astonishment. "To whom?"

Jessie smiled. "Sam, of course."

"Sam! Lord, I had no idea!"

"Neither did he. That's why I had to take matters into my own hands. If I'd waited for him to make the first move I'd have died a spinster."

"I'll bet he was surprised when you told him how you felt."

Jessie grinned. "Shocked was more like it. At first he didn't believe me." She blushed and looked down at her folded hands. "I had to convince him. It took some doing, but he finally admitted he's been in love with me almost since the beginning. It didn't take much to talk him into getting married after that."

"I'm not surprised," Angel said faintly.

"The only time I thought my plan might fail was when I told him about my singing. I waited until after we'd been to the justice of the peace because I was afraid he'd change his mind if he knew." She shook her head. "I was right, too. The minute he found out he started going on and on about how he wasn't good enough for me and how he was going to have the marriage annulled. I don't know what would have happened if Ox hadn't told him to stop being such a damned idiot and be glad I wanted him."

"Ox was there?"

Jessie nodded. "He insisted on being the best man. I only wish I'd thought to take you along as a bridesmaid."

"I would have liked that." Angel paused. "Where is Ox, by the way?"

Jessie looked surprised. "He isn't here?"

"Nobody has seen him since he left with you."

"That's strange. I thought he'd be back by now. I only asked him to escort me to Silver Springs Gulch, which he was more than happy to do since he was on his way to Denver."

"Denver! What was he going there for?"

"I have no idea, but he said he'd be back before the big meeting Friday."

"I certainly hope so. We've worked long and hard for it."

Jessie glanced out the window. "Oh, look," she cried excitedly. "Sam's on his way in from the barn. From the expression on his face, I'd say the meeting went the way he wanted it to."

Sam's grin practically covered his face as he strode into the room a few minutes later. "I think they're going to go for our terms."

"What if they don't?"

Sam shrugged. "Then we sell the Flying T out from under them. You know, Angel, I got to thinking that might be the best way anyhow, since we can't use much of it."

"I know, but it's so much more satisfying this way,"

Angel said. "I'd give up the extra profit just for the satisfaction of watching them squirm."

Martha gave a disapproving sniff. "For revenge, you mean."

Angel's eyes gleamed. "Precisely."

Ox took off his hat, leaned back, and closed his eyes wearily. The train would be pulling in to Cheyenne in a little over an hour, and he was no closer to accomplishing his mission than when he left. His search for Angel proved to be one frustrating dead end after another. She simply wasn't anywhere to be found in the town of Denver. As far as he could tell, she hadn't been there anytime during the last six months.

Ox wondered what game Alexis and Martha were playing. Why would they lie about where Angel was? It made about as much sense as the miniature of Angel and Alexis disappearing. He hadn't seen the picture since he and Alexis discussed it, though he couldn't imagine why she'd hide it from him. Ox wished he had the picture with him now. Maybe if he studied it he'd be able to sort out his feeling for the Brady twins.

Even after all this time he couldn't tell which twin was which. He wondered whether even having them in the same room would make a difference. To be honest, he'd doubted he be able to tell them apart even then. Hell, if he closed his eyes he couldn't even tell which one he was kissing unless he smelled their perfume!

At the thought of their favorite scents, an odd inconsistency suddenly occurred to him. Jared and Shannon had soaked rags with Angel's perfume to make him think of her, but they'd locked him in the barn with Alexis. Couldn't they make up their minds which one they wanted him to marry?

Ox's eyes popped open as an extraordinary idea occurred to him. "Son of a bitch!"

"I beg your pardon!" The woman sitting on the facing seat glared at him indignantly.

Ox blinked. "Oh, I'm sorry. I was talking to myself." Hell, yes! Shannon and Jared knew which one they wanted him to marry. The only one he'd ever met! Ox raked his fingers through his hair as a dozen images of Alexis tumbled through his mind. No wonder none of the things people said about her fit the woman he knew. Challenging him to a race, climbing down a tree in the middle of the night, striking a deal with Mother Featherlegs, wearing a stiletto under her skirt; the socially correct Alexis Smythe would never do any of those. But Angel would, tough, independent, lovable Angel. It had been her all along!

"Damn!" he exclaimed. "How did I miss it?"

"Sir!" the lady on the other seat snapped. "Do you mind?"

"No, I don't mind at all. In fact, I'm rather pleased."

"Well, I never!"

Ox hardly noticed as she rose to her feet in righteous anger and moved across the aisle to another seat. Suddenly everything made sense. He wasn't in love with two women, only one, one gloriously unique, wonderful woman. His impossible dream had just come true. Wait until he told Martha. Ox laughed out loud in sheer joy; he could just imagine what she'd say.

Ox grinned all the rest of the way to Cheyenne, completely oblivious of the woman who sat across the aisle watching him closely, as though he were a dangerous lunatic.

"Are you sure Ox's telegram said he'd be in on this evening's train?" Angel asked nervously.

Martha sighed. "You just asked me that ten minutes ago, and yes, according to the telegram he sent Sam, he'll be here tonight. It isn't likely he'd miss the big meeting tomorrow anyway. He's waited a long time to defeat his grandfather."

"I know. I'm just afraid something will go wrong."

"What could happen?"

Angel gave a brittle laugh. "Nothing worse than Father and Alexis both showing up this afternoon. Do you realize how close we came to total disaster?"

"So what? He didn't see her and won't until she and Brandon confront him together tomorrow morning at breakfast."

"What if Father sees Alexis before Brandon gets back from the ranch? She'll crumble if she has to face him by herself."

"Your father locked himself in the study with a bottle of brandy, and Alexis has already retired for the evening. Besides, all he has to do is look at her. Not even your father would be stupid enough to challenge their marriage when she's due to have a baby any day."

"You're sure Sam knows to meet the train and send Ox here to the cabin?"

"Oh, for heaven's sake, Angel, you told him yourself! Young Treenery will be here and you can plan everything down to the last detail. I'm going home before you drive me to distraction!"

"Good. You can keep an eye on Father and make sure he doesn't see Alexis before Brandon gets here."

Martha threw her hands up. "I give up! You're obsessed tonight. I feel sorry for Ox, truly I do."

"I'm sorry, Martha. I just can't seem to help myself."

"Thank goodness I don't have to stay and listen to you. Good night!"

"Thanks for helping me with dinner," Angel called after her. So much for Martha. There was no way she'd be coming back this evening. Angel glanced at the clock on the mantel. Seven o'clock already! She was going to have to hurry if everything was going to be ready when he got here.

All her years as a successful madam came into play as she prepared for Ox's arrival. As Angel dug into the chest of supplies she'd brought along, she thought of the coming evening with a mixture of anticipation and nervousness. What if Martha was wrong and he didn't want her? And when should she tell him the truth about who she really was? Maybe it was best to play it by ear.

The tall elegant candles on the table cast a soft romantic glow over the room when Angel finally stepped back and surveyed her work. A linen tablecloth with matching napkins in silver rings, goblets of the finest crystal, and a complete array of silver flatware and fine china graced the table. There was a fire in the fireplace to fight the winter chill and give the ambiance of cozy welcome. Perfect!

"Now for me." Angel's fingers seemed strangely clumsy as she unbuttoned her dress and stripped down to her shift and pantalets. A dab of perfume at her throat and on her wrists to give her confidence. She paused a moment, stared consideringly into the mirror, and then applied a subtle touch of the fragrance between her breasts and behind her knees.

The simple green silk dress was exactly the color of Ox's eyes and had been hanging in her wardrobe for nearly two years because she lacked the courage to wear it in public. It was just the touch she needed tonight. The style seemed sweetly demure, but when she slipped it on it hugged her curves gracefully.

A smidgen of color to her lips, a slight darkening of her lashes, and she was ready except for her hair. Gazing critically into the mirror, Angel tried several styles in rapid succession. None of them appealed to her. They just weren't soft enough for the effect she wanted. She was still trying to find the right combination when someone knocked on the door.

Angel's heart jumped to her throat as she let her hair fall around her shoulders. "Who is it?"

"It's me," came Ox's voice. "Sam said I was supposed to meet you here since your father is in residence."

"I'll be right there," she called. "I guess this will have to do," she murmured, running the brush through her hair one more time and letting it hang loose around her shoulders. With one last look in the mirror, she took a deep breath and turned toward the door. The seduction of James Oxford Bruton Treenery the Third was about to begin.

38

"*Welcome back,*" *Angel said,* throwing open the door. "How was your trip?"

"Frustrating . . ." Ox's voice trailed off as he took in her appearance. "Jesus!"

"I hope that means you approve."

"Damn right I like it. You look fantastic."

Angel dimpled. "Congratulations! You just gave the correct answer. You may enter."

"You're in a playful mood tonight," he said with a grin. His smile faded as he took in the changed appearance of the cabin. Maybe playful wasn't the right word. "What's the occasion?"

"We're celebrating." She removed his hat from his hand and placed it on a wall peg. "Your grandfather and my father accepted our terms. They even promised to sign an agreement not to open another stage line anywhere west of the Mississippi."

"Let me guess. That last little addition was your idea, wasn't it?"

Angel shrugged. "It seemed like a good one. I doubt they're going to take this lying down, and I wanted to make sure they couldn't put us out of business the same way we did them."

Ox laughed. "I swear, you think of everything." He glanced around the cabin again. "If I'd known you were going to go to all this trouble I'd have stopped to take a bath and change clothes."

"Ask and you shall receive," she said, grabbing his hand and leading him over to the screen. "Angel told me you always liked a bath first thing when you came in off the trail." She pulled the screen aside to reveal a large hip bath half full of water. "The rest of the water is heating on the fire right now. It will only take a minute to finish filling it."

"I don't know what to say."

"You don't have to say anything. Just take your bath and I'll put supper on the table."

"How could a man refuse a deal like that?" A few minutes later, Ox poured the last of the water into the tub and then spent an appreciative moment watching Angel setting food on the table. Damn, a dress like that ought to be illegal. It could kill a man with a weak heart. He grinned. Oh, what a way to die!

Ox pulled the screen in front of the bath and started to unbutton his shirt. Unless he missed his guess, she intended to seduce him and he didn't mind a bit. The question was, why?

She'd held him at arm's length for months, panicking every time he got within kissing distance. It didn't make sense. As he eased himself down into the water he had a sudden notion. Maybe she'd decided to tell him the truth. Ox smiled to himself. If that was the way she wanted to break the news to him, far be it from him to spoil her plan.

"How about a glass of wine while you soak?" Angel asked from the other side of the screen.

"Sure."

"Are you in the tub?"

"Yes indeed."

Angel's hand came around the edge of the screen, holding the drink.

"I can't reach it," Ox said, unable to resist the urge to tease her a bit.

She reached a little farther. "How about now?"

"Nope."

"Now?" This time her entire arm and part of her shoulder were visible.

"Not quite."

Her head popped around the screen. "Just as I thought," she said, when she saw him sitting there grinning at her. "Do you want me to hold it up to your mouth too?" she asked sarcastically as she walked around the screen and handed him his drink.

"I think I can handle it." He took a sip and watched her over the rim of his glass. "You know, Angel always scrubbed my back."

"She did not!"

"Your sister didn't tell you everything."

"I'm sure she would have told me that."

He smiled devilishly. "It's not something I'd tell *my* sister."

"You don't have a sister." Angel picked up the sponge. "All right, I'll do your back, but not because I believe you. Lean forward."

Ox braced his arms on his knees and Angel dipped the sponge down into the water. She stroked it slowly across the top of his shoulders and watched the rivulets of water run down the contours of his back. She didn't think she'd ever seen anything quite as fascinating. Lovingly she traced muscles developed by years of driving large teams of mules and unloading heavy freight. The sponge glided down his spine, caressing the supple skin until it gleamed wetly in the soft candlelight.

Angel washed the enticing expanse thoroughly, covering every inch at least three times. Then she moved over his shoulders and down onto his chest. Ox obligingly leaned back in the tub and gave her access. If his back had been alluring, she found his chest downright bewitching.

The dark springy curls flattened out and stuck to his skin when the water from the sponge hit them but popped back up almost immediately. Angel was utterly captivated and repeated the experiment several times. But when she started to follow the thin line of hair that wandered down over his belly, Ox grabbed her hand.

"If you continue what you're doing, supper will be delayed significantly." His voice was a deep masculine purr that sent shivers of excitement racing through her.

"We can't let that happen, can we?" she whispered, leaning forward to brush his lips with her own. "Here you go," she said a moment later as she smacked the sponge against his chest and stood up. "You can finish by yourself."

Watching her walk away with an exaggerated swing of her hips, Ox chuckled to himself.

"Supper will be served in ten minutes." She looked back over her shoulder. "With or without you. So you'd better hustle your bustle."

Ox laughed outright at that and picked up the soap.

On the other side of the screen, Angel leaned against the wall and took several deep steadying breaths. The sound of splashing water brought dangerously erotic images to mind. So much for revealing her true identity while he was in the bath. Who would have thought something as innocent as washing his back would affect her so. Lord!

"What am I supposed to wear?" he called out. "Shall I wrap myself in a quilt like I did the first time we were here?"

"I laid out some clothes on the chair."

"You keep a supply of men's clothing on hand?"

"They're Duncan's," she lied. In reality they were Brandon's, lent to her by Alexis. One hint of what Angel had in mind and she'd gone out of her way to make the evening a smashing success.

"The vest and coat are a lost cause," he said a few minutes later, "but the shirt's almost big enough." Ox came out rolling the sleeves to his elbows. "Duncan must have been a mite smaller man."

"He was," Angel said faintly. Brandon obviously was too. The shirt managed to close across Ox's chest, but the seams at the shoulders were strained to the limit. He hadn't been able to fasten the top two buttons, so it gaped open invitingly at the neck. Angel had a difficult time tearing her eyes away.

"I'm ready and with several minutes to spare," he said, eyeing the table. "This looks great. Martha outdid herself."

Angel blinked and then focused on his face. "What?"

"Supper?" he said as he pulled out her chair for her. "I said, Martha sent quite a feast for us."

"Oh. To tell the truth I did it myself. I thought we deserved to celebrate after we worked so hard."

Ox pulled out his own chair and sat down. "I certainly can't find fault with that. What's the plan for tomorrow?"

"The meeting is set for ten o'clock sharp at the office of the Silver Springs Express. I thought we'd make an entrance ten or fifteen minutes late. "

The meal passed quickly as they discussed the coming confrontation and made plans. From there they moved on to Sam and Jessie. Angel's attention kept straying to the open neck of Ox's shirt and to his bare forearms. It was all she could do to concentrate on the conversation.

"So how are Sam and Jessie doing?" Ox finished

his last bite of pie and laid his fork on his plate. "They were still trying to decide whether Jessie would continue singing when I left," he said, picking up his wineglass.

"As far as I know they still haven't completely resolved it." Angel leaned her chin on her hand as her gaze traced the length of his forearm. "I think Sam has finally convinced her she has an obligation to share that extraordinary voice of hers, but she still wants to spend at least part of the time here."

"They'll work it out somehow. As long as they have each other, they'll be fine."

"Mmmhmm," Angel mumbled, studying the dark hairs on his arm. She remembered how incredibly soft they were against her skin and imagined herself wrapped in his embrace again. The picture was a tempting one indeed. His arms were so strong. . . .

"Do you have any idea what that does to me?" Ox murmured.

"Wh-what?" Angel's startled gaze flew to his face.

"I can't carry on a normal conversation when you look at me that way." Ox rose to his feet and walked around the table. "It makes my heart pound so hard I'm afraid it will come right out of my chest." His voice was a soft husky whisper as he took her hand and pulled her to her feet. "All I can think of is how much I want to kiss you."

"Y-you do?"

He cupped her face with his hands and gazed down into smoky gray eyes.

"More than you can possibly know," he said against her lips. The first touch was tentative and uncertain, like the whisper of an early morning mist across the water.

Her mouth was warm and lush as her lips moved against his, caressing them in loving response. Angel's hands trembled where they lay against the hard plane of his chest.

Ox raised his head and lovingly ran his thumb along the line of her jaw. "God, you're beautiful!"

"So are you." She touched the scar on his cheek. "Ox, I want—"

"I know, sweetheart, so do I," he whispered, as her fingers went to the buttons on his chest. "So do I." He took a deep shuddering breath when his shirt fell open. With the sweet fragrance of roses surrounding them, Angel pushed the garment off his broad shoulders and down over the thick muscles of his arms. The shirt fell to the floor forgotten as she ran her hands over his chest, tangling her fingers in the dark silky hair.

"You're incredible," she breathed, gazing at him in awe. With slow deliberation she leaned forward to flick the hollow at the base of his throat with her tongue.

"Jesus," he said, pulling her into his embrace. "Are you trying to drive me insane?"

Angel put her arms around his neck and snuggled closer. "No, just make you a little crazy." She rubbed her cheek against his chest.

"The dress already did that," he murmured, his fingers following the column of her throat to the neckline. He undid the row of tiny buttons with exquisite care, his fingers brushing the sensitive skin beneath and leaving a trail of fire.

Mesmerized, Angel gazed into the emerald green of his eyes as he eased the fabric down over her shoulders in a sensual caress that sent her heart skittering against her ribs. With a whisper of silk, the garment slipped to the floor and Ox scooped her up in his arms.

Their gazes locked in smoldering anticipation. "Are you planning to have your wicked way with me?" she asked, as he carried her the few remaining feet to the bed.

"Why?" he asked with a grin. "Did you have something else in mind?"

Angel shrugged as she traced the inside of his ear with her finger. "Only if you'd rather play a game of cards."

"Maybe later," he said, flopping backward onto the bed with her on top. "Right now I think I'd rather lie down."

She wriggled her body against his. "Are you tired?"

"Not even close." Ox pulled her head down for a long leisurely kiss. "How about you? Are you ready for a nap?"

"I've never been less sleepy in my life."

"Hmm, no cards," Ox said, rolling to his side. "And neither of us feels like sleeping." He pulled the tiny little bow at the top of her shift. "Guess we'll have to think of something else."

"Any ideas?"

"A few," Ox said, resting his hand on the swell of her hip. "Maybe we'll improvise as we go."

Angel walked her fingers up his chest. "I like the sound of that."

"I thought you might," he murmured against her lips.

The teasing mood disappeared in an instant as the kiss intensified. While the first fingers of desire began to unfurl, an odd idea flitted though Angel's mind. Ox seemed to know her body better than she did. A touch here, a kiss there; he played her like a finely tuned violin, creating a symphony of erotic responses Angel had never even suspected she was capable of.

They disposed of each other's clothing in the most sensual way possible, kissing each bit of skin as it was revealed. Even the tips of their toes came into play, as Angel traced the length of a muscular calf with her foot. "I could touch you like this all night," she whispered, against the column of his neck.

"Please do," he murmured, as her lips began an exploratory trip of his body. He managed to lie still beneath her questing touch across his chest and ribs, but when her tongue dipped into the hollow of his navel, he groaned and rolled her to her back. "Christ woman, have mercy."

"You said I could do it all night."

"I changed my mind," he breathed against her ear.

Her legs parted instinctively beneath his weight, and he entered her with one smooth thrust. "I love you," he said in a soft sexy rumble. "I think I have since the beginning, I just didn't realize it." With infinite tenderness he kissed her forehead, her eyelids, and the tip of her nose.

Angel struggled to focus on his words. "Why didn't you ever tell me?"

"Your sister kept getting in the way," he whispered, covering her mouth with his own.

Determined to make it an experience they would both remember for years to come, Ox used every bit of expertise he had, making it last as long he could. Angel responded with the pent-up passion of a lifetime. It was more than a joining of their bodies; their souls touched, expanded, and intermingled. The world ceased to exist as they lost themselves completely. All too soon they reached the top and fell away into sweet oblivion.

Ox wrapped his arms around her and rolled to his side. He closed his eyes and lay there, stroking her hair, as their breathing slowed. "This time when I ask you to marry me I'm not going to take no for an answer."

Angel snuggled closer in his embrace. "Oh, Ox, for heaven's sake. It's not like you ravished some sweet little innocent. I went to great lengths to seduce you and I got exactly what I wanted. Now hush and let me take that nap you offered me a while ago."

He grinned down at her. "Tired?"

"Mmmhmm."

"We have a few things to discuss."

Angel didn't even open her eyes. "I've heard there are two kinds of men, ones who want to talk after they make love and ones who want to sleep. Just my luck to get stuck with a talker."

Ox chuckled. "Sleep now, talk later?"

"Great idea." She yawned. "Wish I'd thought of it myself."

"All right," he said, setting his chin on top of her head. "But after that we talk." Maybe it wasn't all that important, he thought as he drifted off. After all, they had a lifetime to discuss everything.

After his week long search and very little sleep, Ox slept soundly. He barely even stirred when Angel slipped out of his embrace several hours before dawn. She put a pillow on the bed next to him and sighed in relief as he seemed to accept it as her replacement.

The candles had long since guttered out, but the full moon bathed the cabin in a silver light. Her breath caught in her throat; he was so beautiful lying there.

For a while tonight she had thought Martha was right, that Ox would understand the deception and forgive her. But then he'd driven a knife straight into her heart. He'd never said he loved her *because her sister kept getting in the way*. Her sister. To Ox, that meant Angel.

As she dressed and let herself out, Angel wondered if the tightness in her chest could be her heart breaking. Unable to resist, she turned at the door for one last look at the sleeping man. "Good-bye, my love," she whispered past the huge knot in her throat. She was almost to the buggy before the tears spilled over.

39

"I love you, Angel," Ox whispered, liking the sound of it as he drifted in and out of a dream state. Even without opening his eyes he knew she was there. He could smell her perfume. Roses. He smiled and reached toward the body next to him.

When his hand sank into the cool softness of a pillow instead of landing on solid warmth, his eyes popped open in alarm. "Angel?"

A quick glance around the room showed he was alone. He jumped out of bed and struggled into his clothes. Damn, why hadn't he pushed the issue last night? He should have known she'd run, the way she always did when he got too close. Now he might never get the chance to say all the things he'd been thinking, to ask her to marry him, to make love to her again.

Jerking his boots on, he tried to think where she might have gone. Would she go home with her father there? It wasn't likely, and yet where else? Martha! If anybody knew where to find Angel, she would be the one.

The sun's warm rays shone down on a beautiful day, but Ox barely paid any attention other than to curse how late he'd slept. He only took time to saddle his horse because he wasn't sure how far he was going to have to ride. In his haste, he'd just as soon ride bareback and be done with it. The familiar road to Alexis's house seemed miles longer than usual. When he finally arrived, he rode straight up to the house and tied his horse to one of the pillars out front.

He didn't even bother to knock, just flung open the door and stalked through. "Where is she?" he bellowed.

An unfamiliar man was just about to enter the dining room. Ox eyed the stranger belligerently. He was far too attractive to be running loose in Alexis's house. "Who are you?"

"Brandon Johnson."

"The hell you say. If you value your hide you'll stay away from her." With two steps Ox was across the hallway. Brandon saw the punch coming and ducked.

"I'll be damned if I'll stay away from my own wife!"

"She's not going to marry you!" Ox roared. His fist slammed into Brandon's jaw, and the other man crashed to the floor like a poleaxed steer.

"Treenery, what do you think you're doing?" Richard Brady exclaimed from the head of the stairs. "You can't just come in here and start a fight."

Before Ox could answer, the dining room door opened. "Oh, my," Vanessa said, looking from Ox to Brandon and back again.

"Where's Alexis?" Ox asked angrily.

"She's eating breakfast, but—"

"Thank you," Ox interrupted rudely, pushing her out into the hall.

"Treenery's mind has obviously snapped," Richard

said, coming down the stairs. "Who the hell is that on the floor?"

The rest was lost as Ox slammed the door and stomped across the room to the table. The sight of Angel sitting there calmly eating breakfast infuriated him even more.

"What do you think you're doing?" he demanded

"I beg your pardon?" she said, shrinking away from him.

Ox frowned. Since when did Angel beg his pardon? She was more likely to say, "Any idiot can see I'm eating breakfast." He took a closer look at her face. "Christ, you're Alexis!" he said in stunned amazement.

"Yes." She looked dangerously close to tears. "Wh-what do you want?"

"I'm sorry to burst in on you like this," he said, fighting to keep his voice calm. She reminded him of a fragile piece of porcelain. Lord, what if she started crying? "Do you know where Angel is?"

"Angel?" Her face brightened as if by magic. "You must be—"

"Where is the son of a bitch?" The door behind Ox slammed against the wall, and an enraged Brandon Johnson stormed in. "I'll show you . . . "

"Brandon, don't," Alexis said, quickly rising to her feet. "He's Ox Bruford."

"I don't care who he is."

"Alexis!" Richard Brady's shocked voice boomed through the room like cannon fire.

Ox didn't even have to turn around and look at Richard Brady. He knew they were both staring at Alexis with identical astonished expressions. There was no mistaking her obvious pregnancy.

"Brandon?" Alexis said nervously.

"It's all right, love," Brandon said. He put his arm around her shoulder and kissed her forehead before facing her father. "Your daughter and I are married,

Mr. Brady, and your first grandchild is on the way, as you can plainly see. We hope you'll share our joy, but I'll tolerate no interference"—he paused to glare at Ox—"from anyone."

Alexis and Brandon married! Suddenly Ox began to laugh. "Angel knows all about this, doesn't she?"

Alexis looked at him uncertainly. "Of course."

"And that's what this whole charade has been about. No wonder you called her in to take your place." Ox laughed even harder. "Oh, Lord, is she going to have her revenge today!"

"What the devil are you blathering about, Treenery?" Richard Brady demanded.

"Never mind. It will all be clear to you soon enough," Ox said, with a grin. "Alexis, do you have any idea where Angel is?"

"I thought she was with you."

"Then she didn't come back here?"

"Don't tell me you misplaced her!" Martha said, as she came in through the servants' door. "Honestly, Treenery, I've about given up on you."

"At least I finally realized who I've been dealing with all this time. I figured it out on my way back from Denver."

"Hallelujah! It's about time." She set a plateful of sausage on the sideboard. "Don't tell me she ran away when you told her."

"No. I didn't get a chance. She left before I woke up this morning. Do you have any idea where she went?"

Martha sighed. "If the night went the way I suspect it did, she probably left town. She's got some cockamamie idea that it's Alexis you're really in love with."

"That's what she told me too, but I think it's more than that," Alexis admitted. "She's madly in love with you and she's scared to death of it. You've got to find her before she gets away."

"Don't worry. I'll comb the entire town if I have to," Ox said, heading for the door.

"Will someone please tell me what's going on here?" Richard Brady demanded. His face was an alarming shade of purple.

"Calm yourself, dear," Vanessa said soothingly. "I'm sure it's one of those complicated things that will take all morning to figure out. It usually is when Angel is involved."

Ox grinned as he left the house and untied his horse. No wonder Angel had taken her sister's place. There was no way Richard Brady could touch either one of them now. He swung up into the saddle and then paused uncertainly. Where had she gone?

He sat there trying to second-guess her thinking, desperately aware of time passing far too rapidly.

"Ox!"

He turned his head and looked up in surprise. Shannon leaned out of an upstairs window waving wildly while Jared shinnied down a nearby tree. Maybe they knew something the grown-ups didn't. It wouldn't surprise him in the least.

"Have you seen Angel this morning?" he called.

Shannon shook her head. "I haven't seen her."

"Neither have I," Jared said, as he reached the ground.

"Where would she go if she considered herself threatened?"

"If she's in trouble, she goes to Alexis first, then Martha."

"Neither of them has seen her."

"Then she went to a friend." Jared frowned. "Except you're her best friend."

"Maybe she went to another friend." Shannon reached the bottom of the tree and brushed off the front of her dress. "Like Sam and Jessica maybe?"

"Sam! Sure. Why didn't I think of that? Thank you. I owe you two."

"Good. Angel said we had to stay in the nursery until next week for locking you both in the barn. Maybe you can convince her to let us out early," Jared said hopefully.

Ox wheeled his horse around. "Looks like you've done just fine on your own."

"Maybe so," Shannon called after him. "But if she catches us we're dead!"

Ox chuckled as his horse loped down the road. Surely she'd let them out for the wedding. Angel was sure to want all four of her siblings included in the ceremony. *If she married him.* His smile faded. *If he even found her.*

The Silver Springs Express was loading the last of the passengers headed for Silver Springs Gulch when he arrived at the station. Praying he'd guessed right, Ox dismounted, tied his horse to the hitching rack, and sprinted across the yard to the stage.

There she was! Ox could see the familiar flowers of her hat as the driver helped her into the coach. "Wait!" he yelled.

She paused and glanced over the driver's shoulder. Her gaze met Ox's for an endless moment. His eyes were filled with entreaty, hers with regret. After a moment, she bit her lip and disappeared into the coach.

"Angel!" Fully intending to remove her by force if necessary, Ox headed toward the stage with a determined set to his jaw.

The big burly driver stepped in front of him just before he reached his goal. "Do you have a ticket?"

"Hell, no, I don't have a ticket. I'm not going anywhere." He glanced at Angel, already seated inside the coach. "And neither is she." Ox took a step forward, but the driver blocked his path.

"I'm sorry, sir, but you can't come any farther without a ticket. Company policy."

"Fine. I'll buy a ticket; now let me past."

"This stage is full. You'll have to wait for the next one."

"I don't want to get on, damn it, I just want to talk to one of the passengers."

"We don't allow anyone to bother passengers on the Silver Springs Express."

"You're fired."

"Only Sam Collins can fire me."

"That's the trouble with being a silent partner, Ox," Angel said, from inside the coach. "You'd better go now. If you don't, you'll be late for the meeting with your grandfather and my father."

"I'm not going without you. We're partners, remember?"

"Talk to Alexis."

"I already have. She sent me after you."

"I'm going to have to ask you to leave," the driver said, moving forward menacingly. "It's obvious the lady doesn't want to be bothered."

Ox gave him a scornful look. "You can ask all you want. It won't do a speck of good."

"All right by me," the driver said, rolling up his sleeves. "I haven't had a good fight in a long time."

"Look, Angel, I'm going to ask you to marry me even if I have to go through this big galoot and propose in front of all these people to do it. I really don't want to hurt this man, but I will if I have to. The choice is yours."

There was a moment of silence and then Angel appeared. "Don't be such a fool, Ox. He's one of our best drivers. We can't afford to have him off the job."

"I knew you'd see reason."

"The stage is due to leave, ma'am," the driver said. "The company is very strict about schedules, so I can't wait."

"That's fine. I'll just go on the next one out."

The driver eyed Ox suspiciously. "Are you sure you want to stay here, ma'am? He looks kind of unsavory to me."

Angel's lips quirked. "It's all right. I carry a derringer in my reticule."

"And a very nasty knife strapped to her leg," Ox added. "You ought to worry about my safety, not hers."

"If I didn't have to leave right now, I'd teach you the right way to talk about a lady," the driver said.

"You might try," Ox murmured as the man mounted to the driver's seat.

Angel sighed. "This doesn't change anything, Ox."

He watched the stage drive out of town. "Actually, it does. That driver will probably have heart palpitations when he finds out who really owns the Silver Springs Express."

"That's not what I meant."

"I know." He reached out and caressed her cheek with his knuckles. "I guess I'm afraid to say the truth out loud for fear you'll run away again."

"What truth is that?"

"That I love you heart and soul, and that I want to marry you."

"You only want to marry me because of last night."

"I walked into that cabin intending to propose to you." He smiled fondly at her. "It's not my fault you distracted me."

"You had plenty of time over dinner."

"Ah, yes, but then I thought you were waiting for the appropriate moment to confess you'd been playing the part of your sister all along."

"You knew?"

"It sort of hit me between the eyes yesterday on my way home from Denver. I would have figured it out when I met Alexis this morning anyway."

"She *is* pretty obviously pregnant."

"I realized it wasn't you before I noticed that. In

fact, I knew the minute she opened her mouth. You really aren't very much alike."

"What did she say?"

"It wasn't so much what she said it was what she didn't say—namely, to mind my own business." He grinned down at her. "Your sister doesn't have half of your fire."

Angel was incredulous. "I've been lying to you all this time and you don't mind?"

"Mind? I was pleased as hell. It's like having a dream come true." He put his arms around her and pulled her close. "For the last six months, I've wished there was a way to combine you both into one person. I just wish you'd told me at the beginning. Look how much time we've wasted."

She rubbed her cheek against his coat. "I can't believe it. You really love me?"

"I've loved you since South Pass City. I think I was smitten the first time you accused me of charging ridiculous prices for hauling your freight, proceeded to drive a damn hard bargain, and then finished it off with the best home cooked meal I ever had." He grinned. "Of course I didn't realize it was love until later. You were very successful at keeping me at arm's length."

"I was the madam of a whorehouse, for God's sake. How could you fall in love with me?"

"You also owned an extremely successful gambling casino, which I might add you sold at precisely the right moment. Right now, you're part owner in a stage line that is going to make us filthy rich. What you are is a brilliant business partner."

Angel scowled. "So you love me because I'm good at making money."

Ox lifted her chin with his finger and stared earnestly down into her eyes. "No, I love you because you're beautiful and smart and have a heart as big as the Rocky Mountains. You have more courage in your little finger than most men have in their whole bodies. You're the woman I want to share the rest of my life with."

She looked away. "I . . . I'm afraid, Ox. I can't live in a gilded cage like my sister did."

"Gilded cage! Angel, this is Wyoming Territory, as you're so fond of telling me. As your husband I couldn't touch a penny that belongs to you." He waved his hand dramatically. "I'm not even going to pamper you. I fully expect you to be at work every morning just like I do now."

She smiled slightly. "What if I get pregnant?"

"Well, I might give you a little time off for that," he teased.

"You've changed your mind about children then?" she asked.

"Of course. Just think, we could have twins, a boy like Jared and a girl like Shannon."

"That's supposed to persuade me to marry you?" she said in mock horror.

"We might have a Betsy."

"Lord, that's even worse!"

"Well, then, maybe this will convince you," he said, against her lips.

His kiss was like the first spring rain, filled with magic and promise. It weakened her knees and melted her objections. "I don't know," she whispered shakily. "I think I'm convinced, but it might take another one like that just to make sure."

Ox laughed. "Another one like that and we'd wind up doing more than kissing on the street. I prefer a little more privacy myself. Besides, we're already nearly half an hour late for our meeting."

"Shall we let your grandfather and my father be the first to congratulate us on our future of wedded bliss?"

"I think that would be a great idea," Ox said, tucking

her hand through the crook in his arm. "They're the ones who brought us together, after all."

"I'm sure they'll be thrilled."

They looked at each other and grinned.

"Mrs. James Oxford Bruton Treenery the Third. You know, I kind of like the sound of that," Angel said.

"So do I," Ox said, with a huge smile. "So do I!"

Author's Note

Writing historical fiction is such fun. Invariably, I come across some fascinating little tidbit that I just have to use. My research for *Silver Springs* led me to the famous Cheyenne–Deadwood stage line, where I discovered Mother Featherlegs. Though she didn't actually come to Wyoming until 1876, she did run a dugout of ill repute and was well known as a go-between for various road agents in the area. She gained the nickname Mother Featherlegs from the bright red lace pantalets she wore. Since she rode astride, the lace fluttered in the wind like the leg feathers of a chicken when she galloped across the prairie. Now how could I resist that?

I found nothing to indicate she ever went anywhere near South Pass City, and I believe she was a much older woman than I have portrayed. However, she did have a confederate named Dangerous Dick Davis, who is presumed to have murdered her in 1879. A monument dedicated to Mother Featherlegs stands just outside of Lusk, Wyoming, a town that was originally named Silver Springs.

Then I discovered "the great epizootic of 1872." This particular plague was an equine flu that swept through Canada and the eastern United States with devastating force. As many as two hundred horses died of it each day in New York City, and 2,250 horses died in Philadelphia during a three-week period. In many places horsepower was replaced by manpower, as men and boys pulled wagons and trolley cars through the streets. The great epizootic apparently didn't spread to the West, but it isn't hard to imagine what would have happened if it had.

Mother Featherlegs and the great epizootic prove once again that fact is truly more incredible than fiction.

Escape to Romance
and
WIN A YEAR OF ROMANCE!

Ten lucky winners will receive a free year of romance—*more than 30 free books*. Every book HarperMonogram publishes in 1997 will be delivered directly to your doorstep if you are one of the ten winners drawn at random.

Harper Monogram

Let HarperMonogram
Sweep You Away

MIRANDA by Susan Wiggs
Over One Million Copies of Her Books in Print
In Regency London, Miranda Stonecypher is stricken with amnesia and doesn't believe that handsome Ian MacVane is her betrothed—especially after another suitor appears. Miranda's search for the truth leads to passion beyond her wildest dreams.

WISH LIST by Jeane Renick
RITA Award-Winning Author

While on assignment in Nepal, writer Charlayne Pearce meets elusive and irresistibly sensual Jordan Kosterin. Jordan's bold gaze is an invitation to pleasure, but memories of his dead wife threaten their newfound love.

SILVER SPRINGS by Carolyn Lampman

Independent Angel Brady feels she is capable of anything—even passing as her soon-to-be-married twin sister so that Alexis can run off with her lover. Unfortunately, the fiancé turns out to be the one man in the Wyoming Territory who can send Angel's pulse racing.

CALLIE'S HONOR by Kathleen Webb

Callie Lambert is unprepared for the handsome stranger who shows up at her Oregon ranch determined to upset her well-ordered life. But her wariness is no match for Rafe Millar's determination to discover her secrets, and win her heart.

And in case you missed
last month's selections...

JACKSON RULE by Dinah McCall
Award-Winning Author of *Dreamcatcher*
After being released from prison Jackson Rule finds a job working for a preacher's daughter. Jackson may be a free man, but Rebecca Hill's sweet charity soon has him begging for mercy.

MISBEGOTTEN by Tamara Leigh

No one can stop baseborn knight Liam Fawke from gaining his rightful inheritance—not even the beautiful Lady Joslyn. Yet Liam's strong resolve is no match for the temptress whose spirit and passion cannot be denied.

COURTNEY'S COWBOY by Susan Macias
Time Travel Romance

Married couple Courtney and Matt have little time for each other until they are transported back to 1873 Wyoming. Under the wide western sky they discover how to fall truly in love for the first time.

SOULS AFLAME by Patricia Hagan
New York Times Bestselling Author

with Over Ten Million Copies of Her Books in Print
Julie Marshal's duty to save her family's Georgia plantation gives way to desire in the arms of Derek Arnhardt. With a passion to match her own, the ship's captain will settle for nothing less than possessing Julie, body and soul.